BUT DO YOU
LOVE ME
WITH *LOCURA*?

BUT DO YOU LOVE ME WITH *LOCURA*?

Sharon Steeber

atmosphere press

Published by Atmosphere Press

Cover design by Matthew Fielder
Cover painting of tabachín flower by Judith Jenya

Author photo by Mark Johaningsmeir

atmospherepress.com

*For Susana Lucia
& Christopher David*

Table of Contents

Locura *(n., Spanish)*

Passionate enthusiasm; madness

SEEDLINGS

Near León, central Mexico, 1964

Don Alejandro swerved the new Chevy pickup from side to side in an attempt to avoid the ruts in the hard-baked road. His actions were a reflex since his mind was not on the road, nor on the barren hills that rose around him like rumps of brown horses. Nor did he think about the four calves he had just bought and was now transporting to the patio of his house, where he would slaughter them. He lifted his gaze to the rear-view mirror and was startled out of his daydreaming.

Juan Ramón, his ten-year-old son, sat astride the largest calf in the back of the truck. One arm akimbo, the other grasping at air, the boy struggled to keep his balance on the lurching animal. The other three calves, no doubt surprised to find a boy in their midst, pressed in panic against Juan Ramón's legs. The back of the truck whirled with moving haunches and flailing boy.

Alejandro controlled himself long enough to brake to a slow roll. A sudden stop might throw his son under the hooves of the agitated calves. He beat down his panic and a simultaneous desire to backhand the boy.

Alejandro bounded out the door of the cab in time to catch

the defiant look in Juan Ramón's eyes. "What do you think you're doing, *pendejo*?"

The calves continued to jostle each other. Alejandro leaned far over the side of the truck and thrust a hand toward Juan Ramón. The boy grabbed the hand and let his father draw him over the backs of the calves. His shoes, which Alejandro himself had made, trailed through their stiff fur.

"I wanted to be a *vaquero*, a cowboy," he said when Alejandro lifted him to the ground. The boy toed the road's hard-baked dirt.

"That was a stupid thing to do."

His son dared not look him in the eye now. The boy no longer considered himself a *niño*, but he could still be frightened by his father's anger.

"What if you fell under the calves' hooves and got kicked? What if you had bounced off into the road?"

Juan Ramón seemed only mildly surprised by the possibility. He looked up at his father, who cast a dark shadow on the road.

The boy's eyes still gleamed with his adventure as a bronco rider. Yet he took care to angle himself so his left arm, which hung limp at his side, would not be noticed. Alejandro knew this boy. He would never admit that his father, of all people, had been right. The boy had hurt himself. But Alejandro suspected that for Juan Ramón, the ride was worth the pain.

Marbella Beach, California, 1965

"Do something, Mommy!"

Louise observed the green watercolor paint creep across the high-grained paper. In a matter of seconds, it encountered the ribbon of red that Rosie had washed onto the paper minutes before. Green paint, being the wetter, forced rivulets into the red. It coagulated here and there in pools of ugly graybrown, like mud.

"Look what it's doing now." Rosie gnawed the tip of the brush handle.

"Watch," Louise said and tried not to laugh at the distress of her nine-year-old daughter. She picked up another sheet of the watercolor paper they had prepared. "Is lavender still your favorite color?"

Rosie nodded.

Louise laid down a new red wash, then moved away from the paper. "You do it yourself now. Put a wash next to my red one. Try it with blue this time."

Rosie took the brush handle from her mouth and dipped the tip into the blue paint. She frowned with concentration, then washed dark blue above the red. At once, the blue color started to spread.

"It's moving again! That's what I hate about watercolors." She threw down the brush. Sparks of blue flew onto her shirt and over the paper.

This time Louise did laugh. "That's what you will come to love."

Rosie stared at her in disbelief. Then Rosie said, "Look at that!"

They watched the moving paint as if it were a live creature.

"It's lavender! Why isn't it going all muddy like before?"

"The red and green you used the first time are opposites. At least in the world of colors. Those colors look fine side by side. But they don't blend well. This time we used two colors that can mix and make a new color. A pretty one."

Louise flicked her brush and made a few strokes with the rich purple that had formed where the blue and red pooled. "Sometimes, the poetry of watercolors is like the poetry of living. The artist puts down the color with an idea of what she wants. But what results, until she becomes an experienced painter—and sometimes not even then—is always different from what she planned."

"It's creepy how the paint changes itself around."

"To work well in watercolors, you have to be able to accept that. You learn you can work with the ambiguity."

Rosie rolled her eyes. "Ambiguity?" she said in that impatient tone she used for her mother's big words.

"That means not knowing how things are going to go. It's like not having the answers."

"I hate that."

PART ONE

I

EXIT PAPERS

Mexico, Summer 1985

The Mexico City metro car swayed to one side, and I tightened my hold on the strap. I jostled against the man to my left, then the woman to my right. I glanced down at the floor as I struggled to keep my balance. What I saw didn't make sense. At my feet lay my money pouch, keys, passport folder, a bottle of acidophilus pills, and other remnants of the life I had hauled with me from California. In the split second that I tried to understand why my personal effects lay on the subway floor, a hand snaked out from among the other legs crammed there and snatched the money pouch.

I cried out, but the hand disappeared before I could find the words in Spanish to shout what was happening. I looked around for help. At the same time, I grabbed my bag to stop any more hemorrhaging of my things onto the floor. The bag felt uncharacteristically deflated. What should have been solid fabric revealed a gaping hole, with sheared threads of material going haywire in different directions.

"Señorita," said a man's soft voice behind me. I turned and saw an older man in a white embroidered shirt. With a regretful tone, he said, "*Ladrón*," the Spanish word for "thief." I also heard the word "knife" and then the word "machete." It took me a few moments to understand that someone in the metro car had slashed my bag, maybe with a machete. No doubt I stood out as a tourist, an easy mark with that woven cotton bag.

I scanned the crowd to see who might be trying to get away or acting guilty or even too nonchalant. Every face and back of the head I peered at could have been the thief, or not. It could even be the man who had just spoken to me. This moment marked the beginning of what I so often could not figure out during my time to come in Mexico, a shifting scrim of what appeared to be so. The light would come from a different angle, and then I would see that what I thought was so, was not so.

The man dropped down and began to gather my things.

"Gracias," I said, the word too thin for my jumble of emotions. He raised each of my belongings back up to me, one by one. With my bag destroyed, I had nowhere to put the items. Balancing best I could, I wriggled out of my denim jacket and made a sling to serve as my purse. Then the light shifted, and I saw the moment in another way. Each item he lifted to me came back as a gift.

The next metro stop was the one that would take me to my hotel. I wanted to thank the man properly, more effusively, for his kindness. I couldn't miss my stop, though, or I might be lost in the underground. Still, I turned to thank him again. He was gone.

Once out of the metro, I breathed deeply, not caring what I had heard about the air quality in Mexico City. I brought my hand to the safety belt inside my shirt, thankful I had taken the precaution of storing my money in two places.

Close to the hotel was a small outdoor market. I needed a replacement bag, larger and fiercer. I spied just the one, oversized, fashioned out of thick plastic mesh, with sturdy handles, double-riveted. Its plaid design in bright blue was a bit off-putting, but it was the best of the lot. I withdrew two bills from my money belt. It hurt to have lost half my funds to the *ladrón*, but I still had enough to function if I were careful.

Even so, things were not working out as planned when I first conceived the idea of studying Spanish in Cuernavaca, a two-hour bus ride from Mexico City. Surely things would get off to a better start there.

* * *

I tried to sneak into the small purple room, but in a class of four students, I couldn't exactly hide in the back row. Aida, my laser-eyed Spanish teacher for this intensive four-week course for adults, was cutting me no slack for arriving late. She stared right at me, waiting for a fumbled reply to the question she had just flung my way.

"Don't joke, *Coronel*," I managed in Spanish while trying to glide into my seat instead of plopping down with the blue bag and extra-large water bottle.

I blurted out the next line of dialogue we'd been assigned. "Look, *Coronel*! The B-47 is landing!" I was tempted to point skyward but didn't dare catch the eyes of the other three students. If one giggled, we all giggled. Even if we did laugh, I actually believed I might someday need this phrase. I was trying hard to master it and similar ones, just out of the superstition that life has a fatal way of doubling back on you if you scoff at what it hands you.

My destiny at this moment was to memorize odd phrases from old language texts published by the American Foreign Service. But the relentless barrage of total immersion Spanish was harder to keep up with than I had imagined from the other side of the border. Nor did it succeed in walling out my guilt at what I had left there.

Aida, a slim woman who reminded me of a comma—a delicate slice of a woman—shot me another question in rapid-fire Spanish.

Yes! I understood her! I shot back, *"Coronel, alto!* Colonel, halt!*"* I could now see myself becoming a virtuoso in this language, a real powerhouse. I wanted to flare my nostrils like a bull and stamp my hooves.

I had chosen Cuernavaca, this fabled City of Eternal Spring deep in the heart of Mexico, because the poetry of its name held promise that, in such a cradle, I could master Spanish and finally gain a step up in my work as a journalist. In these weeks of saved-up vacation, I could shuck off the dry reportorial duties at *The Marbella Beacon*, safely distant from all those nights of school board meetings that Leland, my philosopher-sadist-editor, had sent me to cover, how I had to pay my dues.

Oh, but Mama. How could I, a single woman, dare leave my single mother to go it alone? It was the duty of the only child to take care of her aging mother, wasn't it?

I was also far from Monty, determined to start anew after almost four years of expecting we would somehow evolve into a serious couple if we just did enough time with each other. I was determined not to sink through Kübler-Ross's five stages of grief over the futility of those lost years, nor over my cowardice in not telling Mama I was going to Mexico for a whole month.

Miss Aida was tapping her long red fingernails on the table the five of us sat clustered around. She assigned another page of dialogue. We took turns reading about the *coronel*'s girlfriend, Claudia, whom he consistently referred to as *La Gordita*, meaning The Little Fatty.

The Spanish school, called *La Divina Escuela de Idiomas*—the Divine School of Languages—was nestled in a neighborhood of walled houses, each with graceful jacarandas surrounding hidden gardens.

With amused determination, we practiced such terms from the old textbooks as "fingerprints" and "the control tower" and "Show me your exit papers."

Ginger, a languid redhead from Dallas, gave her own Texas spin to the military phrases, uttering them like a frightened child. Christian, a thin, intense man from France, made the dialogue thick and throaty, as though all participants in the scene were filtering their lines through exhalations of Gauloises cigarettes. The last to read was Eli, a Dutch woman who looked to be a youthful forty and was the best-dressed student in the school. She could already speak five languages, so for her it was easy to roll out sentences with Dutch efficiency.

"We must hurry," Eli read in deft Spanish as if slicing gouda into leaf-thin pieces, almost translucent. "We do not want to keep La Gordita waiting."

I raised my hand to protest this particular nickname. Aida ignored me and pointed at the wall clock. It marked eleven a.m., time for our morning break, the *almuerzo*.

Those of us at Spanish Level Eight, called the "Morados" in the school's color-coded Spanish levels, sat down together to drink strong coffee and nibble quesadillas from the school's snack bar. The *coronel's* Fat Claudia dominated our conversation.

Ginger slammed her fist on the table. "That *coronel* in his control tower—" For a split second, her twang led me to think she had said "control tire." She went on, "The colonel cannot possibly be getting any from his Claudia if he persists in calling her his Gordita?" Ginger had that Texan way of intoning statements so they ended up sounding like questions. "What an insensitive jackboot? I cannot for my life imagine why the Foreign Service put such cruel language in the dialogue? And to think we have to set it to memory?"

"No," said Eli with an emphatic shake of her dark bob. "*Gordita* is a term of endearment here in Mexico."

"'Fatty' is endearing?" I would lock ranks with Ginger to stand up for the American perspective and women worldwide. "*El coronel* should go back to his control tower and forget about leaving his fingerprints"—I wished I could remember the Spanish word—"on pleasingly plump Claudia."

Christian laughed. "The name Gordita might not be any more offensive than *mon petit chou*. My little cabbage. It's a term of affection in France."

"Quite different," I said. "The *coronel* is attacking his girl-friend's appearance, for God's sake. He doesn't have to point out that she's fat."

"I think that's what he likes about her." Christian inhaled deeply on his unfiltered cigarette. "He will never leave that woman."

I was about to counter that Claudia might instead leave the colonel, but Aida came clacking up to the table, the high heels she always wore to class tapping on the tile floor. She pulled up a chair.

We liked it when Aida sat at the rickety table with us during the break. Most of the teachers at the school had the knack of combining well-honed courtesy with an effort to hear us get the language right. But being descended from generations of virtuoso wall and pyramid builders, they held something back when it came to getting to know the students.

"You must not forget," Aida said in her usual hurried Spanish, "tomorrow is market day in Ixmilco. We all meet here at eight o'clock, so we can walk together to the bus station. It's important we all"—she paused only a second to light her cigarette—"stay together."

Ever since I had learned about this field trip for a group of us—the high-functioning Sevens (*Naranja*, Orange), Eights (*Morado*, Purple), and Nines (*Rosa Mexicana*, Hot Pink)—I had been excited. It was a break from the constant drill and memorization, a chance to absorb more of Mexico's fabled magic.

She flicked her cigarette into the ashtray, long red nails flashing. "Next week we'll throw a party at my house. I'll serve you our typical dishes. Would you like that?"

We accepted at once. Unspoken was shared gratefulness for this chance to peek into the home life of a Mexican. We were voyeurs outside a window at twilight.

A bell tinkled in the distance. We stood up on cue and started toward the classrooms. Aida rested her hand on my forearm. "Rosie, I must tell you something."

I expected her to say, ". . . about the nickname La Gordita." Instead, she said, ". . . about your instruction level. This kind of learning takes time, Rosie. I think you should try Level Seven instead of Level Eight."

Perdón? Hadn't she meant to say "Level Nine" for *Rosa Mexicana,* Rosie the Mexican Rose? How was it possible to feel the blood draining from my face and at the same time be hot with embarrassment? She rushed on, something about my still finding certain items of grammar and vocabulary in Level Seven that would be useful . . . and blah, and blah, and blehh.

She brightened as if she had just thought of something really joyous. "And as a Seven, you may still accompany us on the trip to Ixmilco tomorrow, you know. You can still be with your friends, the Eights."

Aida pointed to the bright orange door of the Level Seven classroom as if I didn't know where it was, as if I needed remedial work in spatial organization and colors or didn't see the giant 7 in tarnished brass on the door. Then she clack-clacked to the purple door of the Level Eight classroom and swiveled inside.

I didn't enter the orange classroom. It didn't help to tell myself this could have been just an administrative decision, that they simply had too few people in Level Seven and needed to even out class sizes. Maybe I wasn't a true Eight—I would never know. But I did know it was time for me, at age twenty-nine, to fill out the form I was meant to have. At *The Marbella Beacon,* I had managed to progress from manning the police scanner to writing obituaries to reporting school board squabbles. After almost three years of journalistic boot camp, my career trajectory still had no rocket ship in sight. I refused to accept I might not master Spanish, grab the bilingual brass ring, and propel my career to a new level.

I was all the further from my language-idol, sandy-haired Günter, a gregarious student from Germany, who, according to gossip at the break, had zoomed past Level Ten and could actually make a joke in Spanish.

I let myself out the school's front gate and started the ten-minute walk to the house of Señora Hernández and my room there.

I hurried through the main square and past the sixteenth century Palace of Cortéz with its crenelated parapets. The midday sky shone a pure and brilliant blue, a watercolor wash redolent with possibility. If only I could find a way to pluck that possibility down and apply it to myself. I walked the tree-lined blocks under a canopy of jacarandas, *tabachines*, and *tulipanes de la India*, trees studded with vibrant red flowers splashy as fireworks. Mexican women of all ages passed by with purpose, women wearing housedresses under checked aprons, women with babies swathed to their bodies, women off to market with mesh shopping bags in all the colors. Why couldn't I be satisfied with their small pleasures, say a steaming bowl of tortilla soup spiced just so? Or a simple job in the Tuesday market that didn't ask me to take it home after eight dry hours in an office? Wasn't it enough to have a steady income and friends I could depend on to make me laugh until I snorted? Surely those gifts would have been sufficient riches for these women or men.

* * *

That afternoon, thanks to Norma and Bernardo and Señora Hernández, I cemented two new Spanish phrases into my Level Seven vocabulary: *to have the wits of a garden slug,* and *the phone line went dead.*

Some students at La Divina Escuela de Idiomas rented rooms in old hotels with thick walls, labyrinthine corridors, and often a swimming pool set amid the greenery like a sudden jungle pond. Actual parrots screeched nearby, let loose from cages for the day. Beauty flamed out everywhere, but friendships with the people of Cuernavaca did not.

My own business arrangement lay with the widow Hernández. Five months ago, circumstances forced her to become a sharp-eyed businesswoman when her husband could not be awakened at four p.m., or ever, from his afternoon siesta. Mexico's community property laws left Señora Hernández a valuable asset: a modest four-bedroom house with no debt.

The house stood just an easy walk from La Divina Escuela de Idiomas. The proximity compensated for it being next to a business, *El Universo de Llantas,* the Universe of Tires, where loud clangs and pneumatic drills carried on from eight in the morning until eight at night. The Señora's other two assets, aside from her excellent health and penurious resolve, were two teenaged children, Norma and Bernardo, old enough to work a little on weekends and help make ends meet.

Outside my small bedroom, the rain fell to a steady beat, muffling clangs from the tire universe next door. Each of the five days I had been in Cuernavaca, big clouds gathered as if by common agreement in the afternoon between three and four o'clock, towering cumulus pileups in a bright blue sky. Then, almost at the siesta hour, the clouds let loose a rain intense but at the same time orderly and soothing.

I sprawled on my bed, lulled by the rain, counting my remaining money again. My thoughts meandered through my demotion to Level Seven, on to the prediction of Christian that the *coronel* would never leave ample Claudia. Despite Mama's pliant fullness, my father had long ago left her. In so doing, he had left me too, when I was six and just starting school. Worse yet, there I was, each morning also leaving her, in a sense, as I waved goodbye at the schoolhouse door. Now I had done it again.

The rain drummed against the broad leaves of a banana tree just outside the window. A knock sounded on the door.

Norma and Bernardo let themselves in and immediately flopped onto the other twin bed in the room before I could issue an invitation. Since my second day with Señora Hernández, the two of them had followed the ritual of showing up uninvited in my bedroom after the main meal to conduct their own version of Spanish class. I liked that they wanted my company and assumed I wanted theirs.

Bernardo, a tall good-natured seventeen-year-old with the tight muscularity of youth, began just as he had the days before, "What did you learn in school today?"

I presented what I hoped was a nifty one-minute summary of the colonel and La Gordita. Bernardo nodded encouragement to everything, as if I were a brilliant polyglot ready for simultaneous interpreting at the U.N. He obviously had no problem with the notion of La Gordita, nor with my Level Seven Spanish.

Norma, a no-nonsense but cheerful young woman of sixteen, who happened to be a bit gordita herself, leaned against the wall, crossed her legs, and pulled out a cigarette from the pack she had in hand. "Do you want to hear a joke?"

Before I could answer, she began to narrate, speaking way too fast for a Level Seven in La Divina Escuela de Idiomas. It was something about a bird and its beak. I knew somehow it was a dirty joke. Weren't they all?

At a certain point, she and Bernardo burst out laughing, the joke over.

I tried a smile. Bernardo helped himself to one of Norma's cigarettes. "I will tell you again," he said, "more slowly."

Bernardo repeated the joke, enunciating carefully. I stuffed the bed pillow behind my back as if relaxing might help me think more clearly. I would have been in the back row of this class if it had rows. I was already up against the wall, in both senses. I liked to think of myself as a person good at inference. I always got jokes in English. But not this joke. Nor had I gotten yesterday's joke, which involved *monjas,* nuns.

Norma knocked the long ash of her cigarette into the empty pack. "Ay, Bernardo, you are too slow. *No seas baboso.*"

I recognized the word for a *slug.* Bernardo wasn't the slug, though.

"Look," said Norma, taking over. "I will draw it for you." She asked for paper and pen, and I provided her my school notebook. She retold the joke, this time with visuals. She drew the bird. She drew the beak, making it huge and sausage-like. She made more lines I found mysterious. She and Bernardo burst out laughing again. Smoke from their cigarettes convulsed in merry loops around my thick gringa skull.

Norma shot me a determined look and began drawing again, pressing down hard. What was clearly a penis took shape on the page. Even as I wondered how a sheltered girl brought up under the hawk-eye of Señora Hernández would be able to render such a detailed drawing while smoking her cigarette to a nub, I felt bad about letting the two of them down after all their effort. Who says a picture is worth a thousand words?

I shook my head to convey deep regret as I maintained what I suspected was a dopey smile. I knew all the words but couldn't put them together in a way that had anything to do with what Norma was drawing with such anatomical glee.

Señora Hernández suddenly spoke, right outside the bedroom door. "Someone is calling you on the telephone, Rosie."

I bolted upright. Should I throw my pillow over Norma's drawing? What were the Mexican laws on this matter? Was I tainting these minors by letting them draw genitalia in my bedroom instead of reprimanding them like a proper authority figure? Yet, what kind of authority figure is someone who has the wits of a garden slug and can't get a joke?

Who could be calling? It wasn't as though I had friends here, outside of the three Purples (*Morados*), and they wouldn't have the number. As I made my way to the door, I ran through the only possibilities in the world: Mama? Dear God, don't let anything have happened and me so far away. Maybe Leland, my sadist-philosopher editor? Dear God, don't tell me he's called to bray that he's turned all my semicolons into full stops, an ongoing philosophical argument between us. What? Newspapers don't use semicolons? Maybe he was calling to say I'd been let go, *adiós, chica.*

I opened the door. Maybe my friend Carole-Ann? God, no. She wouldn't have gotten the city name straight, much less a phone number.

I took the thick black receiver from Señora Hernández. Her face held no answers.

A bluesy voice sang into the phone.

Monty's voice was both distant and near, too near. Now here was a test in any language. I was thankful it wasn't Mama, but this was almost as bad. I tried a yoga breath, deep and long. I exhaled, "Hey there, Midnight Special. What a surprise." Whoops, I shouldn't have used that old nickname.

I imagined him in his orderly office, contradicted by the half-eaten Twinkie and Diet Pepsi that would litter his desk, along with fanned-out files for whatever case consumed him now. The grin on his face flashed between sardonic and playful as the phone held his brown curls in check.

And what image of me was he calling to mind? Being male, he probably pictured me naked: sleepy-eyed, stretched out on a hot rock in the wilderness, my caramel-colored hair tumbling in disarray over my warmed body. Skin glistening. Or did he see me as I stood there in my sensible tan walking shoes, hair wadded into a ponytail, wearing yesterday's crumpled jeans? A pang of despair thumped my chest. How could I even vacillate about which image I wanted him to have?

Did I leave Monty, or did he leave me? To determine that would be like looking for the beginning or end of a Mobius Strip. The two of us, as if in an M.C. Escher drawing, would have trudged on and on, circling back over the same path without end, arriving nowhere. "Pregnant women look grotesque," Monty had idly commented to my friend Carole-Ann, who had passed the stray remark on to me. Emboldened, I cut the strip, sending Monty and me into free fall.

Outside, the rain grew more insistent. I modulated my voice and made it so light and buoyant I felt eerily disembodied. "How did you find the number?"

"Oh, Rosie, what did you expect? I'm a professional."

"I didn't know detective skills in one country translate to another. It's not like you could depend on your usual snitches." I couldn't imagine Monty speaking Spanish, much less applying to a foreign culture the subtleties learned from almost a decade of detective work for the Marbella P.D.

"Easy. The school gave it to me right away. Screw privacy."

I would not dispense encouragement. He was calling way too soon. Months of distance should have passed, or decades. He started to sing again.

How did Monty manage to get through his business day since he was compelled to burst into song so often? You would have thought it was an occupational hazard. Just about any situation or phrase he heard reminded him of a song lyric from the past. That had once been part of his charm.

"Seriously, Rosie, I've been thinking about you. Sandwiched in with my usual thoughts about murderers and child molesters and meth slammers, of course."

My heart, in defiance of its biological limitations, did a half-gainer, a diver's tidy reverse. How dare Monty ruin my escape? How dare he try to beguile me again? I had resolved to move onward without him. Why did he have to make it so hard? And why did I have to let him?

On the other side of the hallway door, Señora Hernández bent over the blue brocade sofa in the living room to unplug the radio and television, just as she did each day after *comida*, the main meal and included in the price of room and board.

The only thing I could figure was she thought unplugging the appliances might save electricity. Or maybe prevent damage during the afternoon thunderstorms.

I bet she yearned to pull the phone plug, too. She padded into the hallway, careful not to meet my eyes as she angled past. Was she signaling by her presence that I had better make this call short? I didn't remember if phone calls cost extra.

"This is kind of awkward, Monty. I'm standing in the hallway here. It's a private home. I feel guilty speaking English as if I'm hatching some kind of foreign plot. There are other people. I can't really talk."

"You don't need to talk. Just breathe deeply into the phone and remember—"

"You're right. I don't need to talk. *We* don't need to talk. We agreed we were cooling down."

"You mean *over*?"

"We agreed to keep our distance and—"

"You're certainly keeping yours. I mean, what's this trip to Mexico really all about?"

A pause for yoga breathing took place on both our parts. "There must be some reason I can't get you out of my mind," he said as if that statement were evidence to clinch a winning argument in court.

"There must be some reason we broke up."

Here we were, doing it again. We could just never stop the verbal jousting. We probably even stood in identical poses, combative phones in hand.

All this sparring once had given me energy, whimsical goofing-off we did to entertain ourselves. That was in the first year when we were still getting to know each other. Energy misspent.

The hallway grew several shades brighter from a lightning flash. The connection sputtered.

"Awww, Rosie. When are you coming home?"

I liked him better like this. It slipped out: "In a couple of weeks."

Wrong and wrong. That was not the thing to tell him. It sounded as though it was just a matter of weeks before we would see each other again. I resolved to put a stop to the way the call was going.

The mysteries of the Mexican phone system did it first. Monty vanished in mid-sentence, leaving only silence and the smell of ozone. Thunder boomed so loud the windows rattled.

I was rattled myself. Señora Hernández materialized again in the hallway. I held out the phone and pantomimed a karate chop.

She held the phone to her ear to be sure, then set the receiver back in the cradle. "*La línea se cortó.*" The line was dead.

The heavens had spoken. In a momentary respite from the next downpour, several loud clangs in a row rang out from the Universe of Tires like exclamation marks.

I pushed open the door to my room and stared into what looked like a thick coastal fog. Cigarette smoke lay curled around the heads of Norma and Bernardo, anointing them.

Norma shrugged and motioned toward the penis sketch. "That's okay." She radiated goodwill. "Tomorrow, we will play cards."

I almost groaned. Instead, I smiled to make up for the fact

I was failing intercultural exchange class, too. I knew what *mañana* would bring. I had never been good at card games, even in English. I wanted Norma and Bernardo to think I was young and cool and hip, like them, not someone closer in demeanor to the dour Señora.

Maybe there's a limit to how much motion and change the human species can manage in a given period of time. I had hurled my body through thousands of miles of air travel, the crowded subway and theft of half my cash, then the commotion of a teeming bus station, the pounding bus ride from Mexico City to Cuernavaca, its streets named after heroes and dates I'd never heard of and other streets not named or numbered at all. All around me were barrages of frenzied Spanish and upside-down ways of doing everything while I was trying to feel how much fun I was having.

Who was the wag that said something is either easy or it is impossible? I was now waiting to discover something, anything, that was easy.

Several hours later, the rain resumed, growing alternately loud and soft. At first, it suited my mood as I lay in bed waiting to fall asleep. Then it began to challenge me: By God, I had to translate it, make sense of it. Was it a welcome rain? Or a sad, regretful rain? A cleansing rain? A singing-in-the-rain rain? A rain coaxing new buds to life? Maybe a rain that makes a woman want to run naked into the storm. I had thought my plan would fall neatly into place. This was more like starting over with a clean slate, a tabula rasa.

Damn, what was that Spanish phrase about needing your exit papers in order?

2

IXMILCO

The old bus crept into the tiny heart of Ixmilco. Big puddles, remnants of the night's storm, pockmarked the muddy streets. Marketgoers maneuvered unconcerned around the pools of water. The seven of us students who had elected to come to this small pueblo burst forth from the cocoon of our bus, excited to see market day already in full swing.

Rows of improvised stalls threaded through the narrow streets. Here and there, vendors strung blue tarps over plastic tables displaying their wares, while others had merely thrown the tarp on the ground and set up shop. I was anxious to shoot pictures of so much rich color.

But once out of the bus, I just stood there, feeling conspicuously foreign. I ducked to one side as an old man angled past, bearing on his bent back two tall stacks of cages with jostled birds that still managed to bill and coo. I tried to keep one eye on Aida as she plunged ahead, leading us like a string of kindergartners smack into the bustle of high commerce.

A knife glinted near the ground. A woman, her face absorbed, hair knotted in a long braid, squatted on her haunches as she sliced needles off a cactus paddle. Her wrist made curt sweeps, rivaling the quick moves of an inner-city street fighter. She paused once to adjust her red shawl, then set the bare nopal onto the thick plastic stretched over the ground. Once devoid of needles, the cactus ovals looked tamed, lying there like large green lollipops. Aida had told us in class nothing was more Mexican than *ensalada de nopales*, the salad of stewed cactus strips seasoned with tomatoes, onion, and garlic.

The woman looked up. *"Nopales, mi reina?"* she called to me in the singsong of the vendors. "What can I give you?"

I smiled. The knife woman had called me *"Mi Reina."* My Queen. I rather liked that, though I admit the endearment was a bit overstated. There she reigned amidst her tribe of nopal sellers, the first one in a row of women who were also stacking their identical defanged paddles on the ground in similar green piles.

I shook my head but lingered there in my American jeans and Perma-press blouse, clearly of the tourist tribe. I just had to take a picture as she set to work on another cactus paddle, her face again hard with concentration. I shifted my bag around and tried to sneak the camera out. But the strap got hung up on something, and I ended up yanking the camera, along with a wad of Kleenex, a half-empty pack of gum, and a baggie of acidophilus pills. All flipped onto the ground in front of her. I dropped to one knee and scooped my stuff up with one hand, grabbing the camera with the other. But this was a good angle for a photo after all, so I brought the camera up.

The woman in the red shawl flicked her eyes from her work to me and back again. My face flushed with heat. It was not like me to be self-conscious with a camera. Journalists are used to intruding on somebody, whether in words or pictures.

Click! I immortalized her. But she had grunted and ducked her head behind the shawl just as I pushed the button. The photo would not capture the person, just the blur of red and her green wares. Maybe she was right to duck from the camera. It was, after all, her soul I wanted. I dropped the camera back in the bag and hurried away.

All around me erupted a crazy jumble of things for sale: used tires stacked in piles, bolts of chiffon, pieces of hardware strewn about on an old Army blanket, plastic bowls and cups in sorbet colors, mysterious herbs, and table after table of what had to be counterfeit copies of the latest movies from the U.S., all sold to the pumping sounds of disco music, also counterfeit.

Despite the thumping party beat, I could pick out Spanish phrases here and there, sometimes whole sentences. What will you take? What may I show you? In all these colors . . . very sweet . . . a sample for you . . . a discount for you.

I had lost track of Aida. Nor did I see any of the others from the school. An unexpected jolt of liberty at being free from my tribe shot through me. We would inevitably bump into each other. I started to wander, intoning to myself, "I am nearly bilingual, a citizen of the world." I was ready to start humming "We Are the World." These assurances let me stave off replays of the previous night's phone call, and its intended yank back to where I'd come from.

The roofed part of the market stood just ahead. The fragrant smell of mango and guava wafted my way. A young woman at the first stall beckoned me with a paper plate of golden mango slices. I reached for one.

The next moment, still focused on the white plate, I lay sprawled on the wet tile. Searing pain encircled my left ankle.

As fast as I was down, a small huddle of concerned people bent over me. I wondered if they were able to telepath instantly: Gringa down on Aisle One. I hunched over my ankle, enfolding it like a mother hen to stop the wild throbbing. My bag with the camera still hung on my arm. Again, the camera had betrayed me, throwing me enough off-balance to send my feet skating.

Collapsed on the cool floor, I just sat there, the center of curiosity. From that perspective, the people surrounding me loomed up tall and elongated. Could I be in a dream?

Two women, who stretched upward like Giacometti sculptures, cooed to me in a chain of undulating Spanish. "Ay, Señorita, are you hurt . . . hurt . . . hurt? Permit us to help you. *Pobrecita.* No, you must not stand up yet. Please, Señorita, please. Who is with you? You are not alone . . . alone, are you?"

I understood them, but it didn't seem to be two-way. I was gibbering something—my accent having flown back to California—about finding Señorita Aida. I tried to see up over their heads, hoping her face would pop into the growing circle of onlookers checking out the gringa on the floor. Where was Miss Aida, anyway? Where was my tribe?

"We are taking you to the clinic, Señorita. You must see the doctor," said a young man in a tee shirt that even in my fuzzy state, I could see spelled out *Old Fart.*

"No, no, I must find my teacher." The last thing I wanted was to go to a doctor in this little town that certainly was not on any Auto Club map of Mexico.

The pain was growing, so I switched to belly breathing. I riffled through my options as my breaths whooshed in and out. I could have somebody phone the school so they might send a car for me. But, of course, nobody was at the school on a Saturday. I could call Señora Hernández and promise to always from now on leave the electric alarm clock unplugged. But she didn't drive, nor did Norma or Bernardo.

I closed my eyes for a moment to better manage the pain.

"Do you want to puke?" It was a female voice in heavily accented English.

Despite my ankle now afire, I smiled at the word "puke" and opened my eyes. A familiar-looking woman with red hair had joined my helpers. Wasn't she the Siren who had lured me with the mango? She knelt beside me and stroked my hair. Overcome by her tenderness, I resisted the urge to teach her *vomit* or *regurgitate* as a better choice than *puke*.

"You have to go to a doctor."

I feared what that would cost. I tried to stand, determined to hobble away with Yankee grit. As soon as I tested my ankle, putting more weight on it was out of the question.

The next thing I knew, two young men improvised a seat with their forearms while a third lifted me into it. The mango-lady bore my legs as if they were fragile boughs. Even so, my ankle bobbed as they started to walk, and I clenched my jaw with each jarring step.

My three Samaritans hurried me deeper into the market—past piles of chiles and bananas and tall vases of pink gladiolas, past stalls with pickled carrots and steaming bowls of menudo, past racks of crocheted infant clothes and stacks of cowboy hats—and out a back door, onto the street and around a corner. Nowhere did I see Aida or a wandering *Morado*.

My ankle continued to bob in pain. I thought I might puke.

* * *

A metal plaque at the entrance of a modest, whitewashed building indicated it was the *Hospital Civil*. We passed through the doorway and into a curtain of cool air held captive by thick brick walls and cement floors. A woman with a clipboard motioned us down a hallway. It turned the corner and opened into a larger waiting area.

At once, I thought we must have blundered in the wrong direction and somehow entered the operating area. At the end of the room, atop a white sheet draped over what looked to be a library table, lay a body.

A doctor bent over it, his hands deft with certainty. A stomach was laid open. The glistening pink and scarlet of human organs and their stark, incarnadine rawness made me feel we had stumbled into a Frida Kahlo painting.

My helpers settled me onto an unpainted wooden chair along the wall, taking care to elevate my dangling foot on another chair. They then melted around the corner, leaving me alone. The smell of blood encircled me. I was pinned there, absorbing a scene that rendered my own situation puny.

To fight the smell of blood, I focused on the doctor and his fierce glare of concentration over the surgical mask. He appeared to be somewhere in his thirties. A shock of dark brown hair hung over his forehead. The somber intensity of his eyes mirrored the determined hands. As if my camera were before me, I kept registering close-up photos: the eyes, the hands, the open patient.

I caught myself. I was ever the tourist, gawking, framing, and reframing. I wrenched my focus away.

A handful of people waited in silence on my side of the room, observing the doctor as if in church or a theater. Two nurses appeared, fluttering like nervous moths. The taller one called to somebody for more bandages, more antiseptic wash. The shorter one passed the doctor instruments with one hand and waved off flies from the open window with the other.

Not far from the patient's feet clustered what must have been the family. They huddled on the floor, faces wilted. One, a slim woman who looked to be a teenager, nursed a baby. Along with the faceless patient and the intense doctor, they formed a tableau.

The curve of the doctor's upper back was visible as he bent over the patient. His hands in the blood-specked gloves seemed the only bit of hope in the room.

The young woman with the clipboard suddenly stood before me, reminding me of my plight. The mango-lady, who had been the bearer of my legs, also reappeared. She whispered to the woman with the clipboard, who gestured toward the scene at the end of the room.

"*El doctor Villaseñor* is in emergency surgery," whispered

back the woman holding the clipboard, "and the other doctor is also in surgery." She peered at my ankle, then cocked her head to one side as if overcome by disappointment. "I am very sorry. Our x-ray machine is not working."

The mango-lady whispered a solution. "We will take you to the dentist."

Perhaps I was becoming Mexican—I didn't understand, but I surrendered. They could take me wherever they wanted. God's will be done. *Si Dios quiere.*

"He will take an x-ray of your ankle." Yes, of course. *Si Dios quiere.*

The blood-spattered doctor suddenly raised his head and looked over his mask in our direction. I wondered if he trusted those eyes as they glimpsed an American woman being lifted out the door. The collar of a blue-checked shirt showed under his white medical coat. The black leather cowboy boots, visible under the operating table, were maybe a sign of the urgency with which he had hurried to surgery. Not seeming to register anyone in the room, he lowered his head again, his passion on display.

As we started to move, I gritted my teeth. We were off to the dentist.

3

EL PATRÓN

noun, masculine: the pattern; the boss

Slowly, Dr. Juan Ramón Villaseñor lowered himself into his office chair. His head was pounding. It had started with the sudden appearance of Magdalena Urbina at the clinic earlier that morning, clutching her side, barely able to stand. She leaned heavily on her skeletal sister, who appeared almost as unsteady as Magdalena.

The pulsing in his temples grew even stronger as he now steeled himself for the phone call he was about to make to the director general. It felt like the hundredth one this month. This time he was determined to impress upon the next person in the chain of command how dire the situation was in Ixmilco.

He dialed the phone. A secretary answered in a rapid singsong. When he gave his name, he expected her to dismiss him with one of the usual stories. The excuse might be that the director general was called to Cuernavaca for a conference with the health director for the state of Morelos or that he was meeting that moment with a delegation from Tepalcingo or Tepoztlán or one of the state's other pueblos, or that he was on vacation—or, or, or. Juan Ramón knew he should go in person to make these requests, but he could not leave his patients unattended that long for what was sure to be a fruitless journey.

The evasively courteous voice of the director general himself came on the line. "Doctor Juan Ramón! *Como estás,* Doctor? What a miracle to hear from you."

They engaged in the traditional ritual as they asked about each other's well-being and their families' well-being, and the well-being of their colleagues. Finally, Juan Ramón said, "Our supplies here in Ixmilco are almost nil, Director. We had another emergency surgery just this morning. At this point, we have only one package of bandages left. We need your help."

"Yes, yes," said the director. "I know the situation is *difícil.*" He gave a big sigh. "It is that way everywhere."

"I am not asking you for much. Well, yes, perhaps I am. But I am trying to be realistic, too. Surely there is a way to request more money from the national health secretary. An emergency transfer of funds."

The director general sighed again. "You are such a good warrior, Doctor. Always fighting for your patients. And that is as it should be."

Juan Ramón tried to keep his tone calm and orderly. "But the hospital here is not as it should be. Why do we even have a hospital, much less a clinic, if we cannot offer medical services? We cannot practice as doctors here without certain indispensable items."

"You know I want to help you, Doctor. I, too, am worried. You know it is not easy for me. In so many ways, my hands are tied. But I will talk to health directors from the other states about this situation. *Vamos a ver lo que se puede hacer.*"

Juan Ramón's calls—the ones that got through—always seemed to end with the same words and the same results: *Vamos a ver lo que se puede hacer:* We'll see what can be done. He knew this polite but tiresome dance with the director general meant he had to resort to unorthodox means to do his job in this tiny out-of-the-way hospital. In fact, unorthodox means were orthodox here.

His hands, which just a little while ago had been so steady as they guided the scalpel to open the abdomen of Magdalena Urbina now shook. He wanted a cigarette. A familiar anger stirred, lashing out in several directions like tentacles of an octopus. This was jungle medicine. He laughed at himself. Were they not in a jungle? What could the two of them—only two doctors in this so-called hospital—do with just a knife and a flame? And he, forced to operate on Magdalena Urbina atop a plain plank table because the hospital's one operating table was already in use. What about the clean bandages the nurses went through in just the first week after each month's delivery? The rightful number never came from Almacén Central, the state warehouse, because the money was skimmed off by someone higher in the chain to cover his country club dues or buy a case of fine imported Scotch. Many months he and *el doctor* Eugenio dipped into their own pockets to buy a tank of propane gas so they could heat water and sterilize. And what about the antibiotics already past their expiration dates when they arrived and the anticoagulants that failed to arrive at all? The Fluothane anesthesia was now gone. He had used the last of it on Magdalena Urbina.

Or maybe his head was pounding simply because of the Presidente brandy with Coca-Cola he had been drinking the night before, lured into a prolonged conversation with his colleague and friend *el doctor* Eugenio. Somewhere in their talk— was it between the transmigration of the soul and the wisdom of privatizing the oil company?—and was that between the three a.m. ringing of the bells and the first cock crow?—somewhere in there he had lost, or maybe just misplaced, the thread of memory. He did remember he had almost glimpsed a crystalline moment, one that would allow it all to make sense to him, the missing piece of the *rompecabezas*, the jigsaw puzzle of his present existence. Life was *bastante difícil*, with its scattered moments of comprehension and momentary peeks at the obscure pattern. It was surely destined to do exactly what the words for a jigsaw puzzle literally said: *rompe cabezas*, break heads.

Doctor Villaseñor reached for the worn hunting jacket hanging on the back of his chair and rummaged in one of the pockets. He found what he was looking for, half a cigarette. It was broken off but clean, which meant smokeable. His hands trembled as he lit it. He inhaled deeply. He was desperate to see some kind of pattern to all this.

Ah, yes. Maybe there was a pattern, if you could call futility a pattern. Here in this village and the surrounding ranchos, he had thought he could perform his small part in assuaging misery, bringing just a little dignity to a people who had even less hope than money. But he could not work miracles. Even Christ had something to start with, some loaves and fishes.

He inhaled again, deeper, until he felt that satisfying clutch as the smoke reached hoary gray hands down into his lungs. He exhaled and considered another puzzle piece that fit nowhere, unless futility was indeed the pattern of his life: a marriage, if you could call it that, when he was twenty. Such bad luck it was to be caught in bed with a foolish girl, and he just as foolish. Caught by her scheming mother.

"You have ruined my daughter!" the mother screamed at him. She pulled the girl from the bed by one bare leg, then turned on him in fury and scratched his arms and chest until she drew blood. "You will do the decent thing! You will be an honorable man."

He was trapped like an animal, ordered by her family—but, worst of all, by his own father—to mouth unholy vows in church. Even his mother did not dare brave his father and contest the decision that he must marry the girl.

He had approached his father and actually begged. "But

Papá, we should not marry. We do not have that kind of feeling for each other. If there is a baby, I will support it. I give you my word."

The marriage lasted two months, but he was marked forever. No girls in this country, Catholic to the core, wanted a divorced man, even less one who had managed only a two-month marriage. The possibility that there could be an annulment was absurd in such a country.

At least there had been no baby. He had left the girl, his "wife," and in so doing, he had failed his father Don Alejandro yet again. But he should be used to that. Trying to please his father was the oldest futility of all.

Sí, Señor! He saw the pattern now. How had he been so blind?

4

DUST TO DUST

Don Alejandro Villaseñor sat upright behind the big desk with its oversized legs carved into lion heads. He unlocked the center drawer of the desk and reached for the bottle of capotena to calm his blood pressure. As he felt into the drawer, his fingers brushed the cold and dispassionate metal of the old Colt 38. He picked up the gun and tested its weight in his hand. The early sun through the arched window caught the stock and burnished it with a dull gleam. He closed his eyes.

He intoned to himself, as he had so many times, that only in self-defense had he bought the gun when he was fourteen years old. The warmth of his hand heated the metal and for the moment brought the gun alive in his fist.

Don Alejandro never knew his mother, who died at the moment of his birth. The year his father was murdered, school stopped. So did God. There had been no rightness in the world. Thirteen years old, he went to live with his father's brother, who, although married, had no children. When his uncle was also killed a year later in the same feud that had taken his father, he knew it would soon be time to go off on his own.

El Avión, the Airplane, was the nickname for the man who had killed his father and then his uncle. El Avión was twenty-two years old, a fighter, and fast. Fast as an airplane, he would swoop down on his enemies. El Avión had vowed to kill every one of the Villaseñor men.

Alejandro, by then almost fifteen, sold his bicycle to buy a gun. El Avión was looking for him—that was what everyone in the village of Aguas Puras told him. Had not El Avión sworn before the Virgin of San Juan de los Lagos that he would kill all the Villaseñor men?

Alejandro began to have bad dreams. In one dream, he was actually shot. He stood on a street, a slight hill, lined with tall, dusty pines, impassive and pale as old ghosts. When the bullet entered his left side, his legs had slowly crumpled, returning him to the soil, just as such a bullet had his father and his uncle. Earth to earth, he cried in his dream, as his legs fell away and his soul floated out of his body. The vision haunted him.

One day as he returned from the marketplace with the chicken Tía Blanca had sent him to buy, he heard the droning sound. Buzz, buzz. Was it El Avión? Perhaps it was just his fear that put the drone of a circling airplane in his imagination. Buzz, buzz, buzz, chanted El Avión. This was no dream.

Alejandro wished he had his bicycle so he could pedal away with his strong legs. A bike was no match for an airplane, of course. He reached inside his shirt for the gun that was pulsing close to his heart, the barrel lodged beneath his belt. Even then, the gun was old and rusty. Alejandro hadn't known if it would in fact work. He withdrew it from his shirt.

Buzz, buzz. He heard it, the maddening sound El Avión made to taunt his enemies. El Avión was coming for him, the agent of death circling as it had for his father and uncle. Earth to earth, dust to dust.

But he was only fourteen years old, too young to die. Everyone had heard the loud bragging of El Avión in the plaza and the dirt streets of Aguas Puras. The boy Alejandro, named after his father and after his father's father—none of whom could help him—started to run. El Avión was coming for him. Everyone had said it would be so.

El Avión was bellowing his name. "Alejandro! *¡Cobarde! Coward!*" The boy rounded the corner, running with the gun in his hand, and turned down a familiar road. Only he had never noticed the two rows of dusty pines before. Yet they must have always been there. They lined both sides of the road as it slanted down the hill, just as in his dream. He heard a scream and realized it was his own.

"Stop, *hijo de una puta madre*," the Airplane yelled. "Here comes El Avión to take you away. Today, *cabrón*, you kiss your father in hell."

Buzz, buzz. The relentless droning was in his ear. Alejandro spun in place and fired the Colt 38. "In the name of the Father," he said, maybe to himself, maybe aloud, sinking to his knees.

El Avión crashed to the earth. His gun flew to one side and thudded against the trunk of a dusty pine, then dropped to the ground and spun once in the dirt.

Alejandro got to his feet, stunned to be alive. He still clutched the market bag of plucked chicken in his other hand. Slowly, he walked the long blocks to Tía Blanca's house. His hand with the old gun was trembling. He wished again he had a bicycle.

Later that night, he left Aguas Puras by foot. Six months later, word reached him in León, where he had found work as a shoemaker's apprentice, that Tía Blanca had gone to live in the house of a goddaughter. There she had died of a complication with the lungs.

His family gone, Alejandro vowed to start his own. At nineteen, he had married Guadalupe Ramírez Ramírez with breasts plumped up like yeast buns, daughter of a baker. At twenty, he became a father. When he saw his infant son for the first time, those clenched baby fists punching at an invisible opponent, Alejandro recovered his belief in God. For almost all his life, he had wanted only two things: A big family and work enough to support that family. These two things finally brought him a sense of rightness with the world. As he gazed at the new life he had fathered, he prayed for forgiveness for the other life, the one he had taken.

Don Alejandro, his eyes closed in reverie, could once again feel El Avión, the agent of death, circling him. He felt the way it had been that day almost sixty years ago as he made his way back from the store, a plucked chicken in the loose net bag his Tía Blanca had given him. This time, though, El Avión was not an airplane at all, but a skeletal woman, La Catrina, the image of death, wearing lipstick on her bony mouth and a large-brimmed hat. He snapped his eyes open to vanish the image.

* * *

Seventy-four years of age, Alejandro was old and revered enough that his friends and employees unhesitatingly inserted *Don*, the title of respect, before his name. Don Alejandro stood now in the kitchen, the large jar of vinegar on the counter in front of him. He unscrewed the lid and sniffed the murky contents. The smell rose strong and pungent. He dipped a finger into the jar, then stuck the finger in his mouth. He smacked his lips with satisfaction. All who knew him said Don Alejandro made the tangiest and tastiest vinegar, and he took pride in their saying so.

He glanced at the clock as he started to strain the vinegar, pouring it into a small bottle that later in the day he would give to his neighbor, Don Ponchito. It was six-thirty in the morning. He pictured his wife Lupita still asleep on her back in their king-sized bed, her soft snoring grazing the darkened bedroom.

The hours just before and after dawn were his favorite

time of day. Since boyhood, he had been unable to sleep past four-thirty. He arose to savor the hours when he had his thoughts and movements to himself, owing no explanations or courtesies to anyone. This was the only time he worked in the house. With the large chrome presser, he squeezed oranges to make fresh juice for his wife and youngest daughter. He spilled water onto the tiled floor and scrubbed grease spots. He tended his cooking projects: the vinegar, the salsas from chile cambrai and chile chipotle, the uncooked salsa with fresh chopped onions he always served with the pork loin he packed in rock salt and left for his wife to roast slowly for exactly one hour and twenty minutes.

When his nine children were still little and all living at home, he had found comfort in having them tucked upstairs spinning dreams while downstairs he wound the clock of domestic events that would mark their day. Now only his wife Lupita and his daughter Ceci were left upstairs to dream. The other children were married and in their own homes. All except Juan Ramón, he thought, with a tightening of the lips and heart.

He placed the bottle of Don Ponchito's vinegar to one side and carried the much larger jar of vinegar outside and across the service patio to the pantry. He set it on the shelf next to the bounty of bottles and cans he had stored there: cases of mineral water, Coca-Cola, El Presidente brandy, jars he had put up himself of pickled pigs' feet, plastic bags of toilet paper, forty-eight rolls to the bag, and formations of napkins and paper towels lined up like a platoon under review. His eye caught three bottles of rubbing alcohol with blue tops, and these medical supplies led him to think again of Juan Ramón.

He returned to his office and dialed the telephone. Juan Ramón answered, his voice thick with sleep.

"I have made inquiries, *hijo*. The new hospital here in León opens in six months."

Juan Ramón was silent. Don Alejandro waited.

Juan Ramón finally said, "Papá, I have obligations here in Ixmilco."

"You have obligations *here*. This is where your family is." Don Alejandro had spoken more sharply than he intended. He would modify his tone. "You have gone as far as you can in a pueblo like Ixmilco, *hijo*. In a city there are opportunities. You have choices." He knew he was pushing, but he grew excited to think of the possibilities for this well-trained son, the only one to have left León, the only one who had to journey almost an entire day when he came home.

"This new hospital will have everything, the most modern equipment. It will be the best in León. The best in the state."

"Gracias, Papá. I will think about it."

"While you are thinking, call the director. He says they are doing the hiring now." Don Alejandro read off the director's name and phone number from a business card. It had taken him several weeks of planning to find the director's name and then arrange for someone to introduce him.

"You do not have to say you want the job. Just investigate it."

They hung up, and Don Alejandro returned at once to the pantry. He faced the jars of pickled carrots and pigs' feet and steadied himself for a moment, resting his forehead against the impartial coolness of the metal shelf. His other sons—Alejandro chico, Tomás, Luis, Martín—all lived less than a kilometer from the family home. They brought their wives and children each Wednesday and Sunday to eat the family midday meal. These other sons quarreled among themselves and at times with him, but still, they stayed near and sought him out. As boys, they had begun to work with the shoes in his factory. Unlike Juan Ramón, they had stayed on at the factory, content, even proud, to continue the work Don Alejandro had begun.

With Juan Ramón, this impetuous and headstrong son, he never could find the right words, the convincing rhythm. Now he had once again used the wrong tactic and the wrong words.

The metal shelf where Don Alejandro rested his head had turned warm and moist, as if now charged with the anxiety emanating from his body. His temporary solace gone, Don Alejandro moved away and resumed his daily routine.

5

SUBJUNCTIVE MOOD

Church bells chimed me awake earlier than I wanted. I urged myself back into a half-sleep and managed to hold on to the end of a dream that needed immediate fixing.

Green, white, red. Green, white, red. The light bulbs blinked the colors of the Mexican flag in sequence, just as they had before a picture of the Virgin of Guadalupe at the bus station when I arrived.

Suddenly, I was on the deck of a small boat. Monty balanced on the edge of a makeshift wooden pier bobbing up and down next to the boat.

"Jump!" I called. "The boat is leaving." But Monty didn't move.

"Jump!" I yearned so hard I could almost see him, make him, do it. The wind ruffled his brown curls. A rippled expanse of water appeared between us as the boat drifted from the pier. I watched with a sad knowledge I must always have harbored of him unknowingly. The stretch of water between us grew wider, and Monty only stared at me with blank eyes. A seagull cawed from above, mocking my yearning. A trace of crooked smile crossed Monty's face, but his eyes stayed blank. He did not jump.

My first urge was to sink back into the dream so I could rewrite it and give it the ending I wanted. That's what I did with disturbing dreams.

I had fallen asleep poring over the Spanish subjunctive mood. Aida had told us, when I was still at Level Eight, the subjunctive mood was the language of desires and doubts, and of potential happenings. That certainly sounded like what my days had become. Aida said mastering it would arm us with the ability to escape from present reality and make statements like "I wish that" and "if I were to" and "if it should happen." Now subjunctive thoughts came to me unbidden: *If he were to jump . . . I wish he were . . . that I were . . .*

But in my half-sleep, a paralysis held onto me. I could not make myself change the dream's ending. For God's sake, Monty had missed the boat. How obvious a sign did I need? The subjunctive mood with its hypothetical "what ifs" refused to be welded onto my dream. I woke up, this time for good, the dream's vaporous trails wrapping me in uneasiness.

I dressed slowly, nursing my ankle. I tried to be silent as I hobbled into the hallway and toward the phone. My semi-suspended foot still hurt like hell, but I steeled myself to endure it, remembering how people in other centuries had to brave all kinds of injuries without pain killers, unless you counted stiff shots of whisky and biting on bullets. I rather fancied the image of myself, alone in a foreign land, courageous and noble through the pain.

On a whim, I lifted the receiver and listened. Nothing. No dial tone, no static, no outside world, no Monty. The line was still dead, *gracias a Dios*, as people here said, seeing Divine complicity in all events and near-events. There was only the sound of my breathing bounced against the receiver. Sweet relief. *Te amo, Telmex*, I whispered to the phone company, sending it my love.

Back in the bedroom, I rearranged myself on the bed,

careful to elevate my foot. I was also saying *gracias a Dios* that the dentist had not been the one to treat it after all. A pudgy man with a tendency to look downward when he talked, maybe from always peering down into gaping mouths, he had summed up the situation at once. Yet again, he had the only functioning x-ray machine in town. When my two helpers and I appeared in his office, he motioned us toward a small cubicle with a dentist chair and a low table to one side.

"Sit here," he said, pointing to the table. "Stretch out your leg."

Even though he was not wearing gloves, his hand felt rubbery and cold as he angled my leg just so on the table. Each tiny movement made me wince in pain. I sensed the dentist was as uncomfortable as I, not used to touching his patients anywhere below the molars. He swiveled the large black proboscis of the x-ray machine around like the boom on a sailboat.

I lay there waiting for the comfort of a thick lead apron. I also expected him to tell my helpers to move to safety. Instead, with surprising alacrity, he zoomed the machine's arm over my outstretched leg, homing in toward my swollen ankle.

Then he let go to scurry into a nearby cubicle. The machine whirred as he snapped one x-ray straight on. I next had to roll on my side for a lateral shot. As I lay there, a recumbent odalisque, feeling exposed, what with no lead apron, I wondered if the x-rays were shooting up my thighs right into my vagina, and from there into my stomach, onward to my throat and then happily into my brain. Would I later trace brain cancer back to this moment of indignity as I lay stretched out in the dentist's office like a patient etherized upon a table? My two cheerful helpers seemed not at all concerned about the devil rays that also had to be ping-ponging off in their direction.

A few minutes later, the dentist studied the x-rays. "Lucky it is, is not fractur-ed," he said in a mix of Spanish grammar and English vocabulary. He sounded in a hurry to be done with me. He uttered a word I took to mean "sprain" and suggested I go back to the *Hospital Civil* for treatment.

He charged me for the x-rays and passed them to me in a brown envelope, not meeting my eyes, as if he were handing me smut. His eagerness to dispatch me roused my suspicion he had overcharged. Then my sweet helpers from the market, who were gaining increasing skill at hoisting, elevated me again for the jolting walk back to the hospital.

The receptionist said the doctor would soon be attending me. My good Samaritans deposited me in a small windowless room and apologized that they had to depart. I did my best to tell them how fortunate I had been to have their help, *gracias a Dios*. They had stuck by me with amazing patience and courtesy. I felt I should pay them but had to save my dwindling pesos for the doctor.

The doctor entered, and I recognized him as the same one who had been operating out in the open when I was first carried into the hospital. He had ditched the splattered white coat but still wore the cowboy boots and checkered shirt. He was of medium height and build, with finely carved features in a narrow handsome face, a still disorderly shock of dark hair, and equally dark, slightly sunken eyes.

Since leaving the dentist's office, I had been rehearsing my Spanish for this moment, but when I finally had a doctor in front of me who could actually be of help, my crafted sentences deserted me. "My ankle . . ." I pointed to it the way a child would. "I fell, and it—" I stopped before I shamed myself by providing the sound effects of a bone cracking. I handed him the dentist's brown envelope, knowing a picture would clearly say more than any words I might string together.

He glanced at the x-rays, then lowered himself onto a stool and carefully lifted my leg. The intensity I had observed in his eyes during the surgery was subdued now but still glimmered. Being so close to someone recently bathed in blood, guts and—

perhaps more than a touch of local glory—left me a little disconcerted. My ankle problem would seem like first aid for Girl Scouts.

He gently rested the heel of my left foot on his knee and rolled up the cuff of my pants several inches. He studied my ankle as he probed it from various angles. He took his time. Such slow intensity made me wonder if the news was worse than a mere sprain, but I managed to relax a little into the firmness of his hands.

He supported my leg in such a way that my ankle did not dangle, and I did not wince as much as I had expected. "You were dancing?" he said with a half-smile.

His tone was so serious I wasn't sure if he were joking. "I was going into the market and suddenly I started to—" I hesitated, considering the best way to frame my explanation. To illustrate, I made a gliding movement with my hand.

"So, then, you were dancing in the market." He shook his head at my folly. "I advise tourists against such displays of felicity at the sight of our *chiles*. Especially after a *tormenta.*"

After a *torment*? So maybe he was joking. *¡Ja, ja!* But I didn't get it.

Then I remembered that *tormenta* was Spanish for *storm*. So he was not joking, and I did not have to think of something jolly to say back, something that risked not surviving translation from English. I did remember the scatological meaning for *chile* that Bernardo and Norma had taught me, but surely he was not talking about *that*. Or was he? No, of course not. At least his words were slow, yet not so slow they sounded as if he were addressing someone with a head trauma.

"I will wrap it. The ankle needs compression." He still cradled the heel of my outstretched leg in his palm. His other hand rested lightly on my shin. I stared down at his hands, long and fine-boned, with a few tufts of dark hair at the wrist. The slim fingers seemed just right for managing the fine maneuvers of a surgeon. I saw him again as I had earlier, bending over his patient with total concentration.

"You must keep the foot raised as much as possible for the next three days," he said, startling me back to the fix I was in.

"Three days?" It wasn't as if I had to hie myself off to work each morning, but I didn't relish the idea of wasting three long days of precious Mexican time indoors, inactive, and under the probing eye of Señora Hernández.

He replied with a slight shrug and a look both serious and scoffing, as though he did not really expect his patients, head-strong mortals that they were, to follow the medical advice he dispensed. Still, the unexpected gentle touch from the doctor as he continued to support my leg helped soothe my rising concern about how I would indeed manage. Just for starters, how would I get back to Cuernavaca?

The doctor withdrew from a glass canister a length of stretchy gauze. He lifted my leg again and with slow hypnotic motions ran the gauze around and around my foot and up my ankle. As he wrapped, still carefully nestling my foot, he made small talk, asking me where I was from and how long I had been in Ixmilco.

When he asked what had lured me to Mexico, I wasn't sure how to answer. I took a moment to compose a response. But I didn't have to answer because someone rapped on the door. The door pushed open, and there, amazingly, stood Aida. I was flooded with relief. I couldn't imagine how she had found me.

The doctor gave a start, which I attributed to the boldness of someone entering without preamble. Then, as Aida leaned in to kiss the doctor on the cheek, I realized they knew each other. Aida, as slight as she was, knew how to fill up a room. She had shed the nylon rain cape she was swaddled in earlier. She wore a hot pink sweater set, tight jeans, and, despite the rain puddles, her customary stiletto heels.

"*Pobrecita*, you poor thing," she said, spying my gauze-encased ankle. "This is what you get for abandoning me."

Her hand went to her hip in mock exasperation. "Doctor, what have you done to my student? Always you find the pretty ones, no?"

The doctor laughed. "Last month another of the *profesora*'s students fell into my hands. That one from eating cream puffs in the central market. *Lástima*, unfortunate that they were not as fresh as they looked." He directed his explanation to me but glanced over at Aida several times as he spoke. "You see, she does not take such good care of her students after all."

"Let that be a lesson to you," Aida said to me, pretending to ignore the doctor, "and to all my other students who are too eager to go off on their own."

I wanted to snap out a spunky retort to match their playful air, but I just couldn't muster the Spanish fast enough. My muteness no doubt continued to justify my Level Seven ranking in Aida's eyes. I lurched between wanting to join in and being disappointed to have the mood in the room so abruptly altered by her entrance. "How did you find me?" I finally managed.

"It was on the radio. The radio at the beet stand." I must have looked disbelieving. Ever the teacher, she said, "The radio in these small towns is like the official town gossip. I heard an American tourist had suffered an accident in the market. And that she was being transported to the hospital. When you didn't show up after a while, I figured that might be my Rosie."

Aha! I had heard her use the subjunctive. Or was it the conditional tense? Whichever it might be, I was pleased I was at least starting to recognize such shadings in the words of others, even if I couldn't yet make those nuances come out of my own mouth. I had also noticed Aida call me "her" Rosie, making it clear that I certainly was not his.

* * *

I lay on my bed back in Cuernavaca, my leg elevated, and under the solicitous care of Norma and Bernardo. Norma had just come into my bedroom, bearing a cup of chamomile tea. "What is it with these *aires*, Norma?" I said as soon as she entered.

She set my tea on the nightstand, concerned. "*Aires?*"

"You know, *aires*—wind, breezes. I heard some women talking in Ixmilco about *un aire* making them sick. Is an *aire* just, well, air? Or is it moving air, like a cold wind? Or is it a spirit of some kind, in the form of a malicious wind?"

Norma flung her hand in exasperation. "*Un aire frío*, that's why I got sick last month. Very bad."

She sat down on the bed as if serious about explaining what she meant. "Señorita Rosie, there is something I want to ask you."

"Yes, of course." I adjusted the pillow, bunching it under my ankle.

"Have you ever had a boyfriend?"

I nodded. "Oh yes. Not now, though."

She tried to suppress a giggle. "I have one, but I don't want to tell anyone yet. Except you."

"It's nice to have a boyfriend, someone to talk to, do things with."

"You are right. It is *so* nice. What I want to know is how not to get pregnant."

My eyes widened. Could the *aires* she had just referred to have anything to do with her being pregnant? Of course not, or she wouldn't be asking how to avoid it. "It's a very good idea not to get pregnant. Especially while you are still in school."

"So, do you know where I can go? Where I can get help? I'm asking you, Señorita Rosie, because I can't let my amigas or my mother know I need this kind of help."

I was on the verge of asking if she was sure she wanted to

go down this path. But the very fact she was asking me about birth control could mean she had already set foot on the path. I placed my hand on hers. It was warm, soft, not as big as I thought.

"You can ask questions, find out where," she said. "I cannot do that."

I flipped through a flurry of emotions on her behalf. "Yes, I can do that, Norma."

The ringing of Señora Hernández's telephone startled us both with its shrillness. The perfidious thing rang twice, forcing itself into the conversation.

"Rosie," Señora Hernández said, her voice muffled by my closed door.

I hobbled into the hallway and took the phone, wishing I could find a way to avoid this call with Monty.

"*Bueno,*" I said, using the Mexican phone salutation. I hoped it would sound distancing.

"Rosie, stop hiding under that Spanish accent. Speak your native tongue." My editor's voice, normally low and wry, boomed loud and crisp through the phone as if he had morphed into a huge no-nonsense Michelin Man and was bobbing up and down right there in the room next to me.

"Leland?" In my three years at *The Marbella Beacon*, he had never called me at home. I couldn't imagine what could now bring him to track me down in another country and another time zone. Was the newspaper in trouble? Was he fired? More to the point, was I fired?

"Time to get back to work, Rosie."

Did this new Michelin-style Leland not come with a memory? He had signed my vacation form himself. I tried to make my voice regretful. "Not yet, Leland. My leave goes for another three weeks. Until June 1. At nine a.m."

"*Perfecto!*" His big new voice boomed.

"*Perfecto* for what?"

"For your new assignment!"

Was this really Leland? The Leland I knew was as dry as a double martini, speaking in a lazy roll from the side of his mouth, threading his talk with quotes from some philosopher he held dear, all the while his single gold ear-stud twinkling. Now he was a tire salesman.

"I have no assignment. Unless you count learning how to express doubt and uncertainty in the Spanish subjunctive mood. That is my job for now. I'm on vacation. *Estoy de vacaciones*," I said, thinking a little Spanish might drive home my point.

"Doubt is good for a reporter. I always recommend it. Besides, I would think you could work a little and be in the subjunctive mood at the same time. All while on *vacación*," he said, adding a little *th* sound to the last *c* of *vacación*, as if he were now shouting at me from the Iberian Peninsula.

"That's pretentious, Leland. You're using an accent from Spain when you know I'm in Mexico. You Americans, you always get your geography wrong."

He laughed. It was as if the laugh let the air out of the Michelin Man, and his voice returned to normal. "I'm thinking we need a story," he said, "more coverage of Mexican issues. We have a growing Mexican readership."

"*Estoy de vacaciones.*"

"If I were you," he began. *If he were me. If I were to. If it should happen that.* Everywhere I turned, I bumped into this mode of doubt, which was ironically the same mode for desire. It was also, I knew, the verb tense for uncompleted actions, the verb tense that fit my life.

I said nothing but wavered within.

Leland dangled bait. "With what I have in mind, you should even be able to leap frog past city council meetings in the future."

I appreciated the board game innuendo when it came to

advancing in the newsroom. It would be a boon indeed to skip the endless city council meetings. On vacation or not, I took the worm. "What do you have in mind?"

"Something cultural. Maybe Mexican art. Or Mexican cuisine."

To my own surprise, I said, "I do want to write an article, Leland, but about something less, er, usual." I had caught myself before saying "predictable."

"Like what?"

"Like birth control."

Leland was a master of the pause. This I knew from experience. He waited about five long beats. "Babies? Very well, write about babies. They always win hearts."

"Yes, this is a country of babies. Lots of babies. So birth control is a subject that's still pretty taboo down here. Or is it? That's for me to find out."

"Birth control. It's a country of babies, and you want to write about no babies."

"Changes are happening, Leland. Readers would learn something new. What are the current attitudes of Mexican women toward birth control? Especially rural women and out in the small towns where people are more traditional."

Before he could further demur, I said it would not be so hard for me to locate my key sources and set up interviews, given how proficient I was becoming in the language. I didn't mention that I sorely needed the extra money.

"Okay," he said, drawing the word out and making it sound downright subjunctive. "See what you can stumble into. But try for something at least picturesque."

As soon as we hung up, doubt came roaring in. "*If it should happen* that *I were* to give up this vacation—*as it were*—to pursue the story. If *I were* to ferret out enough sources for such a piece, and—" Even as I was speaking, I heard in my mind an odd echo. It was as if a simultaneous translator were in my head, although not a very adept one. My brain was whirring, trying to translate my English sentences into Spanish. Yet it stumbled when it came to the subjunctive mood.

I feared I might be tone deaf to the taunting music of the hypothetical and the potential, stuck in the ordinary mood of the indicative, of what already is certain. At least with this article, even though I had unthinkingly suggested it, I might be able to enter the portal of a new mode.

6

MAYBE A RICH GRINGA

María del Carmen, his receptionist-nurse, stood in the door-way. "The americana is here," she said with a listless air.

A short, dark woman with a plump figure like donuts stacked atop one another, María del Carmen looked plumper and rounder than usual. Juan Ramón wondered if she might be pregnant again. Then her words sank in, and he was annoyed with himself for agreeing to this interview, even if it was with an attractive señorita. Green, deep green, that had been the color of her eyes. But he had wrapped the ankle and sent her on her way, and that was that. It was strange enough to have a tourist in this small clinic. He resisted calling it a hospital.

The señorita had called a couple of days ago, and María del Carmen told him she found it hard to make out what she was saying on the telephone. "The lady of the sprained ankle is determined to see you," said his nurse in a voice caught between admiration for the americana's spunk but mostly annoyance at this interruption to their daily routine. Juan Ramón had not wanted to seem rude, but he had not been able to think fast enough to get out of the interview. What was it María del Carmen had said—something about an article the señorita was writing? On birth control, wasn't it? And she had mentioned Aida. Perhaps that was the real reason he did not turn down her request.

María del Carmen showed the americana to the door of his office. She strode in, tangles of brownish-blonde hair flying loose over her shoulders, and he noted she was wearing tight jeans, a long-sleeved red top, with a large blue bag slung on her shoulder. He was startled when she parked the bag on his desk and stuck out her hand.

Now that she stood planted before him like a Yankee flag, what his friend Eugenio said about American women popped into his mind. American women want only two things—orgasms and money.

He wondered if that were true, and if Eugenio had gotten the order right. Well, he would make short work of this interview. What was there to say about birth control in these outlying areas, anyway?

"Rosie Logan." She smiled and handed him a business card. "But we've met, Doctor. You taped my ankle."

"Ah, yes," he said, as if just recalling. She had seemed so vulnerable then. He remembered Aida bustling in to spirit her away. Rosie Logan's Spanish seemed a lot better now, less than a week later. Maybe it had just been the pain and shock from the fall that had made her speak so haltingly.

"Please have a seat." He motioned her to the chair perpendicular to his desk.

"I work for *The Marbella Beacon*. It's a newspaper in California."

He glanced down at her card.

"And," she said in a slightly louder voice, as if to call his attention away from the card and back to her disconcerting presence, "we're doing a story on Mexican women and birth control."

He wanted to say, "What birth control?" Instead, he leaned

down and pulled out the bottom drawer of his desk. He groped for an information sheet he had printed up for his last fruitless presentation at the regional directors' meeting.

"Here are numbers," he said. He tried not to drone. "Numbers on how many people this clinic serves, how many men, women, children, infants. You'll also see the categories of cases we've treated."

"Yes, that will be helpful." She looked at the paper and said, "I'm surprised by the high number of pregnancies. But I guess I shouldn't be." She folded the paper and dropped it into the cavernous blue bag. "I am especially interested in individual cases. I want to get beyond the statistics. Although I thank you for them."

"Very well then," he said. Just that afternoon he had seen Fátima Mendoza, mother of eight, who had to sneak to the clinic twenty-three kilometers from their farm just so she could get birth control pills, without her husband's permission. Juan Ramón would start by telling her of this determined woman, a match for any americana in her audacity.

As he spoke, Juan Ramón watched the reporter scribble the hieroglyphics of shorthand in a school notebook that featured a gray shark on the cover. As she kept writing, he modified his assessment of her. What had, a few moments ago, seemed bluntness was in fact seriousness, even earnestness. For just a second, he felt a flicker of envy at her single-mindedness. She bent over that notebook with such vigor.

He couldn't help but think of his own wasted energy with all those futile calls in search of more money, more supplies. In his two concurrent positions, he had no sense of efficiency or control whatsoever and certainly not vigor. Being Director of the Ixmilco Civil Hospital—just a small clinic, really—and at the same time serving as Ixmilco's Director of Public Health merely doubled his despair. He doubted he would tell this earnest American on the other side of his desk anything of that.

What good would it do, anyway? It's not like she could solve anything for him.

With a surgeon's hunch, he resolved to knife through his frustrations and provide just the basic little stories for her bigger story. Then she could take her fat blue bag off his desk and leave. He could dismiss her without being discourteous. He could get back to his people and his despair.

She was now staring at a large spot on the wall where the plaster had fallen. He was conscious of her taking it all in—the few rooms, sparsely furnished, in need of painting, the makeshift roof, the odd medicinal smells.

He began to tell her about Enedina Cruz. Two of her ten children were born deaf, and a third child with only one lung. From lack of prenatal care and from a diet deficient in protein? Oh, but now he was straying from birth control. Or was he? It was all connected, wasn't it?

"Statistics show teenaged mothers in the rural areas are likely to have their second child before age twenty." He worked again at not droning, yet careful not to betray how these seemingly dry facts were anything but dry to him. They were, in fact, fuel to his daily desperation. "In 1967, the average family had eight children. That figure is dropping nationwide but still high in—"

"Rural women have a second child before they are twenty?"

"Yes, Señorita. That is how it still is in 1985." He waved his hand in resignation. Why should she be surprised? Couldn't she look around and see that? His voice was measured, but he had begun to play with a pen on his desk.

"When do you think I could meet some of these women?"

He could almost envision her looking at her watch, ready to push on according to some tight personal schedule. He resisted a desire to look at his own watch.

"I would like to talk to a teenage mother. Maybe one of those young women I saw in the waiting room?"

Juan Ramón nodded. "Yes, Señorita, that is possible." He picked up a stack of urgent papers and moved it from one side of his desk to the other. She was referring to the line of women down the hallway, stomachs swelling under their plaid aprons, babies in their arms, toddlers on their hems. They were waiting for him at this moment.

"Perhaps you could introduce me. To make it okay for them to talk to me."

He hadn't expected her to be aware the women in his hallway would be shy about talking to a *gringa* from another planet. Surely she wouldn't walk up and hand them a business card the way she had him. "Yes," he said. "I will do that, introduce you."

Even with an introduction from him, though, he was not certain the mothers would reveal their stories to this foreign lady. "I will be glad, Señorita," he said again, "to present you to some of the young women." This was a good excuse to stand up. He started to push his chair away.

She remained seated and was flipping pages in her shark notebook. "Doctor, I'm wondering what kind of birth control is available for young women, perhaps middle-class young women?"

He stared at her. She wasn't asking about birth control for herself, was she? There was plenty available in her own country. She should have come prepared.

"For a young Mexican woman," she said as if reading his mind.

"Well, we have pills from the government and injections."

"How would a young woman go about getting those injections?"

He started to stand up again and was relieved to see she was taking his cue and closing her notebook. "I suppose she should ask a doctor."

She opened the notebook again. "One last question, Doctor.

Could you describe for me your typical day?"

A baby wailed from somewhere down the hall. María del Carmen appeared in his doorway, paused a moment, then slipped away. He glimpsed in Rosie Logan's open notebook what looked like a list of hand-written questions. Beyond the list, the blue bag loomed large in his vision, perched in his territory. He sighed inwardly. Who had sent this green-eyed messenger from another world to call him to task for his sins of omission, a reminder of all the things he had failed to do?

Now she was smiling at him with that same expectant look that had both intrigued him and made him uneasy since she came through the door. His typical day? His typical day was the last thing he wanted to think about. Did she really want a list of what he did at what hour? Did she want to know the dead ends of his typical day, week, month? What in the world did this woman want of him, anyway? He sank back into his chair and did not speak for long uncomfortable moments. She waited. "Sometimes I feel desperate," he said, against his resolve not to look too closely at how he really felt about his chain of days. "I don't know what else to do."

"You mean you don't want to work here anymore?" Her pen was poised, ready to write. He eyed it with suspicion.

His last talk with his father echoed. "Come home," his father had said. "You belong with your family. A doctor can find work anywhere. You will be happier when you are closer to your family."

When Juan Ramón didn't answer, she said, "Or do you mean you are tired of being a doctor?" Her voice was a little softer than it had been.

"Please put your pen down."

She dropped it into her bag.

He sat in silence, and she sat waiting. At last he said, "The people need more than I can get for them." He reached into his pocket for the hard pack of Marlboros.

"And more than you can give them of yourself?" She was looking right at him, almost into him.

He stared back. If her words held an insult, he would choose not to hear it. He extended the cigarette pack toward her.

She looked startled and shook her head.

He lit the cigarette. "I have always thought I could get and give and never mind the consequences to me. Now I don't know. I've become tired." He pursed his lips and blew smoke into the small office. "And that enrages me." He inhaled deeply again.

"That is my typical day, if you want to know. Anger is my typical day," he said in a tight voice.

She was looking down, closing her notebook. Apparently, she did not care to hear about his typical day after all.

"Don't you want to write that down?" He knew he was contradicting himself.

She looked up. "I will remember it. It is important. You are not happy with how things are going."

"Happy?" He tried not to laugh at the understatement. "In the clinic," he said, already ruing his sudden personal confession, "there is never enough money."

"You mean from the government?"

"Clearly, there's not enough from the government. These poor people who come here, they cannot pay me anything. No, that is not right. Sometimes I get a stack of limes here on my desk. Or a kilo of eggs." He started to gesture wildly. "I sometimes have a live chicken squawking and running around this room, more often than you would think. So they do pay me, in their way."

She was smiling now, and for some reason that irritated him. "Those women you saw waiting for me out in the hallway, you cannot expect they would have any money, can you?"

"No, I wouldn't think so."

"How do you think this clinic can survive? It cannot pay for itself. Here it's not like your country." His words were rushing together on their hurried way to an unknown destination. "Here we do not have people with health insurance. Here we do not have people with money. Here we do not have people who want to get a tax deduction for their contribution to a charity."

"Oh, you know about that." She gave a weak laugh. "Yes, many hospitals have donors to help them."

"That's what I dream of," he burst out. "A host of angels to appear with a contribution for this poor clinic. Or not even a host. Just one splendid angel could make a difference."

Her notebook slipped off the side of the desk and clattered onto the floor. He leaned over for it, and as he did, he found himself staring at the nape of her bare neck as her hair fell to both sides. She had leaned down for the notebook, too, and her head was only a notebook's width from his. They both raised their faces slightly at the same moment, and he found his face close to hers. His tirade slipped away. He realized he had been unkind, even rude.

He righted himself and again adjusted the stack of papers on his desk. He patted his pocket for cigarettes before realizing one was still burning in the ashtray. Why not? he thought. Why not? It came to him that maybe, just maybe, this American with her unwelcome questions could herself be an answer after all. She might even know someone who could come to the rescue, someone from her country with money or influence. Americans were rich. "Even just one angel," he said again.

She cocked her head. "You mean, someone to . . . donate money?"

"A little help to keep us going."

"Well, I don't know . . ."

He waited as long as he could, then said, "Maybe there is

someone who can help us? Somebody who is a friend?" He was humiliating himself, asking like this, but what else was there to do? She could be a conduit. This was his chance.

"Well, maybe." She blinked, then said, "I would have to know more, of course."

Ah! She had said *quizás*—the word "maybe." So what if he had put the word in her mouth? Could it be that this green-eyed gringa might lead him to someone who could make a generous donation?

Maybe even she herself could. No, that wasn't likely, not from a reporter, even one with a Yankee salary. But maybe her story would raise a benefactor. He put out his cigarette. "I can give you all the information you need. More than you want even."

"Somebody might be able to help you, Doctor. I am not sure. Perhaps." She gave a small smile as she stood and lifted the blue bag off his desk.

He was sorry to see it leave now.

"Is this a good moment for you to introduce me to some of the women in the waiting room?"

He noticed she was evasive about the money. But he was more than willing to pay the price of his time and information and contacts if that meant she could bring him the angel who might anoint this miserable spot of the world with the holy unguent of cash. He certainly could not depend on the government to dress this wound. But maybe a rich gringa—or one with a rich family or rich friends. For that chance, he would be patient. And the fact that he liked looking at her, well, that was a bonus, a *pilón*, as they said in the market when they threw in extra onions or an apple for free.

He opened the door with a flourish. "Permit me, Señorita, to invite you to accompany me on my rounds to the countryside tomorrow. I think you will find it most useful."

The americana exited his office before him, and he allowed

himself to feel a small spark of hope, the first in months. As if on cue, María del Carmen materialized before them in the hall-way, and he imagined she was astonished to find him smiling.

7

LINGER AWHILE

Don Alejandro knew that Juan Ramón would defy him once again. He would make no move at all to contact the director for the new hospital.

It was just before seven o'clock, and the upstairs began to stir. Lupita came down the stairs and into the room where he sat reading. She glided toward him with the serenity and poise of the older women he saw in the television commercials for cough medicine and detergent. She greeted him with a soft kiss, as she had for more than fifty years.

"What is wrong, *viejo?*" *Viejo*, old man, *vieja*, old woman, words that could convey extreme intimacy and fondness or a surfeit of boredom, or both at once.

Lupita knew him too well. He said, "It's Juan Ramón. He—"

Their daughter Ceci bounded into the room. "*¡Buen día, Papá!*" her voice booming as she kissed him quickly on the cheek, then her mother. Ceci always charged in on a run, jarring his hard-earned serenity. Was there no way to slow her down long enough to stay and talk a while with him? She was a highly-calibrated engine, starting to race the moment she opened her eyes.

Ceci groaned and ran her fingers through her cropped

hair. "*Dios mío*, I forgot I have to make up a quiz in social sciences today. *Qué tonta*. I've been announcing it all week, warning the kids to prepare. They would find it funny to know it is the teacher who didn't prepare."

"We will see you for the midday meal, no?" Don Alejandro hoped to pin her down.

But Ceci, her morning salutations to her parents dispensed with, had pivoted out of the room.

Ceci was the daughter who had not married. The other three—Griselda, Alma, and Gabriela—had married their *novios* well before their twenty-first year, right on schedule. Ceci was twenty-seven now and not even close to marriage. Don Alejandro regretted she had become an old maid. Worse yet, as far as he could see, she did not seem worried about it. On occasion in the late afternoon, she went out for a few hours to drink coffee with young men who came to call. But Don Alejandro had learned from Lupita that Ceci never took these callers seriously enough to feel they merited discussion with her mother or sisters. In some ways, although she lived under Don Alejandro and Lupita's roof, Ceci seemed as apart from the family as her brother Juan Ramón in Ixmilco.

* * *

Don Alejandro steered the immaculate 1957 black Buick the five and a half kilometers to his factory, La Fábrica Quetzal. Unlucky in love, that was what Ceci and Juan Ramón were. When Ceci was nineteen, the whole family had watched in anguish as her *novio*, the boyfriend they all expected her to marry, confessed he could no longer come to see her. He had no choice but to marry another woman, one it gave him shame to say he had gotten pregnant. A terrible accident, *mi amor*, the bridegroom had told Ceci, his voice choked with tears. A terrible accident, that's what it was again when Ceci was twenty-three and had settled into a new *novio*, one that was killed four weeks before their wedding date in a motorcycle crash on a wet, starless night. Maybe as a kind of surety, Ceci continued to dress in the clinging skirts and tops she had favored since girlhood. She was as fit as a teenager, refusing to give in and soften with the passing of years and hope. She seemed to have little interest in the men who less and less came to call.

He parked the Buick in front of the factory where he had spent most of his adult life. Some twenty years ago, when it was first built, its arched colonnade contributed an easy grace to the open lands surrounding it. Now it looked squeezed by the Pemex gasoline station on its right flank and the string of small stores pressing its left. He had named the factory after the colorful green and red *quetzal*, its tail plumes almost a meter long. The flamboyant bird had caught his imagination in his first year of *secundaria*, the only year of middle school he had completed. This early fascination served as a harbinger of a passion that had rekindled in these most recent years of his life, a passion to read stories of Mexico's legendary birds and sacred animals.

He rapped twice on the main door of the factory. Immediately the massive portals gave way, sprung open by the night watchman who knew almost to the minute when his *patrón* would arrive each morning.

"*Buenos días*, Gustavo," he said to the watchman, who, with his shuffling gait and squinty eye, seemed to be a decade older than Don Alejandro instead of a decade younger.

As was his custom, Don Alejandro strolled through all four wings of the first floor. He took in the various sections that marked the stages of shoe construction: the cutters, leather thinners, stitchers, mounters, gluers. Wooden racks of shoe lasts, the cans of glue and nails, all were in perfect order as he had taught his employees to leave them. No, *employees* was not the word—its sound was threadbare. A handful of this work-family had been with him for forty years, from when there had been no factory and they had worked out of a patio and back room at Don Alejandro's house, bathed by the cozy smells of browned rice for *sopas* and flavorful blackened tortillas from Lupita's kitchen. Nine of his current workers were second-generation, their fathers having labored in the factory before them. He embraced his responsibility for this other family.

One day when Juan Ramón was still an adolescent, he said to Don Alejandro, "I saw one of the men hide a pair of new shoes in his satchel."

"He will not take much," Don Alejandro had said, his gaze traveling out over the first floor. "Without these people, none of this would be possible."

On the second floor, he passed the areas for quality control and packing, then went into the *bodega*. Mentally he checked the rows of shoes stored there, arranged first by style, then by size, then by color. Just as he did every day, he walked past rows of dyed leather ready for cutting and shaping.

And just as he did every day, he thanked God for His generosity. He, an orphan boy, had started from nothing and come to this, more than he had ever imagined possible. He rejoiced for his sons and daughters, a loving wife, this prospering business, started and anchored by his sweat and dedication and his faithful workers.

Don Alejandro had known from an early age what he wanted. But what did his youngest son and youngest daughter really want? Ceci, where was she going with long hours at a job that would soon leave her too withered for a husband and children? Juan Ramón, over thirty and still not settled, one marriage already destroyed. What in God's name did he want?

8

LANGUAGE OF
THE BELLS

The swaying of the full-bodied bus threatened to soothe me into complacency, but I resisted, dwelling on sights and thoughts that defied me to understand them. The road looped through pine forests reminiscent of the trip, already several weeks past, I had made from Mexico City to Cuernavaca. That bus had lumbered slowly around the corrugated tops of volcanoes, then sunk down and down into the lower hills of the state of Morelos, resplendent in shades of green. Ah, this is primeval, I felt, entering into the land of the volcanoes, threading in and out of greenery. Here and there rose tall cactus, like fingers pushing out of the ground, rigid and determined.

Now, on this ride from Cuernavaca to Ixmilco, I was seeing even more cactus, scattered amid the vines and broad-leafed foliage. What were they doing in this semi-tropical terrain? I considered cactus to be indomitable desert beings with wills of their own. Were these cactus-paradoxes harbingers of the people I was about to interview? Or were they like me, out of place but nevertheless here?

I looked at my watch. Doctor Villaseñor would pick me up in the central plaza at eleven, on the way to his rounds in the countryside.

It was already five to eleven, and we weren't yet in Ixmilco. To distract myself from the probability of missing the appointment, I recited to myself information I had crammed from the doctor's fact sheet:

By 1985, Mexico has become the second most populous country in Latin America. Forty-two percent of Mexico's population is under the age of fifteen. The national birth rate is 34.4 per thousand inhabitants. One out of every three women over fifteen is illiterate. Only one out of every three women who is living with a man or married uses any form of birth control.

I was in the land of fecundity. I couldn't admit it to my editor Leland, but I was downright uneasy about this self-imposed assignment. After all, I had been living my own form of birth control. In college, I thought I would do like so many friends: marry and spawn children. After college, other things came along to distract me.

I grew up in the silence of my single mother's house. The portraits Mama painted and propped on tall easels in our dining room seemed to be standing in for non-existent family members. And I suppose you could say my absent father was a form of birth control as far as my mother was concerned, given that she showed no interest in men after he left us.

Carole-Ann, whose desk was next to mine at the newspaper, put forth her own impassioned perspective whenever the subject of children arose. "What does it matter?" she once said, smacking the trunk of a pine tree outside my little beach bungalow as if smacking the flanks of a horse—or a man. "You're better off without a kid. Plant a tree instead." She had raised her chin and stared up into the pine as if in worship. "Trees grow tall and live for centuries. They give shade and shelter." She smacked the trunk again. "They'll be there when you die. You'll see them through the window. Your child, on the other hand, may be off hitting tennis balls. Your child may be high on a mountain slope or in an ashram. Your child might consider your life far too extended."

I looked at my watch again, then fished from my bag the list of cognates Aida had given us. Tricky things, these cognates. *Actual* in Spanish doesn't mean *actual* in English. I flipped to the next page. A *compromise* isn't a *compromiso*, at least not in the modern sense of the word. *Suave* in one language isn't the same *suave* in the other. And in Spanish, when you are *embarazada*, you aren't embarrassed. Way past that, sister, you're pregnant.

Here, each night as I lay in bed, a confederation of neighboring dogs barked to one another in urgent code. Each morning, I would awaken to the bells from the nearby church. These bells, which sounded like clanging buckets, didn't just mark the hour and the quarter hours. They seemed to be imparting an urgent message. But it was a message that fell, if not on my deaf ears, then on my illiterate ones. Encircling me were words and codes I didn't understand, and it was taking more energy than I had expected, this being repeatedly on the outside.

I was so relieved to see the doctor still waiting for me that I almost skipped into the plaza. He was wearing the cowboy boots I'd seen before, a long-sleeved white dress shirt with the cuffs rolled, and a pair of dark slacks. Over his shoulder was slung a dark pullover. Contradicting his crisp attire, dark circles showed under his eyes and his forehead was creased. I was embarrassed—not *embarazada*—to be twenty-five minutes late. He shook my hand and didn't seem to notice my tardiness.

We set out at once, and I had to make little skips to keep up with his purposeful gait. A passing car sent dust wafting into my face. The streets were full of new pickups and compact cars, all moving slowly. They were probably trying not to rip out an oil pan on the endless speed bumps set through the heart of town. All these late-model vehicles spoke of the soil's richness here and the money to be gleaned in agriculture.

"Do we go by car?" It appeared we might be circling back to the bus station. "Or do we take a bus?"

"Neither. We're walking."

"Walking?" My voice squeaked upwards. Ixmilco was small, but I didn't see how we could walk as far as the countryside.

"I am sorry for this little change in our plans, Señorita. I hope it will not be a bother that instead today we will visit my friend *el doctor* Eugenio. I have to drop off a packet of x-rays for him. Mañana we'll go to the countryside."

I ignored the interesting fact that the hospital's x-ray machine must now be working again. "Mañana?"

I had bounced in a bus over an hour for nothing. Now I would have to bounce here yet again. I suspected this visit to his colleague would turn into a social call and a waste of time. I wanted to get into the heart of this assignment, if only to get it over with. "It's not possible today?"

"Doctor Eugenio is the other doctor in the Hospital Civil. He may have some information you can use in your research. His home is just a few blocks from here." He pointed to a sidewalk diagonal from where we stood. Even though he had mentioned my research, he didn't strike me as sufficiently apologetic for having changed our plans, assuming I would just take it in stride.

In the sky behind him, white clouds smashed up against each other like bumper cars. Church bells began to ring. If only I could use these idyllic details of the setting to assuage my growing frustration at not understanding what I wanted so much to understand: subtleties of the customs and language and logic of the people.

We crossed the street, and as always when I walked here in Mexico, I spotted things I never witnessed in Marbella.

Two schoolgirls were, for some reason, not at school yet

but crawling out through a ground floor French window instead of using the front door. A blind man with a sombrero of plaited palm sat cross-legged on the narrow sidewalk, extending his hand toward us. "*Caridad,*" he called softly as our footsteps passed, asking for charity in a voice so low it was like my conscience calling. A burly young man staggered down the street toward us, a huge side of beef draped over his back, his destination a butcher shop we had just passed.

The sidewalk narrowed, and the doctor motioned me to cut ahead and take the lead. I did, but had no idea which way to go. I trudged on blindly to the home of *el doctor* Eugenio.

The bells finished tolling eleven thirty, stopped, then revived. I turned back toward the doctor. "Tell me about the bells. They do ring a lot."

"The bells are one of our dialects here in the small towns. Listen to them and you'll learn what's going on."

"I'm not so sure about that." All I seemed to be doing these days was listening, and the more I listened, the less I knew. "I've heard the bells chime the quarter hours. But they're a lot busier than that."

"They also call people to Mass. First call, second call, and the third call, known as the *última llamada*—the final curtain call, you might say. The tolling at the end tells you which call and therefore how many minutes you have to get to church. It's hard to ignore three reminders."

"Much more insistent than a mere wristwatch."

"The bells indicate the kind of Mass, too. You can tell from the type of ring if it's a Mass for the Dead or a wedding—which some people think are the same thing."

I realized he was making a joke and was pleased I caught it. I laughed more loudly than need be. A station wagon passed, stuffed to the roof with onions, only the driver's seat clear. My eyes followed the sight.

"Imagine the aroma in that car," he said, noticing my gaze.

"I hope his wife likes it."

"We have a saying: *Dios, ajo y cebolla*. God, garlic, and on-ion." He surprised me by taking my elbow as we neared the corner. "Like marriage."

"We were talking about the bells," I said, annoyed that I seemed to understand nothing of nothing. Everything here was open to interpretation.

He continued, unruffled. "Do you know that if you wake up too drunk to realize what day it is, the bells can at least let you know if your hangover is taking place on a weekday or a Sunday. Or if it's a day of fiesta."

"That's a lot to listen for. With a hangover." I was tiring of this topic.

"It's automatic. People understand the language of the bells without effort." He smiled.

He didn't have to rub it in. This was just one more thing I suspected I might not master, along with our previous day's interchange at the clinic.

Ever since I left the Ixmilco clinic, I had been replaying the doctor's words about money, all that business about needing an angel. Was the doctor actually asking for some kind of pay-off for hauling me along on his rounds? If I had gone to school today instead of cutting class, I could have searched out Aida and asked her about this. My Spanish was becoming more solid, despite my descent to Level Seven, but today it was chal-lenged on all sides by something beyond language. Perhaps the doctor had been just lamenting the clinic's general lack of funds. Maybe he wasn't expecting any money from me at all. Then again, maybe he was. Had I agreed, without realizing it, to line his palm with silver in some discreet way? Was he wait-ing for that money, or at least a down payment, before taking me to the rural areas? Was today's meeting a test I was about to flunk? Anyway, he wasn't the only one of us needing money. Besides, a doctor surely should have some extra tucked away.

"Did I mention each church has its own particular ring?" he said, almost giddy.

I was glad he was in such a good mood today, but I groaned aloud at this added detail. If it wouldn't have taken me so long to say it in Spanish, I would have pointed out how it seemed more than mere coincidence there were churches on every third corner, and women with an average of eight-point-something kids.

The fragrant smell of tortillas signaled we were nearing a *tortillería*. A line of aproned women bearing buckets or baskets on their arms stretched to the corner. At the head of the line, a tortilla machine was flipping out flat cornmeal rounds like newly minted coins. How fitting they should resemble giant versions of the thousand-peso piece. Tortillas: the golden coin of the realm.

The doctor paused in front of a wooden gate adjacent to the tortilla factory. He tugged on a rope protruding through a hole in the gate, and on the other side a bell tinkled. We waited almost a full minute without speaking. It's hard to make small talk when you know you have to translate it all into another language and it's never going to come out the same. Pleasant chit-chat goes in; garbled stiffness with possible international affront comes out. Nothing small about that talk.

A stout woman in a green-checked apron sprung the door open. Her hair stood out from her head like Medusa's snakes, but her face was open and welcoming.

"*Pasen, pasen, por favor.*" She scolded as if we had been lingering outside the gate sneaking a smoke. Her snakes bobbed as she hurried us forward.

Behind the tortillería rose a steep slope of some ten or twelve feet. We marched up the stepping-stones, engulfed by an abundance of ferns and flowers on both sides. The untrimmed growth bestowed on the old single-story pink house at the top of the rise an aura of benign neglect.

The woman waved us toward the front door. *"El doctor* is on the patio." She then turned and disappeared into the lush greenery at the side of the house. Judging from the thickness of the foliage, I half expected to hear machete sounds as she took her leave into the bush.

Dr. Villaseñor led the way across a small formal living room with the whiff of a museum about it. Here the furniture was in the style of some French king who liked porcelain figurines and red brocade upholstery—I never could keep those Louis's and their chair legs straight. All was tranquil, spotless, in order, and uninhabited. We continued straight through the salon and out the French doors onto a central patio. I had just traversed from the jungles of Mexico to Old Europe and now entered Colonial Mexico.

Doctor Villaseñor addressed what appeared to be an empty patio. *"Buenos días, Doctor,"* he called out to the old walls and worn paving stones.

A tall, thin man shot up from behind an iron table. As we drew closer, I saw he had been squatting next to a green garden hose that undulated across the patio and disappeared behind the table. The two men shook hands, embraced, and, as if on cue, administered each other two brisk pats on the back.

Doctor Villaseñor turned to me. "Señorita Rosie Logan, Doctor Eugenio Padilla."

The hand of Doctor Eugenio zoomed out to meet mine. "You are most welcome to Ixmilco," he said in English, then cradled my hand in both of his. "I most humbly put myself at your service."

Such flowery language. I hoped he wouldn't bow. I might feel compelled to do the same. Or dip into a curtsy. To forestall any bending on his part, I quickly stated my purpose for being in Ixmilco. I felt a bit of a liar, since I hadn't originally come to Mexico for that reason.

"A journalist? American?" He grinned at Doctor Villaseñor

with more pleasure than I thought the fact warranted. Doctor Villaseñor was grinning back.

Doctor Eugenio toned down his smile as he said, "I will be most happy to help you, however I may. You must know our country wears many faces. I can show you some of those faces. But you must convince Juan Ramón"—he nodded toward his friend—"to take you out to the rural communities with him."

"Oh, do you think that would be possible?" I said, no longer minding that I might sound cynical.

Doctor Eugenio bent over and picked up the garden hose. "In the communities of the countryside, you will see our living past. That's something you won't find so easily in the tourist zones of the big cities." As if he just remembered himself, he said, "Señorita, please sit down. Forgive me, I have just a little chore to finish."

In the distance, the church bells started again with their taunting code. Doctor Eugenio knelt with one knee on the stone and began to fidget with the top of a plastic bag.

While his hands were busy, he looked up at Doctor Villaseñor—should I call him Juan Ramón now that Doctor Eugenio had referred to him that way?

"You remember Señorita Araiza?" It was kind of him to address Doctor Juan Ramón in English for my benefit.

Juan Ramón nodded. So! He must understand some English. But what I was really interested in was what Doctor Eugenio was going to say about the woman. I pulled out my notebook. Maybe I would be able to gather information today after all.

"I operated on her this morning. Tomorrow I have to go to the laboratory in Cuernavaca." As he spoke, he shook the contents of the plastic bag and upended it. Something reddish-pink, like a cut of meat, did a slow-motion slide into his left hand.

"Excuse me, Doctor." I sat poised to write. "What is that?"

Once I could see it better, I thought it looked like an organ from a large animal. "Is that some kind of body part?"

Doctor Eugenio turned on the hose and sprayed water over the thing in his hand. "This?" he said with a detached air, all doctor now. "This, Señorita, is a uterus."

Only days before, I had flinched when I saw the woman being operated on in the hospital. This time I willed myself not to look away. No, that's not true. What's true is that I couldn't make myself look away.

"A uterus from a—" I was at a loss for words in my own language.

Juan Ramón finished the thought, "From a woman, of course."

The two doctors were both looking at me with an expression that told me they just might be savoring this moment. There they stood, neither seeming to consider the situation worthy of undue remark.

"See," Doctor Eugenio said, becoming the clinician and slipping back into Spanish as he gained inspiration. "See, here is the opening." He stretched with his fingers the rubbery aperture at one end of the fleshy sack. He then extended the uterus on the wet stone.

There it lay, like a slab of meat for tonight's dinner. Woman demystified. I couldn't bring myself to look at Juan Ramón, to allow him to see my shock. I stared at the female organ in silence. This other doctor was obviously a gynecologist, and I knew I was missing a chance to interview him about his patients and birth control. On the other hand, an extracted uterus was, if ever there was one, a completely reliable form of birth control.

"We have no laboratory here in Ixmilco," Juan Ramón said, maybe feeling my silence needed ministering to. "Later this afternoon, Eugenio will go to Cuernavaca and have the uterus analyzed."

"Analyzed?" I said. "Analyzed for what?" Analysis seemed

beside the point now.

Doctor Eugenio took over again. "For the tumor that is growing on it." He picked the uterus up and stretched it toward me as if an offering. "See? There it is."

The uterus lay in his open palm just inches from my face.

"That yellow part?" I pointed and sought a scientific tone of detachment to match theirs.

He beamed at me as if I were a smart student. "Yes. That's the tumor. That's why I had to remove this uterus."

I stared at it. My feigned detachment crumbled. The disembodied piece of meat now assumed a body. I pictured a distraught woman, full dark hair framing her face.

"Was she young?" I had to ask, to address some inchoate uneasiness inside me.

"Thirty-one."

I imagined a face not much different from my own. The woman's eyes were marked with shadows. She was too young to lose her womb. Somewhere in Ixmilco a woman lay crying, despite the midday sunshine, because she had lost her womb. The woman had considered herself young and immortal. Her face was firm and unlined. She had thought she would have more time.

Juan Ramón said, "I just had an idea, if it would not be too much of an imposition. Señorita Rosie will be taking the bus back to Cuernavaca this very afternoon." He was addressing both me and Doctor Eugenio in what I considered an unctuous tone. "Perhaps she would not mind doing us a big favor. Perhaps she could deliver the package to the laboratory for you."

"Package?" I said.

"The uterus," said Doctor Juan Ramón. "The lab is just a couple of blocks from Aida's school—your school."

All I needed now, I thought, was to hear those damn bells again. Then, because it was exactly twelve noon, the bells broke into a garrulous and indecipherable frenzy, as if speaking in tongues.

9

UN SUSTO

noun: a shock, a fright

I was confused, then exasperated, when Juan Ramón turned the VW Bug back toward the center of Ixmilco instead of the open highway. "We have to make just a little stop," he said. He pulled up in front of the Hospital Civil, a sight that was becoming familiar.

I tried not to let my sigh be audible. It was already after noon on my second day of trying to get to a rural community, and we still had not left Ixmilco. I had yet to talk to a single woman there. Maybe a comment from Miss Aida had been right. Maybe I should have turned to another doctor for my main fount of research.

He double-parked in front of the clinic, turned off the ignition, and came around to help me out. He was wearing jeans, as he was during the emergency surgery when I first saw him, and this time a long-sleeved blue shirt and rolled cuffs. With his sunglasses and straw hat, he looked like a country boy reborn with a touch of city slickness.

"It's okay to leave the car here in the street?" Even as I said it, I realized I had seen quite a few double-parked vehicles here in Ixmilco and in Cuernavaca.

He looked mildly surprised at the question. "Of course." We entered the clinic, but he hadn't said for what purpose.

He stopped at the front desk, where the receptionist passed him several pieces of paper. I stood to one side as he glanced at each, then handed them back to her except for one. It was folded into a small, tight rectangle. After unfolding and reading it, he crumpled the paper into a ball and crammed it into his pocket, but not before an expression darted across his face, what looked for a second like alarm, then resignation.

I raised an eyebrow. "Everything okay?"

"Business as usual." He nodded toward the door. "Let's drive to where the air is fresher."

Outside the cars were curving their way around the Bug without honking, as if double-parked cars were just another swerve in the road.

We were at last on the open highway, hurtling toward our destination. The rev of the VW's motor made talking difficult, and Doctor Juan Ramón seemed lost in his own thoughts.

I contented myself with absorbing the landscape. Many miles to the north, Monty, who for so long had loomed large as a snow-capped mountain in my life, was melting fast, regaining his rightful size. Soon he would reduce to a mere man, then an anthill, then a speck of dirt, then a pile of salts and minerals worth no more than ninety-eight cents, according to my high school biology book. Finally, he'd vaporize into nothing but a memory, along with a drawer full of snapshots and four years of birthday presents. I was happy now to have open vistas in the distance toward which I could stretch my eyes, just as I could from the seashore. At the sight of the uncluttered land, I too regained my rightful size and seemed less important to myself. Thoughts of Mother also rose up, but I at once trained my attention on the horizon. The road flattened out, and on both sides of us stretched fields and fields of rose bushes in full red and pink bloom. Then the rose bushes gave way to hills again. At what looked like an unmarked point in the road, we slowed, then veered right onto a narrow unpaved road. Relentless ruts and rocks caused the Bug to alternately sink low on one side, then bounce high on the other.

"What a bronco ride." I started to laugh, feeling as though I were on one of those electric bulls in a country-western bar. "Is it always like this?"

He seemed startled, as if he had forgotten I was even there. "It's worse when I take the bus. That's on those days when Eugenio's car isn't running."

"Doctor Eugenio usually lends you his car to see patients out here?"

"He insists. He knows how long it can take to come by bus. If the bus is running that day. Or if it runs but has the bad luck to get a flat tire."

"Do you come often to the rural communities?"

"Once or twice a month, sometimes more. This time it's urgent. I need to check on a certain patient."

"Speaking of patients, that reminds me, Doctor—"

"You must call me Juan Ramón."

"Oh, yes, *Doctor* Juan Ramón," I said, trying to lighten the mood. He didn't smile, but I continued anyway. "The other day, Norma—that's the sixteen-year-old daughter in the family where I'm living—yesterday she was complaining again that the *aires* were making her sick, and—" I didn't know how to express it, but I pictured a spiraling miasma of ominous fumes encircling her like a python. "What exactly are those *aires* she keeps talking about?"

"Those are just changes of climate. Or abrupt changes of temperature."

"Oh." They were only drafts—just air, as their name said—and nothing as superstitious or pestilent as I had been imagining. "So sensitivity to them couldn't be a sign someone is pregnant."

He gave a quiet laugh. "People blame a lot of their sicknesses and other conditions on those *aires*."

I was about to lead the conversation into a discussion of the best discreet way for a woman to find some form of birth control, but he was still talking.

"The other thing people attribute their illnesses to are *sustos*. You know, abrupt frights. Scares."

"What kind of frights?"

"Say someone falls off a horse. The sudden accident gives the person a *susto*, a scare. Or witnessing something awful can do that."

The VW hit a large rock and came down hard. Juan Ramón pushed back the rim of his hat, which the jolt had tilted over his eyes.

I braced myself against the dashboard. "Was that a *susto*, Doctor?"

He laughed out loud this time. "Juan Ramón," he said.

"Juan Ramón," I said.

"In summer, the road is like this because of the rains. In winter, the road is still full of holes left from summer rains."

I wasn't ready yet to leave the topic of *sustos*, but I was glad to have him talking. "Why doesn't the highway department fix it, if there is such a thing?"

Juan Ramón emitted what I thought must be the Mexican version of harrumph.

"There are two highway departments, in fact. Until six months ago, this road belonged to the state. Now it supposedly belongs to the federal system. But the federal department doesn't want to accept a road from the state in such poor repair. And the state says, 'Why should we spend the money to fix a road when the road isn't going to be ours anymore?'" He gestured toward the windshield with a broad fling of his wrist and harrumphed again. It seemed as though he were also shaking off his mood a little, and we were actually having a conversation, even if about lousy roads.

He took his hands off the wheel for a moment and folded his arms in front of him in mock indignation. "The federal department answers, 'How can we accept a road that was damaged under your care? It is your responsibility to hand over a road in good condition, no?'" He sighed. "So no one fixes it. The road remains the same."

"In my country," I said, "we call that a Mexican stand-off."

Before I could see how he took my attempt at a joke, the car splashed into a large hole filled with water, and the spray went flying, some drops bouncing in through the open windows.

"That one was big enough to roast a goat in," said Juan Ramón.

"Or bathe it." I shook my arm out the window to knock off the drops.

Juan Ramón leaned over the steering wheel. "Listen," he said, in a voice so low it was almost a whisper. "Do you hear that?"

I couldn't help but whisper back. "What?" I was primed to receive the mystical sounds of nature, the call of a meadowlark, woodpecker or creature of the piney woods, even the bleat of a lost lamb. But I didn't hear anything, other than Juan Ramón pumping the accelerator.

"It's gone."

On its own, the Bug rolled to a stop. Behind and ahead of us the road stretched on, lank as a worn shoestring. No trucks, no buses, no people in sight.

Juan Ramón climbed out of the car. I figured I might as well, too. He lifted the hood in the back of the car. I peered at the small engine as if it might reveal its problem to me.

"The accelerator cable, it snapped." He turned away from the hood and looked around. Then he returned to the passenger compartment and began to poke around.

An old woman appeared out of nowhere and trudged her way along the road, passing right by us with slow steps. Her mahogany skin was heavily creased—she looked to be in her eighties—and she was bent double under a huge bundle of skinny branches. Her open mouth was puckered up like a little draw bag, a sign her teeth were gone.

"*Buenas tardes*," she said in a rusty voice, wishing us a good afternoon as if we were all out for a casual afternoon stroll in the sunshine.

"*Buenas tardes*, Doña Angélica." Juan Ramón stood up, a pair of pliers in hand. "I see you have your cooking wood already."

"*Sí*, Doctor." The woman plodded a few more steps up the road. "Catalino is still waiting for you," she called over her shoulder.

"Catalino?" I said.

"A patient," he said, keeping his attention on the task at hand. "The one it's urgent that I see."

As the woman receded along the road, I couldn't help but wonder how far she had gone to gather those branches and how far she still had to go. And what, except grinding poverty, could impel a woman at that age to wander about daily in search of the day's firewood?

"How often does the bus come along here?"

"We don't need the bus." Juan Ramón said it so fast I realized my question had offended him.

He started off across the field on my side of the car, muttering something that sounded like "wire." I opened the door on my side again and positioned myself sideways on the seat. I pushed up the legs of my pants so I could at least sun my calves in the meantime. After less than a minute, I stood up again. I couldn't really enjoy the sun's warming rays because I kept thinking of that ancient woman foraging over and over for her meager measure of sticks.

Juan Ramón was still in the field, bending down next to a fence. Off to one side a goat stood on its hind legs and extended its neck to nibble at the leaves of a mesquite. I tried to enjoy the beauty of the landscape and the charm of the goat and not think about the old woman, or Juan Ramón's waiting patient, nor how long before I saw civilization again or could do my research for this damned story. I ran over the schedule I had self-imposed:

Today, Day Two: interviews in the countryside, given that Day One had been sidetracked with the visit to Doctor Eugenio's patio;

Tomorrow, Day Three: interviews at the clinic with Doctor Eugenio, who had turned out to be useful after all;

Day Four: one more day of interviews with both doctors and, ideally, a third and fourth;

Day Five: Wrap-up. Goodbyes all around, then departure from the Cuernavaca bus terminal;

Day Six: Land at LAX and start along the coast to Marbella.

Juan Ramón returned to the car, a long piece of barbed wire in hand. He set about pinching off the barbs with the cutter part of the pliers.

"Our new accelerator cable?"

"We'll see how long it holds." In a while he had fashioned a somewhat smooth piece of wire, free of protuberances.

I stood up and watched the doctor as he worked, his hands a blur of tugging and twisting. His jaw was set, and a lock of dark hair had worked loose from the hat and draped over his left eyebrow. He didn't seem to notice. He was as focused as that day I first encountered him in the makeshift operating room, a patient stretched out before him.

A long hour later we were chugging down the road. The further away we got from the main road, the more I tried not to think about the possibility that the wire might not hold. We began to pass rows of corn fields. Soon we came abreast of the old woman, still trudging along with her bundle, bent over so far she gazed at the dirt.

Juan Ramón slowed. "Would you like a ride, Doña Angélica?"

Doña Angélica waved us off.

Imagining her life, I couldn't help but feel sheepish at what I had taken to telling myself lately, that I wanted to "fill out the form I was meant to have." What form was this poor woman meant to have? Or was this it—her wobbling over the hills each day in search of cooking fuel? But then, maybe she really had filled out the form she was meant to have. Who could say she was any less happy than I? Maybe, with her fuel safely on her back, she was even happier, satisfied with her day's accomplishment.

Plain red-brick houses now appeared here and there, small block structures. Newly washed clothes lay spread out to dry over the low branches of the young mesquite trees, making crazy-quilts of color in the sun.

"Welcome to the community of Los Valdez," said Juan Ramón. He had lost his brief lightheartedness. We got out of the car, and I followed his lead in rolling my pants legs so we could wade through the muddy stream that separated us from what I took to be Los Valdez proper.

A string of jubilant children waved wildly to herald our arrival into what appeared to be the heart of the community. There was no center, really. It was just a scattering of bare brick houses, framed with banana palms and clusters of red and yellow flowers. The plants and trees muted what would have otherwise been blunt poverty. There were no electrical lines, no cars. Here and there a little store sold *pepitas* and Cheetos *con limón*, operating from the open front doorway of a two-room house. The children, who obviously were not in school, wore dirt-stained clothing, and one was barefoot. Chickens scattered before us as we walked.

If I thought Cuernavaca was another world, then Ixmilco was another world within that one, and this small community was yet another. I was burrowing into nesting boxes, one inside the other. What further microcosm lay inside this one?

* * *

I perched on a plastic chair within a semi-circle of five women Doctor Juan Ramón had gathered for me. My notebook rested on my knees. The women and I had been talking together for almost an hour already, our chairs in a dirt clearing between two houses. Lacey branches of a mesquite gave us shifting shade. Hanging from the tree's branches, several cages held songbirds that trilled sudden commentary.

A quick-eyed woman named Hortensia squatted at the far end of the circle, next to a fire where ears of corn were roasting. "It isn't that I don't want to use the pill or the condom. It's that my señor does not want me to. He reminds me a child is a gift from God."

The other women nodded in agreement. At first, I thought the nodding was about a child being a gift from God. Then I realized it was about the attitude of the husbands.

"My Fidel has heard there is only 98% protection with the pill," she said. In a quick movement she flipped the corn, revealing the side charred from the coals. "He asks me, 'What if everyone knows you are on the pill and then you are that 2% that gets pregnant anyway? Maybe all the other men will think you were lying to me or even cheating on me. Maybe the baby is not mine.'"

The women laughed in recognition of this logic, a logic that eluded me.

A clutch of brown hens traipsed through the clearing as if searching for something they had misplaced.

"It is not that I want to go against God," said Hortensia. "I would not want Him to take my husband from me. My Fidel is just what I prayed for. A hard worker who doesn't drink. He is the right señor for me."

I said, "How did you know when you had found the right man?" It was something I hadn't been able to manage, despite what I might cynically call years of practice.

Marcela, who sat just to the left of Hortensia and appeared older than the other women, answered before Hortensia could. "I always looked at their shoes," she said, giggling. "I wanted a man who had beautiful shoes. Polished and clean."

Hortensia giggled, too. "Oh yes, the novios," she said, "the boyfriends."

I sensed the excitement as the women leaned in toward one another and lowered their voices, although no men were nearby to hear. They wanted to talk about their novios, the boyfriends they once had. Juan Ramón had said he was going to the village's one-room clinic. I had no idea where the other men were.

Hortensia fingered a small cross that hung at her neck. "When I still lived in Cuernavaca, I had three boyfriends. All at the same time. None of them knew about the other. One was Fidel." She smiled and momentarily dipped her head. "One of the others—Mario Alberto—was rich. His father had a lot of money. He always dressed perfectly, with beautiful shirts and pants. The third novio was very handsome. But he did not have as much money as Mario Alberto."

She lowered her voice almost to a whisper. "I would meet one novio on a street corner, walk and talk with him for a while. Then I'd leave him to go meet another one on another corner. Of course, none of them knew what I was doing."

"Would you kiss?" asked Paola, the youngest of the women. They all laughed.

Hortensia looked around to see who else might be listening, but there were only the chickens. "Oh yes. We would sometimes kiss on the lips. *Besitos,* little kisses."

This information made everyone giggle, including me.

Hortensia leaned forward again. "I didn't know which one to choose. All three were nice. But Mario Alberto had a lot more money. And the other—his name was Cipriano—was short, but handsome. So I prayed to La Virgencita. I prayed and prayed and asked for a sign." She put her hands together as if in prayer.

The other women nodded their heads.

"Then I knew what I was going to do." Hortensia spoke slowly, drawing out her words, relishing her own drama. "I asked each one to bring me a flower. The man who brought me a white flower would be the one the Virgin María meant for me."

She paused to poke at the coals with a stick.

"I said to each, 'Please, would you be so kind as to bring me a *regalito,* a little gift of just one flower? It would make me very happy. Just one, no more.'"

The women were following Hortensia's every word even though, I suspected, they had heard this story before.

"Mario Alberto, the rich one, brought me a beautiful big orchid. It was very grand and wrapped in an elegant box. 'Ah,' I thought, 'so pretty. But this man is not for me.' The orchid was purple. Cipriano, the handsome one, brought me a—"

Hortensia spoke so fast and low that I couldn't catch what she said. The other women stirred and murmured. They recognized the name of the flower.

I broke in. "What's that? What kind of flower did you say?"

Hortensia glanced around as if she might spot one. "It's

like an azalea. A beautiful flower."

"And was it white?" But I already knew the answer.

"A fiery gold." Now Hortensia's voice rose as if in song. "And when Fidel brought me his box with the flower, I opened it slowly. Inside was a perfect white gardenia."

"And so you married him?" I said, half statement, half question. I wanted to add, Just like that. Without a doubt in the world? And also, are you that *loca?*

Hortensia stared at me, taken aback. "I knew he was the one La Virgencita wanted for me."

"And what about the rich one?" teased Marcela.

"Mario Alberto?" Hortensia shifted her focus to the corn on the coals. "He had a bad temper. He died a few years later in a fight."

"And Cipriano?" I said.

"I have never liked short men very much."

I set my notebook to one side. Women in this century just didn't make important decisions in that way. At least my friends and I didn't. But then, why not? To put your trust so completely in a supernatural power, that would be an enormous relief, wouldn't it? Trust someone or something else to untangle your knots, wipe up your spilled milk, rebuild burned bridges with better ones.

"What about you, Señorita Rosie?" said Paola. "Have you had lots of novios?"

I didn't know how to answer this simple question. I thought of the "little kisses" Hortensia had mentioned. Before my eyes, as if I were drowning, rushed a stream of so-called novios, my boyfriends. The gulf between my past and the past of these women yawned so wide I could think of nothing to say.

A chick darted in front of me squawking all the time, then ran right past and out of the circle as if pursued by an invisible phantom. I pretended to be absorbed by its addled path.

The irony was not lost on me: these women might not be able to manage birth control, but they were able to find the right man. Now they were all looking at me, waiting for my story. They wanted to hear about my "signs."

I had none. I had missed the signposts and taken too many wrong roads. I had heard no bells, no tolling reminders, unless I counted the bells I heard in Doctor Eugenio's patio.

The heat, which I had not been aware of before now, bore down. I lifted my hair off the nape of my neck. The women were still gazing at me. I managed to say that, yes, for a long time I once had a novio. He took me to lots of parties and made me laugh. But he was not the right one for me. That was all I could think to say.

Hortensia plucked the ears of corn from the fire and began to unwrap one. She handed it to me on a plate before passing the remaining ears to the other women. They continued to look my way, expecting me to finish the story. "Well, he didn't want a family," I said, to offer some kind of explanation.

They clucked in sympathy. This was something they could understand. I bit down hard on the hot roasted corn, glad Mexican field corn was so chewy I would not be expected to say anything more. Anyway, I had come to interview them, not the other way around.

I held the ear of corn gingerly. "Could anyone tell me where Doctor Juan Ramón or the clinic is?"

"Oh, is he your novio now?" said Paola.

"He is helping me with my research. That's all. I don't know him very well."

The women clucked again. This is just how small towns are, I thought. You talk to a man, and the next moment you are sweethearts, sitting in a tree, k-i-s-s-i-n-g.

Marcela led me out of the clearing and pointed to a small white building up the hill. A sign next to the door bore the letters *SSA*. How unexpected to find a government presence, a branch of the Secretariat of Health and Assistance, in such an out-of-the-way place. Along the front of the building grew stalks of red geraniums, the only landscaping.

I strode up the hill. Inside the tiny room of the clinic, the air hung cool and slightly musty, despite the unscreened door. A plump young man in a white medical coat was standing behind a table in what must function as the reception and waiting area and consultation room. On a chalkboard behind him were the words "To purify water." I had interrupted his talk. Three women sat bunched in front of the table and now turned to stare at me.

The young man, I supposed, was the *médico pasante* who was living there in the rural clinic for the year. Juan Ramón had explained earlier that rural clinics had no directors. Instead, they might be staffed solely by a medical student who had finished his formal studies but, like other professionals in Mexico, first had to give a year of social service to his or her country wherever assigned, even if it meant living alone in Los Valdez.

The *médico pasante* hurried from behind the table to meet me, his high cheekbones rising like little hillocks in the slopes of his face. He extended his hand. "You must be the friend of Doctor Juan Ramón, no?"

My reflex was to reply "no" in response to his "no," but then I remembered that the right response to "no" was "yes," even though Juan Ramón and I weren't friends as such.

"Do you know where I can find the doctor?"

The *médico pasante* explained that I must count nine houses, then at the flowering tabachín turn left and follow the trail until I came to a house surrounded by a fence of *órganos*, the tall straight cactus that looked like organ pipes. That was where *el doctor* was seeing a patient. He sighed quietly, and I took that as a sign I should move on, that this *médico pasante* was a busy man with much to do in the clinic and his village.

I made my way, counting off houses. At the house with the organ-pipe fence, I lingered a moment in the doorway. The door was open, and a strong and unpleasant smell clawed out at me. I peered into the dimness. The tamped dirt floor of the house became visible. As my eyes adjusted to the low light, I could see the room served as kitchen, dining room, and living room. Against one wall rested an unpainted wooden buffet. On a crate set against the opposite wall stood a small thirteen-inch television. Its source of power, a car battery, rested on the floor next to it. On the three walls bloomed a dusty garden of holy pictures, mostly of the Virgin Mary in her manifestations as Our Lady of Guadalupe and Our Lady of Perpetual Help, ringed by floating cherubs with golden curls.

A woman lumbered from a chair in the right corner of the room, her black shawl trailing over her shoulders and partly over the bulge of her pregnant stomach. I couldn't tell her age. She could have been a woman of twenty who looked old or a woman of forty-five who looked young. She did not seem as surprised to see me as I was to see her. She shuffled forward and without a word motioned me toward the adjoining room. A pink curtain hung as a door between the two rooms.

I pulled the curtain to one side and took a step into the small bedroom. The strong smell burned my nostrils, and all at once I found myself staring into stark brown eyes. The boy, who lay on a wooden pallet, appeared to be about ten, and he was swaddled like an infant in a ragged blue blanket. He blinked several times in fright. Otherwise, there was no movement, only the smell of charred flesh.

"You must leave, Señorita Rosie," said Juan Ramón.

I turned at once and went back into the front room, my heart pounding.

"He has been burned," said the woman with the black shawl. She was sitting again on a chrome chair that matched the chrome table's Formica top.

The Spanish phrases I had been working on so hard and had even been using successfully with the other women now abandoned me. I couldn't utter any words, not one.

"He was playing with a blanket, rolling himself up like a candle," said the woman in a monotone, as if condemned by a curse to drone out her tale. "Some other children were playing with matches. They set fire to the blanket." She stopped talking and stared through the window at the geraniums growing in cheerful confusion among the organ-pipe cactus. "They were just children."

From inside the bedroom, I heard the boy whimper. Then came Juan Ramón's voice, as soft as the gauze he was probably winding or unwinding at that moment. "Listen, Catalino, tell me a secret." He said in a conspiratorial whisper, "Do you have a novia?"

I knew he must be trying to distract the boy from his pain as he tended to him.

"Yes, I do. My mother tells me I do." The boy's words trembled but were clear. "My mother tells me *La Muerte* is my novia now. Death is my girlfriend."

My eyes met those of the mother, who was obviously the woman in front of me. "We are ten, with another coming," she said, barely audible. "We are too many."

I translated and retranslated the simple Spanish words.

The meaning stayed the same.

I made for the door, where I escaped into the day outside, bright with sunshine. A couple of hours ago, the sunlight had beamed down, scattering festivity and goodwill like confetti. Now its glare shoved into me with hard elbows.

I peered into the distance, searching for the feathery green of the pines, seeking out the color of hope and solace. But the house was situated in a dimple of land and surrounded by the tall cactus. I couldn't spot the pines even though I turned in a ragged circle looking for them.

When would Doctor Juan Ramón come out? How could he stand to still be in there with that dying boy, that boy willed to die by a mother who had too many children to feed? Didn't he want to run despairing through the cactus and dirt as I did?

"Rosie."

I heard his voice but waited long seconds to compose my face before turning around.

"He's going to die, isn't he?" I hurled the question like a stone.

"Yes. His parents won't let me move him to the hospital in Cuernavaca."

"They are too many, that's what the mother says."

"Yes. They are too many. And it is too late. They know that."

We walked in silence back through the pathways of Los Valdez and waded back through the stream to the car. The multi-colored wash still floated on the branches of the mesquites and the dark-eyed children again flailed their arms as merrily as if Juan Ramón and I were a favorite aunt and uncle come to bestow strawberry candies and *papitas* with *limón*.

We got in the car without saying anything. Like a pull toy on a string, the little car bounced back along the same rough road we had traveled hours before. I didn't care anymore if the rewired accelerator cable held or not. We jostled in slow motion, and my limbs felt heavy.

After a while, Juan Ramón said, "I like driving out through the hills. It's something we did a lot with my father when I was younger." He paused, as if waiting for me to show some interest. "Once a month he took us boys hunting. We also went to the *granjas*, the ranches where cattle are bred." He paused again.

I forced myself to say something, anything. "Oh. Did you grow up in this area?"

"In another state. In the city of León. Do you know where that is?"

"It's in the state of Guanajuato. In the middle of the country."

"Very good, *Señorita Periodista*," said Juan Ramón, turning his head my way as he addressed me as Miss Journalist. "I thought most Americans believed the world ended at the U.S. border."

"That's not fair." I didn't tell him I had spent time on the airplane studying the map of Mexico with its thirty-one states. Otherwise, I wouldn't have had a clue either.

"You're right." He grinned. "I should have said most Americans think the world ends with Mother Europe."

I was too downspirited to respond to the teasing distraction he was offering.

He edged the Bug to a flat area at the side of the road. I thought it might be car trouble again, but he didn't mention the cable, and I didn't hear anything odd from the motor.

Off to one side rose a thicket of pines. The trees grew up high and forbidding, like a barricade. A small pond mirrored the tallness of the pines upside down. It was just the way I felt, upside down.

"Are you—how do you say—an outdoors lady?" He said that in English.

Before I could answer, he sprinted to my side of the car. He yanked open the door and reached for my hand. "Come. I want to show you something."

I leaned toward the floor to pick up my notebook.

"No, leave your shark book behind this time." He tugged at my arm. "You need both hands to climb."

I wondered what had him so animated. I let him lock my notebook in the car. Then we tramped through the wild grasses and into the stand of pines.

"You've been here before?" I hoped he wouldn't take that as lack of confidence.

"Many times. It helps me."

A carpet of pine needles muffled our footsteps. I breathed in the fragrance from the trees. Juan Ramón was striding briskly, and I had to hurry to stay up. At least if I were to dislocate my knee, he should know what to do. And he already knew my ankle.

The pines disappeared, and we entered into a meadow of knee-high grasses and yellow wildflowers the size of dimes. Ahead rose a huge slope, dense with trees.

"That hill we will climb," said Juan Ramón, startling me again with English. He gestured toward the so-called hill. I would have put his hill in the Alpine family.

We began our ascent, and he was right: I had to use both hands. Mostly, I concentrated on climbing and dealing with the moist ferns and trickle of water that flowed in tiny rivulets here and there. I was forced to lodge my feet into any small foothold I could spot and grasp a handful of fern or tree branch to grope my way up. A few times, Juan Ramón reached back and hauled me up by one hand. In those moments, I dangled in space for a few beats, linked to the mountain only by his arm and fist, my feet floating, no choice but to trust him to hang on to me.

We seemed to climb for maybe twenty minutes, maybe more. Suddenly, the shaded slope of the mountainside opened and afforded a vista of the top.

We were both breathing heavily, but I gasped to see the stone structure that capped the hill's summit. "A pyramid?" I said, not trusting my eyes, even though the carved stone edifice that rose before us most obviously was that.

Juan Ramón seemed pleased to see my amazement. "Built before there were gringos on this continent. Made in America by the original Americans. Centuries even before that famous mapmaker Américo Vespucio, so even before the word *America*."

We ascended the weathered steps leading to the top of the

small pyramid, which was maybe thirty feet high. It flattened off at the apex, opening to a broad stone platform. We let ourselves down onto the edge of the ancient escarpment. We sat like children, resting our legs on the steps below, gawking at the panorama.

Mist looped and swirled in ribbons over the tops of pines, a wave of green that washed down the slope of the mountain. This side dropped off in a gentle descent and in the far distance below opened into a lush and leafy valley.

"Like the navel of the earth." I breathed in the scent, the view, the hope. Then it all hit me again. "I can't imagine how it is to be a doctor. Face to face with death."

He pulled a cigarette from the pack in his shirt pocket and lit it. "We all have a time."

"That doesn't make a child's death easier to accept. Or understand."

"I suppose not. Unless you believe, as the people here do, that when you die, you are going to look upon the face of God."

The face of God. If there was a God. That was something I desperately wanted to believe but could not sustain. The language of doubt.

"Is that what you believe? That you will look upon the face of God?"

He shrugged as the smoke from his cigarette floated out like a cloud and lost itself in the mist. "I try to. And you?"

"How could any kind of God I would want to believe in let that boy be burned like that? And die like that?" I drew my legs up and rested my head on my knees.

He waved his arm out over the vista of green before us. "The face of God. I think we're looking at it right now."

I lifted my head and nodded. "There's something primordial here.

"It's the kitchen of life."

But, I thought, the brew of life came in twos, Adam and

Eve, animal pairs in the ark. Without warning, the image came to me of the boy Catalino swaying with bare-ribbed Death, his *novia*, in the dance of rotting flesh. Then, just what I didn't want to do, I let go of any remaining attempt to maintain a semblance of journalistic cool.

"That boy—" I choked on my words. "That mother is just going to let her boy *die*? She's not going to fight for his life?"

Juan Ramón turned toward me, his face the opposite of the dispassionate doctor as his eyes met mine. "In her way, she is fighting. She is fighting for the survival of her family. The more children a woman has, the more likely her children will suffer malnutrition."

"Can't we do something?" I tried not to wail, but how could this doctor—not a farmer, not a plumber, not a waiter, but a *doctor*—remain so calm? Didn't he care? I felt mired in mud, up against his impassivity. There were too many things I didn't understand. I was staring into the face of old ghosts, old faiths. Juan Ramón shrugged. "We can change the bandages. Make Catalino more comfortable. That's about it. Tomorrow I will send the *médico pasante* another package of anti-inflammatories to help cool the boy's pain. I told him he must continue to pressure the parents." He again sounded resigned to forces beyond him.

"And if you get him to the hospital?"

"That is just the first step of many in these cases. The small hospitals provide only aspirin. The family would have to pay for his medicines. And, well, that is not so easy."

"Maybe I can help." I didn't know how it would happen, but I said it anyway. "Just get him to the hospital."

"Rosie, it will not happen. It is too late."

"But isn't there a law? Can't the parents be held responsible? Can't you, as the doctor?"

He shook his head.

"You seem so accepting."

He waited awhile before answering. "To lose a patient, a child, is something I never accept. I am not, as you charge, 'accepting.' Only experienced." He hesitated before adding, "And you, forgive me for saying, are not experienced. That's why you think I should be able to go in and change things that have been this way for . . . centuries."

I finally saw the sorrow in his eyes, the sag of his shoulders. I found a Kleenex in my pocket and wiped my nose.

"This boy will not live. His parents know it. The mother's words sound harsh. But his family has found a way to accept what they cannot change."

He placed his arm around my shoulder. The two of us sat there, staring ahead as if watching a movie. The panorama before us was more encompassing than any offering on a modern screen. Clouds formed and reformed into odd creatures of the sky, their long limbs trailing white and filmy, with touches of purple, red, and flaming pink.

"There," said Juan Ramón, pointing to the brilliant brushstroke of pink in the sky, "that color is what we call *rosa mexicana*. That is you, Rosie. That is your heart as you become more Mexican."

I wasn't sure if he was teasing, but I hadn't the energy to argue. His bringing me here had been for me, to assuage my shock, but it had also been for him.

As we continued to sit there, the strength of Juan Ramón's arm steadying my shoulder, the gossamer soul of a ten-year-old boy lifted up through the pines. Turning slowly, as if waltzing with an unseen partner, it swirled closer and closer toward the edge of the world.

* * *

There was no way I was ready for another day in the countryside, but after we left the pyramid, Juan Ramón insisted he had to take me to another village the next morning

"You must trust me."

"This will help my article?"

"This is what you need. I think you will thank me." He was noncommittal beyond that.

I was not excited. The drive was as long as the drive to Los Valdez had been, but uneventful. When we finally unfolded ourselves from the Bug, we stood alongside it for a few moments, stretching our legs and arms. Juan Ramón pointed to a tiny adobe house where he said his patient lived. I dreaded it. He left me at the car and went to check on her.

He returned shortly. "She is due to deliver any time. The midwife is with her now."

"So if there is a midwife attending her, you are needed too?"

"No. The midwife knows what to do. Only in the last few months has a doctor even been permitted to attend a birth in this village." He asked me to wait there again. He returned to the house and disappeared inside. I wondered just what I was going to get for my article from this situation.

Juan Ramón reappeared and beckoned for me to come. As I drew near, he put his finger to his lips, indicating I shouldn't make a noise. He guided me to the rear exterior of the house and right into a bed of plants. I had to tiptoe not to trample the vines. He placed his forefinger against his lips again, then nudged me in front of him and against the house's back wall.

An open window—no shutters, no screen—was only a foot away. Juan Ramón gestured toward the window. We waited there in the loose dirt and vines, me wondering what this was all about.

Then I heard the singing. At first it was soft, high, and feminine, almost like the voices of young girls in chant. The words were in some other tongue, not Spanish, more guttural.

"They're singing in Nahuatl," said Juan Ramón, barely

breathing. "That's the ancient language of the indigenous people in this part of Mexico."

The chanting rose, expanding into full-blown song, women's voices in harmony, at once ethereal yet grounded in earth.

I cocked my head toward him as if to ask.

"The birth song," he whispered. "*Ya se da a luz.* They sing because the baby is being born now."

I could see nothing of what was happening inside the room, but I could imagine it. The baby's head was coming out, *crowning* as we say in English. In Spanish, the mother was *giving her child to the light, giving light to her child.*

"Here it is the tradition for certain of the village women to gather and sing the new soul into this world. It's their song of welcome."

The song kept coming, flowing through the room and out the open window, produced by perhaps no more than a few women. They lifted their voices in rapture, inhaling the new soul into this world with the force of their own breath, linking its breath of life with theirs.

I wanted to make sounds within me, though I couldn't even hum the unfamiliar melody.

"Gracias, Juan Ramón," I whispered. "Thank you for insisting I come here."

No, this day wasn't about allowing me more interviews with the women or with Doctor Eugenio.

It wasn't about birth control, but he was right; it was what I needed. The outrage I felt over the burned boy still smoldered, but a new awareness arose, setting me in balance and tempering the harsh complications in this insistent land.

10

TO CATCH A SOUL

For the next two days I could not rouse myself from bed. Malaise and uneasiness draped over me like a mosquito net, and all my joints ached. I postponed the interview with Doctor Eugenio, throwing off the tidy schedule I had planned. The third day, I managed to drag myself up, fortified by some mystery drops.

"This is what you need, Rosie," said Norma. "I got these drops for you at the pharmacy. They will make you want to rope a steer."

By the time I climbed the steps through the Eden in Doctor Eugenio's entry, it was four thirty in the afternoon, just after the midday meal and smack in the heart of the drowsy hour. During the interview with the doctor, his housekeeper Imelda repeatedly swept the already tidy paving stones around our chairs in the patio. A few times she stopped nearby to push her tendrils of unruly hair back into the loose bun on her head and peer my way.

I now had compiled pages of data—statistics and histories that Juan Ramón and Doctor Eugenio provided me. But I wasn't satisfied. When, at the end of our interview, Doctor Eugenio invited me to accompany him to the hospital where two of his patients were in labor, I agreed. Even though the fact of women about to give birth was the other side of the coin from birth control, I now saw it was still part of the coin. I waited on the patio as he disappeared inside the house to gather his things.

"Permit me, Señorita," began Imelda as soon as he was out of sight. "Permit me to say you do not need to go to the hospital just yet. Not if you wish to see the women *dar a luz*."

"No?"

"The moon is not yet full. Those señoras will not deliver for another two days." She pointed to the sky, even though there was no moon to be seen at this time of day. "I didn't intend to listen to your conversation, Señorita. But what could I do? There I was with the broom."

I lifted one shoulder in a half-shrug, trying to convey that eavesdropping was inevitable, part of the job.

"*El doctor* Eugenio is a good person, an excellent doctor. But there are some things he can't tell you. He doesn't think they are real." She hesitated a moment, then lowered her voice. "I have one child, my son Constantino. He wasn't born until I was almost forty-five years old. Day and night I thank Our Lord in Heaven who gave him to me. But there is someone on this earth I thank, too. That person is not a doctor."

She had prayed and prayed for fruit to issue from her loins. In desperation, her husband was turning to drink, his manhood in question. Imelda had turned to a *curandera*. This healer promised to unchain Imelda's womanly power. The *curandera* would cleanse Imelda's spirit and body in the ritual called a *limpia*. Imelda would catch a soul in her womb before that year had passed.

She hurried her words. "Señorita Rosie, I will take you to a curandera." She began to untie her checkered apron. "My work here is finished for this day. I invite you to accompany me now." The humble people trusted in these healers for everything, she whispered. Not just to bring babies, but to stop more babies from coming. The curandera could heal wounds, alleviate headaches, vanish infections, some said even cure cancer.

I did want to take advantage of this opportunity though it might seem to be leading me away from birth control. I had insisted to Leland I wanted to learn the women's real feelings, had I not? A healer was the poor people's psychologist, was it not?

Doctor Eugenio strode back into the patio, black bag in each hand.

I explained I wouldn't be going to the hospital with him, not just then. "But if you wouldn't mind, maybe I could go with you day after tomorrow?" I quickly added, "Surely you will have another woman ready to give birth in a day or two?"

I caught Imelda's eye so she would know her medical prognostication for the two women supposedly in labor right now was safe with me. She busied herself again with jamming back in her bun several curls so wayward they seemed to serpentine their way into the dark background of vines behind her.

The three of us left Doctor Eugenio's house together, marching in single file down the vertiginous steps toward the tortillería. It was closed at this hour, depriving me of the earthy fragrance of hot tortillas. Outside the gate, Doctor Eugenio turned right. The housekeeper and I turned left. We made many more turns and ended up walking along an unpaved road on the outskirts of Ixmilco.

"Who will I be watching? Who will be having this *limpia*?" Imelda lifted her eyebrows. "Well, you, Señorita."

I jerked my hand up as if to stop traffic. "Oh, no, no. I'm just going to watch. I only want to get information."

Imelda smiled again. "This I know. But *la curandera* will not want *la señorita* journalist only to watch and ask questions."

I insisted I had to maintain my professional objectivity by just observing. That was my job. It's what I did.

"Señorita Rosie, you are too worried. I promise on my life you are in safe and decent hands. You should not miss this chance for a cleansing with a healer who has allowed her body to be taken over by the spirit of the *curandero famoso del norte*."

"The famous healer from the north? I don't know about him. Tell me." I looked back up the road we had just traveled, increasingly uneasy about this subject of healers and cleansings.

"Only one time I have been out of Ixmilco. It was without my husband's permission. Before the birth of my son." She had journeyed with her own curandera, the one who finally cured her barrenness, to the state of Nuevo León, and from there to a remote village. They visited the shrine of the celebrated Niño Fidencio. "Do you know, Señorita Rosie, that each year tens of thousands of people go from Mexico and the United States to visit the tomb of this miraculous healer?"

I shook my head.

"His spirit lives on, here in Ixmilco." She stopped in the middle of the road. "I have not told you all the story. In exchange for my baby, I allowed the spirit of Niño Fidencio to enter my body. I myself am the curandera you are going to see."

I came to an abrupt halt. "You? You're a curandera?" Unfortunately, I had come too far to find my way back alone.

Where was the line between natural healing and quackery? Out of nowhere, the words of Carole-Ann echoed, her proclamation that mind and body were one.

"Sure, the mind can influence the body," I more than once argued to Carole-Ann, "and vice versa. But if the mind and body are one and the same, how could the death of the body augur for any kind of afterlife? It seems to me that if mind and body are one and the body drops dead, the mind drops dead, too. So what's left?"

"Spirit."

"That seems like a contradiction, Carole-Ann. A spirit without personality? A spirit without any spirit to it?"

Imelda said, "I will not charge you. You need only to have faith."

I smiled weakly. If I had not been able to muster faith when I so desperately needed it after seeing the burned boy at the ranch, I didn't foresee any upcoming leaps of such. No point in conveying that to the housemaid Imelda—now curandera—whose own leap of faith shot over the moon.

Here and there stood a house. We were coming into a community. We stopped in front of an unpainted red-brick house like the hundreds I had seen since arriving in Mexico. Imelda placed her hand at the small of my back and guided me to the door.

"You must not struggle so. You are a person of too much thinking all the time, no?"

"No. I mean yes. I mean, I don't know."

Minutes later I was lying eyes closed atop a green chenille bedspread on what I assumed was Imelda's marital bed. Outside a window high in the wall, treetops tossed in the wind with azure sky beyond. I knew a chicken had run into the room when I heard it cluck, and the aroma of the black pig in the pen just outside the door wafted in.

Imelda began to trace over my clothed body with a branch of *pirul*, what in California we called a pepper tree. I lay perfectly still and allowed myself to close my eyes. Could some kind of subconscious impulse have propelled me to this dim place that smelled of *pirul* and melting candle wax and a pinch of pig?

A limpia indeed. Imelda had not asked, but I wondered what I might want to cleanse from my life. I didn't intend to go along with this, but suddenly the word "career" appeared. I had once looked up the word "career" in the dictionary. It derives from *carriera*, from the old Provençal language, and refers, literally, to my "road." As I lay there, I acknowledged my road was as flat as an Iowa interstate. I stole a peek at Imelda, now fully curandera. She was anointing the branches of the pepper tree with what I took to be herbed water. To her side stood a pregnant girl who had silently joined us. The pregnant girl balanced a white plate with three eggs rolling slowly side to side. She seemed to be a sous chef to the curandera's ministrations.

Imelda continued feathering the pirul branch up and down my outstretched body. Fragrant water wafted into the air and mixed with the other scents: hot candle wax, pirul, chicken, pig, musty brick. Imelda began to pray in a low rapid chant. I closed my eyes again and tried to give in to the experience. My career could do with a limpia after all.

What other memories should this limpia scrub? I dug deeper into the dirty clothes hamper. I didn't like to think of him, but there was my father who—now dead or alive, I didn't know—had bowed out of my life early on, leaving only the residual smell of gin and cigarettes. In quick succession came Monty, then my gnawing realization I might not be "relationship material." Like my mother and her mother before her, I would sail my adult life in a single-passage cabin. Oh, Mama, she must be missing me and worried. I drifted, and then suddenly I pictured the marks of age that had claimed my mother's face and were starting to claim mine.

Imelda was right. I did think too much.

She took hold of my left wrist. "You must not struggle so," she said again, gently, then let go and began to make light rubbing motions over me with one of the unbroken eggs, then the next and the next. "The eggs will draw out the bad things that trouble you."

I expected to feel something happening. But I didn't. I tried to visualize the "bad things," amorphous as amoebas, streaming out of me and into the beckoning eggs. If anything, though, I only surged with resistance.

After the limpia, I still felt no different. But I had done my research, and whether or not these notes made their way into the actual article, I took some enjoyment in imagining Leland's eyebrows as he read about this cleansing. He would admire my ability to ferret out the unusual angle. He would have no reason to suspect mine was the body and mind under the pirul's sweep.

* * *

Juan Ramón fished in the pocket of his jacket for the lighter and brought up a wadded ball of paper. He didn't need to open the ball to remember it was the note he had gotten a few days ago, the third such death threat he had received in the last few weeks. Each, scrawled in pencil with the same wobbly uppercase letters, betrayed how much effort it had cost their author to form them. The threats were from Cecilio, of course. As health director, Juan Ramón had to expect such things. He crushed the note back into a ball, stuffed it in his pocket and walked into Aida's party, determined not to dwell on the inevitable.

Twice a year, Aida invited her current students to her home on the outskirts of Cuernavaca, near the road to Ixmilco. That was one of the things he admired about her, that she would allow her students to breach the stone walls and enter her more private world.

He greeted Aida's housekeeper, Doña María, a seemingly passive woman but with quietly alert features. He passed under the series of arches that led through the house and out to the courtyard. The patio was festive and full, with students from La Divina Escuela de Idiomas as well as a few people he knew from Cuernavaca and Ixmilco. Salsa music pounded from the speakers, and a banquet table near the back wall displayed a colorful panoply of regional dishes.

He was startled to find Rosie, the American journalist, looking at him from across the patio, seeming as surprised to see him as he her. She flashed a smile and crossed the patio toward him. This was the first time he had seen her in a dress. It was blue and fitted close to her body, unlike the oversized shirts she seemed to favor. The blue bag was nowhere in sight. She had even replaced her tennis shoes with sandals on a little heel.

"How are you?" he asked, leaning toward her for the traditional kiss on the cheek. From the corner of his eye, he noticed Aida, who had also noticed him and was drawing near, a brandy glass in her hand.

"Better now," Rosie said.

"Better? You were sick?" He would have said she looked healthy as a running bull.

"After we got back from Los Valdez, I took to my bed for almost two days. I don't know what was wrong with me or where it came from."

"Some kind of susto, I imagine," said Aida, entering into the conversation. She stood close to Juan Ramón and lifted her head to receive his kiss on the cheek. She was wearing her inevitable tight jeans with stiletto heels, and a flowing yellow hostess top of filmy material. A small gold cross hung just above her breasts.

"I am glad you could come," she said to Juan Ramón. She handed him the glass of brandy. "Don Pedro brandy is still your favorite, no?" She didn't wait for a reply. "I see you remember Rosie. You taped her ankle."

"I remember her very well. In fact, I've been helping her with some research."

"Really?" Aida looked swiftly at Rosie, who had been observing their exchange.

"I took Rosie to Los Valdez a few days ago. To meet some of the women there."

"How generous, Doctor." Aida suddenly reached out and snagged hold of Leonardo, who was ambling by at that moment, balancing a plate of *sopes* lined up like oversized buttons. She then pivoted toward Rosie. "Have you met Leonardo Cortés?" She beamed a wide hostess smile.

Juan Ramón supposed it was her duty to introduce guests to one another. Leonardo's face lit up.

"He has a pharmacy close to the school," said Aida as she swiveled Leonardo toward Rosie.

Rosie smiled at the pharmacist just as she had smiled at him only a few moments ago. Juan Ramón reminded himself Rosie was a woman who had a job to do. As soon as she got the story she wanted, she would pack up and go. But he doubted she would get anything valuable for her article from soulful-eyed Leonardo, a known *mujeriego,* chaser of women. Leonardo and Rosie dropped into conversation, and Juan Ramón turned to look for Eugenio, who must be there someplace.

The air thickened with smoke and conversation. Spanish was being spoken in a stew of accents, German, French, and a variety of American intonations. Somebody ratcheted the music higher, and several couples began to dance.

Now he spotted Eugenio. He was one of those pulsing to the music, his head higher than that of anyone else on the patio. Eugenio held his shoulders motionless, in good salsa fashion, and let his hips make the moves. He caught Juan Ramón's eyes, and Juan Ramón gave a short self-conscious laugh. Eugenio must have been watching him since he entered the patio, reading his mind.

"*Aguas, hombre*—careful, man," Eugenio mouthed. Juan

Ramón gave a deprecatory wave of his hand, pushing away Eugenio's concerns.

At the table that had been set up as a bar, he poured himself another Don Pedro and then glanced in the direction of Rosie and Leonardo.

They had been standing together near the patio's long main table for some time now. Leave it to Leonardo to make a play for the americana. Juan Ramón would have liked a chance to talk to her himself. He wondered how her interviews with Eugenio had gone. He started to smoke a cigarette, but ground it out halfway. Taking his time, he started to chart his way through the patio.

Leonardo was smiling at Rosie as if besotted. He lifted Rosie's empty glass from her hand, gave a little bow, and angled off to the makeshift bar.

Juan Ramón came alongside Rosie. "When you get a free moment," he said in a low voice, "I would like to show you something."

She turned and stared into his eyes, hers green as the pines outside his living room windows. A few pale freckles, not normally visible, dotted her cheekbones.

Leonardo returned to Rosie's side, his Lothario face intruding on Juan Ramón's line of vision. Leonardo handed Rosie the new drink, then busied himself lighting a cigarette. "*Oye*—listen, Doctor," he said to Juan Ramón when finished. "Did your medical studies ever include a visit to a curandera?"

"Of course not, Leonardo. I can't imagine why you ask."

"Rosie has been telling me about her visit to a curandera yesterday. Fascinating." He pursed his lips and propelled smoke out over the table.

Juan Ramón set his face, keeping it impassive. What the devil was Rosie doing in the clutches of a curandera? Who had put her onto one of those people? And why was she telling this oily *payaso*, this clown, something she had not told him? She had spent at least part of yesterday talking with Eugenio, and he was sure it wasn't Eugenio who had sent her. And probably the curandera, when she saw a gringa face, charged double. Rosie wouldn't know that. Or perhaps care. Was it a case of her doing anything for a story? Or maybe it was a little adventure she was after.

He stared at Rosie, ignoring Leonardo. She dipped her head slightly and looked back at him.

Leonardo pushed up his sleeve and made a show of consulting his watch. "Señorita, I am so sorry I must take my leave. Forgive me, but I have to say a few words to Aida before I go back to the pharmacy. Who knows how much traffic there will be on the road to Ixmilco. I hope to see you again, no?" He kissed Rosie's one cheek, then the other, then, as if in slow motion, her hand. He quickly tapped Juan Ramón's shoulder and shook his hand. Then he was gone.

"So the curandera made you clean now?" Juan Ramón folded his arms and tried to keep the cynicism out of his voice. "Did it work? You have to believe, you know."

"Well, I'm not sick anymore. From the susto." She grinned and lifted her glass. "In fact, I feel great. *Salud*." She clinked her glass against his and took a sip. "Does that mean I have faith?"

Was she serious, or was she flirting? He wondered if the **Don Pedro** brandies were already affecting him. Maybe she was the one the drinks were affecting. She seemed more relaxed, as if she were finally having a good time. She stood there, her legs planted firmly with that unsettling Yankee confidence.

Something in him wanted to shake up that confidence, wobble her cool northern stance. "I think it's the drinks," he said as if giving a medical diagnosis, "not the limpia."

"Not the drinks. That I can tell you for sure."

"No? Well, then." He hesitated but could not stop himself

from saying, "Beware the *chapulín*, Rosie."

"*Chapulín?* The grasshopper?" She started to laugh. "What's that? A local drink?"

"It's your friend the pharmacist. The one you've been talking to the last hour—"

"Ten minutes. At most."

"He likes the ladies. He hops from one to the other like a grasshopper. That's how he got his nickname."

The expression on her face told him she couldn't tell if he was teasing. Then she said, "I can manage. The *chapulín* is a small creature. Almost domesticated." She took another sip of her drink. "It's the wild creatures I'm not so sure about."

He was about to say, "Like me?" but might need another Don Pedro for that.

"What is it with these nicknames? Doesn't anybody go by his real name? I mean, I hear *el Gordo* and *el Flaco* and *la Momia*—the fatty, the skinny one, the mummy."

"What's wrong with that? Those names fit, and they make a person easy to remember."

"—and there's *el idiota*. And *el panzón*, for those with a belly hanging out. Do nicknames always focus on somebody's defects? Aren't there any nicknames that are, well, nice? Or that express affection?"

"Let's see, *el idiotita*—dear little idiot? That's loving. And we have *la panzoncita* to show we adore that little belly, and—"

"What's your nickname?"

"I don't have one. Everyone else in my family does, though." He met her eyes. "You can give me one."

"Yes, I'd like very much to do that." She rubbed her hands together and peered at his face, then looked him up and down. "You're a . . . hmm, you're a . . ."

Juan Ramón waited.

"This is sort of like naming a newborn."

He stood still and allowed himself to feel self-conscious as she continued to study him. What might have been only seven seconds seemed like a minute as she inspected him, her head tilted, twirling the empty glass between her fingers.

"Okay, help me. Are you more animal, more vegetable, or more mineral?"

He shrugged.

"Well then, what are your defects? Surely you have some faults."

He rolled his eyes upward, then shrugged again.

"All right, what are your good traits?"

He said nothing at first, then, "We'll have to get to know each other so you can find out."

"Then you'll just have to wait to get your nickname."

He pretended indignation. "That leaves me like one of those newborns that lie around unnamed for weeks as their parents mutter a litany of names, searching for the right relative or saint." Juan Ramón took the glass from her hands. "We don't have weeks."

"No, we don't."

That word "we" was strange, even exciting. It had been so long since he and a woman were "we." He was, of course, deluding himself. He briskly reached for her glass. "Let me get you another drink. What can I bring you?"

"I've been drinking mineral water. But really, I don't want another. I want to ask you, though—you had something you wanted to show me?"

So it wasn't the drinks that accounted for her more open demeanor. He ran his hand along his chin, trying to find the words, words he regretted would change the mood. "I found more numbers. I have statistics from each of the states on birth control use for the last two years. That's the kind of research you need for your article, Rosie. Not a limpia with a curandera, something never meant for you in the first place."

She lifted an eyebrow. "And why not?"

He touched her shoulder lightly with his index finger. "You're not Mexican. For you, having a limpia is like going to a tourist attraction. It's a lark in a foreign country. Something you can tell your friends about. You're not a believer."

She touched his shoulder in return. "And you? You're entitled to go to the healer because you're Mexican? Because you are a believer?"

"I believe in science. And I believe in psychology. The healer works through psychology. But some people rely too long on the curandera's power of suggestion. They don't know when to turn to science. To a medical doctor."

"Ever since that limpia I do feel better, different, even though the change didn't happen right away." She paused. "So you don't use psychology?"

"Of course I do. I look for patterns and for revealing words. It helps to know what is troubling the person besides physical symptoms."

"Be careful. You don't want the other doctors to hear you. That sounds like medical heresy."

The patio brightened for a second as someone's flash went off. Across the table he caught sight of Aida, lowering her camera. She had just taken a picture of the two of them standing close in conversation, not aware they were arguing.

Rosie blinked from the flash, then said, "You are such a surprise, Doctor Juan Ramón. You are not what I expected, either as a doctor or as a person. You might even be a heretic. I think your nickname should be *el rebelde inesperado*. The unexpected rebel."

He was surprised she could roll the phrase out so smoothly. "All that for a nickname? I need something shorter. Easier."

She was staring at his hands. "What long fingers you have, Doctor. You could be—what is the word for somebody good with his hands?"

He couldn't stop himself from looking her up and down.

"That depends on what you mean."

"I mean—" He could see her backing away from where they were going. "I'm not sure what I mean. Well, I know you must be good with your hands—you're a doctor and a surgeon. But you're also different from what I would have thought."

She had said that before.

"What were you expecting?"

"Wait—I know, how about *la sorpresa*—the surprise?"

"I can't be a *sorpresa* all the time, Rosie."

She sighed. "Well, then, I'll just call you Juan Ramón." She repeated his name slowly, as if she had just discovered it. "I like the rhythm of it. Besides, it's the name that carries what you are made of, isn't it? It's where all your memories reside."

There was again a flash as Aida took another picture, then fast upon that another.

Rosie looked over her shoulder at Aida. "This is strange. Usually, I'm the one shooting the photos. I'm starting to feel like a celebrity. Is Miss Aida a member of the paparazzi?"

Despite Rosie's light tone, she was obviously uncomfortable with the picture-taking. He could imagine this series of photographs, he and Rosie facing one another, drawing closer. The curve of Rosie's bare arm, the fall of her hair—those were details the camera could capture. Could the camera also capture the intangible? Did Aida's camera discern the energy between them, just the way some people could see auras? Oh, listen to him, the man of the stethoscope, ruminating about energies, and after he had scolded Rosie for her visit to the curandera. He might as well be waving willowy pirul branches over the two of them.

Perhaps he was a rebel after all. Or was he a believer after all?

If he were to turn that camera on himself and Aida, could it also detect a diminished energy, one no longer there? Were there residual traces, a palimpsest of sorts?

Oh, Aida. How long ago was it that Aida had made her choice? More than two years, certainly. It was all for the best, though. He could see that now. She was a believer, and he had not been able to come between her and her staunch Catholic beliefs. She had seen to that. In her mind, he was still a married man.

He glanced in Aida's direction, but she and her camera had moved on. He turned back toward Rosie.

II

THE PINES

I wasn't being contrary. I did feel better after the limpia. I hadn't realized it until I heard myself saying so. Juan Ramón was a medical doctor trained to his empirical view of things. I couldn't have explained the sensation, and it wasn't a burning bush kind of thing, but I was what? Lighter. Or maybe I was just getting used to being in Mexico and speaking Spanish all the time. Now that I would be going home so soon.

Spots were still floating before my eyes from Aida's camera flashes when Juan Ramón leaned forward and suggested I stop by his apartment to pick up the new data he had collected. "Your time here is limited—in fact, I may not have a chance to see you again before you go home to California."

I was reluctant to leave the party. I hadn't yet had a chance to bid goodbye to the other *Moradas* and the *Naranjas* from the school, but duty compelled me to see what he had assembled for me, aware I might be passing up something essential if I didn't go. I could get whatever information he had and hurry back to the party.

Juan Ramón's apartment featured high colonial ceilings and floors of stone slab called *laja*. In each of the three main rooms—the living room, a bedroom, and a combination kitchen and dining area—tall French windows invited the light. Or they would have if it wasn't already nearing sunset. The building rested on the side of a hill where, Juan Ramón explained, the mid-afternoon sun dipped early, shadowed by a still higher hill.

By late afternoon, the apartment was cold and sulky, even in summer, unless the corner fireplace in each room was lit.

Soon after we arrived, he puttered about and lit a small fire in the living room fireplace. I stood by the desk in the corner of the room and leafed through the small pile of papers he had handed me. On one side of the desktop lay a scatter of photographs and some coins. The sight of the money brought back to me my low supply. Would I have to embarrass myself by borrowing from this doctor? No. I couldn't just write him a check as I left the country. He couldn't cash it. I wrenched my focus away from money and onto the photographs. The top one showed four children, obviously poor, maybe about five years old. They grinned and clowned for the camera, eyes gleaming. The children appeared to be on the hospital's patio.

I had a sudden idea and turned to ask Juan Ramón about my helping out in the clinic during my remaining few days. A loud knock at the door jarred the stillness.

Juan Ramón's voice was low, but I could hear his words, patient with politeness. "*Buenas noches*, Don Cecilio. I've been expecting you."

I stepped closer.

Juan Ramón turned to me and said in English, "You should wait in the bathroom."

"I have come to settle a score, *Doctorcito*," the man at the door said, his voice slurred. He appeared to be somewhere in his fifties, a worn-out mule of a man, his features blurry from too much drink. His face twisted into a snarl accentuated by the flickering light of the fireplace.

Juan Ramón kept his attention trained on Don Cecilio. "We

must talk. I want to hear what you have to say." He spoke with the diplomatic air of one who wished to confer with a colleague over the details of a difficult case.

I should go. I had Juan Ramón's materials in my bag. I could still find a taxi and make it back to the party. I took a tentative step nearer the door. Neither man looked my way.

But there was no way I could walk between them, nor walk out and leave Juan Ramón alone. I backed toward the hallway that led to the bathroom but went no further.

Cecilio's mouth was contorted, his feet unsteady. "Now it is your turn to die. You should have accepted my money. It was a splendid amount. One you were worthy of. That is what I—" He laughed and coughed at the same time as if caught up by something funny. I couldn't make out his muffled Spanish.

"Come, Don Cecilio." Juan Ramón motioned the man toward the dining table. "I'm not interested in your money. Sit down and let's talk about your restaurant." He made a ceremony of setting two glasses on the table, then lifted a bottle of brandy from the sideboard and began to pour.

What was he thinking? Even from where I stood unobserved in the shadows, it was obvious Cecilio required no further alcohol.

Juan Ramón took his time pouring the drinks. I wondered at his equilibrium. His gestures seemed to say Cecilio was an honored guest, not someone who had come to make this his last night on earth.

The dynamics of power were creeping about the room like a wary animal. Around the two men slipped a ring of masculine knowledge. Maybe this wasn't a matter of different cultures but of different genders. Men squared off against each other would sniff like animals, sensing how far they could test one another. They emitted a separate set of signals. I stood outside that ring, more female and foreign than I had ever felt in my life.

Cecilio didn't sit. Suddenly he pounded the table. "You have killed me, Doctor! You have closed my restaurant. You spurned my money. You disgraced my name." He arched over the table, stabbing his index finger at Juan Ramón. "You have turned me into a *fantasma*. Yes, a ghost. A ghost who will have his revenge."

Cecilio kicked over the chair Juan Ramón had pulled for him. He bolted down the *copa* of brandy and dropped into a crouch.

Juan Ramón rose as if in pre-arranged choreography. Something in his gestures, a sudden tightness in his back, or maybe it was a betraying awkwardness to his smile, something told me he must be afraid after all. The bravado was all calculation.

Cecilio made a sudden lunge into Juan Ramón's right shoulder. Juan Ramón pushed back against him and grabbed Cecilio's arm. Interlocked, they lumbered in a circle, a clumsy wheel of fortune, still in their masculine ring. They rotated full circle, then wheeled again and stopped. Cecilio stumbled to the floor.

My neck felt damp. I was sweating.

Juan Ramón extended his left hand to pull Cecilio to his feet. "There is a solution," he said, as though nothing had passed between them. "I assure you there is a solution, Cecilio." He righted the overturned chair and pointed toward it. Cecilio didn't sit.

Juan Ramón lifted the bottle of brandy and poured another drink for each of them, the dark amber spilling hope into the snifters. "We shall make our plan."

I held my breath, watching their faces, straining to catch their words.

When Cecilio didn't move, Juan Ramón lifted his shoulders. "Do you really want to kill the health director? Should you succeed, that will bring you true disgrace. Your restaurant closed—that is an inconvenience, not a disgrace. You can choose, of course, to kill me and bring true disgrace to your family."

Cecilio had not stopped glaring at Juan Ramón. Like a circus bear performing a tired trick, he slowly lowered himself into the chair. I let out the breath I was holding.

"The meat is not so bad," Cecilio growled. "The price is good."

Now it was Juan Ramón who pounded the table. "The price is too high if it causes people to fall sick and then causes your restaurant to close. Isn't it a disgrace, hombre, when people get sick from the food you serve?"

The two men glowered at each other. Cecilio suddenly put his head down and started to sob.

"Let me help you, Cecilio. Let me help the people at the same time." Juan Ramón's voice rose. "Who is this *ratero* selling you bad food? You can find a better place to buy meat, hombre. I can help you with that."

Cecilio raised his head, eyes pooled in misery. "My sons can't find work. They have come back to live with me. One brought his five children. The other has three. These *mocosos*—they jump on the beds until the wooden legs collapse. They fall down and rip holes in their clothes. They want to eat lunch as soon as they finish breakfast."

He went on, half sobbing, half angry. Day and night now he worried about money. The children, they were eating it all. What he had offered *el doctor* was the last of his money. "I cannot afford to pay more money for better meat. That is the truth."

"You must, Don Cecilio. Pray to God that He shows you the way."

This God talk again. The essential irony was that the children were at once part of the cause of the poverty and part of the hope for the future. Why couldn't Cecilio just send the five kids packing with their parents? Yet such a solution was un-thinkable. At bottom lay an unshakeable assumption that ran deeper than a man's ability to sire offspring like some kind of stud horse, deeper than a man's duty to care for his family, deeper than an insurance plan for care in his old age. To spurn a child would be to argue with God. To attempt to redesign the blueprint He had drawn for your life. Who would be so fool-hardy as to arm wrestle with God?

Juan Ramón stood and placed a hand on Cecilio's shoulder.

It was resolved then, I said to myself as Cecilio struggled upward. Juan Ramón guided him to the door, his arm slung across the man's shoulder. Cecilio's shuffling left dull sounds on the hallway stairs as Juan Ramón turned to face me. I just stood there, a few feet into the living room.

"Why didn't you stay in the bathroom?"

"How could I? I've never had a death threat. I've never even known anyone who has. I was scared for you."

Juan Ramón shook his head as if to clear it. "Wait here," he said and angled past me toward the bedroom. A few mo-ments later, he emerged with a blue and white serape draped over his shoulders like an old-fashioned Mexican from the movies.

He opened the French doors that led to the balcony. "Let's get some fresh air." His tone was determined.

I stepped through the doors into cool evening air. The bal-cony was a narrow rectangle, a protruding eyebrow for the building, its mate to the right protruding from the bedroom.

The balconies, designed for flowerpots, left scant room for two people to stand. We bunched together alongside the clay pots like two more plants in the row, two gangly ones.

The railing was damp. It must have rained while Cecilio was there. The air held the soft promise that follows a rain. Below us a scattering of lights marked out little Ixmilco.

Juan Ramón lifted one side of the serape and dropped it

over my shoulders.

"You will go to the police?"

He gave me a look to say I had just introduced a quaint and frivolous notion. *"No vale la pena—*it's not worth the effort."

"You should at least inform them. Just in case. Maybe they can stop him. The man threatened to kill you."

"I know only a little of how the laws are in your country. Here we have health laws to protect the public. But in these small towns, the laws sometimes go unheeded. These matters come down to a question of money, as you heard. Unfortunately." He shrugged. "That's all."

Maybe he felt an explanation unnecessary for the scenario I had just witnessed. Or maybe he just didn't want to talk about going to the police, supposedly a fruitless act. Or maybe he retracted at my separateness, the outsider who could not understand. Truth was, I was a bit homesick for known territory. I wondered if a Mexican woman would have stayed in the bathroom.

We gazed down at the town's lights in silence. Finally, Juan Ramón said, "Tell me about where you come from." He said it in English, perhaps giving up on my Spanish.

I followed his lead into my own language, relieved to be able to sink back into the soothing rhythms of the familiar. "I live in California, in a town by the beach. It's beautiful there."

"The beach—of course it must be beautiful." He pulled a cigarette from under the serape, lit it, inhaled deeply, and exhaled the smoke away from me. "What do you like most about it?"

The words came tumbling out. "So many things. The crash of the ocean. The smells. Light on the water. Changing colors during the day. The rocks at the jetty. The warm sand. The shore birds." I saw and felt each of those things as I named them.

"Do you miss it?"

"Yes, I do." I hadn't realized the extent until I said it. "I am not used to being landlocked. Sometimes it's hard to breathe here."

"Landlocked?"

"That means surrounded by land all the time. With no ocean near."

"Locked in. I see." He exhaled again. "Trapped. That doesn't sound very nice."

We returned to silence. I feared I had insulted his part of Mexico. "But it's pretty here. Are you from Ixmilco?"

"My parents and brothers and sisters live in León. It's several hours from here."

"I'll ask you what you asked me—do you miss them?"

"Yes and no." He was looking straight ahead, staring at the lights that had begun to twinkle. "I know so little about you, Rosie. Tell me something more than the ocean. Tell me about your family."

"My family?" I never liked this topic. I tried to lean into the railing for a moment to gather my thoughts but bumped against the clay pots lashed to the wrought iron.

"Start with your parents, then brothers and sisters."

I almost snorted. "It will be a short story. There's just my mother. And me, of course."

"That's all? What about your father?"

"I barely knew him. He left us when I was little."

"Why did he leave?"

I took a deep breath. "I used to try to figure out reasons when I was little. I'd try out each reason on my mother, hoping I would strike the right one and solve the mystery."

He turned to face me. "Why did you think he left?"

"I thought it was something I must have done wrong. I had been sassy. I had begged for a new Barbie doll. Left shoes in the middle of the floor. My room wasn't in order. I believed I drove him away. My mother always said no, it wasn't my fault he left. I was sure it was."

"That's the way kids try to make sense of painful things."

"I don't think my mother knew why he left either. Or at least she didn't say."

"That must have been hard for you. And for her. Not to know."

"It was a movie in my head that never ended. It just broke off, and we were left with no future installments, just a chain of 'maybe.' Maybe he left us because he liked to drink a lot. My mother hated that. It frightened her. Maybe he just wanted to go off and drink by himself. Or maybe with other drinkers." I couldn't believe I was jabbering about all this.

"Your mother, what is she like?"

I brightened. "She's kind and wise. And resourceful and clever. She manages to live mostly by her painting." I was proud of her for that, meager as her income was.

"She is an artist?"

"Yes."

"Ah, then she must be very clever. And good at her art."

"She has her painting students, too. She gets by . . . we got by."

"How does she feel about you being so far from home now?"

"She would prefer I stay close by," I said hurriedly. "Maybe even set up a tent in her backyard," I added, trying to make light of what had nagged at me since I had made the plane reservations.

"Close by? You don't live with her?"

"Oh no. I have my own place."

"Your own place?" He laughed. "That would almost never happen here in Mexico."

I tugged at the loose part of the serape between us. "I've told you about my family, my little family of two. It's your turn. Tell me about yours. I bet it's a family of two times ten."

"More if you count all the children. I have four brothers

and four sisters. And lots of nephews and nieces."

"I don't know what I would have felt growing up with all those bodies and their many moods all the time." It sounded like a merry-go-round of chaos. "Do they all live with your parents?" I asked, to make a point.

He smiled. "No, but they live nearby." Then nudging me, he said, "And I have a mother who, like yours, is also clever. And a father. He's the biggest one of us all."

"Your father is big?" I pictured a giant, maybe even a pudgy giant in cowboy boots.

He stared into the distance again. "My father is the one we all obey. Well, almost all of us." He grimaced and even in the dim light I could see he didn't like this topic about the father of the family any more than I had.

"He keeps a tight hand on all of us. Even though we're adults, he still has to have everything his way." He looked me in the eyes. "Whether they stay or go, Rosie, fathers impose their will one way or the other."

"I hadn't thought of it that way."

"You could say my father is also the most clever of us. He became an orphan when he was just fourteen and has built everything he has. He did it by himself."

"That's impressive, but nobody really does it alone. Surely your mother helped."

"Of course. She ran the household. He built the business."

"It sounds to me as though he couldn't have done it without her. Especially because there were nine of you kids." Juan Ramón didn't reply for a moment.

"You're right, Rosie. I hadn't thought of it that way. I don't think he has either. Or he doesn't admit it aloud."

"Lucky us to have clever mothers."

He peered into the darkness. "Listen—do you hear it?" He gestured to the far right, to the point where the sparse lights disappeared and the unknown prevailed. "Do you hear the whispering of the pines? They're talking now." I stilled myself and listened.

"They're speaking Nahuatl. The language of the Aztecs." The pines swooshed and moaned, and for a moment I was hearing the ocean back in Marbella.

"Oh, I do hear it. The pines have a rhythm. Like waves," I said, marveling at the discovery. "I wonder what they're saying."

"I will recite a Nahuatl poem for you. I believe it's what they are saying." He turned and looked almost sheepish. "It's a very old poem." He began to recite in what I assumed was the Nahuatl language. "It says that no matter what thing it is, even jade or gold or the feathers of the quetzal bird, it does not last. Like us, it's here in this world just one moment."

"Like that dying boy in Los Valdez," I said, losing my attempt to stay lighthearted."

"Like us as well. Just one moment."

I shivered, despite the weight of the serape draping my shoulders. "Juan Ramón, there are too many new languages here. The bells, the sustos, the movements of the hands, the relationship between men and women, what's right and what's wrong, the talking pines. And now Nahuatl philosophy. I have enough to do with just Level Seven Spanish."

He laughed. "Those are not new languages, Rosie. They are all old ones." He reached for my hand. I was startled by the firm warmth of his.

"I think we both need a change of mood, no?" He pulled me back inside the apartment and toward the kitchen. There he flew into a flurry of taking things out of cabinets and the refrigerator. In just minutes we were standing side by side at the kitchen counter, crunching our way through a humble feast: heated tostadas topped with refried beans, cheese, and avocado, onto which we tipped generous spoonfuls of red salsa.

Equilibrium was coming back to me with each bite. "I didn't know violence would make me so hungry," I said, crunching my way through my second tostada.

"Who is waiting for you at home, Rosie?"

"Do you want to know if I have a roommate? Or are you asking about my mother again?"

"Don't be silly, Gringa," he said, taking hold of my wrist to pull the tostada away from my face. "I'm asking if you have a boyfriend. A novio waiting for you."

I pulled my wrist back and lurched into an extra big bite of tostada. "Not anymore," I said between swallows. "I had one for a long time. But—" It was always so hard for me to encapsulate, even to myself, what had happened. I knew very well what had not happened.

"It's over?"

Yes, I told myself, and felt my heart lift up. "Yes," I said out loud. "And you?"

"It's all 'no.' I have no novia and no children and no family of my own. My family in León, it thinks in the old ways. They can't understand my way of seeing things. And my clinic—I cannot run it the way I think it should be done." He stopped eating and set his tostada down, suddenly pensive.

"I want to know about all of those things."

"Well, that would take a long time."

"Then we have to hurry and start right now." I held onto his shoulders from behind and propelled him toward the sofa in the living room, then pushed him down and plopped beside him. I surprised myself with my boldness.

"Juan Ramón, you say you have no girlfriend. Yet I had the feeling at the party that Aida and you are more than friends."

"Ah, you are a detective."

For just a second Monty's face fleeted into my mind. I shooed him away.

"You are half right. Friends, yes. More than friends we are

not. But we were."

"And what happened? I saw how she was looking at you."
I was again surprised at my directness. In those years with
Monty, I had trained myself to avoid direct questions because
I never got a direct answer. How easy it was, and at the same
time how unexpected that I was able to ask these questions of
this man, practically a stranger, who did not share my language, nor my set of references, other than what we had experienced together in the last week, and who was now clad in
a blue serape. How much more foreign could he get? But
maybe that's what made it easy for us to talk freely, like people
seated next to each other on an airplane, with no expectations.

"What is it you want, Rosie?"

"You mean for my article? Or my career? I know I want to
go further with my work, get more challenging assignments.
What do you want?"

"*Seca*. Your answer is too dry, Rosie. Let me teach you
how. I'll go first." He got up and threw another log onto the
fire. Sitting back down beside me, he said, "I have not been
happy with my life. It is not what I meant it to be in any way."

His statement took me aback, the openness of it. "You are
talking about your work? You mean money for the hospital?"

"My work is a problem, yes, but not the biggest. I have too
much to do and, as you have seen, little money. But I like to
work. My father taught me to work before I was ten. I have
always worked hard. I want to continue to work hard. Not just
for myself. And not only for what the poor people here get
from me. I want to work hard for a family, too."

"You've never been married?"

He took a big breath and let it out slowly. "I want a wife
and children."

How easily he said the words, as if he had simply opened
a chamber of his heart and without fanfare shown me what
lay there.

"I went first, Rosie. Now what do you want? Beyond your work."

My thoughts darted back and forth. "I don't know. Right now I want to concentrate on that, on my job, on advancing."

My statement was bald next to his, and we both knew it. "And beyond your work?" He started to rummage through a box of cassettes on the floor next to the sofa.

I had no answer. I pretended to be distracted by his looking through the cassettes.

He found one and sank it into the player. Out floated a female voice, rich and pure, plumped with emotion. The song was a ballad, slow and impassioned. I could easily understand the lyrics. They spoke of *Un Cariño Nuevo*, where the new love has already woven itself into the singer's life.

"How romantic the words of this song are," I said. "So many Mexican songs make me want to swoon."

"Romantic, yes. That's how we Mexicans are. Mexican music is supposed to make you cry, in an anguish of yearning—and alcohol, of course."

"An anguish of yearning? I think I'm getting there, even without the alcohol." The poetry, the music, the death threat, a man so different from what I had known. "No, no, Juan Ramón. I don't trust all this, these extremes, the romanticism."

I moved to the edge of the sofa and angled back to face him. "The picture on your desk, the one of the children at the hospital's clinic?" I paused just a moment. "I was wondering if I might be of some help there in my last week."

"Week? I thought you had only a day or two left."

"I called my editor and told him I needed a little more time."

"To do what?"

"To work. To help. That is, if you have something I could do. I told my editor it was for research. In a way it is." I wondered if I dare mention that maybe he could even pay me a little something. But I knew that wasn't possible.

He sighed and laughed at the same time. "Of course. No romanticism in the clinic. There will always be something for you to do. If you can handle constant need."

"I can," I said, not knowing whether I really could or not, but ready to live up to the certainty in my words.

He extended his hand and pulled me up. "Let's dance."

I held back. The music was beguiling, but I didn't want an "anguish of yearning," as he had termed it, induced by beautiful music. I had to keep my mind on the research and now on my upcoming work with the children. I hadn't come to Mexico for romance. I dug my toes into my sandals. I shall not yearn. I would write it in the night sky.

"Rosie, you must not resist so," he said, gently taking hold of my wrist, his thumb covering my pulse.

Those were almost the same words the curandera had used. I stood stock still. Then the resistance in me let go.

When we kissed, I tasted in him smoke and brandy and something that did not waver in its directness. The kiss lasted a long time, stopping only when the music did. In the silence where the music had been, I listened to our breathing and the whispering of the pines. Yes, of course, the pines were murmuring, breathing along with us, yes, of course, their natural voices filling up the room. *Just a moment here*, they said again.

Very well then. I was succumbing to Mexican romanticism, ancient in origin.

* * *

It was as if Norma were lying in wait for me when I reappeared at the house of Señora Hernández two days later. She stood at the kitchen counter, ably peeling a mango. I was so anxious to get to the clinic that I had left before the school's *laboratorio*, which most of us called *dormitorio*, since it took place at the end of our five hours when we were all worn out from deep drafts of Spanish.

"Who is he, Rosie? He is a Mexican, isn't he?" Golden drops of mango plopped onto the counter. When I only laughed, she said, "You must sit and tell me all about it. I want to know every little detail."

I laughed again.

"I mean it, Rosie." She held my gaze, wanting woman-to-woman knowing.

"What, Norma? No hugs after not seeing me for two days? First you must give me your news. And I do have some news just for you."

She raised an eyebrow as she fanned out the mango slices on a plate.

I lowered my voice. "About the birth control. Where to get it."

It was her turn to laugh. "Oh, my boyfriend and I broke up day before yesterday. I won't be needing it after all."

"Oh, but you did need it, didn't you? It still is important to know. In case—"

"No, Rosie, I don't want to think about that now."

I wanted to have the conversation with her anyway, as if I were her mother or guardian. Obviously, I would have to choose a better time. But, in fact, I was relieved not to have that conversation just then because I was so anxious to get to the clinic.

When I saw Señora Hernández in the hallway, she said nothing, but her usual scowl deepened. Her knowing was another kind of woman-to-woman knowing. Bernardo was as cheerful as ever, silently telegraphing that what had transpired was perfectly right with the world.

I boarded a noisy bus for Ixmilco, excited about seeing Juan Ramón and being part of his world, if only for another week. A man outside the bus was hawking sandwiches, and I passed money out the window for a cheese and ham sandwich on soft white bread. It came with a tiny slice of jalapeño stuck inside, like a consolation prize for the tasteless sandwich. I also bought *pan dulce*, a sweet roll that truly was a consolation prize. It was my first day of volunteering at the clinic, and I wanted to make my presence felt, to make a difference even in some small way. I entered the reception room where maybe four or five women and a couple of men were waiting to see Juan Ramón or Eugenio. All eyes went to me, and for a fluttering moment, I again felt awkward, out of place. But I let myself take note, then dismiss the self-consciousness. I had come to help, not stay drawn up into myself.

The door to Juan Ramón's office was closed, so I sat down next to a slight woman who had two children leaning against her knees. I smiled at the children, a boy about five years old and a girl a little younger.

They smiled back and then hid their faces in their mother's skirt.

"Are you waiting for Dr. Villaseñor?" I said to the mother. Not that it was any of my business.

"*Sí, Señorita,*" she said.

"There are a lot of people waiting today."

"*Sí, Señorita.*"

"Have you been waiting long?"

"*Sí, Señorita.*"

"Did you—"

Juan Ramón's office door swung open. A young patient with a large pregnant belly tottered out, trailed by three children sized like Russian dolls, each taller than the one before it.

María del Carmen, the receptionist, looking pregnant herself, informed the woman next to me she could now go into the exam room.

Juan Ramón caught sight of me. "Rosie," he said, his accent

on the "s" making my name sound rosier still. He glowed with pleasure. We had to be satisfied with only the traditional kiss on the cheek, but I hadn't known the custom could be so electric.

He turned to the woman. "Señorita Rosie will take care of your children for you while we talk."

Panic passed over the woman's face. She was turning her children over to this complete stranger, this gringa, maybe even a kidnapper who would sell them to foreigners desperate for adorable children.

"*Sí, Doctor*," she said and rotated the children back toward the waiting room. The doctor had spoken.

The woman continued into the exam room while the receptionist herded the children my way. Seeing the door close and their mother disappear, the children erupted into a wail, their mouths rubbery with desolation.

I invited them to follow me, but they continued to bellow. Everybody was watching. What did I—a single and childless woman and an only child myself—know about taking care of little children, compared to any person in this room and probably in this town? I swooped into my arms the littlest one, the girl, and took the boy by the hand.

"We're going to the patio. I have a present for you there." I had no idea what it would be, but I was determined to get the children out of the waiting room so Juan Ramón and the mother could confer in peace behind the closed door. I also didn't want anyone witnessing how green I was around little ones.

Both children stopped crying in the same second. I was amazed. Just the movement, the change of venue, seemed to have calmed them. Or they thought they were off on an adventure, one promising a present. I held tight to the girl in my arms, and I was suffused with the little kid smell of her, the pressure of her skin against mine, and something sweeter, the weight of her body in my arms, depending on me totally to bear her up.

The patio behind the hospital's clinic was nothing more than a stark stretch of concrete, surrounded on all sides by high brick walls. I set the girl down and let go of the boy's hand. He immediately tugged on my pant leg.

"*Mi regalito?*" He wanted his present.

What to give them? I fished in my blue bag. A pen? My hands closed around the *pan dulce* I had been saving since the bus, the flat sweet roll called *orejas* because it's shaped like rabbit ears. I unwrapped the treat from the napkin and then made the *orejas* dance about like a rabbit gone berserk. I hummed a silly tune to accompany the rabbit's frenzy.

The children's eyes at first grew still and then big at the sight of the treat. They followed my every move. I broke the orejas in half and regaled each an ear.

"Gracias," they said in soft voices, then lowered their eyes and gobbled their portion down. "Can I have another one?" asked the boy. "Please," said the girl. They stood waiting.

It dawned on me the children were hungry. But I had nothing else to give them.

"Your mother will be finished with the doctor in a moment. She will take you to eat," I said. The second the words left my lips, I regretted my glib promise. I had no idea if this mother had the spare change to buy a simple treat at a street stand, much less a meal.

I was trying to think of some kind of game to distract them when suddenly the boy dropped to all fours and began kicking his heels in the air. He made the sound of a braying donkey. The little girl giggled as if her brother the donkey was the most hilarious thing she had ever seen. She laughed so hard she plopped down onto the concrete. Her merriment was contagious, and I joined in their laughter.

As the boy turned in a circle, kicking all the while, I

suddenly riveted on his shoes. One sole was full of holes, like a slice of Swiss cheese. The other sole flapped loose from the shoe, barely attached. How could a child possibly walk or run in those shoes? He started to add variations to his donkey repertoire, happy and absorbed in play, seemingly oblivious to the fact that he was hungry or shoes could be any different from the ones he wore.

María del Carmen appeared to tell me the children's mother was done. She called the children to her and led them into the clinic. They toddled away without a look back. I was sorry to see them go. But soon I had another child to look after, and then another.

At one point, I realized Juan Ramón was standing in the doorway to the patio. I didn't know how long he had been watching. "Gracias, Rosie," he said. "Muchas gracias." Then he disappeared back into the clinic.

Some three hours passed, and evening was drawing on. Juan Ramón was still seeing patients, so I hurried to the central market, the same one where I had my fateful fall—was it less than three weeks ago? I was afraid the market would close before I could find what I had come for. Some vendors were already stretching tarps over their wares.

Money be damned. I bought an inflated beach ball, four little plastic cars, and modeling clay in yellow and red. I then rushed through the other aisles of the market. I was tempted to buy a couple rolls of toilet paper but had to save my remaining pesos for what I really wanted. On the far side of the market, I found it, a pair of cheap tennis shoes in a size that looked right for a five-year-old boy.

Relieved to have the shoes in hand, I let myself be drawn to the scene of my fall on the wet floor, hoping to thank again the young woman who had helped me that day. She was not there. Instead, I bought two oranges from a wizened man about to close the stall for the night.

The provisions as heavy in my arms as a child, I almost ran back to the clinic. I had not really made much of a difference there, but contentment flooded me anyway.

In the distance, the rows of pines Juan Ramón had pointed out were swaying slowly in the breeze, no doubt gossiping among themselves about what I was up to. I knew I would not be returning to Spanish class. It's not that I feared being demoted again, this time to Level Six because of my absences. Even if I could not yet make a joke in Spanish, I felt as though I was finally soaring beyond Level Ten.

12

LOCURA

That weekend Juan Ramón once again borrowed Eugenio's car. He set out alone for León. The first part of the trip was the hardest as he had to loop around obese Mexico City and its clogged arterial system of highways. He tried to go home at least every second month, sometimes by bus, sometimes by grace of Eugenio's car. His family made it clear it should have been every weekend, of course, or twice a month as a barely tolerable minimum of respect.

Now he chugged along the outskirts of Mexico City, almost to Highway 57. His shoulders relaxed as the world's largest city itself relaxed, releasing its cares onto open fields dotted with mesquite, huisache, and cactus. He was free to think about the clinic and Rosie. The rest of that week, he had made sure he stole a few moments between patients to glance into the patio and catch sight of her there. Most of the time she watched over children while the mothers met with him or Eugenio.

Even though he was busy with a steady stream of patients into the evening, he liked having Rosie as even a small part of his day. She somehow knew when to look up and catch him watching her, and they would lock eyes. Her presence and that steady gaze allowed him to gloss over the bleak reality of the pitiful hospital where there was never enough.

He gripped the steering wheel more tightly and shifted in his seat. Another bleak reality: he had not yet told Rosie he had been married. There was no way of predicting what it would mean to her, but he had experienced what it had meant to other women: the period at the end of the story, the closing of the book. Even if he might never see her again afterwards, he still must tell her to make things right. He had to find the perfect moment. Only a few days remained.

This morning as they had left Ixmilco, he took Rosie with him as far as Cuernavaca, a logical stop as he drove northeast toward Mexico City in route to León. When he had awakened in the dawn's half-light, he propped himself on one elbow to study Rosie as she slept, one bare leg extending from the sheets. It came to him suddenly and clearly what he wanted to do during this visit with his family.

He angled the car onto Highway 57, merging with buses and trucks heavy with everything from automobiles to broccoli to men standing upright in the back, squeezed alongside each other like pencils in a box. He prayed this visit with his parents would go well. The part with his mother would. It always did. It was the part with his father that was like two bulls charging each other. But he would make it different this time. He would not be a bull.

As a boy, he had hungered to know more of this father who had little time for him, preoccupied with earning a living for his growing family of growing children, all intent on devouring his attention and time. When he was nine, Juan Ramón had built a wooden worktable in the laundry-patio of the house, picturing in great detail the hours he and his father could pass there, working side by side.

When it was done, he had tugged on his father's hand and said, "See what I made—" He had meant to add "for us," but his father had quickly uttered "*Bien, hijo*" as he glanced at the table, then said he had to hurry and buy more leather dye.

Twice Juan Ramón had written letters to his father, thinking that he who loved fine words might respond better to that kind of request than one made in his small person. "*Querido Papá*," he had painstakingly inscribed on stationery purloined from his mother's dresser, writing paper as sheer as he imagined the soul to be. "El Pípila Secondary School plays Benito Juárez School this Friday in the most important soccer match of the season. Excuse me, Dear Papi," he wrote, using the term of endearment, "I know you are very busy working, but I hope you can find time to come see me play." It had been his wish for the last two years, despite the futile letters, that he would suddenly spy his father in the thicket of other fathers at the playoff games. His father would stand a little behind the others, perhaps having arrived late, but following his youngest son's every play, admiring him. *Eso es mi hijo*—that's my son! But his father never came.

Juan Ramón pulled off the main highway. Immediately he had to slow the VW for a cow that had broken her tether and wandered onto the road. The dingy white cow moved in aimless ambulation, its bony haunches like pistons in slow motion.

At sixteen, when Juan Ramón started to work with the leather at his father's shoe factory, as had his brothers before him, there had been Don Alejandro's traditional way of stitching the soles, a method that could brook no innovation, no challenges. Nothing Juan Ramón suggested—perhaps he suggested too eagerly or too often—was good enough.

More serious was his own decision some years later to go to university instead of devoting himself to the family shoe factory and working alongside the other males of the family.

But most serious of all was that forced union—he could never dignify it with the word "marriage"—when he was twenty years old and found in a compromising moment with the daughter of a family friend. He had been sold at a price, like meat on the hoof, to preserve a friendship between the two families. No wonder he and the bride—it had been impossible to think of her as *his* bride—never saw their first anniversary, or even two wedded months together. And not a civil ceremony, but in the *church,* the parents had insisted, forever branding him. From the first glimmerings of adulthood, he had been a divorced man in a Roman Catholic world. No, he could not tell Rosie all that. Not just yet.

He turned off the narrow road and onto an even smaller one paved with cobblestones. At the road's end, he parked in front of the family home. The two-story house had changed little through the years. Bougainvillea in hot pinks and purples tumbled in brilliant display against its whitewashed walls and tall symmetrical windows. To the left, a planting of agave and *nopal* cactuses rose behind a profusion of red geraniums, all inscribed within a circle of stones, also whitewashed, as were the lower trunks of three mature poplars forming a small triangular grove to the house's right.

He reached behind the seat to pull out his valise. His mother's voice, soft as a caress, came through the open car window. "*Mi hijo,* my son." Suddenly his youngest sister, Ceci, was there, too, joining his mother in embraces and a chorus of *¿Cómo estás?* The three of them walked arm in arm to the front door.

"*Hermano*—brother," whispered Ceci when their mother pulled a little ahead, "you actually look happy. You must have a secret."

"*Loca!*" said Juan Ramón. He shot his arm out and tousled her bobbed hair, leaving parts of it standing in points.

"No crazier than you. Who is she?"

"*Ay,*" he said, flinging his wrist in her direction to dismiss her probing.

As they entered the house, he glanced around at the familiar furnishings and paintings. "And Papá? Is he home?"

Ceci nodded as she started up the stairs, promising to return in a moment.

His mother stopped and said, "Your father is waiting for you in the *sala*. But first let me look at you." She held his hands in front of her and scanned him from head to toe. "It is good to have you home, *hijo*."

Each time he saw his mother, she looked a little older, more fragile and shrunken into herself, and he always felt sad about that. Her gray hair fell in waves to her chin, framing skin that had the texture of *atole*. She was dressed in a dark blue skirt and blouse, with pearl earrings. A matching pearl cross hung from a black ribbon at her throat. Still grasping one of his hands, she led him into the *sala*. The skin of her hand felt papery, but her grasp was firm.

His father stood by the stone fireplace, his face, as ever, unsmiling. He took a step forward, then stopped.

"Papá," said Juan Ramón, and immediately crossed the room to embrace him. His father, too, seemed to have grown thinner, even though it had been only a little over two months since the last visit. They embraced with two brisk pats on the back, as if each had to reassure himself of the corporeal reality of the other.

His father lowered himself into one of the two brocaded chairs and motioned him to the other. Positioned on the coffee table in front of them was a bottle of brandy and two small snifters. His mother took her place on the sofa.

Father and son each poured themselves a drink and then made small talk as they smoked together, his father asking how the journey was, what the traffic was like, how long it had taken him to get through Mexico City. It was their conversational ritual.

They poured themselves another brandy, and Juan Ramón,

in turn, asked his father about the factory, the number of orders coming in these days, how Gustavo and Cristóbal and the other long-time workers were.

Ceci bolted through the doorway with a large bottle of Coca-Cola and three glasses of ice clutched against her chest, as well as another brandy snifter. "When do we eat? I'm dying of hunger. I thought you'd never get here, Juan Ramón." She poured each of them a glass of coke and herself a straight brandy.

"*Salud*." She lifted her brandy to toast their health.

His father lifted his glass but didn't smile or say anything. "We can eat soon, when the others get here," his mother said. "Mari has everything ready."

Juan Ramón knew it wasn't just Mari the maid who had everything ready. It was his well-organized mother, who even at this age could tend her own kitchen and had a better hand for seasoning than any of his sisters ever would, certainly a better hand than Ceci, who refused to learn how to cook.

Ceci shooed everyone to the dining room. When they were seated around the glass-covered table in their customary places—his father at the head of the table, his mother next to him, and he and his sister across from each other, the next part of the ritual began, the hypnotizing feast.

"The others are coming to celebrate your being here," Ceci said. "Tomás asked his wife to bring her *jericalla*, that pudding you love so much."

He took a deep breath and let it out slowly. "I would like to come again next weekend, too. If everything works out."

Ceci clapped her hands like a child. "Of course it will! And you can come to the festival at my school and see my children in the play we wrote."

"*Si Dios quiere*—if God wishes," said his mother, just for insurance purposes, but clearly pleased at this *milagro*, a miracle to have her son home two weekends in a row.

Juan Ramón turned to face both his parents but directed his words to his father. "I would like to bring a friend with me. There's someone I want you to meet."

"Aha!" said Ceci. She smirked her approval.

"A woman friend," he said.

Ceci made a motion with her upturned hands as if to say "of course."

His mother widened her eyes with surprise. "Who is this friend, *hijo*?"

"Her name is Rosie." He paused a few seconds and addressed his father again. "I am asking for your permission, Papá and Mamá. I want you all to know her. She is beautiful, a beautiful person."

His mother's voice was quiet. "Where is she from?"

"California. She works for a newspaper there."

Ceci clapped her hands again. "¡*Una americana!* How did you ever unearth a gringa there in poor little Ixmilco?" She crunched into a tostada with *panela* and said, her mouth half full, "I know, you must have raided a language school in Cuernavaca. Lots of gringos and gringas there."

"Well, she *is* studying Spanish in Cuernavaca. I mean, she was, until—" He flushed with heat just to think of the nights he and Rosie had spent together at his apartment, nights which kept her from getting back to morning classes in Cuernavaca.

Outside, the sound of car doors shutting and voices in the hallway interrupted their conversation. Then they were all there: his brothers Alejandro chico, Tomás, Luis, Martín, with their wives—women who grew up in León or the surrounding area—and his sisters Griselda, Alma and Gabriela, with their husbands. A procession of their children bubbled into the room. Each child greeted each adult with a soft, dutiful kiss on the cheek. The procession grew longer each year as more children were added to the family. They were all there celebrating because he had come home to them, and they would be there again tomorrow, as was their custom, for Sunday dinner.

His father moved to a central position at the table, the better to take part in their conversations. His mother stationed herself across from his father. Both his parents, Juan Ramón noted, had their children drawn up around them like a blanket. He now was seated at the far end of the table with Ceci squeezed in next to him.

Mari delivered a steady stream of platters—*lomo* baked in rock salt, chicken stewed with potatoes *cambrai* and onion, *barbacoa*, red rice dotted with a confetti of carrot, peas, and corn, fresh *nopales*, bowls of sliced radishes and cucumbers, *panela* and *ranchero* cheeses, two salsas, one green, one red.

Juan Ramón let Mari fill his plate again. Ah yes, this was home. This was the good part. His father was saying, "—and your Tío Sergio was unable to walk because—"

Juan Ramón couldn't concentrate on the story his father was launching into. His father always held sway with something about a family event, a baptism, or maybe a wedding party that took place years ago. Always retracing and reliving. Some of the stories he heard his father tell on these visits home were about León and the land, going back and back until even the Spaniards and then the Chichimecas and Otomí indigenous peoples before them, until the tales were magically woven into his father's life. Juan Ramón wanted to know where all these stories were when he was still a boy. Starved to have time with his father, he would have deeply inhaled any words or stories directed his way then, no matter the topic. Now he had to force himself to pay attention to the phrases that fell in great plenitude, and it seemed compulsively, from his father's lips.

His father's story finished. Several conversations were swirling about the table at the same time, with loud laughter and the clink of glasses.

"Juan Ramón." The voice was insistent. His second oldest brother, Luis, two seats away, was speaking.

It took Juan Ramón a moment to realize Luis had called his name. A tall, slim man now almost touching fifty-five, Luis made an unusually angular sight, with a pointed face like that of a fevered saint.

"So, Juan Ramón, I hear there's a chance you are moving back to us. Finally."

"Moving back?"

"Papá told me about the new hospital. He's spoken with the director and said you would be applying. You'll be accepted, of course."

His father and everyone seated at this lower half of the table had simultaneously stopped talking. Juan Ramón felt as if he were on stage, the spotlight beaming down, making him sweat.

"I haven't applied."

"Not yet? You can stay and do it Monday."

"I'm not ready."

Luis raised his eyebrows. "You're not interested in the position?"

"No."

For a few moments, nobody said anything.

Then Luis said, "We could all be together. You're the only wandering bull."

Juan Ramón caught the allusion to the mariachi song in which the repeated desperate wailings of the trumpets eventually guide the lost and lonely bull home.

His brother Martín chimed in. "You could put all those years of studying to good use. Working at the new hospital here, you could start to make some real money."

His father poured himself another brandy and slowly pivoted toward Juan Ramón. "You are always welcome here, my son. This is your home." He took a sip and set the glass down with a loud clink against the glass tabletop. "But it is not a good idea for your gringa to come with you. It is not a good idea to bring her to our home."

His father had a way of saying the word *gringa*, making it scornful, whereas on Ceci's lips it had been just playful.

Again, nobody said anything.

Juan Ramón could have said two dozen things. He wanted to burst out that it was 1985, not 1885. Ceci grew busy trying to erase a smudge on the tabletop with the pad of her index finger. His mother played with the cross at her throat.

His father lit a cigarette and, as they all held their breaths, knowing this man well enough to know he had not finished speaking, he exhaled a blue smoke cloud.

"It is time, Juan Ramón." Ah yes, it was the tone his father reserved for the rhythmic narrating of old stories and admonitions. "You are thirty-one years old. It is time for you to get serious about your life. Time to recognize who you are, who your family is, and where you belong. Time for you to find a woman of your own world. Time to begin your own family. Here."

"Papá!" said Ceci. She had stopped working on the smudge and folded her arms over her chest.

Don Alejandro did not look her way.

Juan Ramón knew Ceci's small outburst was as much for herself as for him. It was useless to argue with his father, but he owed it to himself and to Rosie to present his point of view in the most earnest terms he could.

"I am not talking about getting married, Papá. I'm only talking about a visit. I just want her to meet all of you and for you to meet her. I know you would like her. She's kind and well-educated and *alegre* and—"

His mother broke in. "*Mi hijo*, you have been working so very hard. It is natural to want company, a woman to be with when you come home, to cook for you and maintain your house. Especially at your age. Maybe you have been spinning fantasies about this Rosie, unable to see clearly what your future might be with someone who—"

"Forgive me for interrupting, Mamá. I'm not talking about the future. I just want you to meet someone I like being with. Now. *Nada más*, nothing more." He raised his voice to make his point. "To me it's only natural that you would want to know this part of me that is her. And I want her to know this part of me that is you." Despite its volume, his voice seemed weak and puling to him.

"This sounds like more than a friend," Luis said.

"Well, of course she's more than a friend," Ceci said. "She's a woman, and she's important enough to Juan Ramón that he asks Mamá and Papá if he may bring her here all the way from Ixmilco, or Cuernavaca, or California, or wherever."

"Yes, she's more than a friend," said Juan Ramón. "She's my—" He searched for the word. What word could represent the place she held in his heart? And, truly, because she was leaving in such a short time, what word could there be that didn't sound presumptuous, or worse yet, frivolous?

There was the sound of scraping as his father pushed his chair back and stood. "We would welcome a woman of your own kind with complete respect and love in our hearts."

His mother reached for his father's plate and placed it on hers. "This time we want you to make a good marriage, *hijo*."

As if they had nothing to do with the failure of the first! Juan Ramón reminded himself he would not be a bull. "I'm not talking about marriage. I'm simply talking about bringing a friend home to meet you." He should not be arguing, but he had to.

His father set his empty glass on the table. "I do not want my grandchildren scattered everywhere, in distant places far from us. What could they know of who we are? Or of who *they* are?" He poured his snifter full of brandy again, then picked it up and left the dining room.

Juan Ramón experienced a silent sucking of air created by his father's departure. He knew Ceci, too, felt the vacuum. She quickly stood and began to collect the dirty dishes.

Mari, the maid, hurried into the room to take over the clearing of the table.

Juan Ramón chided himself that he should have been prepared for his father's utter refusal. And his mother had once again fallen in behind his father. But he had not expected his father to respond as if his request were a breach of custom or even of family loyalty. Juan Ramón saw the request as loyalty in the utmost. He could have just shown up at the front door with Rosie. No, he could not actually have done that to Rosie— or to his family. Well, at least he had not been a bull.

Suddenly he slammed the table. The remaining glasses vibrated with the blow. Everyone turned to look, first at him, then at the glass tabletop, then back at him. Mari kept her head down as if they were all invisible.

This matter with his father had turned out just as Juan Ramón had expected, and as it always had. That was the pattern, wasn't it?

In a blur of anger, he somehow managed to get out of the house. He tore through the back patio, past the chorus of cooing, chirping birds his mother kept in cages, and let himself out a side gate. He started down a rough path that would open to a large meadow. Then he made an abrupt turn back toward the house. It was clear he could not stay here. He had to break the pattern.

He wanted to see Rosie, to go home to Ixmilco. Now. In this place, in this house, everything had to be his father's way, the job he would hold, the place he would work, even the woman he would take as his wife or merely spend time with.

He hurried back to the dining room and announced in a loud voice, "I came only for the day."

All went silent. They stared at him.

It was risky, even foolish, to drive at night in the countryside. No telling what errant farm animal may have wandered onto the road, or what *ranchero* might suddenly loom up in front of him, barely chugging along in an old truck with no lights.

"What are you talking about?" said Luis. "That's crazy, a *locura*."

"I have to leave." He faltered before adding, "I have something important to do tomorrow. A patient who needs me." He didn't give them a chance to probe the details of this sudden alleged patient. He instead promised he would be all right, that he would drive with caution, and that anyway, night was a good time to pass through Mexico City because the traffic would be so much lighter.

"But why not get up early tomorrow morning?" his sister Gabriela said. "Stay with us tonight."

"It's dangerous driving at night," Griselda said.

"It is better this way," he said.

His brother Tomás called out, "Hey, Juan Ramón, what kind of car are you driving these days? Aren't you still using that old *vocho* that belongs to your friend? That battered heap isn't safe anywhere, day or night."

Juan Ramón ignored Tomás's jab and threw himself into a frenzy of cheek kissing for the women and quick embraces with back pats for the men. When he got to his mother, he tried not to focus on the fact he was kissing tears on her cheek.

"God be with you," they all said as he turned his back on them and hurried toward the door.

Ceci insisted on accompanying him to the car, which the rising moon had burnished a blackish orange. The old car was almost beautiful now, even tinged with something supernatural. On both sides of it were parked the shiny new trucks that belonged to his brothers.

Honeysuckle scented the late spring air, and the trees stood oddly motionless for this time of year, with not even a lick of breeze. Under the moonlight, the cactus to one side of the house flung a sinister shadow across the driveway.

"I'm dying here," Ceci said. "Take me with you." She fell in next to him, hurrying to keep up with his determined strides.

"I want to move out. I want to get an apartment with two other teachers from my school. We've been talking about it."

It took effort to uncoil himself from his churning. "What did you say?"

"I'm almost twenty-eight, and I want to be on my own. I'm old enough not to have to clear all my activities and actions with my parents." She was a little breathless from trying to keep up. "My papá is opposed, of course."

"Of course. And Mamá?"

"She cries whenever I mention it. She says I have everything I need right here, good food, a soft bed, a family that adores me."

His first impulse was that Ceci should indeed stay right where she was. Why, in fact, would she want to move away from her family and its advantages? He was in agreement with his parents on this matter. They took good care of her. She was safe and protected.

Then Rosie's face appeared in his mind. How independent she was, free to live alone or with friends, to come and go without permission, to learn how to be responsible for herself, to travel without her family, to discover new places, to follow her heart, get to know a man from another country, have untold experiences his sister never would. Should Ceci, with all her bounding energy, be restrained in a parental prison while Rosie flourished, free to live and love and venture?

No, it could not be true that Ceci had everything she needed in her parental home, or she would not be burning to move away. He also realized, and was uncomfortable doing so, that he could see not only both sides of this situation at the same time, but he could at the same time feel the rightness of each.

"I will call Mamá," he said at last. "Maybe she can persuade . . ." He left his sentence unfinished. His father had taken his stand, both with Ceci and with him, and nobody could ever sway him.

He pulled his sister to him in a final embrace and kissed the top of her head. She knew why he was leaving. They both knew she could not leave, not yet.

* * *

Juan Ramón retraced the branching veins of roads leading to Mexico City. Even though it wasn't late yet, traffic was already less heavy. He just wanted to get back to Rosie, to the solace her arms offered, smooth and enveloping as silk scarves. He was pushing the VW engine harder than he should but making good time. About two hours later, just as night had settled over the land, he heard the thump-thump-thump of a flat tire.

Hijo de una puta madre. He eased the car onto the shoulder of the road and got out. It was the right rear tire, collapsed like a bean bag. He tasted the night air, now ripe with the imminent promise of rain, even though the rainy season was still weeks away.

He checked the trunk. Yes, there was a spare! But it too was flat. He swore again and looked around to get his bearings. No lights, no little villages nearby. He was somewhere in the middle of nowhere.

Raindrops started to fall, intermittent splashy ones at first, plopping slowly with the promise of more, bigger and harder. Griselda had been right—it was too dangerous to drive the roads outside the cities at night. He knew that, of course.

Everyone in the whole republic knew that. To try to hitch a ride and then get somebody to come out in the rain on a Saturday night was more than dangerous. And, even in the rain, there was no guarantee Eugenio's car would still have all its parts when he got back to it.

He kicked at the treasonous tire before he flipped the front passenger seat forward and curled himself onto the small back seat, his legs hanging to the floor. Instead of a night next to Rosie's warmth, he would lie half awake, cramped on the narrow ledge of the VW's back seat, jolted fully awake whenever a semi howled by. An owl was hooting in the darkness as he tried to relax into sleep.

He did not realize how long he had been asleep, or even if he had been asleep, when voices and then a knocking on the back window jarred him. He sat upright. The clouds had cleared, and in the moonlight he could make out three men. For a few seconds, moonlight gleamed on the blades of their machetes.

One of the men began to jiggle the lock on the door. "Not like that, *güey*," one said and bent down for a rock.

He smashed it into the window, and glass flew inward onto Juan Ramón.

The man reached through to unlock the door, then swung it wide. Gesturing gracefully, he said, "Please hurry and get out. It's not so warm out here, and we want to go home to sleep."

Juan Ramón lumbered out of the car and onto the side of the road.

"Please excuse us," said the tallest of the three, "but we must relieve this noble vehicle of its tires."

The men deftly set about removing the VW's four tires while Juan Ramón waited at the side of the road, charging through a silent litany of swear words.

At least, he thought, they are getting only three good ones.

Now he just wanted them to hurry so he could get back to his roost and stuff this miserable night into his past. At dawn he would figure out what to do next.

The tall man said, "And let's not forget the back seat."

It took them little time to maneuver the bench seat from the car. When they were finished, the three gave a little bow to Juan Ramón and, heavy with their booty, backed into the nearby field and then the darkness.

Juan Ramón slung himself into the driver's seat. He hunched over the steering wheel and did his best to fall asleep as he waited for morning light. *Hijo de una putísima madre,* he swore over and over, varying the phrases with staccato creativity.

13

CONTINENTAL DRIFT

The matter of the missing tires ate up all the next morning and afternoon. A little after six p.m., Juan Ramón pulled up in front of El Universo de Llantas, its clanging tire irons silenced on a Sunday evening. Rosie opened the front gate, blue bag in hand. She was wearing a red sweater he had seen on her before and particularly liked. She threw her arms around him, oblivious to the fact he had spent the night awake on the highway, collapsed over the steering wheel. The solid reality of her against him soothed his jangled nerves. He wanted only to get the both of them back to Ixmilco as soon as possible.

His phone was ringing as they entered the apartment. He picked up the receiver and was blasted by a loud crackle of static. In mangled Spanish, an American voice, male, asked for Rosie. The caller seemed to be identifying himself as Leland.

Rosie took the phone, and Juan Ramón listened as she greeted the caller with enthusiasm by his first name. He was startled to hear how quickly the English words spilled out of her once she was connected to that other world. As if a machine on fast-forward, she seemed to be playing out a summary of information she had gathered. He caught only phrases: "high mortality rate . . . two thirds of the married

women not using contraceptive . . . disapproval of the husbands . . . against God's will." Long pause. The male must be
talking.

"Yes, I'm having a great time." Her voice rose on the word
"great."

What would that declaration mean to the man on the other
end of the line? Juan Ramón tried to follow the words, curious
about what kind of man enjoyed the intimacy of Rosie's voice
so close in his ear just now. What might this Leland mean to
Rosie beyond her work? It was, after all, a Sunday evening,
not a Monday morning. He pictured a lumpy man in his fifties,
silver-framed pictures of his lumpy wife and toothy grandkids
on the desk. That reassuring image held but a moment, meta-
morphosing into an intellectual thirty-four-year-old bachelor
who lifted weights, sported a thicket of hair and an even
thicker wallet. Juan Ramón wanted to ask Rosie about this editor, but she would probably interpret his questions as bad
manners—wasn't that what she had said last week?—that jeal-
ousy was bad manners where she came from.

Sure, he thought, bad manners to lash out about it, maybe,
but to feel it—that had to be universal. Even in such a rich and
powerful country, they probably had not yet been able to beat
down an emotion so basic and essential it was surely an in-
stinct. Even the animals shared it. And why would Americans
want to suppress an instinctive reaction so threaded into basic
human nature? For what purpose, those *pinches gringos*?

The velocity of Rosie's words shut him out. In the open
field visible through his French doors, a mongrel dog was
chasing a white pig up an embankment toward the pines. The
pig squealed, and the dog barked as the pig began to wheel in
circles, like a fat man surprisingly light on his feet once out on
the dance floor.

Rosie leaned against the dining room table as she talked.
He perked up when she said his own name into the phone,

sending it spiraling into that other domain and against the tympanic bone of a man he would never see. Then her tone became placating, or so he interpreted it.

She pivoted his way and smiled at him as she cradled the phone against her shoulder. Shafts of dying sunlight eased through the balcony door and lit up her hair, casting an aura that set her apart from the practical and commonplace things of his apartment and his daily routine. In the middle of it all was Rosie, uplifting it simply by her presence. Echo of his heart, bright with her distinctness, she was no longer foreign to him.

Silence hung in the air. The unseen man was doing the talking. Juan Ramón sat down at the dining room table to wait for the end of this miserable call.

"Who did you say?" She shot a quick look in his direction, then turned away. He could no longer see her face, but heard her mutter something in a low voice.

More silence. Then she said, "Could you tell the receptionist I prefer not to announce when I'm coming back?" More talk on the other end ensued.

"In three days? This Wednesday? But—"

The words struck him with a jolt. Then she said, "No thanks, I can manage. I'll take the airport bus."

This phone line, this umbilical cord, had with just a few flicks of someone's finger re-attached Rosie to a life completely separate from his. It crystallized for him that she was indeed leaving. Her words on the phone reverberated: *No thanks, I can manage.*

Outside, the white pig had the advantage. The dog was no longer chasing it; the pig was now chasing the dog, which had stopped barking and was running away full throttle, stretched out lean as a greyhound.

Rosie hung up. "That was my editor. You could probably tell."

"How did he get my number?"

"I thought it best to leave the number with Señora Hernández, just in case he needed to reach me. Especially now that it's nearing my deadline."

"You said Wednesday. Why do you have to leave so soon?"

"I've already used up my vacation and extended my stay past that. I have to go home."

"I don't want you to go."

He had always known Rosie's time here in Mexico would come to an end. In just days, she would return to where she— he hated that the word his father had used came to him so readily—"belonged." She was going back where she belonged.

* * *

The next morning, the hospital was unusually busy. Eugenio, his forehead furrowed, at one point appeared in the doorway to Juan Ramón's office. "We need to talk. Alone. New storm."

"*Ay*, Eugenio, how you know me. That is just what I was thinking, too. I'll come by your house after *comida*."

When Juan Ramón arrived in mid-afternoon, he found Eugenio with his feet propped on a chair, a newspaper tented over his sleeping frame.

"*Hola, güey*," he said, intending to startle Eugenio awake with affectionate insult.

Eugenio opened one lazy eye. "*Cabrón*," he said, returning the insult.

Juan Ramón didn't broach the subject of what was on his mind. Instead, they talked in the easy way of old friends, a loose weaving of rambling thought, explosive observations, and expletives heavy with sarcasm: the *Club León* soccer team, a few words about a common case, and the lack of an anesthetic they needed at the hospital, an update on William Schroeder in the U.S. and his Jarvik 7 artificial heart, and especially the huge interest rates in Mexico and the flight of capital to the U.S.

"And your gringa, Juan Ramón?"

His? Hardly. "She's leaving."

"Of course. When?"

"Wednesday." A gravid silence followed. It bulged with expectation that the other would have something to say about that, some cynical bit of philosophy or practical wisdom or even a witticism.

"That doesn't bother you, does it?"

"What do you think?"

"You know what I think, *cabrón*."

Juan Ramón picked at the platter of salted mango and papaya sprinkled with chile that Imelda had placed before them. "I know it makes no sense." He speared a piece of papaya on a toothpick and held it up. "I should look at her as a *botana* of papaya, a snack. Sweet but not filling. Not the main course." He popped the papaya slice into his mouth. "That's the logical way," he said between swallows.

He fell silent again. So did Eugenio.

Juan Ramón speared another slice. "She has her world and I have mine." He tightened his jaw as he said "world." That, too, was his father's word.

Eugenio sat straight up. "What you do is this, *hermano*. You exchange pictures. You promise to write letters. That way, you don't have to say goodbye forever. Then the letters will come—and go—less often. A gradual drift." He gave a mock sigh and waved his thin arm to and fro like the phlegmatic ebb and flow of low tide. "Gradually you are busy with someone else. So is she. Voilá. It is *fini*."

That was just what Juan Ramón didn't want to imagine. A gradual drift and there he would be, several months later, alone, his days marching to the desperate cadence they had before Rosie came to flip her business card into his hand and plant her big bag on his desk. Even if she couldn't bring money to the clinic, she brought hope, a fresh and optimistic spirit. He refused to picture Rosie "busy" with someone else, as Eugenio put it, their merging cracked apart like continental drift, with the possibility of geographical reunion too massive to envision.

Eugenio sank back again in his lounge chair. "Leave it alone, Juan Ramón. You are torturing yourself, and for what? Realistically, hombre, what can you do? She has no life here. *Punto final*. Anyway, if she were the woman for you, she would have been short and Mexican. With a platter of *chilaquiles* in her hand." He kissed his fingertips and smacked his lips. "How delicious, just the thought of it. How could you possibly want an American woman?"

Juan Ramón barely summoned a grunt.

"Anyway, you have to put that matter aside. I have important news." He sat upright again and pulled from his shirt pocket a piece of folded paper that appeared to be some kind of official stationery.

"Our poor hospital is getting poorer still. La Secretaría de Salud—our wise and all-knowing health department—is swinging its machete." He handed the letter to Juan Ramón who unfolded it slowly, resisting the desire to just crumple it up and hurl it at the vine on the other side of the patio.

He read the letter once, then once again before refolding it and passing it back. "I am so sorry, Eugenio. When did this come?"

"Saturday morning, after you left for León. And this morning there was no time to tell you about the cuts."

"You sit there so calmly. You are losing your job in two months, and here you are patiently listening to me moan about Rosie." La Secretaría de Salud had determined there was not enough money to keep two doctors at the hospital. The situation was clear: Juan Ramón, having seniority and the two directorships, would stay. Eugenio would go. "What will they lop off next? Our right legs or our *cojones*?"

"They've already got mine," said Eugenio.

Juan Ramón stood and patted Eugenio on the back several times, trying not to reveal the despair that was imposing a dark shadow over him. "We will figure this out, *hermano*."

Eugenio walked with him through the house and to the front steps that led down into the thick greenery. "Something else. More bad news, I'm afraid."

Juan Ramón had already started down the steep steps, his head lowered to see where he was placing his feet. He jerked his gaze back to Eugenio, who now looked thinner and paler still.

"Catalino, the burned boy—"

Juan Ramón did not have to hear the rest to know what had happened. What he didn't know was how, or even if, he could tell Rosie.

14

LOCURA II

The old bus was crammed full, and loud ranchero music boomed from its speakers, setting a tone of lightly reined-in mania. Even from the back seat I could see the procession of saints glued on the dashboard, small plastic statues in ready formation to ensure our safe journey.

Juan Ramón and I sat huddled together in the back of the Pullman de Morelos bus that was leaving the terminal in Cuernavaca. We were on our way to Mexico City and then the airport. He apologized for not being able to secure Eugenio's VW Bug with its new tires and back seat. I apologized for having to borrow money from him for my ticket.

The bus began to move. *Adiós,* Catalino and *niños* of the clinic. *Adiós,* Norma and Bernardo and Señora Hernández. *Adiós,* Aida and Doctor Eugenio and Imelda. *Adiós,* City of Eternal Spring and Ixmilco.

As if he could read my thoughts, Juan Ramón said, "Are you saying your goodbyes to what you've found here?"

I tried to smile. "Yes."

"Your Spanish is better. You got what you came for."

"And more. I've got research I'm excited about and—"

He took a deep breath. "I don't want to make you sad, but

I have to tell you that the burned boy you saw that first time we went to the countryside has died."

I stared out the window and didn't speak.

Juan Ramón squeezed my hand. His touch brought me back to the moment, this busy bus crawling up the looping highway to Mexico City.

Juan Ramón squeezed my hand again, and I managed to return the squeeze this time. I thought of his directness, his energy, his passion, and compassion—traits to admire. Not to mention his dark hair, his chest, his hips, his heartbeat, his graceful and able hands. All we had shared these last few weeks was ending. Me, from the U.S., "O beautiful for spacious skies." He from Mexico, "Viva México," always alive.

The bus driver swerved toward the side of the road to let somebody on. A thin little man who looked to be in his late sixties, brown and corrugated as a walnut, limped down the aisle, his guitar in hand. He positioned himself a third of the way down the aisle and, still standing, propped his feet against the base of a seat as the bus started to move. He strung the guitar over his shoulder and exhaled into mournful song. His face screwed up in agony, as if overcome by the sorrow of it all. At the end of his wail, passengers rewarded him with a handful of coins.

He limped further down the aisle and launched another song, this one fast and raucous—a dance tune that set heads to bobbing. At the end, he extended his hand and garnered more coins.

He next lurched his way to the very back of the bus. Fixing his attention on us, he smiled a crooked, knowing smile. He began his song, a slow one. The languorous words sounded familiar.

"Remember this song?" said Juan Ramón. "It's *Cariño Nuevo*, A New Love."

It was the song we danced to in his apartment our first night together.

The old man, seeing us absorbed in his song, unleashed more fervor, his voice quavering. His facial expressions dramatized the words as the melody lifted to a crescendo, then subsided to tenderness again. Juan Ramón began to sing along. I recalled Juan Ramón's pronouncement that the point of romantic Mexican music was to trigger in you an outburst of emotion.

I wasn't sure what to make of a man so unabashedly romantic, but I liked it. When the song ended, Juan Ramón pulled away to fish for coins in his pants pocket, and soppy as I knew it was, I already missed his nearness.

Clutching his take, the old man looked directly into our eyes and, almost chanting, beseeched God to bless us, to succor us, to preserve our good health, to protect us, to give us a long and loving life, and more. Then he slowly rocked his way back to the front of the bus. The driver lurched to a stop and discharged the man onto the road's shoulder.

The bus doors swished closed, and Juan Ramón turned to me as if galvanized by this visitor surely from the spirit world. I sat transfixed, still under a spell.

"What is it you want, Rosie?" he said, stepping into the spell.

"That's what you asked me the first time I went to your apartment."

"And I asked you to go first."

I took a deep breath. "I don't know what I would have done these weeks without you. But it's not just about my research."

"I have been afraid of this day."

"I can't say goodbye, Juan Ramón."

"Nothing will be the same. I'm afraid of losing you. I just found you."

I nudged him in the side. "Correction, Doctor. I found you. You were there in your clinic. Waiting."

He smiled for just a moment. "When will I see you again?"

The words hung suspended. He slipped his arm around me again. "I understand. There's your mother. And there's your job. And your friends. Your house. Your beautiful ocean. Everything."

"Not everything." I was flailing in the immensity of that ocean, and my heart was pounding. "I want to see you again, Juan Ramón. I just don't know how that would work."

"We're from two different worlds." He grimaced as he said it.

My heart sank. I didn't want him to be aligned with that scoffing voice within asking why I was trying to meld two things that didn't belong together.

"Of course I want to see you again," he said. "In fact, I have to." He shaded his eyes with his hand, though no sun was lighting the back of the bus. He started to laugh. "But it would be *locura*, Rosie."

"*Locura?* What's that? As in *loco*?"

"*Locura* is madness. Craziness. Losing your mind. Losing control."

"We can shape the kind of life we want. Go where we want. What's so crazy about that?"

"*Gringa loca.* Do you think it's that easy, *mi chiquita linda*?"

It was the *chiquita linda* that got me. I was like a bird pivoting on the edge of its wing in the air current, going as high as the drafts lifted it. I was soaring on the edge, in control and out of control at the same time, riding the current.

Just as suddenly I was plummeting. He was right. It was *locura* to think we could pluck the life we might want right out of the sky and live it.

The bus was now running fast along a straight stretch of highway. To the left flashed a pine forest. To the right the road's edge plunged into a canyon dotted with cactus families. I looked down into the abyss and immediately wanted to recapture that feeling of soaring.

"I just might come after you, *chiquita linda*."

And he might not. Exquisite Mexican courtesy compelled him to say he might.

The bus swerved around a curve, and we had to grab at the metal bar of the seat in front of us. He tightened his hand around mine, casting me a look that was flirtatious and challenging and, I knew in my bones, serious. I held fast to his hand and savored the feeling I had soared off the edge with *locura*.

15

SAL SI PUEDES:
LEAVE IF YOU CAN

The boy's eyes still gleamed with his adventure as a bronco rider. Yet Alejandro saw that his son took care to angle his body so his left arm, which hung limp at his side, would not be noticed. He knew this boy. Juan Ramón would never admit that his father, of all people, had been right. The boy had hurt himself. But Alejandro suspected that for Juan Ramón the ride was worth the pain.

Don Alejandro gave a start and spurred his horse just to feel it respond and to bring himself back to the moment. He had fallen into a reverie so deep he wondered if it had been a dream. But, no, it had happened. He remembered clearly that day on the road with Juan Ramón. He could still conjure up the smell of the calves, agitated from fright, and the smell of his own nervous sweat.

This was the first time, though, he had drifted off while riding his horse. He had saddled up as soon as the phone call from Juan Ramón terminated. Right away he pushed the horse into a hard gallop, riding with the wind in his face, trying not to think, not to react. Yet parts of the conversation pursued him and insisted on repeating themselves.

"Why would you want to abandon your family and go to another country, *mi hijo*?" he had asked. He was trying to be gentle with this son, the one most like him. But inside, he was seething.

"Because I want to be with a marvelous woman, *papá*."

"There are many marvelous Mexican women, *hijo*."

"But I am not in love with a Mexican woman, *papá*."

"In love you say!" In spite of himself, his voice hardened. "*No seas estúpido*. Don't be stupid! You are giving up everything. What about your work? The hospital? You want to leave your friends? Your family?"

"This is what I have to do."

"You don't belong in another country. You are Mexican."

First Ceci had talked about leaving their house. Now Juan Ramón talked about leaving their country. It had been bad enough when his son insisted some years back on accepting the medical post in miserable little Ixmilco in the state of Morelos, so far away, and a place without opportunity for riches or advancement.

Don Alejandro had already lived seventy-four years and fathered thirteen children, nine still living. At times he yet felt like the orphan he had once been. Whenever one of his boys or girls talked about leaving to live in another city, he again became a fourteen-year-old boy, no mother or father, desperate for a family. Now Juan Ramón wanted to escape the family Don Alejandro had fought so hard to build. This son wanted to live in another country with a gringa he claimed was *maravillosa*, marvelous.

"*Maravillosa*," Don Alejandro said aloud and spit. Ahead, scrubby trees lined both banks of a dry riverbed.

He had raced the horse until it broke into a lather, then eased the reins and allowed it to walk as they neared the trees. That's when he must have drifted off for a few moments, lulled by the rhythmic clopping of hooves. The horse had whinnied, sensing its rider was no longer fully present, summoning him back.

The conversation came back too: Juan Ramón with his wayward plan to follow this *norteamericana* back to her country, as if he could fit in and make a home just anywhere he took it in his mind to alight—and Don Alejandro to be left with his grandchildren strewn all over the continent. With his children and his children's children spread so far apart, how could he ever know them? How could he pull them around him to shut out the cold penetrating his bones?

Juan Ramón had called for his blessing. He could not give it. Even if his son had come in person for the blessing, as he should have, he still would not have given it.

Perhaps, if he had spent more time with Juan Ramón while he was a boy and Ceci a girl, their roots would have grown deeper and taken permanent hold. Yet how could a father have done more than he when there had always been more mouths to feed, more shoes to make, more workers to supervise and support?

He felt tired and chilled, despite the bright sun. He turned the horse back toward the house.

Dismounting, he led the horse past the large living room window. Ceci perched there in her customary reading position, her feet propped on the coffee table, a book open on her knees. What was this *locura* about getting an apartment on the other side of León? She had stood before him and announced she wanted to be closer to the school where she taught, as if that were an explanation. What decent girl would live by herself—or even with other misguided girls—if her family were nearby to protect and care for her? Just because other girls were starting to do that now, it still made no sense.

He entered the house and stomped loudly through the hallway. He would let his daughter know her father was present. He glanced at the living room as he passed it, but Ceci was no longer there. Then he remembered this was a school day and she would be in her classroom at this hour. His mind was playing tricks on him. Now he was feverish and cold at the same time.

"You'll be back, Juan Ramón. You can't leave. This plan is doomed. Mark my words, you'll come back sooner than you think." Those had been his last utterances to his son.

"You'll be back, Ceci," he now intoned to the empty living room. He could picture the expression that would cross his daughter's face—a set look of resentment and rebellion, the same look he had observed before on Juan Ramón.

Don Alejandro stomped all the way up the stairs to his bedroom, although only his wife and the maid, whose undulating laughter sounded from the kitchen, were in the house to hear him, had they been attuned. This foolish Ceci would get over her foolish, foolish ideas. This defiant Juan Ramón would come back, humble and ashamed, to his own people.

He rummaged through the closet shelves for his blue serape. It was long and woven of heavy wool, with animal designs against the rough blue background. Had any of his children been present, he would have pointed out the symbols and explained the meaning they held to the local people who still celebrated the old indigenous traditions. He would have lingered on the symbols for the hills and rivers that made up the sacred land, and he would have lovingly embellished those explanations.

Now he remembered. He had given the serape to Juan Ramón several years before.

He yanked the bedspread off his marital bed and draped it over his shoulders in a hurried attempt to warm himself.

PART TWO

16

HOME

The rocks were slick, and I chose my steps with care. Another wave crashed onto the breakwater, sending white spray exploding into morning light. This is how I liked my ocean, wild and sassing back.

Mornings at the beach in Marbella were my favorite time and place. It was easy to get up and dress in half-light, then start my jog. After running barefoot along the tideline on the cool, wet sand, I often made my way onto the jumbo rocks that formed the two breakwaters. The best place to be was where the water met an unmovable object with relentless insistence.

I picked my way over the rocks to the far tip of the southernmost breakwater and peered into the churning water. Rumor in the beach community was that a ship had crashed on these rocks in decades past and lay sunken below the water. As usual, I searched for a glimpse of it, a tall rusting tower, or a mast if it had been a sailing ship, but the water held dominion, and I spied nothing but restless swirls.

Another wave slammed against the breakwater, and cold saltwater rained over me. I felt anointed by the sea god, welcomed home. I had missed this. But I couldn't linger because I had to go see Mama. It was my first full day back from Mexico, and it was time to put up, show what I'd been doing on the summer vacation that had morphed into something much more.

The gorgeousness and unexpected differences in Mexico had beguiled me while I was there, but it was so damn good to be home and embrace its own gorgeousness. As I walked back to my house, I reappraised the familiar contours of my neighborhood with its eccentric collection of cottages. My house was not oceanfront but sat on a side street some two hundred yards perpendicular from the waterline, at the top of a small berm and within a cluster of similar houses. The red and pink ivy geraniums I had planted to introduce sparks of color near the carpet of sand, grew leaves prolifically but had yet to burst into color. One lone pine stood in front of the house, a sentinel of green that managed to flourish in the salty air. At times during a summer day when the tide was low, I caught the fragrance of pinesap along with the tang of seashore, and I would breathe deeply. At night, I stayed attuned to the constant heartbeat of the waves pulsing the shore. Late last night, finally home in my bed, I tried to picture what Juan Ramón might be doing, what he was feeling about my absence, and what he might feel as the weeks, then months, wore on.

I turned onto my sidewalk and weighed what I would tell Leland. It was time to show him my notes for the story on the rural Mexican women and the sample draft for how the notes could be developed further. I hoped what I showed him would justify in his mind the extra time I had spent well beyond my official vacation.

* * *

I held my breath as Leland finished reading the computer printout of my notes, which, in a sudden burst of energy on the plane, I had reshaped as a tentative article. He was at his desk, and I sat across from him, suffering and quiet while he perused. Leland was a handsome man, in an ascetic way. Straight brown hair pulled back in a ponytail that hung a few inches down his back, strong angular features, a determined chin, wide thin shoulders curving inward, these features made him a cross between a rock musician, Clark Kent, and a hungry monk.

Surely he had been reading for twenty minutes, but it might have been only five. I tried squinting at the hole in his earlobe for the little gold earring he wore when not on the job. Watching and waiting while a person reads something you have written is an especially fine-tuned form of torture, one that a person's enemies should consider. The sheaf of papers I had handed him was meant to be the roughest of drafts, not the final product. He would pass my body of notes to one of the senior writers.

As he read, I reflected on how far I had been transported in some four weeks, from lush greenery and brilliant flowers everywhere, a countryside of sadness yet blessings, a stark waiting room with big-eyed children, to now the white noise of the newsroom. I was getting caught in *The Marbella Beacon* maelstrom again, eager to please my editor, hoping to wring even a measly compliment from him. It could soon be hard to feel I had ever been in Mexico.

Finally, Leland focused on me over the half-rim of his spectacles perched partway down his nose, making him look older than his thirty-eight years. He was positioned one hand on hip, one leg resting over the metal trashcan next to his desk, his characteristic pose for pondering. "Not bad. I think you've got it."

"Thanks. I mean gracias."

He switched legs, giving the opposite one a rest on the trashcan. "Now tell me, did you spend those leftover pesos I gave you before you disappeared south? Drink some cervezas in my honor?"

"Multiple times. Just to get it right. In fact, you owe me more pesos to cover all that I drank in your honor."

Leland nodded his head in approval. "I wonder with *whom*." He drew out the word, enjoying his grammar. "I'm sure you weren't drinking alone."

"With my sources, of course. *Whom* I must protect." I felt a twinge of betrayal, referring to Juan Ramón in such a flippant manner, demeaning him to just a useful source.

"Drinking on the job, then. In the tradition of the investigative reporter. Bravo."

"I do my best to revere holy traditions."

"A bit of trickery it was to telegram on the very day we expected you home. Announcing you were extending your stay yet again. And by a whole week." He arched an eyebrow, and I expected harsh words.

"No pleasure whatsoever? Only work, work, work while you downed those cervezas and chased those leads?"

"If you look carefully, you'll find my notes are flecked with the suds."

He hesitated, then smiled faintly. "Well, then, I approve." He turned his attention again to my draft. He flipped pages and then lingered on a particular paragraph. "This part here, about the curanderas—yes, that we can definitely use. That's very good, actually."

He garbled the word *curanderas*. I flushed because I liked his praise. Then it came back to me just how the curandera Imelda had seized my hand. But that dark adobe room of saints and candles was a faraway realm. No scent of pirul branches here. Not even of newsprint. Only the sanitized air of a huge open room with the low hum of computers. Instead of pictures of saints tacked to the wall, there were cartoons carefully scissored from the pages of *The New Yorker*, along with yellowing political caricatures of Ronald Reagan from the op-ed pages of assorted newspapers, including *The Marbella Beacon*. To my surprise, even a caricature of Miguel de la Madrid, the current president of Mexico, hung there.

The scolding I'd received from Juan Ramón for my visit to the curandera also came back, and I squirmed inside as if being found out. Juan Ramón had implied I was a tourist playing with having an adventure. Was I now betraying hallowed beliefs by including this visit with Imelda in my story, displaying it as merely a bizarre bit of local color instead of the more multifaceted part of the culture that it was?

Leland pointed to another paragraph. "This about the fertility rate—include the previous five and ten-year rates by way of contrast. Also find the U.S. birth rates for the same period." He started to grin. "Good work. Have I been too 'constipated,' as you would say?"

Some months back, in a moment of exasperation, I had accused him of being miserly with his compliments, downright constipated. His was "not a fluid and generous nature," I had charged, half serious, half teasing, when it took so much effort to squeeze a drop of approval from him. "No, Leland," I said now. "You were not constipated this time. Two words of praise? You were gushing."

"How sentimental of me. Next time I'll cut back. Why use two words if one will suffice?"

When I had first informed Leland his issuance of compliments was meager, he had actually been astonished. "Am I really like that?" he had said, his voice rising an octave, as if pleading with me to take it back. It was one of the rare moments he let me glimpse him suffering a doubt, and it had endeared him to me. I had been referring to more than just the stories I wrote, and I was sure he was responding to the broader implications in my accusation.

Leland and I had known each other since I first landed at the *Beacon*, burned out after three years of teaching middle-school English and admonishing students not to chew gum, pass notes, or stomp on the classroom turtle, while inviting them to revel in the finely tuned lines of Walt Whitman, Gwendolyn Brooks, Langston Hughes, and Emily Dickinson.

Leland covered city council and county supervisor meetings then, as well as wrote frequent editorials. I started out handling obituaries. I know, I know, a dead-end task. Another twenty-something reporter, Carole-Ann, came aboard at the same time and dazzled us all with unexpected but timely viewpoints about women's issues, and with her rebellious red ringlets. She wrote for the section of the paper titled "A Woman's Touch," which she said might as well be called "The Ladies' Room" for all the shit in it, and which she had successfully lobbied to have restyled as the more unisex *Currents*. During my first year on the paper, the three of us had formed a tight knot: coffee breaks and lunches together, unwinding after work at Zev's Deli, sometimes taking in a foreign flick. Then Leland had been promoted to editor; I began to cover city council meetings in his place, and Carole-Ann had parlayed her concept for *Currents* into her own interview show on local cable TV.

Leland and I enjoyed the kind of friendship that always seemed on the verge of becoming something more. Fired by an easy rapport and an involvement in each other's work, flirtatiousness hovered on the edges of our conversations, and sometimes Leland would stare at me as if he were about to make some kind of declaration.

But he had never, and I had never. That was a relief. There was always the chance that what I took to be an unacknowledged fancy for each other's cantor was nothing more than his peculiar gait. His way was marked by a mild chivalry that involved mock jousting and parrying which was, at heart, no blood sport. So why should either of us risk slaying a mutually enjoyable work relationship for a passion that wasn't there?

Leland pushed my sheaf of papers across the desk. "Here, I made a few suggestions. You'll need these when you write the story."

"Excuse me? Did you say I'm going to write the story?"

"I want you to write the feature. It was your idea from the get-go. Not mine. Nor that of one of the other writers. You're ready, more than ready."

I had wanted this for a long time, to write a feature story. I was thrilled and I was scared. This was not constipated Leland at all. At the same time, a little voice inside was uneasy with the possibility I may have cheapened or sold out what I loved in Mexico just to get this plum.

* * *

Mama opened the door. Her light-brown hair was drawn back in its customary bun, and she was trying to smile. It was good to see her, my tinge of guilt at leaving her alone so long notwithstanding. "Mama, I'm home! And I'm happy to find you home."

"I'm always home. Waiting for you." She suddenly threw out her arms and embraced me. "I thought you'd never get back here. Where you belong, I might add."

"You're not *always* home. You're often gadding about."

She led me into the small kitchen. "Rosie, I don't know if I like my trips out of the house referred to as 'gadding about.' And, by the way, you're the one who's always out."

"Oh, did I hear welcome home?"

"Would you like some coffee?"

As Mama busied herself with the ritual of making coffee, she said, "Here you are, finally home, not even knowing what's been going on in your country this last month. Have you heard about all the tornadoes in the Midwest killing so many people? Seventy-six! Did you hear about the Unabomber mailing some kind of explosive to a professor at Berkeley? Of course you didn't. When did you finally get in? And you must never do that again! Taking off with nary a word and then a battered postcard appears in my mailbox twelve days later."

"Last night. Late," I said. "I had to leave town like that. Else you would have talked me out of it. Listen, Mama, there's so much I want to tell you about Mexico and all I saw and felt." I began to tell her about my research and the clinic and Leland's giving me the actual article to write. Suddenly I was saying, "There's someone I met there."

"A man."

"A man." I beamed.

"A Mexican man?"

"There are lots of them in Mexico, Mama."

"Oh? And now I suppose there will be one more here."

"Oh, he's not here. I don't know if he can come. Or even really wants to."

"I see."

"You will. At least I'd like you to." I laughed nervously. I didn't know what I was asking her to see. There was nothing solid.

"I've met every one of your boyfriends since you were sixteen. So why should this time be any different?" She paused, then added, "These last four years, though, you've appeared settled on Monty. That seems a good thing."

The sociable aroma of fresh coffee filled the room. Mama sighed. "Don't tell me you've given this man the stir-fry test."

My laugh turned into a snort. "I'm surprised you remember that." I had once confided how I could tell a lot about a man by how well he could stir-fry. Early on, I would invite a man over for stir-fry, then innocently ask him to stir the pan as I tossed chopped onions, sliced green beans, or florets of broccoli into the hot oil. Some men were overly cautious, barely moving the vegetables, exposing them to the risk of scorching and sticking. Others were too awkward or exuberant in their moves, shooting an onion missile out of the pan and onto the floor. Rarely was somebody just right, controlling his strokes so that the dish turned out juicy and readied to perfection.

"He does know how to cook, Mexican style. You should have tasted the fabulous meal he surprised me with in our first week together."

"Week together? I can't help but wonder what 'together' entailed."

Before I could think of a reply, she said, "Don't tell me. And Monty?"

I cleared my throat. "Monty and I were not going anywhere. Not 'together' anyway. You knew that."

Mama didn't say anything.

"It's been four years, Mama. There's no flavor left in the bubble gum."

She still didn't say anything.

"Four years is a long time. Monty doesn't want anything more than he's always had with me. I mean, he certainly doesn't want to get married. He doesn't want children either. When he's fifty, he'll marry a twenty-two-year-old and have his first kid."

"Maybe."

"Maybe. That's just the point." I tried to hold at bay the note of annoyance creeping into my voice. "I don't want to talk about Monty, Mama."

"Oh, so this sounds serious. What's your new beau's name?"

I wished she had used another word besides "beau." It diminished him, implying his position in my life was frivolous, merely decorative in an old-fashioned antebellum way. That's what Mama really wanted him to be—just a beau, a grace note, not a major chord.

"Juan Ramón."

"Oh. Nice. I was afraid he might have a name I couldn't pronounce." She sighed again. "Well then, if he gets up here, you'll have to bring him to dinner. I'll make a cheesecake."

"Oh great, can't you make something else, Mama? Something that wasn't Monty's favorite dessert?"

She sighed again, loudly. "Well, damn it, I've gotten used to the guy and whipping up cheesecakes for him. You must admit I do make a first-class cheesecake."

It was my turn to sigh. This, too, was home.

* * *

Fog had gauzed over the evening by time I got back to the beach. The phone was ringing as I came into the house. Against the drone of the foghorn, I heard Juan Ramón's voice.

This sudden meeting of my world and his took me aback. "I am coming to be with you, *chiquita linda.*" Once he got together his documents that proved he was rooted in Mexico with a job and bank account, he would go to the embassy in Mexico City and apply for the visa.

"Are you using vacation time?"

He would explain everything when he got here. He thought he could be with me in a week or thereabouts.

Mexico was coming to me. Just like that. I wasn't sure I wanted this adventure. Then I immediately couldn't believe I'd had that thought. But could it really be this easy? The fog layering the beach and the ocean always hypnotized me into a dream-like state where I could not trust the familiar to be where it was supposed to be and had to grope instinctively. The foghorns continued to signal the route for ships at sea but were no help to those of us on land. In fact, they made things worse, causing sounds to suddenly enlarge in one area, then diminish, then call out loudly in another. Here—no, there—

now over here. "*Fabuloso,*" I said. "I am waiting for you." I didn't know what else to say. I had a feeling that home was about to change irrevocably.

17

A FAMILY OF TWO

Color hunger was creeping up Louise's arms. She tried to ignore it as she studied the painting before her. The energy on her canvas was wrong. That had been happening a lot lately, her not being able to capture the essence, the inner spark of what she saw. It wasn't a matter of her draftsmanship. It wasn't a matter of perspective. It wasn't a matter of so many things. Elusive, the missing energy taunted her to come discover it, to get down and dirty in her mission. She just couldn't.

The color hunger was almost fully upon her now. For most of her life, she could be overcome on certain days with a longing to rest her eyes on a particular color, to take it in, gobble it up. The colors she sought were as varied as the colors in the big box of No. 64 crayons she'd begged her mother to buy when she was seven years old. Sometimes she hungered for cadet blue or forest green or violet or even burnt sienna. It wasn't enough to fill a page with a given crayon's color. She would also tear through her mother's magazines, flipping pages in search of the very hue, moistening her forefinger as she had seen her mother do to turn a page. Now an adult, when the color hunger rose up, she fed it by taking a walk, straining to spot that precise color along her way. Today she hungered for red.

She opened the door, anxious for the search. At this hour, chances were good her neighbor, Mr. McGee, wouldn't spy her stooped over the pansies and marigolds flourishing along his front fence. She didn't want him to misinterpret her interest in his flowers as an excuse to linger in the vicinity of his house and certainly never to—she winced at the thought—induce him to come out and get chatty.

Early summer flowers were now in full display, but his spring tulips were what she liked best about Mr. McGee. "Teddy," he had insisted one day when they had run into each other on the front sidewalk. He had given her a look any woman knows how to interpret. "Call me Teddy."

She had shrunk from even that degree of intimacy. Mr. McGee he remained. Still, to plant in his front yard some two hundred tulips that burst forth each spring, that revealed a trait she could admire in a man. She pictured him poring over bins of bulbs at the nursery, or most likely he ordered them from glossy catalogs. Then he would have had to push aside the orange juice cans and ground round in his freezer to make room for two hundred bulbs. When he had fooled the pregnant bulbs into feeling they were in the middle of a mean Dutch winter, he dug holes for hours in his front yard and sank a frozen bulb into each. It was generous of him, she admitted, to plant a row along her side of the fence.

She started to hurry down her sidewalk, pleased to note a few hardy tulips still standing among the summer flowers. Then there it was, just steps outside her door. The red. Not brick red, maroon, or orange red in the No. 64 box, but the exact color of the crayon labeled simply "red." She took her chances that Mr. McGee might appear as she balanced her sketchpad on the fence top.

Peering into the bowl of the tulip nearest her, she absorbed its redness. The riddle of the universe lodged there in miniature. With deft motions of her charcoal, she began to render the essence of flower: pistil, stamen, ovule. Cervix of flower, she mused, vagina of tulip. And to think Georgia O'Keefe claimed those interpretations were certainly not her intention. Who could believe her? Exuberant celebrations of female organs, for certain. If only Mr. McGee knew what he had festooned about his yard. Or maybe he did.

She heard a door opening, and there he was, walking right toward her, leaving no graceful way of escape. He was an elongated man whose profile reminded her of pictures she had seen of Abraham Lincoln—craggy, not handsome but strong and determined. The odd thing was that when she looked at him head-on, his face grew rounder, softer, displaying another facet, gentle and patient. It was like seeing two sides of a coin at once, depending on how she tilted her head.

Mr. McGee smiled at her and made for his front gate with long set strides, just the way she imagined Abe would have walked. She gave a perfunctory wave, then ran up her steps and into the house before he could force her to be amiable. She shut the door quietly, trying not to give the impression she was slamming him out, although she was.

Once inside, she pulled the flower sketch from the pad and propped it against the wall over the bookcase. It was her practice to set each sketch in a place where she could absorb it as she went about her day. She didn't consciously think about the forms of nature she depicted. Instead, she breathed them in, letting them seek their own path through her. When she was ready, she would start to paint. Sometimes it took just a few hours; other times it took days.

That afternoon, she stopped several times to stare into the flower. She was held in place by the mystery of the tulip's essence, its quick. Here was the seat of the matter, red, full with fruition, mute, spilling secrets her eye and brush could intuit.

Louise tried to imagine this Mexican fellow who had followed Rosie home. She saw a short man with tan skin, lively brown eyes. He would have a mustache, of course. He would be very polite and probably shy. It wasn't much of a picture. Sheepishly, she realized she had just envisioned one of the young men who bused tables at the Italian restaurant where she and her friend Margie ate every Tuesday. She quickly erased that mental sketch and replaced it with a different Juan Ramón: tall, slim, imperious, a bullfighter with family from the Old World. Oh no, he wasn't holding a cape in her mental picture, was he? The persistence of her stereotypes dismayed her.

The image of Monty arose, clear and unmistaken: a compact wiry build, long pale face with a slight sprinkling of freckles, eyes green like a cat's. While her daughter was partial to his mass of reddish-brown curls, she herself had always enjoyed the changing planes of his face. Most of the time he bore an alert, impish expression, but when in repose, or the light struck from the side, the steep cheekbones and pointed jaw took on a different appearance, more troubled, as if something sad had happened to him as a child. Louise wondered if that look of sadness would settle over his face once he learned about Rosie's new friend, her souvenir of Mexico. She missed Monty. Now she had to pretend he no longer existed.

* * *

Rosie's new beau, this Juan Ramón, sat on the other side of the small dining room table, not eluding Louise's attempts to fix him in her eye as he angled his fork into a generous slice of strawberry pie. Well, he was taller than the busboy she had first envisioned. Nor did he flash the arrogant mien of a matador. He also didn't sport a mustache, and he didn't strike her as shy. He was extremely polite, though. Already he had called her "Señora" several times. He had shaken her hand upon meeting her, then bent to kiss her right cheek. He held her chair before they sat down to eat, and he had waited for her and Rosie to pick up their forks before he did.

"Yes, for eight years I have been a doctor in Ixmilco," he said in answer to the question Louise had just asked.

She couldn't make out the last word he had said. She strained to cut through his accent, aware Rosie was observing her.

"Ish-mel-low?" Louise tried. Marshmallow? Is mellow? She wasn't sure if the word was English or Spanish. She would be embarrassed not to have recognized an English word because, in turn, he would be embarrassed that she could not penetrate the bog of his accent.

"Ix-mil-co!" said Rosie, exaggerating the syllables. "That's the little town where I was researching the story, Mama."

"Yes, of course," said Louise, humiliated but relieved.

"And your family, Juan Ramón? Do they live in Ix-mil-co, too?"

"They live in León. Everyone except me."

"León? Is that near Mexico's border with the United States? Near Texas?"

"León's a big city, Mama," put in Rosie. "It's in the middle of the country. In the richest area for growing things."

"West of Mexico City," he said.

"Do you have many brothers and sisters?" She would move away from geography to a subject she could handle better.

"Eight now," said Juan Ramón. "But we were a family of thirteen children." Louise sucked in her breath. "Very different from here. Big family, different customs," he said. "You and Rosie are a family of two, no?"

"A family of two? Yes," said Louise. But she wasn't thinking of the fecundity or the number thirteen. She was thinking of the number four. Eight children plus Juan Ramón made nine. Nine from thirteen left four. It would be inappropriate—too soon—to ask what had happened to the other four children.

She pushed the plate of strawberry pie in his direction. "Have another piece, Juan Ramón."

He placed his hand on his stomach. "No, Señora, I cannot. I am satisfied." His eyes sparkled. "It was very delicious, your pie."

"I'm glad you liked it."

"You like to cook, no?"

"No?" Louise was a bit confused because the answer was *yes*, not *no*. "Yes, I do like to cook. But just desserts."

Rosie giggled from across the table. "Just desserts," she repeated. "Is that an intentional pun, Mama?"

Juan Ramón's brow wrinkled in concentration.

"It's a type of joke," Rosie explained before Juan Ramón could ask. "A play on words."

"A play on words?" said Juan Ramón.

"Double meaning," said Rosie. "*Doble sentido.*"

"Ah, yes," said Juan Ramón. He continued to smile, but shifted in his chair.

Louise was stymied. Should she go on to explain the word "play" in this context? "Well, actually, it wasn't much of a pun, Juan Ramón." She glanced at Rosie, who was watching her expectantly. "But where were we? You said you're a doctor." She chose her words carefully now, trying to avoid phrases he might not grasp, like *practice medicine*. She decided on, "What kind of doctor are you?"

"I'm a general—how do you say?—practitioner. *Médico cirujano*, we say in Spanish. Surgeon doctor."

Well, that was something, thought Louise. Clearly, he was no dummy. Nor was it lost on her the easy, confident way he rolled out the two words in Spanish compared to his more halting English. He must be a person of compassion to have labored as a country doctor. Not to mention that haunting loss of four brothers and sisters. What she most wanted to ask him, just to assuage her anxiety, was whether he treasured Rosie and would be kind and loving to her, and just when would he go home.

"Rosie has told me you are an artist. May I bother you to show me some of your works?"

"Well, yes," said Louise, touched by his interest, even if just courtesy.

Rosie pointed at the tablecloth. "Here, Mama painted this."

"You paint tablecloths?" He looked down at the cloth covering the table, clearly baffled.

Louise tried to see the whorls of burnt sienna and gashes of charcoal gray as a new pair of eyes might see them. She could well imagine Juan Ramón had expected a different sort of artist than one who made swirling messes on tablecloths like a child at finger paints.

"Mama was depicting the soil," said Rosie. "The soil, the earth, where our food comes from."

"Ah yes," said Juan Ramón. "A poetic idea."

Louise didn't know whether she was being patronized. But then it wasn't the first time someone had been at a loss for words upon viewing her abstract painting, the work that stood apart from the portrait painting she did for hire.

"Maybe you'd like to see some of Mama's other work? Something more typical?"

Louise was sure Rosie wanted to say "understandable." Following Rosie's cue, she led the two of them to the second bedroom, the one that now served as her studio and which many years before had been Rosie's bedroom. The tulip sketch was propped on the bookshelf where Louise had moved it while tidying up for Juan Ramón's arrival.

As soon as they entered the bedroom studio, Rosie said,

"Here's one Mama did of me when I was nine years old." She pointed out a framed picture on the wall of a beaming child with sun-streaked hair pushed back with a headband. "This was done when Mama still painted people for pleasure. Now it's only for money." She looked back over her shoulder at Louise and winked.

She is happy, Louise thought. As soon as they entered Rosie's former bedroom, Rosie seemed to assume an invisible mantle that allowed her to take charge, and Louise was content to let her do so. She stayed in the doorway. She was tired, suddenly drained of energy. One of her weary spells, she told herself. That was what she had told Dr. Foster, too. The spells came over her as quickly as hot flashes had some ten years ago. When they were upon her, there was nothing to do but endure.

Louise said, "That's right. I'll only paint your picture now, Juan Ramón, if I can distort you into a radish or a peony. Then I'll send you a bill." She moved to the daybed and allowed herself to sink onto it. As Rosie continued to chatter about the paintings, Louise wondered if he knew what a peony was. She should have mentioned a more universal plant, like a tomato vine or ear of corn, something native to the New World. But that would have required too much thinking ahead.

From where she rested on the daybed, she studied Rosie and Juan Ramón, their bodies close together. She could see his appeal for her daughter. He was intelligent, good-looking, intense, attentive. He laughed easily. But then, didn't Monty, too? At least Rosie and Monty spoke the same language and could get each other's jokes.

Each of the men Rosie had brought home over the years, Louise had been able to match to a different aspect of her daughter's nature, from the student race car driver, to the cautious economics professor, to the whimsical and witty and neurotic Monty.

Rosie started into the hallway to show Juan Ramón "the portrait gallery," as Louise referred to the preliminary sketches for portraits she had painted over the years—sketches that once had peopled her dining room walls as though invited to a dinner party.

Rosie threaded her arm through Juan Ramón's. "You see how the status of these portrait sketches has sunk in my mother's eye? Here they are, stuck in a dark hallway."

Rosie had the other arm extended, pointing to the row of faces. As she gestured, Juan Ramón swayed in the direction of Rosie. Her body, with a kind of thermal sensitivity plants possess, swayed to meet his in autonomic response.

Would this happiness last, or was it as ephemeral as the red tulips remaining in Mr. McGee's garden, soon fading into the next season? She wanted to warn Rosie, to beg her to learn from her own disastrous experience, but knew she couldn't trespass on whatever shard of memory Rosie might have of her father.

18

MONEY AND ORGASMS

Juan Ramón was relieved to see U.S. Labor Day over with and gone. He didn't want to be reminded of what his labor consisted of now. He hunched in the thinker position on a large rock in the breakwater, watching the roiling waves. Two breakwaters, formed from boulders tumbled together in a straight line some four meters in width, jutted into the sea. The northernmost breakwater, half a mile from its twin to the south, defined the mouth of the small marina. At the far end, the waves reared up, held their fury for just a second, then crashed down on the stolid rocks, flooding sea foam into every crevice and cranny.

Juan Ramón sniffed the storm on its way. "It probably won't rain," Rosie had said. "We only get winter rains." He might be from a landlocked area, but he knew a storm was coming. He was glad of it. The weather here tended to blandness, specializing in coastal fog with no sudden changes. As morning wore into afternoon, the fog might burn off and the sun's rays finally penetrate. Or the fog might coyly resist the sun's advances, blanketing everything under relentless haze. This morning's haze still hadn't lifted. Fog horns penetrated at intervals, long and mournful.

He missed the summer thunderstorms of Ixmilco and León with their quick shifts in temperature. The atmosphere here needed a good crisp charging, a rough and tumble of ions, a bursting exchange of pent-up forces.

When he was fourteen, he and his next oldest brother, Martín, had climbed out the window of their bedroom one summer night while the rest of the family lay sleeping. They had ridden their bicycles down the road from the house and into a midnight thunderstorm. Lightning cracked open the night sky, exposing its veins of purple and black and illuminating trees caught in its brilliance. Trees seen this way were not trees at all, but mysterious beings belonging to some other world, a world of purple and gold. He and Martín stood up tall on the pedals of their bikes. They yanked and pulled at the handlebars as if clutching the manes of untamed horses. In ecstasy they hollered into the deafening thunder that rolled over and into them, pushing before it all their caution.

"*Pendejos, cabrones!*" their father would have yelled, had he known. "Riding bicycles in a thunderstorm!" They, of course, could have been struck by lightning. That was part of the voltage that kept them pumping and screaming, whirling their bikes in circles under the illumined pine trees. They pedaled fast, driving at each other out of the flashing darkness and light, swerving at the last possible second, their clothes so soaked they would have been as well off naked.

Here in Marbella, thunderstorms rarely occurred, or at least that is what Rosie told him. It was the rainy season now in Ixmilco, but here they had felt not a drop in the weeks since he arrived, just the steady blandness of fog. For contrast, there was the ocean, stirred and furious now.

Not long after he had arrived, Rosie took him a few blocks from her house to where the ocean pulsed in close to the road. "There," she said, pointing close to the waterline. "Two houses used to stand there." The ocean, in one of its tempests, had simply reached up and snatched the houses into the sea.

Now there was only bobbing gray-blue water. No sign people had lived and loved on this noisy margin between terra firma and sea. Such was the power and caprice of the ocean. That was what Rosie loved. He was trying to.

This barren beach was far from the green and golden beaches he knew in Mexico. The water here was never warm; no palm trees lined the shore; the wind whipped up almost every afternoon around four o'clock with force. The unsparing salt air licked paint off the sides of houses and from deck railings.

Still, the waves summoned him down to them each day. They offered some relief from the web of fog but did nothing to assuage his feeling that he was bobbing aimlessly here.

He looked at his watch—eight fifteen a.m.—then picked his way back along the rocks, slippery with sea mist. He had to be at school in forty-five minutes. His day consisted of English classes in the morning, work in the afternoon, Rosie in the night, unless she was at a meeting.

The California Medical Boards were offered every six months. But this December was too soon. No way would his English be strong enough for the test. His teacher in the Adult Education course was doing her best, but his fellow students in the ESL course were merely playing. A significant number arrived late, unprepared and unmotivated, and the pace of the class dragged as the teacher slowed and backtracked to accommodate them.

"We can find you a better class," Rosie said. "Maybe a private language school. Some place where the students are serious, and you can move ahead."

"A private school will cost more money. A lot more."

"I'll pay for it. It's just for a while until you build up your vocabulary."

He grabbed her hand. "Rosie, I cannot let you do that. You

are paying too many things already."

She had insisted, and he had resisted, and was continuing to resist.

The house was quiet now. He barely had time to shower before leaving for this new miserable class. Rosie had gotten up a couple of hours before and left early in her running shoes, muttering something about being forced to interview some politico while he jogged, the only time the guy insisted he had available for her. He must be in good shape if he could jog and answer questions, Rosie said, or maybe it was his ruse for providing brief, truncated responses.

"Or maybe he doesn't want you to take notes," said Juan Ramón. "Probably he just wants to see you in running shorts." Rosie had laughed and rolled her eyes.

Like many houses on Marbella Beach, Rosie's bedrooms were on the ground floor, the living room and kitchen upstairs with a view of the ocean and surrounding community of wooden houses—casitas, really. The queen-size bed was freshly made, a task Rosie insisted they perform together each morning. There was something significant, she believed, in taking responsibility for the bed you slept in by ceremoniously putting it in order. He didn't know about that. He would just as soon let a maid take care of the matter. Except there was no maid, just a gay cleaning crew, the Merry Wizards, who appeared every two weeks as if in *Fantasia* costume, toting their own brigade of brooms, mops, buckets, and dust cloths.

He emptied on the bed the loose change and dollars from his pocket and counted the money. One ten-dollar bill, four ones. A little more if he included the change: two quarters, a dime, some dull pennies worth no more than they looked. The topic of money was one he was accustomed to dwell on only when it came to the *Hospital Civil*. For his personal needs, he had never required much.

"Come to León," his father insisted during his first year in

Ixmilco. "The big money's here in the city. There in Ixmilco you won't earn enough for *cacahuates*, not even peanuts."

His father had been wrong. Here in the U.S. was where the big money was. Everything was big here. People stood big, talked big, laughed big, earned big, spent big—except for the poor he had seen sleeping along the sidewalks, those who eked along without jobs, without good nutrition, without doctors, sometimes begging for change, just as they did in his country.

He dropped the money back into his pocket. The coins clinked against the house key. He used the comparatives he had learned in English class: big money, bigger money, biggest money. That's what he needed to take care of Rosie and himself here.

* * *

Paco's Tacos allowed its employees thirty minutes for lunch. He was hungry, and it was a reflex to grab a taco there. But if he never again saw one of those so-called tacos or *chimichangas* or flying saucers, that would be a blessing from God. He should have sought work in a faux-Greek restaurant instead of a faux-Mexican one. Perhaps then the oozy Mexican food here could serve as a bit of comfort instead of annoyance.

"You don't have to work there," Rosie told him almost as soon as he got the job. "I can ask around. Maybe one of my friends knows of something. Something that pays better."

He would stay where he was, he told her, until he could find something better on his own.

"Bur-reed-o," he said on the job when he had to repeat a burrito order from a customer. He had learned to slur the Spanish words, not roll the *r's*, and extend the vowels so customers would understand him. If he pronounced the Spanish words correctly, the customer would often blink without comprehension.

Bur-reed-o. Even Rosie, once back here in her country, re-verted to this slurring: Loss Anj-luss, San-a-Bar-Bruh. He let the thought of Rosie linger in his mind, even with her skewed pronunciation. Her bare body cupped against his as they slept. That at least made a right out of so much wrong.

Two weeks before, he had gone into a Security Pacific bank to change the last of the pesos he had brought from Mexico. Standing in front of him in the Security Pacific line was a man without shoes. A trickle of dirt formed a delta between the man's big toe and the one next to it. Juan Ramón's attention moved to the cut-off shorts, evidently once a pair of blue jeans. A pale blue thread swayed from the ragged edge of one pant leg. The man turned at that moment, as if sensing Juan Ramón's scrutiny.

"These lines take forever, don't they?" the man said in a confident way.

Juan Ramón was astonished to hear the smooth, modu-lated tones of the man's voice. In Mexico, only the extremely poor—or deranged—went barefoot in public. And they cer-tainly would not dare step foot in a bank. Juan Ramón had ex-pected a guttural grunt from the man, not the polished inflec-tions he associated with the educated. Why was a man like this barefoot in a bank? He must realize his attire made him look poor, dirty, and ignorant. *Por el amor de Dios*, why would a man not carry himself with more dignity?

Juan Ramón crossed the street and paused in front of the Marbella First Alert Clinic. It occupied the corner of the block and was about the same size as the *Hospital Civil* in Ixmilco. He stepped on the grooved rubber mat, and the similarity to the *Hospital Civil* ended. Automatic glass doors sprang open with even more alacrity than an obsequious *mozo* or servant could muster.

A silvery receptionist's desk was posted in the large open entry. Flat gray carpet flecked with white covered the floors, absorbing and muffling inappropriate sounds. Music wafted from the walls, but not so loud as to interfere with the soft paging of a doctor over the intercom.

"May I help you?" asked a perky voice pleased with its efficiency. A slim young woman with three diamond earrings studded up her left ear and even more up her right, was looking at him, friendly but glazed. Behind her, enshrined in little cubicles partitioned for privacy, sat two other women, each with a bone-colored computer monitor and keyboard on her desk.

"Would you like an appointment with a doctor?" Her manicured fingernails hovered just above the keyboard as she waited for his reply.

Over the long weekend, he and Rosie had talked and decided it would be best if he found work more closely related to his field than wrapping up greasy tacos in orange-colored paper. Even in a clinic such as this, he knew it would be something menial, at least for now. In his hurry to leave Ixmilco, he had not had time to make arrangements with a school to qualify him for the F-1 student visa or the F-3 professional visa. He asked just for the tourist visa. That meant he was not supposed to work. But a man had to eat. He had to pay his share of the expenses. It wasn't correct to live off Rosie so much, no matter what she said.

"It's only temporary." She was ruffling her fingers through his hair as they lay in bed. "It's just until you get your license for practicing medicine here. I certainly don't expect you to be paying our expenses in the meantime. Or even want you to. I just want you to study for the medical boards."

He tried to read in her eyes if she meant that. Either way, though, he could not accept her offer. If he couldn't support them both, at least he could contribute his share until he was finished with the exam. Of course, if he didn't pass all sections of the exam the first time, the process could take years. He had worked since he was nine years old, starting in his father's shoe factory. He wasn't afraid of menial work, and if he could work closer to the medical world here in Marbella, he might feel more at home.

Paco's Tacos was just a few blocks from Rosie's house, and in spite of his accent, it hadn't required any show of working papers. The restaurant gave him a chance to hear a little more English and a lot more Spanish. His fellow workers were good to joke with, quick with slangy witticisms in off-color Spanish. He just couldn't get any substantial talk out of them about Mexican politics, or even U.S. politics, and nothing about history or medicine.

The personnel office of the clinic was as modern and streamlined as the entry room. The coddling music, the neutral gray and white tones of the décor, the cushioned chair he waited in, all lulled him with a too ready sense of . . . of what? That there was no sickness and disease in this country, and by extension, the world beyond? Or that impersonal, mechanical science could cure whatever ailment a body might be suffering? Or that medical insurance was as good as a high-tech drug, dulling the harsh realities of a serious illness? That a place where bodies were cut open was no more jarring than a bank, where uniformed helpers stepped softly and fed your hope with the latest designs in medicine and technology?

Or that he might secure a job in such a place, any kind of job, even sweeping the floors, when he didn't carry the right papers, didn't possess a green card?

He entered Rosie's address in the appropriate blanks of the application the receptionist handed him. He balanced the clipboard on his knee and stared at the column of little boxes. What was it called, the job he wanted? A list of positions ran down the left side of the page, a box before each. He didn't know what most of them referred to or how to pronounce them. Could he just write "anything" at the bottom of the list?

But he wasn't sure how to spell even that.

He started to sweat. The secretary had stepped away, and there was nobody to ask. An older white man with pock-marked cheeks bent over his own application. Juan Ramón stood up, the neutral gray and white stripes of the room criss-crossing before his eyes. He set the clipboard on the secre-tary's counter, removed his application from the clip, and crumpled the paper in his fist. His curriculum vitae with years of tending the poor and desperate in Ixmilco was not enough, he knew that.

He crossed the street, back to Paco's Tacos. The rest of the afternoon he spooned salsa into little plastic cups. Strangely, this mindless task provided him some satisfaction. The rote motions of his hands, steady and quick, pleased him, remind-ing him how capable his hands could be, given a chance.

As he worked, he tried to push down another observation that troubled him. Here, on her own terrain, Rosie was differ-ent. He pictured her just beyond the length of his outstretched arm that reached for her. She had friends she chatted with for *hours* on the phone; she had her job that sent her spiraling away from him every morning.

But most of all was her subtle knowledge of how to get things done, that awareness of what's possible and what's not possible that a person begins to breathe in at birth by virtue of location, just the being there. Rosie had the right word for the right situation: how to make light when she'd just trampled on someone's toes in the movie theater or, more difficult yet, when a latecomer entering the row had just trampled on hers. She knew the words to coax a parking attendant into letting her leave the car in a no-parking area of the lot. She would have known how to strike just the right tone with that man standing shoeless in the bank. She could do all these things without a betraying accent and syntax, something odd or wrong in how the English words came out. English congealed in his mouth like refried beans grown cold on the plate.

These last few weeks, Rosie did not laugh as much as she first had as he passed on his analysis of things here in *gringolandia*. One evening in their living room he reenacted a walk through the supermarket aisles. "I can't believe Americans eat like this. This isn't food. It's recycled plastic. It has never been alive. Twinkies, in a prior life, probably were old phonograph records. Hamburger Helper, Pop Tarts, Kool-Aid, Jell-O. This is food?"

Rosie picked up right away. "Jell-O? You dare attack Jell-O? I saw Jell-O on almost every street corner in Ixmilco. People were even selling homemade Jell-O out front of the Pemex gas stations. Just because you call it *gelatina*, what's the difference?"

"I should not have included Jell-O," he said at once. "*Gelatina* is honorable. Especially in my family. My aunt used to—"

"Even if it's mostly sugar?"

The phone rang in the middle of their exchange, and he answered.

A woman's voice he vaguely recognized said, "Hello, Rosie there?" The voice did not identify herself nor say hello to him.

"Please, who is calling?"

"Marianne."

He connected the name to the voice and recalled a middle-aged woman with freckles and graying auburn hair. She worked as a fact checker at the newspaper. The three of them—Rosie, Marianne, and Juan Ramón—had talked for a while at an office party Rosie had taken him to a couple of Fridays back. He handed the phone to Rosie without bothering to say hello to Marianne, either.

He waited for Rosie to finish her phone conversation. As soon as she put the receiver down, he said, "She didn't even greet me."

"Greet you?

"She didn't even say hello to me. Even though we've met."

Rosie stared at him with that look her face sometimes assumed now. He supposed it was the face of someone under siege, called on too many times to explain the off-beat or the violent or the inexcusable.

He said, "Is that polite, her not greeting me? She was talking to me just last week. I don't think that's right. Do you?"

"Well, no, it's not exactly polite. It's just our way. It's done all the time."

"She had to know by my accent who I am."

Rosie looked tired. "I don't know what to say about her, Juan Ramón."

"I'm going to be as rude to these callers as they are to me. 'Is Rosie there?' they say, as if I'm just an answering machine. I'm going to say, 'Hell no, what do you want, anyway?'" He slammed his hand on the table as if it were a phone receiver, then glared at her. "What do you think of that?"

"I think it's rude."

"And that person who just called, what she did isn't rude?"

"I agree with you. It's not polite." Rosie was straining to keep an even tone. "But a lot of people are just that way. They don't intend to be rude." Rosie went on, slowly, "I believe that people who do that, I mean people who don't take time to say hello to the person answering the phone, they feel you probably don't want to waste time talking to *them*. They don't want to trouble *you* by taking up your time. In fact, it can be seen not as rude but as courteous on the part of the caller."

He hated how she twisted things around. He seized on her words. "Time, that's the most important thing for you Americans, isn't it?" The phrase "you Americans" carved a wide gulf between them, but he couldn't stop himself.

She folded her arms. "I don't like standing for the entire American society. I don't imagine you would like to represent the entire Mexican society, would you?"

He reached into his shirt pocket for his cigarettes. "Why not? At least we treat people well." How could he stop himself from these pointless statements that weren't even true? A sick feeling washed into his stomach from the way he and Rosie were barking at each other. The worst thing was that neither of them was speaking the whole truth and neither of them was ready to stop.

Rosie unfolded her arms and placed them on her hips. "Treat people well? The Mexican society treat its people well? Oh sure, on the surface. When it comes to greeting people on the street or in a restaurant, or on the phone, you Mexicans are all handshakes and smiles—on the surface."

He was pleased he was getting to her. She was losing her temper, showing some fire instead of that terrible patient control. Her voice rose in pitch and volume. "Meanwhile, you're letting your indigenous eat snakes, and your street people eat worse, if at all. Probably rats."

"That's not true. Who told you that?"

"I read it. Some sixty, or probably seventy, percent of the people in Mexico are poor."

"That's crazy. That number is wrong. Where did it come from? A so-called researcher who spent five whole days in Mexico on his—or her—big American ass at the beach? Or maybe a newspaper reporter sitting in front of a typewriter making up fictions so her story gets attention?"

"That's a low thing to say."

He ached to stop this. But each time he thought he would let a comment pass, a retort welled up in him, unstoppable as a sea wave. He said, "Most of the things I hear in this country about Mexico are bullshit."

"*I* have never sat at my typewriter, as you say, making up 'fictions' just so I can have a good story."

"Did I say *you* did it? Did you hear the word *you*?"

"You implied it." Rosie's voice broke. "That's just a coward's way of saying something he can't say directly."

"Are you saying I am a coward?" He groaned to himself as he heard the way he sarcastically echoed her words, and he felt really bad that she was now crying. He yearned to jump up and hop around the room on one foot, to run over and tug at her ear and muss her hair, for the both of them to burst out laughing at how trivial and ridiculous and cruel their argument had gotten. They had become two countries on the verge of war, each with camps pitched on the border.

He slammed out the door and started for the shore in a fast walk. In the distance he heard thunder. Yes, he was right about that, too. There would be a thunderstorm here in Marbella. He ran up and down the length of the beach for a long time, from breakwater to breakwater, until their fight reshaped itself and became sadder and more embarrassing than raw.

He stayed outside for hours, welcoming the storm, allowing himself to be drenched from head to toe as he had at fourteen. Finally, he returned to the house. Instead of going right in, he waited for several long moments outside the front door, making sure his mind was right. He rested his hand lightly on the doorknob.

At once the door swung open.

"You're all wet," Rosie said. She was wearing a blue bathrobe with a red scarf draped around her neck. "In fact, you're soaking." Her voice was subdued, but she took him by the hand and led him inside. "To cheer you up—to cheer us both up—I've been cooking. Sort of," she said, as if trying to take refuge in the light and easy.

He was relieved. "You have?" He sniffed the air for some telltale signs. All he caught was the sea smell borne through the still open door behind him.

"First, Juan Ramón, I want to tell you I'm sorry. I didn't

mean all those things I said. I was just mad. I was striking out wildly."

"I'm sorry, too. I went too far." She allowed him to embrace her, wet as he was.

They stood that way for long moments, rainwater dripping onto the small vestibule floor.

"Now, what did you say you were cooking? Let's go back to that."

"It's your favorite. Something traditional. In both countries. It didn't really come out right, though."

"Tell me."

She whipped off the red neck scarf.

"First, I have to blindfold you."

"Oh? Like a taste test?"

"Hmm. You could say that. You also must take off your clothes."

"I'm liking this meal already." He let her unbutton his wet shirt. She stripped off his shirt and pants, then tied the scarf around his head, blindfolding his eyes. She grasped his hand, hers soft but insistent in his, and led him toward the hallway. She asked him to wait while she slipped out of her clothes, too.

He reached out in the direction where he imagined her to be and caught the smooth angle of her hip. "Maybe I could lift the blindfold just a little?"

"No peeking."

She led him into the bathroom, and he heard the sound of the shower curtain being whisked to one side. She guided him into the bathtub.

Instantly he drew back his foot. "What's that? Is this a trick?" He had stepped into something cold and viscous. She stepped into the tub with him. He started to laugh with the ridiculousness of it all—he naked with a blindfold, the two of them standing in this tub of cold . . . rubber?

She pulled him down with her into the pudding-like stuff.

It was strange, even sensual, as it gave way beneath them. It smelled sweet and familiar.

"What is this?" he asked again.

She lifted the edge of his blindfold. "Don't you recognize it? In its earlier life, it was probably a plastic coke bottle." She smeared a finger's length of the substance across his lips.

"Raspberry? Strawberry?" He burst out, "Gelatina!" He laughed and pulled her against him. The Jell-O, not yet firmed up properly, warmed between the curves of their bodies. As they moved, it squished and oozed and spurted like some primordial mud.

"It looks like a battlefield here," he said as partly congealed red gelatin washed up over their bodies and climbed along the sides of the tub. A scene of slaughter. That's what they had to do, he knew, slaughter their jingoistic selves. They had to pass beyond international boundaries to a new country of their own devising.

He snuggled more closely against her. "Didn't I tell you?" he said, "about my Tia Leticia?"

"Tia Leticia? Uh, no, you only started to. Before we—"

"She had twenty-three children. All live births. All still living today."

"Twenty-three?" She shifted to her side and rolled on top of him in a swift frictionless slide. "Do I believe that?"

"Yes, twenty-three." He licked the Jell-O that dappled her breasts.

"I've long thought they give Nobel Prizes for the wrong feats."

"Tia Leticia herself supported them all, all twenty-three. Her husband was a bum who didn't work."

"Maybe he was tired from all that—" He stopped her with a long kiss, deep and berry-flavored. The Jell-O made soft sucking sounds.

"How did she do it?" Rosie asked when the kiss ended. "Do

what?" he asked and with his knee parted her legs. The Jell-O was melting into a warm syrup from the heat of their bodies.

"Support her twenty-three kids," breathed Rosie.

"*Gelatina, mi amor.* She made gelatina every evening of her adult life. In the morning, she sold it on the corner to passing workers and school children. Look what gelatina did for her."

Rosie moaned in mock terror. "A fertility potion!"

Over the edge of the tub, in the trash basket next to the sink, Juan Ramón caught sight of a mound of empty Jell-O boxes and plastic bags that had held ice cubes.

Outside, the waves pounded the beach, but devoid of the storm-driven anger of their earlier crashing. The unseasonable summer storm had moved on, leaving the shore in sweet delight.

19

ME ENCHILÉ:
LITERALLY, I MADE
MYSELF TOO HOT

Leland peered at me over his glasses, which had slid down his nose. "Carole-Ann is planning a party for you. Next week. She says it's essential you mark the occasion with festivities."

I tried not to laugh. "She remembered this year. Usually I throw the party myself, and when she arrives, she's surprised that it's my birthday."

"I'm glad you said that. She's giving you a surprise party."

I laughed out loud. "So why did you tell me?"

"The surprise is that the party's at your house. Some complicated story about an ex-boyfriend of hers who lives in the same building and whom she doesn't want to invite but would have to if the party were at her apartment." Leland managed to look amused and disdainful at the same time. "Local soap opera." He turned away as if distracted, then quickly turned back. "Oh, and the rest of the surprise is that it's not a birthday party. It's a celebration because your Mexican birth control story has garnered a prize."

"What? Say that again."

"Your story won an award."

"Award? I didn't know it had even been nominated. What's this about?"

"Foreign Features with Concern for the Human Condition," he said absentmindedly. "I submitted the story."

"And everyone has known about this—the story winning an award—before me?"

"Seems so, Rosie. Otherwise, what kind of surprise would it be?"

* * *

I didn't remember Carole-Ann ever mentioning an ex-boyfriend in her building, but maybe this had all taken place when I was in Mexico. A party at my house? My little beach place had undergone a change in the last months since Juan Ramón moved in, not so much in how it looked but in how it felt.

I had shoved my clothes together in the closet to make room for his. Stolid men's shoes stood neatly next to my coquettish female footwear. When I got home each day after work, I heard Televisa, the Spanish language station, prattling away in the living room. I bought enough chiles and pinto beans for the whole week and maintained salsa and a pot of refried beans in the refrigerator as if each were a sacred temple light never to be extinguished. I had taken to hurrying home right after work so Juan Ramón would not be alone there after his midday English classes, bored by the same off-white walls. I felt the need to be home more, and when there, I had started to trim my hour-long phone chats so I wouldn't seem to be ignoring him. For the years Monty and I had been together, we kept our separate living arrangements. I just wasn't used to having a man around the house.

"You won't have to lift a finger," Carole-Ann said when I quizzed her about the surprise party. "I'm between tapings, so I have time to take care of everything. Nothing for you to do but shine and enjoy yourself. That's also part of the surprise—you don't have to do anything. This launch into an expanded career must be festive, a positive portent."

When I told Juan Ramón that evening about the surprise party, he said, "Perfecto. I get to celebrate with you, and I get to meet more of your friends from the newspaper."

I was pleased to see him animated. I had been so busy these last few weeks I hadn't had a chance to ask him whether he was restless being in the house so much of the day. Spending long hours in my cramped beach cottage had to be a let-down after the first rush of excitement about being in a new country, a new town. I feared the reality of what he had done was growing in him.

"Carole-Ann is throwing the party here, at my house." A syllable too late, I wished I had said *our* house. But it actually was *my* house. I kept talking, hoping he hadn't noticed. "Carole-Ann will come here next Friday afternoon to get things ready. I told her you were good in the kitchen." I was tempted to add, "And not just in the kitchen." But I had grown more circumspect, less spontaneous. I wasn't sure how my compliment might translate. I always had to think twice now.

"Of course, I'll help, too, *mi amor*. I'll add to the surprise—I'll surprise you with some food you like." But he said it in a more subdued way. His earlier animation also tamped down.

He could be concerned about his English. I knew firsthand it was tough to understand and speak a foreign language in a crowded, noisy room. In fact, it was tough to have personality at all when jokes and repartee in a foreign language flew fast.

The day of the party, I spent part of the morning and all of the afternoon at an overlong and tedious meeting of the Board of Trustees for Marbella Community College. The party was scheduled to start at seven o'clock, but I was already worn out by time I got home at six thirty. I would have much preferred to collapse into Juan Ramón's arms in front of the TV than have to perform in the spotlight as the star of my own surprise party. From the kitchen already wafted homey and enticing aromas. It would be a good long while before I could collapse and rest. Still, I should attempt to have a good time.

"I notice Carole-Ann has been busy in the kitchen," I said, resting against the door jamb. "What smells so good?"

"That's part of the surprise." Mischief danced in his eyes. I was glad to see it.

I barely had energy to make it to the living room. I stood in front of the sofa and stripped off the straight skirt and blouse I had worn to work. The skirt fell to my feet with a soft plop. I was on the verge of kicking the heap across the room with a last muster of energy when I became aware of Juan Ramón watching me.

Suddenly, he took two stretched out steps and was standing against me. He caressed the length of my bare back. "*Mi chiquita linda.*" He kissed me long and hard.

I was distracted, though, that here I was standing almost buck-naked in my living room when my friends would be here in a matter of minutes and I would have to be *on*, not to mention clothes on. I could not hold the kiss.

He drew back and peered into my eyes as if to ask a question.

"It's just that I'm tired." I tried not to sound whiny as I added, "I have to be lively until God knows what time of the morning or everybody's feelings will be hurt. I couldn't do that to Carole-Ann."

Juan Ramón turned away to pat his pockets for his cigarettes. He said, "You will feel better once the party gets started. You will get more energy from having a good time with your friends."

He gave up his search for cigarettes and reached for my hand. This time he kissed me lightly on the forehead. "I'll make you a drink. Tell me about the friends who are coming to your party."

I sighed, but not so loud he could hear. He was trying to be kind, but I felt too worn out for even that little bit of chatting. The doorbell rang. I snatched up the mound of rumpled clothes and hurried off to get dressed in something besides my birthday suit.

Within fifteen minutes, the whole staff of *The Marbella Beacon* seemed to have turned out. At the start of the festivities, I introduced Juan Ramón to almost everyone who came through the door. I wished there were time for each person to engage in conversation with him, to make some kind of connection, but more people kept appearing. Carole-Ann, or maybe it was Leland, had invited even some of the staffers who had gone on to other jobs in the last year. I was forced to swirl from one person to another. Sometimes I truncated conversations in mid-syllable as new faces appeared.

Carole-Ann had bedecked the dining room table with my favorites. A fresh tomato salsa dip was next to a global arrangement of herb-broiled shrimp. There were fresh chips, refried beans, guacamole flavored with cilantro and serrano chiles. In the center of the table presided a steaming platter of chicken and pork tamales. My favorites. I gasped to see them.

Two hours later, it was just as Juan Ramón had predicted. I had forgotten I was ever tired. To the contrary, I sipped margarita after margarita that Juan Ramón managed to hand me until we lost track of each other. I shimmered, twinkled, grew wondrously witty, or at least felt I did, which was just as much fun.

I elbowed my way through the press of people standing in the living room to get where Leland stood by the patio door. Not more than twenty-four hours had passed since Leland and I had been in hot analysis of the Marbella Beach political race for a county supervisor seat. We picked up almost to the word where we had left off.

"You claimed Fenton was a dark horse," Leland charged.

"He's a horse's ass, and all the other horses know it."

"It's your guy who's the jackass." I loved nothing better than trading political insults with Leland, our earlier analysis having now degenerated into one-liners.

"Did you hear his press conference on the seawater intrusion problem? 'Put tiles under the agricultural land.' Oh sure. Underground tiles covering almost two hundred square miles." The little gold earring in his right earlobe sparked in indignation.

I spotted Carole-Ann replenishing the shrimp display. Next to her stood Margaret, a short brunette who wrote headlines and spoke the same way—crisp, succinct and attention-getting. Cathy, a shy round woman who took classifieds over the phone, was munching through a fistful of tortilla chips.

I slipped my arm around Carole-Ann's waist. "You've given the perfect party. Me as the star, and you doing all the work. And handmade tortillas! I can just picture you up to your armpits in all that work." I kissed her on the cheek.

"Not all the work," said Carole-Ann. "It's Juan Ramón who worked all day."

"He did?" I glanced around the living and dining room. "Where is he, anyway? I haven't seen him for a while."

"He's in your kitchen. Where he's been since early this morning."

I looked at her sharply.

Not at all daunted, Carole-Ann went on, "He wanted to surprise you with the tamales. He told me in Mexico they were your idea of an aphrodisiac."

Thanks to the margaritas, I giggled. "When I was in Mexico, everything was my idea of an aphrodisiac."

Carole-Ann didn't laugh. She seemed to be weighing whether she should continue. Then she said, "He also made the shrimp and the guacamole. The tortillas, too. Hand-patted by his own hands. He made everything but the salmon cheese ball and the dill bread. Those were my tiny contribution. You can't believe how hard he's worked."

Margaret, who had been standing next to Carole-Ann all this time, said in a loud voice, "A man in the kitchen. Don't let that one get away, ladies." All the while she was ladling lots of salsa onto her tamale.

"Be careful," said Cathy, who was watching her. "That stuff really burns. Rosie, you better tell the chef to turn down the flame."

"Some like it hot," boomed Margaret, giving me a wink. "Is your Mexican friend—what's his name, Juan something? I know, Don Juan!" She laughed at her own answer as she forked into her mouth a large chunk of tamale bathed in salsa. "Is he just visiting?" she asked through the mouthful.

"Juan Ramón is living here. We're—"

"Good God!" Margaret sputtered. "You're right, Cathy. We'll have to sue Juan the damn cook. This salsa is too fucking—" She didn't finish because she had taken to fanning her open mouth with her hand. The yellow-red mixture, all wet and mushy, rested in lumps on her outstretched tongue.

I was too distracted with concern for Juan Ramón to laugh or commiserate. I handed her a tortilla. "See if this helps." Actually, I was pleased Margaret's eyes were watering and that she was panting without decorum. Juan Ramón's salsas were too hot for me too, but I wasn't about to say so. Where was he, anyway?

Cathy turned her attention from Margaret, who now had a mouthful of tortilla and puffy cheeks. "I take it you and Mr. M are no more?"

I lowered my voice. "That's right."

"Really? After so many years?"

"Monty and I are all done, all gone." I threw in some Spanish, just because I could and because it seemed appropriate. "*Punto final*," I said, not bothering to translate.

I was acutely concerned now about Juan Ramón's where-abouts, and I was washed with guilt. I hurried to the kitchen but didn't see him there either.

Finally, I found him, out front of the house, alone in the damp salt air. His face was chiseled with anger as he spit out the words, his eyes aflame. "You ignored me. You talked to everyone but me."

* * *

Saturday morning I was even more exhausted than I had been before the party began. I awoke late and with a headache. Juan Ramón had spent the night on the sofa but was nowhere to be seen. I was in the kitchen making a fresh batch of salsa. I poked another *chile de arbol* into the pot of chopped tomatoes and onion and turned up the fire. The salsa was up to seven chiles. Each time I had made salsa since Juan Ramón arrived, I increased a little the amount of chiles, and still Juan Ramón wouldn't admit the salsa was too hot. In fact, he seemed to take it as an insult each time I asked.

"No," he would say in a gravelly voice, waving his hand to dismiss the presumptuous question that evidently challenged his virility.

I stirred the fragrant mixture as it came to a boil and forced each long red pod under the water, making sure it released whatever hellfire it contained. In my head, I composed another line in the letter I had started to Juan Ramón. I would tell him in writing so he could read and reread it: "No one has ever yelled at me like that before. I was humiliated by your tone of voice."

These chiles better be screaming hot. Here I was, pondering what, until recently, had been inconsequential things in my life: chile peppers. Could they go stale? Was there something wrong with the chiles I bought? Had they maybe been languishing in the store too long and lost their sizzle? I had switched stores. I now bought chiles at a Mexican market where, because of the frenzied turnover, a chile could never be suspected of doing anything so uncharacteristic as languishing.

Chiles were anything but inconsequential to most Mexicans. When we were still in Ixmilco, Juan Ramón told me about his Uncle Paco, the one nicknamed the Pink Panther, for his slinky gait and limbs like oiled wire. He dared not travel anywhere outside Mexico without lugging an extra suitcase with chiles secreted about: *chile verde*, *chile jalapeño*, and *chile güero* for munching raw with his meals, *chile pasilla*, and *chile piquín*, and the liveliest of them all, *chile habanero*. His suitcase was like a doctor's medicine bag, at the ready should he pass a bland pot bubbling on the stove.

As I waited for the next phrase of my letter to come to me, I wondered if the Mexican mouth, after steady years of eating hot peppers, had already lost its sensitivity by the age of fourteen or so, twice the age of reason. A reasonable mouth would have deduced twice over that it was—*ay, caramba*—afire. Maybe most Mexicans were somewhat like numb lepers in this regard and had lost their sense of feeling. They could not be counted on to identify a salsa as hot or mild. So often they said, disappointment in their tone, "*No pica*"—it's not hot.

Put battery acid in the salsa, a nasty little voice inside said. That should bring him to his knees. Another sentence for my letter bobbed up: "You yelled out those accusations, and you never considered their effect on me." I continued: "Those words will stay with me for a long time." I made a mental note to revise "those words will stay with me" to "those words burn me." On impulse, I slipped in an eighth, then a ninth pepper.

I couldn't bring myself to tell him how terrified I had been when I finally found him out front of the house, the breakers slamming in the background. "Your friends don't know how to talk to me," he said.

I was getting obsessive but couldn't stop composing. "You say I ignored you at the party. That I stuck with that 'editor *cabrón*' for a long time, laughing and teasing in a way I don't do with you." Juan Ramón charged that he had sweated like a pig all day, while I had roamed around like a goat nuzzling for everyone's attention.

I slung back. "It was *my* celebration." My letter would inform him, "I can only think you have not been to many parties in this country." Oh well, of course not. He just got here. I should revise to say, "parties with Americans and Europeans. Our customs are different. Couples usually split up and circulate separately."

I imagined myself translating this letter into Spanish, even though we had agreed to speak English in California and Spanish in Mexico. But when, just last week, I left him a couple of notes in English, he had paid more attention to the individual words than to the messages I had written. The last time he had stabbed at a word I had written and burst out with "*Thought*? That word is *thought*?"

He had thrust the notepaper in my direction. "Say *thought*! Let me hear you say *thought*!"

"Thought."

Immediately he got what I thought was overly excited about how he had heard only three letters and what were all those other letters doing in the word and what an illogical language English was, and how he would never learn it right, and it was *pinche. Punto final.*

I had half expected him at that moment to switch forever from speaking English to only Spanish and in his heat rise up to declaim verses by long-dead poets from Mexico's War of Independence. We were both lost in a flame-throwing linguistic defense.

Oh God. This letter I was composing, how didactic and

self-justifying and sniveling. It was true some couples at parties did not go their separate ways. It was just that for all these years, Monty and I had been in the habit of fanning out from each other, then coming back together at the end of the party to entertain ourselves with our exploits as we had sailed our separate ways around the room. Those couples that clung together, how dependent and insecure they looked. I sighed. On the other hand, they also looked united, making a public stand of their desire to be with one another, the value of each other's company, their commitment.

The ninth chile pepper was bobbing on top, not yet submerged. I stabbed it down into the boiling water. One thing I had no doubts about was my recipe for salsa. That's because it was Juan Ramón's. It seemed more and more of my recipes were. In just a few weeks he had become the acknowledged chef, the artiste of the household, accorded the respect and acclaim worthy of a graduate from the Cordon Bleu cooking school in Paris. I, who actually had sat in on cooking demonstrations at the Cordon Bleu during a drizzly Parisian spring on a sudden vacation with Monty a few years before, was deemed a mere mechanic in the kitchen, a slave to cooking manuals, a follower of recipes.

Observing that Juan Ramón's "recipes" never had any fixed amounts, only fixed ingredients, I ventured to increase the quantity of chiles. I wanted to see him mop his brow, fling his wrist and say, "*Me enchilé.*" I wanted to make a salsa that was the licking flames of hell. Let him burn. I wanted him to suffer. I wanted his respect.

I dumped the rest of the bag into the boiling brew. The fumes ascended and struck me in the eyes and chest. I started to cough. I was barely able to breathe. What were the remedies? No time. I was coughing too much from the fumes, which had flashed their way through the kitchen and were surely lighting up the living room. I hurried down the stairs, threw open the door and ran out onto the steps, nearly tripping on the unopened newspaper.

Juan Ramón was coming up the sidewalk, apparently back from a morning run on the beach. "What smells so good? Is that what I think it is?" he said in a perfectly natural voice, no trace of anger. "I can hardly wait."

"About last night," I began, suddenly ashamed. "I shouldn't have—"

He pulled me to him although I was still coughing and he was all sweaty. He said, "I am sorry. I don't know who I am here, Rosie. I don't recognize myself."

I surrendered the rest of my anger. In its place arose a steep regret that I had indeed abandoned him at the party where he knew almost no one and where he had toiled so hard for hours to regale me with my favorite Mexican dishes. He had wanted only to celebrate my accomplishment.

20

¡OH DIOS!

Juan Ramón first learned of the earthquake from two students in his English class who had heard about it that morning on a Spanish radio program. On September 19, at 7:17 in the morning, a massive earthquake struck Mexico City. It measured 8.1 magnitude on the Richter Scale. It was felt as far away as Houston, Texas, more than 900 miles away.

That evening, Juan Ramón and I could not separate from the television, where the first pictures were appearing. What we saw were searing flashes of devastation, flashes of chaos:

Flash: tall sleek buildings broken in two or their top floors shattered away;

Flash: multi-story apartment buildings oddly buckled, leaning to one side as if melted in the sun, defying gravity;

Flash: towering mounds of rubble where schools, hotels, factories, homes, and businesses once stood;

Flash: desperation in the streets with the dead, the dazed and the barely breathing hauled out of buildings on stretchers or in someone's arms;

Flash: piles of toppled concrete hunks, steel rebar poking out, twisted and bent as if no more than a blade of grass.

My shoulders hunched with the misery of the images and

what I was imagining under the rubble. I tried to rub Juan Ramón's neck as we sat side by side. He, too, was tense with the immensity of it all. Knead and massage as I did, my fingers could not release the knots in his neck and shoulders. He sat slumped, head between his hands.

"Hundreds of buildings have collapsed," the broadcaster announced.

"And how many thousands of people are buried alive?" Juan Ramón asked.

Nobody knew.

"Do you have friends in Mexico City?" I asked.

"Some that I haven't seen in a long time. But all of these suffering souls are my people."

Juan Ramón called in sick the following morning, September 20th, and remained stationed in front of the television.

¡OH DIOS! screamed the enormous headline in one Mexico City newspaper. A huge aftershock of 7.5 struck that evening. Panic ran rampant through the already turbulent streets. People poured out of buildings that had not fallen the first time, resolved never to return.

Between news reports, Juan Ramón paced in front of the television, then perched back on the sofa edge when the reports resumed. Each broadcast brought worse numbers. The death toll climbed into unknown thousands. Over and over we heard news of the victims, and we saw clips of television personalities killed while on air. One story focused on a stricken Placido Domingo, who lost an aunt and uncle, a baby nephew, and two cousins in a collapsed apartment building.

We hung on the words of geologists, on both the English and Spanish channels, who explained why so much of the earth under Mexico City was unstable—as if these merciless facts somehow assuaged the terror. The quake's epicenter was located off the Pacific coast, some 350 kilometers from Mexico City, but the clay soil of the ancient lakebed of long-ago, Lake

Texcoco, had amplified the seismic waves, waves that buckled more than three minutes.

"Six years ago, in 1979, we had a strong earthquake in Mexico City, but this one is in another category," a broadcaster said, his eyes wild as another aftershock struck while he spoke. The city's telecommunications center was badly damaged, frustrating rescue efforts. Three hospitals were down, major sections destroyed, and over eleven hundred patients killed by the collapse. Juan Ramón barely spoke.

I sat next to him, not saying anything either. My fears ran everywhere. I knew he wanted to be there, administering to the injured. He was powerless here. He belonged there. Without his saying so, it was clear he needed to leave. Should I tell him to go? And then what? I could not bear the thought of his leaving, and would he, like my father, never come back?

He groaned at the sight of a sobbing toddler and his mother being pulled from the rubble, the mother dead. He braced his head in his hands.

I said it. "You have to go."

"I have no ticket." His voice choked. No money is what he meant, though he couldn't say it.

That all along had been an unspoken thought in both our minds this last week. "We'll get it. There's got to be a way. Even if we have to borrow from my mother."

"No!" He stopped, then heaved a sob. "Yes."

* * *

Even now, as we hurtled down the freeway in Mama's old red Comet—she had insisted on driving—I didn't want him to go, and I did want him to go. He had to be there. This was who he was.

Juan Ramón had grabbed Mama's hands in his as soon as she pulled up in front of the house. "Thank you for this, Señora

Louise," he said repeatedly. "May God repay you for all you are doing."

"At least I can help in some way," Mama said. "Always I sit helpless as I see these tragedies on the television. I can do this little bit."

I was thankful Mama suggested we sit in the back seat so we could be next to each other. He spoke to me in a breathless flow, half Spanish, half English, as if Mama were not there in front of us, peering into the darkness through her driving glasses, hands gripping the steering wheel at nine and three o'clock. If she heard, it didn't matter—now it was all in the family.

"Rosie, *mi amor*, I will come back, I promise. I cannot live without you."

We insisted Mama accompany us into the airport waiting lounge so as not to leave her alone in the dark. She held herself apart so we could say goodbye in private. Then the flight was called, and Juan Ramón disappeared. He was lifted into the night sky, gone as suddenly as he had come less than four months ago. *Oh Dios.*

That night as I lay in bed, I wondered if these last months had really happened or if I were having an extended dream. I would wake up in Cuernavaca, late for my Level Seven class at La Divina Escuela de Idiomas, and have to angle by the gimlet eye of Señora Hernández on my way out the door and into a world without Juan Ramón.

21

THE WAY THE PAINT MOVES

A golden hen gamely lay belly up on the plate before each of them. Rosie lifted the pitcher of margaritas, which she had prepared at Louise's request, and refilled their glasses with pale, frothy promise.

"*Salud, dinero y amor*, health, money and love." Rosie lifted her glass to Louise. "Juan Ramón always says that." She held her glass suspended and sighed.

Louise raised her glass to meet her daughter's. She intuited Rosie's unspoken fear. She did like Juan Ramón but mostly thought it just as well he didn't return. Mostly she hoped their time together had played itself out. Mostly. Her uncertainty was perhaps just the margaritas mixing with whatever was ailing her lately.

They clinked glasses, then ate hungrily, with almost no conversation for the first couple of minutes. The ringing phone interrupted the scraping of forks.

Rosie answered it. "Long distance," she said, covering the mouthpiece to muffle her voice. "In Spanish." She winked, suddenly animated.

Rapid-fire words issued from the receiver. Spanish words,

tinny from distance, came faster now, incredibly fast. The unintelligible language began to crescendo. From across the table, Louise was hearing desperation.

As in confirmation, Rosie rose halfway to her feet and froze, unable to fully stand or sit down. She stared straight ahead, turning wan, the shape of her mouth unreliable as she struggled to control it. "No! No!" she said. More agitated Spanish followed before Rosie let the receiver into its cradle.

"Juan Ramón has to leave Mexico City and go to León at once. It's Ceci. His younger sister. There has been—he didn't know—an accident of some kind. Ceci is in the hospital. She's very bad. That's all his brother Martín was able to tell him. Juan Ramón is going to León tonight."

A half-eaten hen lay congealed on Rosie's plate. "He didn't have time to tell me any details. Or about Mexico City—he just said his work there is sad and grueling, with no rest." She fluffed her napkin like a blanket and tossed it into the air, then watched it plop back onto the table. "It's all so vague. I know nothing. No plans to come back. I'm worried for him."

Louise carried her drink of frothy promise to the kitchen and poured it down the sink. Even if she didn't want Juan Ramón to return, she didn't want this wrenching uncertainty for Rosie either. Or for him to be sad. Or the people in the Mexican capital to have suffered such losses. Every which way, there was misery.

* * *

A week later, the morning was clear and hard with bright sun as Louise stepped out earlier than usual for her morning sketching. Mr. McGee's purple and yellow petunias had given way to chrysanthemums. Before she got halfway down her walkway, Mr. McGee flung open his door and hurried toward their common fence. He held out an enormous bouquet of fall flowers—lavender chrysanthemums and bright marigolds.

"I see you bending over my flower beds in the mornings. Looks like you're making notes or drawings, or something like that." He pointed to her sketchbook with his one hand and with the other extended her the bouquet. "Thought you might enjoy seeing the flowers close-up."

Louise accepted the large bouquet, which she could barely manage with one hand. "Thank you. They really are lovely."

The polite thing would be to reciprocate in kind, maybe invite him in for a cup of coffee or at least chat for a while. But she didn't want to make idle talk, nor want him there in her house stretching out his long legs, folding and unfolding his arms behind his head, with sharp angles of elbow, knee and bony knuckle. She didn't want any man crossing her threshold, unless, of course, it was one of Rosie's friends in temporary visits not directed her way. A flicker of ingratitude toward Mr. McGee told her that now she would have to plan her daily strolls at a different hour, maybe even at dawn. Or she could turn in an opposite direction, toward a stretch of neighborhood that held less erotic interest than Mr. McGee's fertile flower beds and sodden soil, and away from his itchy green thumbs. Still, the autumnal beauty of the bouquet was undeniable.

She thanked Mr. McGee again and used the excuse of needing to immediately stick the flowers in water to return to the house. There she trimmed the stems and began lowering each flower into the vase. A wave of fatigue descended over her again, one of her spells. If it had not been that the flowers would wilt, she would have abandoned them at the sink.

Wilting, that's what she herself was doing. She must remember to see Dr. Foster for a check-up. That would also give her a chance to ask about the occasional ringing in her ears.

She sliced the stems of the remaining flowers on an angle and poked them into the water. To extend the life of the bouquet and keep the water from getting slimy, she would add a teaspoon of bleach. The word *wilting* reminded her of something Rosie had said a couple of days before. "I see the bowl of serrano chiles every time I open the refrigerator door. They look forlorn there on the chrome shelves under the glare of the refrigerator bulb. I can't bring myself to throw them out." Louise pictured the chiles, waiting for Juan Ramón as they pined away in fading shades of green and red like some abandoned biology project.

A few evenings later, Louise joined Rosie and her friend Carole-Ann for dinner at a nearby Thai restaurant. Louise was delighted to be included. She always craved to hear the perspective of Rosie's friends and the tidbits they let drop. Those tidbits were diamond chips, little gleams of light into Rosie's world.

"You and Carole-Ann offset one another well," Louise told Rosie in the car on their way to pick Carole-Ann up. "She's more opinionated and spontaneous, you more analytical. You are each other's glue." That was how Rosie and Juan Ramón were, too, though she didn't want to give Rosie that or bring up the subject of Juan Ramón, who hadn't called back again.

At one point in the meal and after two enormous margaritas, Carole-Ann said, "So when is Juan Ramón coming back?" She elbowed Rosie playfully. "Or is he?"

Rosie stared into her plate. "I don't know. His sister is in the hospital in León."

"Oh. I am sorry about that. I hope it's not serious." She paused a moment. "Rosie, you know I love you and want what's best for you. Forgive me for saying this, but I'm surprised you two lasted as long as you did. I'm trying to see this situation from your perspective, presumptuous as that is of me. I know opposites attract. And I know Juan Ramón is a fabulous man. Even so, in the face of so many differences, how would you expect to keep the flame burning—if I may scramble my metaphors?"

Carole-Ann looked at Louise as if soliciting a mother's confirmation of this pronouncement, perhaps sensing she had spoken too plainly. Rosie opened her mouth, about to say something to Carole-Ann. Instead, she too turned to Louise. Both young women were waiting now for her to pass some kind of judgment shaped by the wisdom of her years.

Louise was shocked by Carole-Ann's thoughtless words, even though she had often wondered the same thing. She picked her own words carefully. "I can see the attraction to a man like Juan Ramón," she began, then stopped. She was talking about Juan Ramón as if he were a distant object. Rosie was sure to catch that. Louise felt a vague disloyalty at odds with the affection she had come to feel for Juan Ramón in these last months, affection she had in time developed for each of her daughter's boyfriends, even going back to the teenage years. Maybe in some way these young men were the sons she never had, the other children she had once hoped for, missing limbs of her phantom family.

Rosie spun back to Carole-Ann. "What do you mean, 'lasted as long as we did'? You talk as if Juan Ramón and I are history."

"Look, Dear One, let's not sentimentalize the situation. You've got a boyfriend who can cook and has a cute ass." She broke off a piece of bread, slathered it with butter and popped it into her mouth, all the while not meeting Rosie's eyes. "These kinds of relationships are hard. It seems you don't have much in common. That's why I said you're opposites."

"We don't have enough in common? Bullshit, Carole-Ann! And what makes you think for one minute we're through? You're right—you're being presumptuous. You see only the part of him that doesn't speak English very well and doesn't get all your jokes. You . . . you probably don't know how to talk to him to even get to know him." Rosie swerved back to Louise. "Do you think Juan Ramón and I are opposites?"

Louise took a slow drink of her margarita. "Mixing people is like mixing paint. Some blend and form a new and beautiful color. Others can look good side by side but can't blend together. Often," she added, hoping this bit of philosophy was getting her clear from having to take a stand, "it takes a while to know which kind of colors you make together."

In truth, Louise had been surprised that Rosie, who was devoting herself to the written word, would choose a man who barely spoke English. Of course, Louise had no idea what their relationship in Spanish was like. Or in bed. That was another kind of blending.

Rosie said, "I bet you didn't think that much about mixing colors when you and Daddy met. Or maybe you just weren't trusting what you already knew."

Louise sucked in her breath. It was true that in choosing Carl, she had not made a harmonious choice for one who purported to be a colorist, one so sensitive to shadings and their combinations that she instantly knew which ones belonged together. When it came to what mattered, Carl did not speak her language either.

On the way home, Rosie dropped off Carole-Ann first. The two of them alone, Rosie said, "I didn't tell you. Juan Ramón and I talked on the phone for a few minutes this afternoon. He told me there were 'complications,' and that he was at the hospital in León all the time. He says he still has hope. His word is *quizás*. It means 'maybe.'"

"He has hope? It's that dire?"

"Apparently so."

"But what happened?"

"All I know is some kind of accident. There's something Juan Ramón won't, or can't, tell me."

"A car accident?"

"I told you what I know." She was struggling to stay patient. "He doesn't say. All he says is '*Ay, chiquita hermosa*, I don't know yet when I am coming back.'" Rosie paused. "I hate to say this, but I wonder if he had been drinking a little. His words were kind of slurred. Or maybe it was just hard for him to speak English after these weeks of being away from it."

Louise raised her eyebrows. She tried to picture a Juan Ramón under the influence. His hair might be unkempt, his eyes burning with grief. There would be a looseness in his walk, his steps slow and syncopated as if he were testing a footbridge likely to give way. No—that was not it. He would be wild and electric. He would walk and talk with angry bravado to cover his grief.

As soon as she got home, Louise flipped open her drawing pad and sketched another Juan Ramón, emotions naked. She then stood back and studied the sketch. Startled, she saw she had caught elements of someone else. Oh, surely Juan Ramón was not a Carl, a man who could leave Rosie twice abandoned.

No, he was not a Carl at all. She ripped the sketch from the pad and tore the paper in pieces, then dumped them into the kitchen trashcan to mingle with eggshells and coffee grounds.

While in the kitchen, she poured herself a snifter of cognac and returned to her sketchpad. How did *she* look when she'd been drinking? Could she capture the lines of irony etched around her eyes, eyes that once observed her earlier revulsion toward any form of alcohol, not just Carl's, and just as clearly watched its attraction to her now, decades later, an interest that had risen phoenix-like from the cold ash bed of her marriage?

She was careful not to drink to excess. To stumble, to grow sloppy, to fall, that was out of the question.

She poured herself another snifter and moved the easel and oil pastels next to the mirror. She rendered what she saw there: a woman with thick reddish-gray hair pulled back from her face with high combs, a few tendrils escaping around her temples; a face grown blurry at the edges; a straight proud nose, long and, she liked to flatter herself, patrician.

The eyes she couldn't get right. She sketched them as slight ovals, almost circular, revealing in their pale blue an unspoken disappointment. Then, not liking or wanting to believe what she saw, she redid them. This time she would make her blue eyes gleam with hope, even enthusiasm. Maybe being happy was no more than a decision like this.

She depicted the eyes of an aging coquette, lashes long and beckoning. But her trained painter's eye could detect the pentimento, the under-picture buried there. It emerged even now, still visible through the cosmetic repainting, the bones of sorrow asserting themselves amid the determined painted merriment.

Louise gave in to the warmth of the cognac. It intensified her fatigue and dizziness. She stretched out on the daybed, thinking of Rosie and fearing for what lay ahead. She recalled a scene when Rosie was twelve years old, and she was trying to teach her to watercolor. Louise had been startled by the urgency in Rosie's voice, but hid it under a laugh.

"It's creepy how the paint changes itself around."

Louise smiled. "You learn you can work with the ambiguity."

Rosie rolled her eyes. "Ambiguity?" she asked in that impatient tone of voice she used when her mother happened to use big words.

"That means not knowing how things are going to go. It's like not having the answers."

"I hate that."

The truth was that Louise hated it, too. How had she managed the ambiguity in her own life? She was adept with a canvas or watercolor paper. But her marriage with Carl, that was another story. She wondered, perhaps for the first time, what role her own inability to handle uncertainty had played in losing her marriage. What role did it play in her being alone now?

22

QUIZÁS:
PERHAPS

I didn't realize I was drumming the eraser end of a pencil on the table until Leland looked my way and arched his right eyebrow. I lay the pencil down and tried to concentrate on the agenda in this week's editorial meeting. It had been well over a week since I heard from Juan Ramón, and even though calls from central Mexico to California were expensive, I felt he should phone anyway. I resented being in the dark. Above all, I deeply rued not having the presence of mind to ask for the family's phone number the last time he did call.

I studied the three writers lined up on the opposite side of the rectangular table. Richard, the main political writer, a fifty-something man with a wart on his nose, sat straight across from me. He had doodled an extra busty Wonder Woman on his notepad and was deeply involved in decorating her heroic panties with stars and diagonals. I was tempted to draw him and his wart, but then he might be offended if I inked it as exuberantly as he had inked superwoman's bustier. So far, there was no indication he was going to add Wonder Woman's famous Lasso of Truth to his depiction. Such a lasso should hold irresistible appeal for a political writer.

To his right sprawled Bruno, who, like me, was a local news reporter. Bruno had mastered the art of sleeping with his eyes wide-open. He fixed his stare on Leland as if mesmerized by his observations about *The Marbella Beacon's* editorial stance, but a more careful study of his features revealed no affect at all, no indication he was in fact hearing what Leland said.

In all honesty, I wasn't either. I picked up the pencil again and tapped it lightly on my knee. This time I did it under the table where nobody would see.

Leland was stacking papers, the signal he was adjourning the meeting. No telling what I had missed in my distracted state. Everybody was standing, preparing to exit, and Richard and Bruno had already locked Leland into some kind of discussion. I felt pressure on my arm and turned to see Margaret.

She had edged around to my side of the table. She let go my arm and extended her hand toward me. "I just want to say congratulations. Another nomination."

"Well, yes. It was quite a surprise. I had no idea." I turned to see if Leland was free now. But neither Leland nor Richard nor Bruno was to be seen.

"You know that Leland is awfully fond of you," she said. "He likes pretty faces. He must have been riffling frantically through the prize categories to see where else that Mexican story fit. Lucky you. I guess he eventually found a place."

I felt clammy. "I wouldn't know anything about that." I made up some kind of excuse about having an appointment and moved away.

Damn Margaret anyway. Why couldn't she at least let me have a little time of pure astonishment and delight that I had even been nominated again. I had just wanted to savor it a little, even to believe it, and now she had planted the possibility that my story wasn't really worth mention and that Leland had ulterior motives. Typical *Marbella Beacon* backstabbing. I wished she had postponed her insinuations long enough to let me feel I had accomplished something worthwhile, that I was finally a real journalist.

The phone was ringing when I got home. I almost sprained my ankle all over again, clambering over the ottoman to get it. The ringing stopped. I ached with the possibility that the call had been from Juan Ramón and I had missed it.

A while later the phone rang again. This time I was prepared and answered promptly.

"Rosie." Juan Ramón said my name and paused. I would not have recognized his voice if it had not been for his accent.

"This morning we had Ceci's funeral."

I stood astonished as his words sunk in. "Oh, Juan Ramón. What can I say to you in the face of such tremendous loss? Talk to me. Tell me what happened."

He said that he, a doctor, had made no difference in the end. He said a few more things, a jumble of emotion and hurt and anger and self-reproach. At times he just stopped talking, too distraught to continue.

I felt small for having resented his not phoning earlier this week or the week before. Nor could I tell him what was going on with me, about my tiny and trivial pique at Margaret. I had no idea now how to ask when he was coming back. Before he hung up, I did remember to get the phone number, but his voice was detached and dispirited as he droned the numbers.

I dropped the receiver into its cradle, my limbs leaden. I ached for him, and selfishly I ached for myself because he couldn't come back to me. I didn't know how to minister to him from afar. He had not asked me to come there. He bore his pain without me.

Worse than not knowing what had been happening all that time was now knowing Ceci was dead. But how could that be? I spent the next two days in a blur as I replayed our conversation over and over. He, of course, was paralyzed with grief. I grew heavy with my imaginings. Why hadn't he told me what happened with Ceci? Why hadn't he said anything about returning? I would be patient.

Each day, I hoped the phone would ring again.

I had to stop this waiting and resume some kind of normal rhythm. To do so, I would go grocery shopping after work and restock my larder. I would even prepare myself a real meal and enliven it with a glass of wine.

I was in the meat department, reaching for a glossy package of two thick pork chops, when I heard a tuneful call behind me singing "Only the Lonely."

In an instant I knew whose plaintive Roy Orbison voice that was. I spun around.

Monty was beaming at me. He was wearing jeans and a lavender-checked cowboy shirt—when did cowboys start sporting lavender?—with long sleeves rolled up his forearms. His hair was shorter than it had been, but still long enough to curl. "Mmmm," he said, eyeing the package I had picked up, "I see you're buying pork chops for two." Before I could say anything, he asked, "How's your Zorro?" He traced a sharp Z in the air. "You're still together it appears."

"I'm going to walk away from you this instant, Monty, and not look back. Ever."

"You've gotten so serious, Rosie. I was just teasing. Trying to get a little humor into you and a little rise out of you."

"Juan Ramón," I said, pronouncing his name with the best accent I could muster and a flourishing roll of the *r*, "is in Mexico. Temporarily."

"Oh?"

"For the moment." I hoped to God that was true. I wanted to ask Monty how he knew whom I was seeing now, but I already suspected his answer, that he was "a professional." He prided himself on sniffing out such things.

He paused, then said, "So you're going to hog both of those

pork chops yourself?"

"Yes, I'm just such a swine," I said with a giggle, and gave what I hoped was a dainty snort.

It was oddly soothing to hear Monty's banter, that is, if I overlooked the Zorro comment. Yet I did feel as if I were being untrue to Juan Ramón in even this mere exchange. But then maybe I just couldn't brush away four years of my life so easily.

He grabbed my upper arm. "Listen, Rosie, I've missed you. I've been wondering how you are. Really."

"I'm fine." His grasp was firm, and he didn't let go until I added, "Really."

"Tell me something. This new relationship, is it something serious?"

I didn't have a good answer. I hardly knew what to think, what with Juan Ramón so distant, the shocking turn of events, and no word of longing to come back to me. I was annoyed at how long it took me to respond to Monty's question. Finally, I said, "Yes," because that was the truth on my side.

I went home by myself, prepared an early dinner, one mournful pork chop, and saved the other for the next night. I overcooked it, and the pork chop tasted dry and unsatisfying. I wished I had made some refried beans to mush it in and some salsa to brighten both its taste and looks. I also wished I hadn't run into Monty. It sent my thoughts tumbling.

In need of a gyroscope, I resolved to call the family home in León and ask for Juan Ramón. I fished out the strip of paper where I had jotted the number. For several moments, I just stared at the paper as it dawned on me there weren't enough numbers for calling another country and city. The phone book would have the right sequence. After all, people called Mexico all the time, especially from Southern California. I skimmed the thin pages until I spied the right section, devoured the directions for international dialing, landed on Mexico, flew down the list of cities until I spotted León, and then scribbled the numbers: the access number for international long distance, then the country code for Mexico, then the area code for León.

I dialed the chain of numbers and waited.

The call didn't ring. I dialed again. No luck. I dialed the numbers again, in slow motion. This time I got a beeping sound. Maybe it meant I had dialed too fast or a wrong combination or skipped a number or the circuits were all busy. Maybe it just meant the line was busy. It certainly didn't sound like any busy signal I'd ever heard. I reread the phone book's instructions, just in case I had missed something. I dialed again, in even slower motion than previously. No ring. I tried several more times.

Finally, almost sobbing in frustration, I heard ringing. A recording in Spanish answered. By this time, I was too agitated to comprehend the mechanical message spewing forth in static-laced Spanish. I tried a couple more times to complete the call, then stopped.

Fog must have crept over Marbella Beach because the foghorn was blaring its warnings at monotonous intervals. I was glad I had a perfectly good reason to get out of the house, fog or not. I had promised Mama I would help move her canvasses from one room to another that evening. My pork chop dinner-for-one heavy in my morose belly, I drove to her house.

It was rare for Mama to ask me to do anything for her, even though I repeatedly offered. Pick up some bananas at the market? Drop off a book at the library? She had been considering re-hanging some of her portraits for a long time, and now the spirit was seizing her. I was thankful for this task, not only because I was eager to help in some way, but mainly because I wanted to divert my thoughts from Juan Ramón's loud silence and, I had to admit, Monty's sudden reappearance.

"Let's take down that whole wall," Mama said, pointing to

four paintings hanging in her living room. "There are some flower paintings in the studio I want here instead."

I was able to lift two paintings off the wall by myself and lean them on the floor. The other two, being larger, needed four hands. As we were lifting the first, I said, "You'll never guess who I ran into this afternoon." I hadn't meant to mention our chance encounter, but there it was.

"Monty."

I laughed, causing my end of the painting to wobble a little. "Well, at least you could have made a few wrong stabs first."

"You asked me to guess. He's the logical one. I've been expecting him to show up again. Those detective-types like to go over and over the evidence, then revisit the crime scene."

"Crime scene? Hardly. We were in the Safeway. In the meat aisle, to be exact. Peering at rows of shrink-wrapped animal limbs."

I was edging tiny steps backward through the living room, Mama hobbling forward with her end of the canvas. "What I don't know, I confess, is what I do with all this knowledge about Monty." We shuffled into the hallway together toward the studio. "Mama, isn't this painting too big for the studio?"

"Um, I don't think so. What kind of knowledge are you talking about?"

"Minutiae, that's completely useless to me now. But I'm sure it could be helpful to someone else, like a woman just starting out with him. I know how he likes his coffee—a spoonful of sugar, a quick splash of real half-and-half. I know the television programs he uses to blot out thinking and the ones he can't stand to miss. I know what time he likes to get up in the morning, how he likes his eggs—no runny yolks. His favorite restaurants, favorite vocalists. His favorite color is blue, and he drives only American-made cars, unless a rental car on vacation. The co-workers who are asses and those he respects. All this is useful information to someone. Shouldn't I set it down in a kind of Operator's Manual and pass it on to his dates? 'How to Use this Product. Read this first. Safety Requirements.'"

"How about 'What to Do if the Product Doesn't Work'?"

"Oh, that. I should add there's no guarantee."

She stopped at the doorway to the studio. "We're going to hang the painting on the left wall."

Passing on an instruction booklet to Monty's dates—I turned the idea over in my mind. Of course, Monty must have dates. If nothing else, he would need somebody to go with him to all those blues concerts. Well, he was entitled. After all, I had Juan Ramón. I realized the same observation about an Operator's Manual could also apply to Juan Ramón. And would he have dates now that he was back in Mexico? Was he thinking longingly of Aida, tired of his *aventura* with the gringa? Maybe he had learned from his months with me at Marbella Beach that what he really wanted was to be with someone whose language and customs and way of being were mother's milk to him. No doubt Aida still had his Operator's Manual handy.

Mama and I waddled a few more steps into the room and leaned the painting against the drafting table. As I pivoted right, I spotted a picture on the easel, one I hadn't seen before. Clearly, it was Mama's self-portrait. Yet I was startled to see in it none of the charm and verve I associated with her.

"Why did you make yourself look that way?"

"What do you mean?"

"So . . . tired." I had been about to say "worn out."

"I paint what I see."

"That's not what I see." As soon as I said that, though, I couldn't *not* see the dark circles around her eyes and scores of tiny lines. "Mama, are you okay?"

"Of course. I just get fatigued more easily. That's natural as you get older. Now, let's move these flowers into the living room." She pointed to several 2 x 3 sketches on the floor, leaning against the wall. The sketches were matted and framed in thin, inexpensive black frames. The top sketch was a stylized close-up of the inside of some flower, blood-red and vibrant.

"That's a tulip," Mama said, aware I was studying it.

I flipped to the next. It, too, was a close-up, distorted and wavy, this time of a purple and yellow iris. I wouldn't have known that if, over my shoulder, Mama hadn't quietly told me what I was looking at. The last one showed a white rose, again a close-up of those most delicate organs, the pistil and stamen.

"Pretty sexy," I said. "To a botanist."

"Or an artist. To anybody who sees forms the way I do."

I carried the framed sketches into the living room and rested them against the now barren wall. Mama plopped down on the sofa and for once did not take over when I offered to make us each a cup of chamomile tea.

I let the tea bags dunk in the hot water, then opened the garbage can to dump the spent bags. Several large pieces of torn artist's paper caught my eye. I was snooping, but I felt compelled to fish the torn fragments from the garbage. I arranged them on the kitchen counter and was startled for the second time—I should say the third—that evening.

There, staring back at me, was a distraught Juan Ramón. Hair disheveled, lips slack, eyes hooded and more worn out than Mama's in her self-portrait. I had never imagined him that way. What had Mama seen that I had not? And why had she torn up the sketch, relegating it to the garbage? What was it she did not want me to see or know?

I was too embarrassed to say anything to Mama about my discovery, to admit I'd been snooping in her garbage, but I couldn't just toss the pieces back in the can. I blotted the torn segments with a paper towel and wrapped each in another paper towel to absorb the residual dampness. I would find a way to smuggle them into my purse and take them with me.

When I got home, I pulled from my purse the wad of paper towels with the ragged portions of torn sketch. I fit them together on the bed like pieces of a puzzle. Juan Ramón again emerged before me, desperate with grief. His face filled up the room. I saw something I hadn't seen before. My father's face was watching me. Juan Ramón's invisible presence occupied the bed with me, but I felt a greater sense of aloneness. It wasn't Monty's banter I wanted; it was Juan Ramón's sincerity and steadiness and passion. But would he return? Or would he be like the father who didn't?

To block a growing fear, I went into action. I had been blaming this separation all on Juan Ramón, making it his move, waiting for him to call, to reassure me, when it was I who should be reassuring him. His being a doctor had made no difference—he had said those very words.

After my earlier attempt to reach him, I had put the number for safekeeping in a logical place in my purse. Now I dumped all its contents on the floor, but I didn't find the strip of paper. I thumbed through the bills in my wallet, thinking I may have absently stuffed it there.

I was getting frantic again. Methodically, I started over, examining every crevice and fold in my purse, then my glasses' case, then my wallet with all its compartments. Finally, I spied the paper, in a semi-logical place, over a snapshot Carole-Ann had taken of Juan Ramón and me on Marbella Pier. I retrieved the paper and smoothed it out.

I tried every variation I could divine in the string of numbers, sometimes dialing fast, sometimes slowly, then like Goldilocks in a manner I hoped was just right. I rehearsed what I would say to whomever answered. I prayed it would be Juan Ramón.

To my surprise, the phone was ringing. A real person answered. The male voice was higher than Juan Ramón's and with a staccato rhythm. It didn't sound old enough to be his father. Without explaining who I was, I asked for Juan Ramón.

"*Cómo no. Por cierto. Un momento, Señorita,*" the voice said, fluid with courtesy.

That meant Juan Ramón was there. Who would the people in his family think I was, this foreign caller? I wondered if he had told them about me, if they even knew I existed.

"Hello, Rosie," said Juan Ramón in a subdued way I could not read.

Next thing I knew, I was blurting out, "I can't stand this. I cannot be apart from you, Juan Ramón. Not with all you're going through."

"I miss you, too, Rosie."

I could not define the tone. It was weariness and sadness and something else. "I want to go to León. To be with you."

He was silent. "Maybe," he finally said. "I must talk to . . . to my father. I will call you back as soon as I can."

"Yes, of course." How shortsighted of me not to have considered this, that they might not want a stranger in their midst, especially at this wrenching time.

Outside, the foghorn resumed its low nocturnal keening. "Well actually," I said, making it up as I went along, "I was thinking I could stay in a hotel. Not to be a bother. Somewhere near you."

He did not say no; he did not say yes. What he said was *quizás*, "maybe." After our brief call, I continued to turn *quizás* over in my mind. "Maybe" I could come. Why didn't he just tell me to hop on the first plane south?

My call clearly had not comforted either of us. Nor did the foghorn, capricious as ever, moaning up close one minute and mourning far away the next.

23

STORK TREES

Under Don Alejandro's boots, the dead leaves crackled and rustled on the orchard floor. The night was too dark to see the leaves, but he could feel the thick carpet they made underfoot. He drew the new serape tighter around him and shouldered the rifle. Tonight there were stars, brighter than usual against the deepness of the night sky. Stars scattered like distant *cohetes*, fireworks that had exploded so high in the air that no sound reached down to earth.

The actual *cohetes* his sons had shot into the sky all the week after Ceci's death still made noises in his ear. Seven days of *cohetes* for his unmarried daughter. At his insistence, they had prepared her body in the old style, dressed in the manner of her patron saint, Santa Cecilia. The points of the silver crown on Ceci's head gleamed the way the cold and silent stars were gleaming now, visible through the leafless branches of the peach trees. Her face, seen through the netting of the saint's veil, had not looked like her face at all, robbed in death of its vividness.

Here at the country house, the air was always colder than in León proper, but especially now in December. The rains long past, those parts of ground devoid of leaves lay hard and packed. Don Alejandro leaned his rifle against the trunk of a peach tree and loosened the bota bag strung over his left shoulder. He held it above his head and let the brandy stream into his mouth and down his throat. The burn of the alcohol warmed every place it touched, blazing its way through him with its star trail.

He resettled the leather bag on his shoulder and picked up the rifle. In just the minutes it had been out of his hands and next to the tree, the wooden stock already had grown cold, as if finding its own kind in the dormant wood of the peach tree. He planted his feet on the dry leaves, swung the butt of the rifle into the hollow of his shoulder, and lifted the barrel toward the sky. Catching in the rifle's sight the gleam of a faraway star, he held his breath and pulled the trigger. The retort of the gun was loud and sharp. Tears blurred his vision, and the star seemed to splinter into hundreds of tiny shards, forming other more distant stars. *Cohetes,* more *cohetes* for Ceci, skyrockets and fireworks and stars. He raised his gun and fired a second time.

Ceci had defied him again. Since she was little, it seemed she had always tried to break free of him. He had not given his permission, of course, when she said she wanted to move into an apartment on the far side of León with another teacher, a woman friend. What father would? To be closer to her school, she claimed. Although Ceci knew many book things, she had not known what temptations lay beyond the protection of the family. This unmarried daughter, unlucky in love, was yet again unlucky. Carrying the baby of a married man, another teacher, from her same school. The shame of it and the sorrow. Don Alejandro, her father, had been right and she, his daughter, wrong. If only she had been the one who was right.

He drank deeply again from the leather bag of brandy, then reloaded the rifle and took sight on another cold star. He pulled the trigger, and again the speck of light seemed to fracture into a meteor shower of smaller stars. The more he fired into the sky, the more stars gleamed there, taunting him with their distance and invincibility.

His rifle shots brought echoes of long-ago *cohetes* for the babies he and Lupita had lost over the years—*angelitos* they had sung into their graves, throwing rose petals onto the small white coffins and intoning "Adiós, adiós." Everyone lost babies. He had never complained to God. His other lost *angelitos* God had taken from him while he was still young and strong. But this child, this Ceci, where, dear Father in Heaven, would he get the strength to endure her taking?

Don Alejandro laughed out loud into the night. *Cada uno sabe donde le aprieta el zapato* went the saying: Everyone knows where his own shoe pinches. Perhaps he had been too strict with Ceci. Maybe she would not have felt the need to prove herself if he had let her run without trying to slip a harness over her head. Trying to control her, he had made her a rebel. *Echando culpas*, he was the one to blame. Too late, too late.

The night air grew colder in its stillness, and he drank in another stream of brandy from the bota, then drew his hands into the warm folds of the serape. From the road that ran along the far side of the orchard, he heard the cry of a *cigüeña*, calling from its post high in the giant ash trees, the *fresnos*. The stork, disturbed in its dreams by all the gunshots below its roost, protested. Or perhaps one of its young had fallen from the nest. Don Alejandro reloaded his rifle and with his index finger, squeezed again and again into the night sky a fusillade of rockets, aiming for the stars, *cohetes* every one of them, for all his lost children.

* * *

Three good-sized rattlesnakes lay outstretched on the table. Lupita had turned up the oven in the country kitchen and brought him a sheet tray. Don Alejandro lifted the lifeless snake closest to him and eased it onto the tray. He arranged the other two alongside it. Three parallel lines of killer snake, harmless now. As he opened the oven door, he welcomed the wave of hot air that swept across his arms and face, relieving for a moment the cold that now seemed a permanent part of his condition, a cold apart from the rough brick floor and the tiled walls of the kitchen. He slid the tray of rattlesnakes onto the oven shelf and closed the door. Then he sat down at the kitchen table to face Juan Ramón, who had been watching him.

"They still work, Papá? Those rattlesnake pills you make?"

Juan Ramón was observing him with a half-mocking smile. No surprise a modern doctor would be skeptical. Today's medicine made little room for the old ways. "The rattlesnake helps my arthritis," he said, shrugging in apology. Better not to mention how his compadre in León, Don Ponchito, took the pills to control his diabetes. Some people claimed the rattlesnake pills even worked against cancer.

To say such things would start an argument with Juan Ramón. Don Alejandro didn't have it in him now for such sparring. He was aware Juan Ramón's eyes followed his every move. Yet it was as if his son were seeing him without seeing, lost in his own thoughts.

These days since Ceci's "accident," as he thought of it—he could not bear to say botched abortion—marked the most time he had spent with Juan Ramón since his son left home more than ten years ago to pursue his medical studies. With that act of leaving, his son repudiated the plans Don Alejandro had made to ensure Juan Ramón's future, and his own. Such headstrong ideas Juan Ramón had spouted while growing up: one day he would be a race car driver; one day he would own a cantina; one day he would be a bronco rider in the *charreadas*;

one brief month he would even become a priest. Never did he say he wanted to follow his father's steps, never caring about the manufacturing of shoes, the business that had given him his life and secured him a ready-made place in the world.

One defiant child in the ground and here sat the other, enduring his mornings in a kitchen chair, sunk in a trance, smoking one cigarette after the other, grinding them out in slow circles. Since Ceci's death, he had spoken little. The family had together observed the week of rosaries each night at the church. Having somehow survived that searing first week with its stream of visitors to the house and the sobbing that restarted with each new visitor, Don Alejandro and Doña Lupita had enclosed themselves in their country house, Juan Ramón along with them. Alone together, they could begin the slow process of absorbing this fresh loss into the rhythm of their lives. God's will be done.

Doña Lupita, wearing a heavy black sweater over her plain dark dress, joined them at the table. Don Alejandro knew, looking at his wife, her face ghostly against the grim black, that he would never see her in pink or red or green again. With this freshest blow, she would henceforth be like the *viejitas* he had seen in his boyhood pueblo of Aguas Puras, older women who donned the black for a year to mark the passing of a sister, another year for the passing of a grandmother, and another three years for the passing of a husband. Lupita, like those women, would dress in permanent mourning.

"The infection," said Lupita, beginning their daily ritual of discourse as she rubbed the fingers of her hands to put feeling in them. "If the infection had been treated three days sooner, could that have made a difference?"

Juan Ramón, head tilted, blew smoke toward the ceiling, away from his parents. Then he lowered his head and looked them in the eye. "Not in this case. Ceci should have asked for help at once. She wasted too much time trying to treat the infection herself."

Don Alejandro and Lupita could not stop themselves from this catechizing of Juan Ramón, the man of medicine in the family, a high priest of science. Each day they had to go over and over the details, the three of them. Sometimes the ritual took place as they walked across the green expanse of lawn that encircled the house. Or they analyzed with the intensity of theologians as they walked together down the lane where the storks roosted, or they recited their "if-onlys" as they yanked up pussy-willows from the edges of the pond so Lupita could make a bouquet. Together they counted and recounted the days that each stage of Ceci's dying had claimed, each stage of the infection that had poisoned her system and finally overcome her. They clung to Juan Ramón's words as if he, with his knowledge of things they did not understand, could make sense of this incomprehensible thing.

"How much antibiotic were you giving her at the end?" asked Don Alejandro, shifting in his seat at the table.

"Two million units of penicillin every four hours," said Juan Ramón, enunciating carefully as if it were the first time they were hearing this.

"There was nothing stronger?"

Juan Ramón shook his head. "The doctors, they were good doctors. They, we, did everything we could." His voice grew pinched. "If only she had turned to me right away. I would have helped her—in spite of the law."

Doña Lupita rested her hand on his arm. "There was no way she could do that. You were working day and night in Mexico City, from one hospital to the next. Even Martín could not locate you until he remembered the name of your school friend and called you there. He never really expected to find you."

"It was already too late," said Juan Ramón.

"We didn't know that," said Don Alejandro.

The dusty aroma of roasting snake, not unlike the smell of dried shrimp, began to fill the kitchen. Lupita went to the cabinet for the *molcajete*, the heavy black grinding bowl fashioned from volcanic stone. Don Alejandro lined up gelatin capsules on a plate and carefully separated the two halves of each amber cylinder. He would grind the dried snake in the *molcajete*. Then he would funnel the resulting powder into the capsules. With the three snakes, he would have enough capsules for six months, one hundred and eighty days in which the healing properties of the venomous snake would begin to lubricate his limbs and let him move as a younger man, even if his heart would never beat younger.

It was a *milagro*, a miracle, to find the snakes at all in the winter. He liked to think Ceci had sent him the snakes, placing them on that rock in the weak midday sun so he would discover them on his daily walk from the house to the old rural chapel. And it was Ceci who had inspired him that day to carry a hoe as his walking stick. He had used the hoe to sever the nerves in the heads of the sunning snakes.

He thought again of all the things he wanted to tell Ceci. Every night he dreamed of her. Sometimes he was not sure if he had actually been dreaming or lying sleepless, thinking about her. Her presence was never so palpable as when night gave way to dawn. In the dim light of the morning, her spirit hovered near the bed where he and Lupita slept, an angel guarding over them.

How turned around things were. Wasn't he, the father, supposed to be guarding over her? Sometimes he let himself chide her for her foolishness. How could she, a woman who was educated, let herself fall in love with a married man? How could she go against God's will and, sin of sins, try to get rid of the baby? In these moments, Ceci listened to him, taking her lessons with a more obedient face than she had shown in life. Mostly, though, he didn't chide her. He told her about the heat that had gone out of his body, and he told her stories she would like to hear, stories she could pass on to her students. Even in death, she could find a way to use those stories.

Erase que se era, once upon a time, he crooned to her in his dream. He recounted the Mayan tale of *El Adivino de Uxmal*, the Wizard of Uxmal. It was the story of a small man born with nothing except two women who love and tend him as if they were his mother and grandmother. Through the wise teachings and arcane knowledge of these two women, he rises to power. In time, he becomes the king of Uxmal. But he grows too arrogant. He will listen to nobody whose opinion differs from his. "Make yourself listen before you speak," his old grandmother tells him just before she dies. He doesn't follow her counsel. In time, for his arrogance and his stubbornness, the Wizard of Uxmal loses everything he has attained.

* * *

He and Juan Ramón made their slow way along the road where the storks roosted in the *fresnos*. The tall ash trees were noisy again, full of chatter from the white birds. Far overhead they dotted every branch, dabs of white amid the dark green, some moving, some stationary. The ground below the trees was littered with pieces of bark and trailing branches the birds had either broken off while scavenging for nesting materials or that had just sloughed off.

While Lupita was taking a nap, he and Juan Ramón followed their old hunting trail out beyond the ash trees and across the *prado*, a meadow at this time of year filled only with tall dry grasses the color of wheat. Here, some seventeen years before, Don Alejandro had taken his sons tramping through the high grass in search of quail, his sons padding behind him like goslings trailing a goose.

He was glad the sun was warm, but not too warm. To take

this walk with his son today, he had given up his usual siesta. A hot sun, while warming his core, would have only increased the sleepiness that threatened to overcome him.

Juan Ramón wore old pants and boots. With a straw hat tipped back on his head, he appeared like a son of the land, one of the campesinos who dressed just this way and walked with just this same easy knowledge of the ground underfoot. Here on this terrain, with its scatterings of mesquites and huizaches and the curves of the distant brown hills arcing around them, it was hard to picture Juan Ramón in his white starched medical coat, a stethoscope lassoing his neck. Even less could he picture Juan Ramón in whatever he wore when he was in el otro lado, the United States. He wondered if his son might have taken to going around in old jeans, a tee shirt, and white tennis shoes.

"Remember when mi primo Pepe Chuy was so mad?" said Juan Ramón out of nowhere. "He was yelling he was going to kill me, even if I was his cousin."

Juan Ramón pointed to a slope that dropped to a flat area three meters below. "I slid all the way down this hill, thinking I was going to die before I turned twelve." He gazed down the slope, western sun lighting his face. "I remember this spot being steeper. The hill taller." He turned toward his father and laughed. "I can't even remember what Pepe Chuy and I were fighting about. But I really did think he was going to kill me."

"Where was I?" said Don Alejandro. He did not remember this incident at all. Even with the details Juan Ramón was providing, he still couldn't place it. Here his youngest son had been afraid for his very life, and he, the father, could not recall the incident, he who had prided himself on being a watchful papá. Could it be he had forgotten now simply because he was suffering the effects of having missed his siesta?

They walked a while longer until the sun began to wane. Then they retraced their steps across the meadow and back along the road where the fresnos stood.

"Papá," said Juan Ramón, "there is something I want to ask you." He didn't look at his father, but kept his eyes on the dusty road stretching before them. He cleared his throat. "I wonder if you would have any objection"—his voice grew louder and more determined—"if I were to invite my friend Rosie to our house?"

"*La americana?*"

"Yes. The woman I have been with in California. I would like her to know my family."

Don Alejandro gazed down as if studying the well-tended leather boots he had fashioned for himself thirty years ago. "Well—"

They stopped walking and faced each other in the middle of the road. Off in the distance, to one side of his son, rose the impressive peak of the Cubilete. Atop the mountain stood *el Cristo Rey*, a towering statue of Christ with outstretched arms. It was said this peak marked the geographical center of the country. For Don Alejandro, it marked the center of the universe and his family. How was he to go around the obstacles this son and he had put between themselves? How much did they really know of one another anymore, apart from each other's style of resistance?

He thought of Ceci and the harness he had never stopped trying to fling over her neck. She had continued to bolt like a colt, refusing to be broken. Don Alejandro was tired of fighting.

To the right of Juan Ramón and high above his head rose the *cigüeña* trees, full of dozens of scolding white storks. Don Alejandro looked up into the fluttering white of the stork families, chattering and fighting among themselves. One white bird broke loose from the tree. With a series of loud squawks, it flapped up into the air and circled the tree several times, all the while scolding at the other birds below. Then, with nowhere else to go, it settled down on its limb again and was quiet.

Don Alejandro felt sleepy. He wanted to lie down and re-consider what was becoming of his family. But there stood his son, waiting for an answer.

"Your friend—how is it—Rosa?"

"Rosie. I'm sure she wouldn't mind being called Rosa, though."

"This Rosie," he said with a great loosening of his heart, "she will be welcome."

He did not speak to his son of the deep misgivings that still lay buried in him. He did not know how it would be to have an americana in their midst, one who had taken away his son once and would try to do so again. But what stole from a father more permanently than *La Muerte*, Death herself?

24

LA MATRIZ:
THE WOMB

I sniffled with the head cold I brought with me to Mexico and tried not to let my face or shoulders draw near the cold glass of the bus window. Dark of night and the medicine I had taken for congestion combined to make me feel I was floating through a dream. The bus from Mexico City to León, although first class, made frequent and mysterious stops in the dark along the highway. I peered through glass into deep obscurity, wondering why a bus would stop in a place where no buildings or even lights appeared. Then the darkness would stir, and I could make out amorphous shapes, a shadowy underworld populated by people who waited by the road and that somehow the bus driver sensed. Alongside the bus, men draped in serapes stamped their feet to keep warm, their breath leaving smoke trails, light gray against the onyx night. Only here and there a light glowed, as if frosted by the cold, and I would make out the dim outlines of a building.

My first Christmas away from home. Home was very far away now. Home was where there was sun by day, heaters by night. Those tourist posters I'd admired of sun-drenched beaches never gave any hint Mexico could be this cold. What about all those people riding horses in the surf and wearing bikinis year-round?

"Bring warm clothes," Juan Ramón had advised. I donned sensible corduroy trousers and thick-soled boots.

Mama had assured me I should go to León if that was what I wanted. No, she did not mind being alone at Christmas, not really that much. Besides, she wouldn't be all alone. She had her friends. Despite her protestations, I did feel I had abandoned her. Our family of two, divided in two again, left one. But, in my bones, I had no choice.

As the bus drew closer to León, more and more lights appeared. I looked at my watch. How simple and predictable I was at core, I realized, as my heart pounded with anticipation. In just ten minutes, I would see Juan Ramón and feel his warmth. The ten minutes evaporated, and in the press of holiday travelers thronging the bus terminal's main room, there he was.

We stared at each other. He was paler, thinner, and the crinkles alongside his eyes deeper.

"*Ay, mi Rosita.*"

His use of the endearment was the signal. I pushed against him in an urgent embrace.

"*Mi chiquita linda.*"

I wanted to surrender to the honeyed sounds of the Spanish endearments, but his haunted eyes and the deep lines around his mouth stopped me. I also caught the whiff of alcohol.

He slowly ran a finger along the side of my face, as if he didn't know where to begin. "We won't be how we usually are. It will be hard for you."

"Oh, Juan Ramón, I am so sorry. You've all had a terrible loss. How are your parents doing?"

"Everyone cries. Especially my sisters. My father is the only one who doesn't cry." He steered me by the arm toward the parking lot.

"And you, *mi amor*?" I said. "How are you doing?"

He guided me to an old black Lincoln Continental. "As you might expect." He shot me a wild look as he opened the car door on my side. "Sometimes I think the only way to get through something like this is to be drunk the whole time."

I slid in. Hold that thought so you can follow up on it, I told myself as Juan Ramón walked around to the driver's side. But how could I follow up? This was clearly not the time to chide anyone about the why and wherefore of drinking. Nor did he seem to be drunk.

Juan Ramón turned the key in the ignition. "We're going out to the countryside. My entire family always gathers there with my parents for *Noche Buena*—Christmas Eve. This year you will have a Mexican country Christmas instead of an American Christmas at the beach."

The car began to purr, and the chance to probe passed. I didn't know how to wrench the conversation back to Ceci, and most of all, to what he was thinking and feeling. "This car?" I said, awash in the yawning gap between what I was desperate to know and what I heard myself saying. "Who does it belong to?"

"My father has had it forever. It's a '57. This car will last longer than all of us." He seemed to warm to the topic, relieved. "My father drives it little. He goes to the factory and back, a distance of around ten kilometers round trip—about six miles."

Half an hour later, the car's headlights illuminated a large grassy yard, its perimeter outlined by tall trees, and a house—built in an octagon, Juan Ramón said. Its main room glowed with light through floor-to-ceiling windows, rendering the people inside visible as fish in an aquarium. Juan Ramón's family.

My chest was pounding again. The sharp cold intensified

the wall of grief I was about to penetrate. Alerted by the head-lights that had swept the room, the people in the glass house now streamed toward the front door. I was the reason they were congregating there.

My first impression as I stepped into the main room was of a black curtain: dark pressed slacks, inky skirts with fashionable hemlines, dark decorated sweaters, black hosiery, black high heels. Everything dark and well put-together. I felt dowdy and road weary, not worthy to meet the formal dignity of this family in my drab and wrinkled traveling clothes.

A tall, elderly man in a green and white serape, the only person not wearing black, stood to one side of the group.

"Papá, this is Rosie Logan," said Juan Ramón in a tone I found somehow foreign, more respectful and less scoffing than I usually heard from him. Juan Ramón was leaning toward his father, almost bowing.

His father appeared to study me as if trying to understand something that puzzled, even displeased him. I extended my hand to this much older version of Juan Ramón.

His hand was cold, his grip firm. This, at last, was Juan Ramón's father. This was the bullheaded old gent who had become a legend to me in Juan Ramón's stories about growing up.

"Alejandro Villaseñor," he said. "*A sus órdenes*, at your service." He dipped his head slightly in my direction but did not smile.

I met his gaze. "I am very sorry, Don Villaseñor, to learn of the death of your daughter Cecilia," I said in what I hoped was the appropriate way to express condolences in Spanish.

The old man nodded again, this time to acknowledge my statement. I let out the breath I had been holding, then slowly breathed in again. His formal correctness made me question what rash act had propelled me to come here, where clearly I did not belong and where only his stiff courtesy kept him from telling me so.

At once, an older woman with light olive skin and prominent cheekbones stepped forward.

"*Mi mamá*, Guadalupe," said Juan Ramón.

"You must call me Lupita." She smiled and caught my outstretched hand in both of hers. "*Mi casa es tu casa.*" Her skin, warm and soft, offered no resistance. I glanced down and was startled, then pleased, to see hands I recognized, long hands like those of Juan Ramón.

Everyone still stood at attention as Juan Ramón launched into a lengthy presentation of the family. Like an automaton, I nodded, smiled and shook hands with each in turn: Juan Ramón's brother Martín, his wife Carmen, their three children—Martín chico, Tonio, Magdalena; his brother Tomás, his wife Sonia, and their five children—Tomasito, José Luis, Jacinta, Isael, and Andrés; his sister Griselda, her husband Luis, and their four children—Luis Miguel, Guillermina, Delia, and Adriana; his sister Alma, her husband Ignacio Rodrigo and their three children—Nacho, Franco and Alma Luisa; his sister Gabriela, her husband Carlos, and their two children—Carlitos and Gaby; his oldest brother, Luis, his wife Karina, and their four children—Karina, Karen, Luis Alejandro and Miguel Angel. I stood stunned.

Each adult shook my hand; the children in turn glided forward to stand on tiptoe and kiss my cheek as I arched down for them.

The first wave parted like the Red Sea to reveal another phalanx: three aunts, Tía Blanca, Tía Rosario, Tía Sofia; one uncle—Tío Pepe Jesús, the husband of Tia Rosario; and two *primos hermanos*, first cousins, whose names by now I was far too overwhelmed to even try to remember.

Juan Ramón turned and winked at me. "Tomorrow, I'll teach you everybody's other name. Their nicknames."

I was relieved to see a flash of lightheartedness on his part.

I pretended to groan. "You don't suppose they would mind wearing name tags?"

I wanted nothing more than to rest, so gratefully I took the chair they offered. We all sat down around three long tables placed end to end in the dining room. I was the main fish in the aquarium now, and they were watching me do a version of the Mexican crawl.

The ever-polite questions began: Could they get me something to drink, a *copa* or a *refresco*? Surely I would like a *copita*, just a little brandy to warm me after the journey? How was the plane trip? Did I have any problems at the airport? How was the traffic? Was there a long wait at the bus station? How was the weather in the capital, *el Distrito Federal*?

I mustered my best Spanish—aiming for Level Ten—aware of courteous scrutiny. I wanted to do right by Juan Ramón. I was the reason he had left country and this family. Simultaneously, I flashed again on how I had made a terrible mistake. They must all wonder what I, an outsider, was doing among them during this private time of mourning.

Even the children seemed to be inspecting me, perplexed by my accent, staring at the way I wore my hair, the simple bracelet on my wrist, my red nose, the thick-soled boots I was trying to tuck far under my chair rungs, the heavy tan trousers that had just spent four hours on an airplane, two hours at a bus station, five hours on a bus.

As if to a silent signal, chairs pushed back, and everyone stood up. Jackets and heavy sweaters appeared. Griselda, I think it was, brought me my jacket and explained. "We are walking down the road to the rural chapel for Midnight Mass."

As soon as I stepped outside, cold country air nipped my cheeks. Overhead hundreds of bright stars speckled the clear sky, and just the sight of them lifted my spirits. Buoyed by the two Contact pills I had chased with a *copita* of brandy, I drifted along the road with the family, my arm crooked through Juan

Ramón's. Soft snatches of Spanish conversation lapped at my ears. Out here in the dark, with only the canopy of stars overhead for light, I felt more than ever that I was in an exotic dream, and one where I didn't belong.

We passed alongside tall winter-bare trees looming in the dark like burned-out torches marking the road. Ahead of us, the younger family members, confident in their tight jeans and short leather jackets, and with young eyes, led the way. Juan Ramón and I flowed in the middle of the pack with the other brothers and sisters, some walking arm in arm, shadows of shadows under the moonlight. At the rear came Don Alejandro and Doña Lupita, as if shooing the flock along in front of them.

The old indigenous chapel was surprisingly small, with room for no more than maybe forty worshippers, sitting and standing. The Villaseñor family alone filled up its handful of wooden pews. Other worshippers arrived from the nearby ranchos and stood with crossed hands along the walls, spilling through the open doorway into the brick courtyard.

Light in the chapel was dusky and uncertain. It wavered from two candelabras that flanked the altar and from sconces on the side walls. The priest and two acolytes marched up the aisle from the front door, and Mass began. Intermittently, sniffling came from one side of me, then the other. One time I glanced behind me for a moment, and there were Griselda, Alma, and Gabriela, three mounds of black, leaning against one other in the wavering candlelight. Each had a wadded tissue in hand, and I had the impression they were bunched that way to hold each other up.

Mama would want to paint them just like that, a collapsing letter *m*, no spikes, all roundness. There was no harshness to them in their mourning for the absent fourth sister. A sudden desire to call Mama seized me, to tell her I wished we were together, here, there, or anywhere, just together.

After Mass, we retraced the dirt road in near silence. As

we passed beneath the tall trees lining both sides of the road, a bird cried out from the branches high overhead.

"Egrets," said Juan Ramón, who saw me look up. "The people around here call them *cigüeñas*, which are storks. But they're really egrets."

Someone touched my elbow. It was Gabriela. "This isn't our usual Christmas," she said, her voice heavy with regret. "We wish we could have made a big celebration for you. We would sing songs and stay up to see the sun rise."

"You are apologizing to me. I should be the one apologizing."

Juan Ramón squeezed my hand. "There's nothing for you to apologize for."

We returned to the house and to our places at the long tables. Juan Ramón took my hand again out of view. Bottles of brandy reappeared. Don Alejandro and Doña Lupita stayed side by side, and Doña Lupita raised her glass to the family gathered around.

"*Salud*," she said.

"*Salud*," we all responded in unison, raising our glasses to hers. Don Alejandro did not raise his glass. He sat looking ahead of him with the blank eyes of a Greek statue staring into eternity. Perhaps he was as exhausted as I was. I just wanted to finally be alone with Juan Ramón.

How the next couple of hours passed I was not sure, but they involved food. The sisters melted away from the group, then came back. A marvel of irresistible dishes appeared on the table. Platters of carnitas, homemade tortillas, fresh cheeses, baked chicken in chile ancho stuffed with picadillo. Each plate appeared one after the other, borne in the hands of a different sister or sister-in-law.

Don Alejandro presided at one end of the table, and both the men and the women tended to him. They replaced his plates, refilled his cup. More salsa, Papá? Another tortilla? A slice of cheese, an extra napkin? A cigarette, Papá?

I was thankful Juan Ramón stayed by my side, even though there was no chance for any but the most public statements between us. He was caught up in the conversation that rolled like a lazy ball from one end of the table to the other and back again.

At one moment, everyone fell silent, as if all seized at once by the same thought. I was relieved when talk resumed and even more when it started to crescendo, even though it meant I had a hard time following the quick exchanges. Juan Ramón began to tease his brother Tomás at the other end of the table. The brothers flipped one-line quips at each other, and everyone seemed to laugh in a kind of relief to discover themselves still capable of it.

Except I didn't laugh. Shades of my afternoon with Norma and Bernardo in Ixmilco. Jokes were still my weakest spot. I could tell from their tone Juan Ramón and Tomás were insulting each other, but I just couldn't catch the punch line, the double meaning, the delicious nut meat where the humor lay.

Twice Juan Ramón looked and saw the question on my face. He started to explain in English the *doble sentido*, the double meaning, which didn't sound funny in translation. It wouldn't have been so bad if the family had not been waiting for me to break up in gales of merriment. I tried to oblige at the end of the translated joke by emitting a few chuckles. I didn't want to appear dour or disappoint them. This situation was one Juan Ramón and I had been through in Marbella, but now our roles had reversed.

After another period of happy outburst, the family fell still again. I didn't know what was worse: the lively moments when the talk and jokes flew so fast I couldn't keep up, or the moments when the collective sorrow inside them pushed its way out again as brooding silence.

One of the sisters seated to my other side—what was her

name again?—leaned over and said, "You must forgive us. We are not doing what we normally do at Christmas. Usually it is *pura pachanga*, nothing but partying."

"I understand. You've lost your dear sister. How could it be any other way?" I added, "Thank you for allowing me to be here," even though the statement didn't sound quite right.

On my way to the bathroom a while later, I passed the open door of a bedroom. I glimpsed two sisters inside, a black huddle. Was it Alma and Gabriela? They sat crying together on the end of the bed, embracing each other.

I couldn't just pass as though I hadn't seen them. I managed, "I'm sorry, so sorry," then hurried into the bathroom, fearing my words had intruded. I shut the bathroom door and braced myself against the sink. The night was too long. I shouldn't have come. It was too soon for them to have a newcomer in their midst. It was my fault for forcing the situation with Juan Ramón. I peered at the mirror, and my face, paler than usual, stared bleakly back.

When I returned to the table, they were all laughing again. Laughing or crying, either way I was outside the circle. I thought of Mama. What was she doing tonight? Had her assurances been false, and was she really spending this Christmas Eve alone? Always the two of us decorated the tree together on this night. We had taken to inveigling Monty to help with the stringing of the popcorn and cranberries and positioning of the star. Better change the subject.

It was nearing four a.m., and I could no longer concentrate on the conversation that rose and fell around me. I needed to go to bed, but did not know how to excuse myself. To my surprise, Doña Lupita had earlier shown me the room that was Juan Ramón's. "We put your suitcase here, Rosie," she had said, guiding me by the arm. "This is where you will sleep." I wished I were in that bed, finally lying next to him again.

A few of the other members of the family slipped away. My

gaze wandered up the wall to the domed brick ceiling overhead. It was called a *Catalán bóveda*, Juan Ramón had told me earlier. The arched dome had a Moorish flavor. Again, I thought of Mama, wishing she could see this high brick ceiling that seemed to have no beginning and no end.

The direction of the conversation caught my attention.

". . . when the delirium began, by then it was too late?" asked Mario.

The family was quizzing Juan Ramón. Obsessed with unraveling the thread of the matter, they pressed question after question to him about Ceci. He sat there a study in stoicism, answering their probing with the attention he would dispense to the family of any lost patient. Doña Lupita and Don Alejandro said nothing, not taking part in the barrage. There was no way I could leave now and go to bed, not when they were stumbling together to make some sense out of this death. Over and over the details they went, and just when I thought they had quelled their anguish, another person picked up a thread, and they began again.

In the wee hours nearing dawn, when the rest of the family had drifted off and gone to sleep, Juan Ramón and I finally had the room to ourselves.

"They are all so sad," I began in a shaky voice I hadn't intended. "And there's nothing I can do. Nothing anyone can do." I struggled not to let Juan Ramón see my tears. I had no right. They were an infringement on the family's sorrow.

From outside came a sudden fusillade of gunshots.

I gave a start. "What's that?" I was afraid to imagine what kind of malice might be taking place in the dead of Christmas night.

"*Mi papá*," he said as if it were all perfectly natural. "Every night he tramps around in the peach orchard. Shooting off his gun."

"Why?"

"It makes him feel better."

"They were asking you some pretty hard questions tonight."

He looked resigned. "They're trying to understand. It's futile really."

"How are you, Juan Ramón, about—" I waved my hand aimlessly. I was desperate to break through to him. "About all this?"

He picked up the brandy bottle and refilled his glass. "I'm just getting through it the best I can." He emptied the glass.

The silence between us grew heavy.

"It just makes me wonder what kind of doctor I am. That's all."

During what was left of that night, we lay side by side in the bed, not touching. I felt bad I had abandoned my own family this Christmas, even more so because it was just Mama and me. This death had marked us all. Unseen and unheard, I let the tears come until, from total exhaustion, I drifted out of consciousness to the distant crack of a gun going off in the orchard.

* * *

I awakened to festive sun pouring through the window. Juan Ramón's side of the bed was empty, and I was embarrassed to discover it was almost ten o'clock. It was only eight o'clock in California. The slug-a-bed gringa. I dressed quickly and hustled to the living room.

Gabriela and Alma were busy behind the tiled counter that marked off the kitchen area. A tantalizing aroma pervaded the air. Don Alejandro, minus the serape, stood at the sink, to my surprise scrubbing a grill. Another of the women—I was horrified to realize I could remember hardly anyone's name—was setting plates around the table. I was still dizzy and tired, the aftermath of the trip south and sleep deprivation. But the sun flooding through the long front windows and the bustle of normal activity helped buoy me.

"*Buenos días, hija.*" Doña Lupita came forward and greeted me with a kiss on the cheek. "Did you sleep well?"

I was surprised and pleased to be called *hija*—daughter—even though I knew it was a general not literal term of affection. I warmed to the domestic activities in progress around me. How would I have been different if I had been born into a large family like this one? A big, bustling family was what I had yearned for as a child. Here it was, overwhelming in its actuality. So many people to consider. I was made uneasy by what I had often purported to want, once it was smack in front of me.

"*Buenos días,*" chimed everyone in the kitchen as soon as they spotted me. With no hesitation, each came to kiss my cheek, and I returned the greeting and kiss. Gabriela and Alma stood next to the stove, patting balls of masa into tortillas, then placing them on the *comal,* a long flat grill plate extended over two of the stove's burners. This was the source of that delicious smell.

"The maid isn't coming today. For the holiday," said Alma.

"May I help?" I asked.

Doña Lupita and the two sisters looked at me as if I had shot them. *Help?*

"*Ay,* Rosie, muchas gracias, but no, no, no, no," said Griselda, her voice sliding over the string of *no's.*

"*Siéntate,* sit down and have some coffee," said Doña Lupita, motioning me toward a chair.

"I've never made a tortilla. I've always wanted to learn." I studied Alma as she scooped up a handful of the masa, the yellow corn flour mixture, and started to form it with a series of pats, a delicate clapping of hands quick as bird wings.

"No, no," again sang the sisters and Doña Lupita. I was not to work. Please, I should sit down and rest with a cup of coffee.

I had passed a long journey yesterday. I should rest.

"I would really like to see if I can make a tortilla."

"*No no no, mi reina.* You did not come here to work," they all agreed.

"Just one little tortilla," I said. "Then I'll sit and relax from my hard work."

They laughed. "Just one," said Doña Lupita, "because you must not work."

Satisfied, I reached into the pan of masa, just as I had seen Alma do. Extracting a fistful, I began to pat it between my hands, attempting to flutter them together like bird wings as she had. Right away I had trouble. The masa must have sensed foreign hands. It stuck to them like taffy. Instead of forming into a flat disk, the masa was determined to adhere to my right palm in hillocks, little peaks and valleys.

Where were the bird wings? I felt four years old, trying to make my first mud pie. "What am I doing wrong?"

Gabriela eyed my distorted handful of cornmeal. "Perhaps you should pat faster?" she said with compassion.

"It takes practice," said Alma.

Doña Lupita drew near and peeked over my shoulder. "*Ay, Rosita.* Begin again."

I scraped the masa up into a ball and did begin again. I went about the patting with a flurry of concentration. This time I managed to keep the masa compact. Something that at first looked like a rhomboid started to emerge as a circle, wobbly around the edges. I continued patting until the circle broadened and thinned.

"It's ready," said Alma. "Throw it on the *comal.*"

"Throw" was too blasé a word for my creation. I lowered it gently onto the hot grill and watched with a mixture of pride and embarrassment. There it lay cooking, obviously different from the other rounds of cornmeal, but still recognizable for what it was, a tortilla, one that had escaped Darwin's survival of the fittest.

I wondered where Juan Ramón was. See, I wanted to say, see what I made. Turning to scan the area for him, my gaze locked with that of Don Alejandro, standing just the other side of the counter.

"Look, Don Alejandro," I burst out. "See, I made my first tortilla." I then felt doltish because Juan Ramón had impressed upon me what a strict and perfectionistic figure his father was, but I couldn't stop myself.

Don Alejandro looked, whether out of simple courtesy or amusement I couldn't tell. "*Muy bien*, well done."

When the tortilla was ready, Doña Lupita scooped it up and set it on a plate. She cut a slice of *queso ranchero*, fresh country-style cheese, and placed it on the hot tortilla. "Salsa?"

"Sí. Of course."

She dribbled a stream of fragrant red sauce over the white cheese and into the golden-brown tortilla. I carried my plate to the table and sat down across from Don Alejandro.

I bit into tortilla and cheese. At that moment, I had to acknowledge that the mixture of fresh tortilla and fresh cheese and fresh salsa were the most mesmerizing and indulgent and lavish food I had ever tasted. I could get used to this; I knew at once.

Don Alejandro had his black billfold in hand and was rummaging in one of the compartments. He withdrew two photographs and extended them toward me. "Here," he said, just as I popped the last of my heavenly cheese taco into my mouth. "This is a picture of *la vieja* and me when we were young." He handed me a worn sepia-toned photograph.

I swallowed the final bite, wiped my fingers on a small paper napkin, and took the photograph. A smiling young couple sat across from each other in a rowboat. The woman's dark hair was drawn back on one side with a flower. I wondered if Don Alejandro had given Doña Lupita that flower. She was smiling into the camera. The man, who held the oars, sported the trim physique of youth, with broad shoulders and narrow hips. A hat perched rakishly on his head, and a shadow from a willow tree along the bank obscured part of his face. I placed the photograph in front of me on the table. "How beautiful," I said, and it was.

Don Alejandro passed a smaller photograph, a head shot. "This is another. Of me."

Here was Don Alejandro when he must have been around Juan Ramón's age. The long nose, elongated face, fierce eyes— all the same, father and son. But I would never have mistaken this picture for one of Juan Ramón.

"How old were you here?" Yet what I really wished to say to Don Alejandro was how handsome he was in this photo. But it didn't seem right to speak so intimately to Juan Ramón's father. Nor did I want to imply he no longer was what he had been.

"I was thirty-one or two. I had five children."

"A handsome picture," I ventured.

"I was a young man still. But with a family."

For a second, I pictured my own father, as best I could remember him. How would he look now, if he were even alive? He had been blond and athletic when he and Mama had married. I had seen the pictures of him in his sailor suit, leaning against the fender of an early 1950s car. When he still lived with Mama and me, he was lean and rangy, like a cowboy, in work dungarees with a cap pushed back on his head and parentheses of frustration around his mouth. When he had come into my bedroom to kiss me goodnight, he cast over my bed an incense of alcohol and cigarettes.

Don Alejandro was no longer at the table, and it sounded as though he were opening and closing cabinet doors. He returned to the table with a large clear jar of some kind of liquid, along with a smaller jar. He unscrewed the lid of the large container and bowed his head, sniffing deeply of the contents. "Try it." He pushed the jar across the table.

I bowed my head as he had done and breathed in the pungent smell. "Vinegar?"

"Stick your finger in and taste it."

I did as I was told. I licked my wet forefinger and savored the taste of homemade vinegar.

He was watching me intently. "Do you like it?"

"It's so mild, not at all harsh. I like it very much."

"Then I will give you some." He pointed to the murkiness floating in the bottom of the jar. "That is the *matriz.*"

Something vague, like a jelly fish, was barely resting on the bottom of the jar. "What is it actually?"

"Pineapple." I would never have recognized it as pineapple.

"I will give you a bit of the *matriz.* The *matriz* is the mother of the vinegar. That is what you need to make fine vinegar."

He reached down into the jar with a knife and long fork. Holding the *matriz* steady, he detached a piece, then lifted it out and placed it into the smaller jar. Carefully, he tipped the large jar and poured a little of the vinegar onto the piece of mother.

"My son Juan Ramón is accustomed to pungent flavors," he said. "You can take this vinegar with you when you go. That way you will both think of us here in Mexico, *hija.* You will carry a little flavor of our family with you."

I thanked him and held the small jar close to me. Perhaps the father knew the son better than I did. I wasn't sure at all that Juan Ramón would be going back to California again.

25

LIGHT AND SPACE

The spotless black Lincoln Continental, one of the last, Juan Ramón told me, to enter Mexico legally in the '50s, slid smoothly along the two-lane road leading to Ixmilco. Don Alejandro had insisted Juan Ramón take his car. It would be faster and far more comfortable than the bus. I ran my hands over the Lincoln's upholstery. This was how a car should be made, a sofa on wheels, flying Juan Ramón and me through the countryside in plush, old-fashioned splendor. Too bad we couldn't continue along in this bubble. Together alone we were usually fine. It's when we stepped too far into each other's worlds that we lost our way.

A large unplanted field extended to my right, where a lone man crouched over, hitching his burro to a plow. The orderly fields of vegetables in the Bajío, the rich growing region around León, had given way to a whimsical pastiche of landscape as we drew near Mexico City, then morphed into concrete and freeways. On the other side of Mexico City, nature sprung up again, this time in curving slopes and pine trees. As we dropped lower into the valley leading to Cuernavaca, desert cactus punctuated the hills along with small houses hugged by banana trees and tropical flowering vines. Here was no adherence to rules about climactic growing zones, no design I could recognize. Or perhaps it was just a different sense in this latitude of what belonged together.

I had stopped taking medicine for my cold, but still was worn out. For a while at the country house in León, I had rallied as I sipped the hot teas Doña Lupita insisted I take, teas flavored with honey and Don Alejandro's vinegar. Now on the open road, with the scenery whizzing by, I was still light-headed. Maybe, after all, human beings were not meant to hurl their bodies through space at this speed in a mechanical contraption. Perhaps the pace of a horse or burro was more in keeping with the natural rhythm of our corporeal and ethereal bodies.

Juan Ramón's attention was trained on the road. For the last half hour, we had barely spoken, me with my cold, and he—I didn't know.

"Do you feel nostalgic?" I said, breaking the silence, "being so near Ixmilco again?" I spoke in Spanish as I had been doing since the bus station. It was a tacit agreement: English up there; Spanish down here.

"I've come face to face with my former self on the road I left by," he said. "There's a split now. What I was and what I am."

"Are you so different now? It's only been a little over six months."

"A lot has happened."

"You mean Ceci?"

He took his attention off the highway a moment to glance at me. "She's part of it, of course. And the awful aftermath of the earthquake. I saw things I never want to say. You, that's another part. Moving to Marbella Beach. The English classes. My taco job." He followed the word "job" with a truncated laugh. "Those long hours in the house waiting for you to come home. Listening for the sound of your car instead of memorizing my list of English vocabulary." His tone deepened. "The waves never stopped their pounding in my head, even when they were not crashing on the beach. Thinking, thinking far too much. You know how some couples start looking like each other? Well, I found I was starting to *think* more like you."

It sounded as though thinking like me wasn't a good thing. "What were you thinking?"

"Everything. My life. Your life. Our life together. My future. Our future."

I took a shaky breath. "What did you decide?"

"Nothing! Trying to fit together the *rompe cabezas* but missing too many pieces of the puzzle. That's the worst of it. No decisions."

I could imagine the things he hadn't mentioned in his list. The phone in Marbella he was reluctant to answer. The squinted expression on the face of store clerks and some of my friends as they tried to follow his sentences entwined with Spanish syntax and intonations. I had just caught that same expression only two days before when it froze the face of Juan Ramón's brother Tomás as I tried to answer a question he had asked about my work. In Marbella, Juan Ramón had accumulated months of squints, but I had been at the country house less than a week. All my trips in Mexico together totaled less than four weeks. I was way behind on the squint count.

Juan Ramón's frustration over not having enough money must have changed him, too—his expectation that in the U.S. he would surely have more than in Ixmilco. Except for classes he took in the morning, his intellectual and emotional and financial world had been forced to revolve within mine. One evening he asked, "What's a *spic*?" We were in the kitchen, and I was dropping rounds of zucchini into a boiling pot of soup.

I let go of all the remaining zucchini rounds at once. Hot broth spurted up. I turned to face him. "Where did you hear that?"

"I overheard two guys talking."

"To you?"

"They didn't know I was there. Just two guys talking."

I explained what a *spic* was—an insulting name, maybe derived from the word *Hispanic* or maybe from the phrase "No *spic* the English" or who knows where. Over the course of the next week Juan Ramón made sardonic jokes, referring to himself as my spic. I finally had to tell him to knock it off. Although small, the word had marked him.

Ahead, a flock of sheep was blocking both sides of the road. Juan Ramón stopped the car and waited for them to pass.

"Did you like living in Marbella?" It was a question I had taken to trotting out every couple of months. As I heard myself repeating it now, it sounded as though Marbella was in his distant past.

"I like living with you." He had said this before, too. "That I like very much."

"But Marbella, the town, the beach? Do you like it?"

He shrugged. "It's where *you* are." He seemed detached, even preoccupied. A chill coursed through me.

"It will be different for you once you pass the medical boards." I had said this before, too, always with cheerful optimism, as though that one event would make all the difference. I had to believe it.

He turned to meet my eyes. "There is something I want you to know about me that I've never told you." He lifted one palm off the steering wheel and wiped it on his pants legs. "I was married before. A long time ago, when I was twenty."

"Married? You've been married?"

"Yes."

"And you never even hinted at it all this time?"

"I was afraid to." In his first year of medical school, he had an affair with a girl about his age. Her mother found them in bed together one afternoon and began to scream. He had destroyed her daughter! She had trusted him, the son of her *compadre* Alejandro, with her own daughter! After that, there had never been any question about marrying the girl. His father had informed him he would do the honorable thing for the sake of the two families and the child there was sure to be.

"The wedding was a farce. I was drunk throughout the ceremony and drunk all that night."

"How long were you married?"

"Less than two months."

"And you never mentioned it all this time," I said again, anger building. "Did you get it annulled?"

"This is Mexico. It is not so easy to get a marriage annulled even now. Eleven years ago, it was a sealed door."

"Then you are divorced?" It was too staggering to imagine he might not be, after the years that had passed and now after our months together.

"Yes, divorced. Stamped and sealed. Bearing the stigma."

"Why are you just now telling me? Why didn't you tell me this a long time ago? When we first . . . got together?"

The sheep were on the other side, and he started the car again, darting his eyes toward me and then back to the road. He exhaled sharply. "I didn't want to lose you."

I pounded the seat with my hand. "Please pull over. I don't want you looking at the road. Look at me."

The car rolled to a stop on the shoulder. Juan Ramón gripped the wheel but turned to face me. "Two times before, once in my mid-twenties and once when I was almost thirty, I told a woman I cared about that I had been married." His words came fast. "Even if the girlfriend might not have cared, the families did. Whatever there was between us was over before I even got the words out of my mouth. Remember that this is one of the most Catholic countries in the world."

"So right now, you're expecting me to fling open the door, too? You think I'll abandon you? Or were you counting on the fact that I'm older than they probably were and . . . and a less finicky gringa?"

"A little before I left Marbella, before Ceci—" He faltered. "A little before I left you in Marbella, I went to see a priest." He emitted a mirthless laugh. "Isn't that odd? That I went to try to speak in English to an American priest? I had to talk to somebody I could trust. Only the priest wasn't American after all. He turned out to be Filipino. His English was more accented than mine. He said I had to take the chance. He said we couldn't go forward unless I told you."

I felt clammy. "Do you even want to go forward?"

"The question is whether you want to go forward now that you know."

I raised my arms and lifted my hair off my neck, heated and astonished by what he had confessed. It must have underscored everything that had passed between us, at least on his side. "You could have told me, Juan Ramón. Really, you could have. Having been married is not a terrible thing. Divorce is common. It's keeping it secret that bothers me."

"In Mexico it ruined me. Especially at that time. I felt my life was over. I was married in the church. I couldn't—can't— marry in the church again."

"You want to marry in the church? That's something else I didn't know about you."

"It was the girlfriends who wanted that."

I forced a little sound of relief. "When I heard you say you had been keeping something from me, I thought you were going to tell me something I might not be able to accept."

"Like what?"

"I was afraid you had killed someone." It was out of my mouth before I could choke it back, this innocent remark he might see as an oblique reference to Ceci.

He was silent.

"I mean, in a fight or something. You know, in anger."

Finally, he said, "Then it doesn't change things between us?"

"I'm moved and annoyed at the same time. Touched to know you feared you might lose me. Annoyed and hurt to realize just when I thought I knew you, I find I do not." It didn't change things, shouldn't change things. Still, it did bother me he had hid this part of himself. "And these two women? Who were they?"

"They were women I cared about but are now in my past."

On a sudden hunch, I said, "Was one of them Aida?"

"Yes." His voice was even, his eyes on the road again, though the car was not moving. "But that, as I said, belongs to the past."

"It better," I said, attempting more levity than I felt. I released my arms and let my hair fall. I wanted to touch him, his leg, his arm, his face, to reassure myself with some kind of solid, physical connection. But I held back.

He started the Lincoln again. In less than a minute we came to the crossroads that marked the entrance to Ixmilco and its magnetic pull. I was grateful for the distraction.

* * *

Except for the bright piñatas that swung from the corner of the buildings in honor of the Christmas season, everything seemed the same. The rows of brick houses, some painted popsicle colors of pink and orange, the plaza in the center of town with its curvy iron bandstand, the papaya-colored church, narrow stone sidewalks, young girls in tight miniskirts and señoras with blue-checked work aprons over knee-length skirts, all as unchanged as a Grecian frieze. I was about to declare everything was just the same.

A young woman in jeans suddenly appeared at an open door and tossed a bucketful of water into the street. The water sparkled in the sun for a split second before splashing down right in front of the Lincoln.

"So many changes," said Juan Ramón in marvel. "See, the hardware store has moved down the block. And where the bakery stood there's a tire store. Señora Cruz is walking with crutches, and her husband shaved his mustache. Don Beto's *papelería* sports a new coat of paint." He pointed to a small somber storefront on the left. "Look, Don Cecilio's restaurant is closed." His gaze roamed the storefronts on both sides of the road as the car edged along. "*Ai, caramba.* Over there, Don Cecilio's new restaurant! He found a smaller place."

"I hope it's cheaper so he can spend money on better meat."

He didn't seem to hear me. He had rolled down his window and was waving to a boy on the sidewalk. Juan Ramón stopped the car at the corner, causing a slim, middle-aged man who was just then getting out of a white pickup to give a start of surprise. The man hurried in front of the Lincoln and, beaming, thrust his arm through the open window to land two strong smacks on Juan Ramón's shoulder. "What a miracle! You're back, Doctor."

"Nice car, Doctor," intoned an elderly woman from a fruit stand next to the curb. Her face was as crinkled as a brown paper bag long wadded into a ball, but her voice girlish and flirty. "When will you take me for a ride? I'll give you two bags of jícama, one for you and one for your pretty amiga."

"How can you resist?" I said, softening to his reality. "I don't think I can."

"In a little while, Doña Maru," said Juan Ramón to the woman.

The Lincoln inched along until we came to the *Hospital Civil.* The car rolled to a standstill as he stared hard at the modest building. More than ever, I needed to know what he was feeling or thinking as he saw this world he had left behind.

He was right, after all. Neither he nor Ixmilco was the same.

Nor I. It was not just that everything I was now seeing played out against my new knowledge of him, knowledge he had kept secret and yet was so central to his core.

"How does it look?" I asked as he let the car go again, leaving the hospital behind. I was searching for some route to open the subject of all he had abandoned on account of me. More than that, I wanted to know what more lay buried within him.

"There's Señora Reyes out front," he said of a thirty-something woman standing in the open doorway of her house. He was either not hearing my question or not wanting to open the door for the harder question he might suspect lay in wait. "Pregnant again." He chuckled and sighed at the same time as he waved to her.

"Adiós," they called to each other in singsong, drawing out the last syllable. Ah yes, what was it the Beatles sang? You say goodbye, I say hello. In passing by, you say goodbye in Mexico, we say hello in the U.S.

The familiar fragrance of roasting tortilla enveloped us. We turned the corner and were outside the familiar house of *el doctor* Eugenio. In Ixmilco flourished a little patch of world that oddly enough was now a part of me too, although so far from Marbella, Mama, my job, my friends, everything I claimed as mine.

To think that here in this pueblo so far from the *Beacon,* I knew where to buy a homey meal of chilaquiles, and the street stands where you could get the best tacos you ever tasted in your life, and where there was a *farmacia* with a "grasshopper" pharmacist. I also knew where to get a limpia from a green-eyed curandera, and which church bells banged like buckets and which ones sang in euphony. I knew about Don Cecilio's struggles with his restaurant. I was acquainted with handfuls of señoras I had interviewed and with their children. Oh, those sparkly-eyed children. This dusty corner of the world had entered in and become a part of my "totality," just as the old man on the bus had sung when I was leaving Ixmilco.

The wooden gate sprung open, and there stood Imelda. She scowled at us for a split second until she recognized who we were. Then she began to pump Juan Ramón's hand, her black hair-snakes dancing around her face. She wrapped her fingers around my hand, and the pressure summoned up her words during the limpia: You must not struggle so. The pressure in her fingers said I need not make too much of the fact that for some six months Juan Ramón had not told me he had once been married. I need not parse and analyze Monty's phone calls and Leland's too subtle cues. I need not fret over Mama, who for many years had taken care of herself just fine, accepting little real help from me. I need not make any conclusive decisions about my job and where it was likely to lead me. Nor was I to worry over what would become of Juan Ramón and me.

Imelda gestured us toward the wobbly stone steps, and up we tottered. We ascended like explorers through the same untamed confusion of plants and vines and bushes that, for some reason, each time made me think of Juan Ponce de León hacking his way through the swampy flora of Florida, thirsting powerfully for the Fountain of Youth. Imelda escorted us to the patio.

El doctor lay sprawled in a recliner, his eyes closed under the winter sun. I searched overhead for the orange flowering vine that had formed a shady canopy last spring. To my disappointment, it had been trimmed back to a mere single strand. Yes, much had changed.

"Doctor!" said Juan Ramón in a volume meant to startle. It was clear how happy, even excited, he was to be back in Ixmilco. Eugenio's eyes flew open. In one fluid move he reassembled himself and stood. He shook our hands, embraced us, and patted our backs with such automatic sureness it was as if this were his calling, what he had been born to do, be an ever-ready official greeter.

"*Por fin!* At last you're here! I was afraid I'd have to leave for Picholco before you arrived." He hastily explained he had promised to see a midwife's patient in the pueblo of Picholco. "The phone message Juan Ramón left with Imelda mentioned only that you would arrive by the end of the week, but not which day." He scanned Juan Ramón up and down. "He looks a little thin, Rosie. What are you feeding him?"

"She gives me only Jell-O," said Juan Ramón. He caught my hand in his. "You know how these americanas are in the kitchen."

"*Gelatina?*" Eugenio raised his eyebrows as he pulled out a chair for me and as, on cue, Imelda appeared with a tray of glasses, a pitcher, and a bottle of brandy. "Well then, are you satisfied with that diet?" He directed his question to Juan Ramón, who laughed and, for a fleeting second, appeared self-conscious.

"*Pues, cómo no*, well, how not? But, Eugenio," he said, no longer teasing, "tell me about you in your new position. Are you hating me for leaving you as director? And tell me about Ixmilco. I want to know everything. Every little thing."

Imelda poured me a glass of *agua de sandia*, a watermelon iced tea. She set it down and looked hard at me. "*¿Está bien?* You are all right?" she said in a whisper.

I nodded. Imelda held my gaze. "You must take care of yourself, Señorita Rosie." She then disappeared again into the house.

I settled back in the chair and let the conversation stream past. The fast Spanish was studded with names I didn't recognize, slang and innuendo.

The sunshine in this part of Mexico was hypnotic, even in winter, and my eyes closed. I inhaled its smoothness, grateful after the rigid cold of the open fields around the country house. Imelda was right. I needed to take care of myself.

* * *

I had dibs on the back seat. Juan Ramón insisted we accompany Eugenio to Picholco, and I realized with another pang how much he had missed all this. I sat sideways in the back of the Lincoln, my legs stretched out full. The panorama of the countryside now unfolded with leisure as Juan Ramón swung the Lincoln around the highway's many curves. The road circled up the side of what Eugenio informed us was an ancient volcano. As we looped back and forth through tunnels of green, I grew dizzy and again sleepy. I shut my eyes and half listened to the conversation—was I forever to be relegated to the role of listener when in Mexico? I caught something about more money being found for the *Hospital Civil*, meaning they could provide more services. I was asleep before I could hear Juan Ramón's response to this bit of good news.

I woke up when the car slowed. We were pulling into a settlement laid out along the volcano's slope.

"This is the metropolis of Picholco," said Eugenio.

The town consisted of one main road, paved, and a network of alley-like streets, unpaved, branching off from it. Small, unfinished dwellings of adobe or red brick lined the main road. On the dirt shoulder stretched a pair of yellow dogs, dozing in the sun. Mollifying the starkness of the pueblo were wild outbreaks of flowers—red, pink and white geraniums, bright azaleas, flamboyant bougainvillea—along with flowering trees that rose above the rooflines. Not far ahead, a scattering of ubiquitous chickens pecked in the dirt.

Beyond rose the church, unlike anything else in the village. Wide, imposing steps of concrete led from the road to the church's triangular façade, formed like the prow of a ship.

Large and modern, the apex of the roof exhibited a multi-colored abstract design in stained glass. On the ground and protected in an open crate of wooden slats rested the church's bell, not yet installed. I wondered where the bell would go. The sleek pyramidal design in concrete and glass made no room for anything as Spanish-colonial as a bell tower.

We got out of the car and stood together for a moment, stretching our legs. Eugenio, leather medical satchel in hand, pointed out the small adobe house where the patient lived. "The midwife called me in because this is a more complicated case. Today I'm just checking on the patient's progress." Juan Ramón gestured toward a place I could sit and drink a *refresco* while I waited for them.

I turned in the direction his finger pointed and saw a house that looked like all the others, only it had a metal Coca-Cola sign affixed to the side of the open doorway. I had no desire to drink soda pop, something I didn't do even in Marbella. Instead, I ambled toward the church, drawn by the curious architecture. After climbing the phalanx of steps, I discovered the huge front doors of the church shut tight. I hesitated, not knowing what to do next, when an old man in a Panama-style hat appeared from around the corner of the building. The crown of the hat was small and dimpled, the brim flat and grooved as a phonograph record and spotlessly clean.

I hoped he was the caretaker and that in my fatigue I had not taken to seeing phantoms. I introduced myself as a friend of Doctor Eugenio and told him the doctors were visiting the señora about to have a baby. I pointed down at the adobe house. I had hoped to visit the church and wondered if he knew whether it might be possible. I was mustering up subjunctive mood all the way, and proud of it.

The old man brightened. He would be honored to show the señorita the beautiful new church of Picholco. He motioned for me to follow. We circled around to the rear of the building, where he stopped before a plain door and withdrew a ring of noisy keys from his jacket.

This church was unlike those I had seen before in Mexico. The others were Spanish colonial structures tending toward the rococo in their ornate, dark décor, and in the thorn-crowned and bleeding tragedy of their Christ figures. I didn't like the stern lines of this church's exterior, but the interior beckoned with light and space. Sun streamed through the stained glass high in the façade, spilling a palette of color over the center aisle.

I was pleased when the old man said, "I will wait for you outside. There is no hurry."

I selected a pew in the center of the church and plopped down, fearing I was having a reaction to the higher altitude of the village.

The front altar was formed of *cantera*, a carved stone with a scalloped design. Possibly the largest crucifix I had ever seen hung above the altar. Along the side aisles, saints posed atop more modest altars. There was Saint Cecilia, the patron saint of music, with her harp, and Saint Martín de Porres, the Black saint, said by some to be the second most popular saint in Mexico. The statue nearest me wore shepherd's clothing and held a string with a pig at the end. A saint with a pig! I warmed to the idea of such a down-to-earth fellow and to the whimsy of the statue-maker for including the saint's porcine companion.

My hands and lap lay tinted in lavender and yellow light filtering from the stained glass. I could imagine this temple filled to capacity for Sunday Mass, the faithful bathed in downpour of rainbow. I moved my hand from side to side and observed the colors changing from violet to rose to blue.

I did not have my mother's faith, the faith of my childhood, the faith of Juan Ramón's family, the faith of most of this country and probably of mine as well. Was it so simple a matter as just choosing to believe, willing myself to believe? What was it the Danish philosopher Kierkegaard had said—where reason fails, faith begins? I had not been able to make the famous leap to belief. But if just wishing to believe would suffice, I was numbered among the faithful.

I stepped outside where the old man was grinding out a cigarette. "You are right. A beautiful church. Thank you for unlocking the door." I dropped a few coins into his hand.

He beamed with paternal pride. From the top of the concrete esplanade, I looked out over Picholco, taking in the unpainted and unfinished little buildings, the raw dirt, a child playing in a tree, a woman hanging wet clothes on a fence, the fragrance of roasting chiles, along with the magnificence of the pine trees on both sides, holding the pueblo up and gluing it all together. Mama would find much here for her canvas.

Juan Ramón was climbing the steps toward me. Saying nothing, he took me by the hand, and we stood gazing out over the tiny community.

Standing there in the sunlight with my hand embedded in Juan Ramón's, I felt something stir within me, some kind of awareness. I surrendered, letting go the anger about his marriage secret. I let go the desire to understand everything, be it Spanish or English. I simply let go. The same buoyancy and light I had known in the church flooded through me. Certainty dawned, knowledge powerful and sure, carnal and female.

I brought my other hand to rest over my stomach and turned to Juan Ramón. "I'm pretty sure I'm pregnant."

"Sí, mi amor."

The light in his eyes, the way I saw myself reflected in them, just as he must see himself reflected in mine, told me he already knew. I wasn't sick. I was pregnant. Leave it to a doctor to figure out things before I did. He stepped close behind me and slid his arms around my body, placing his hands atop mine.

"I will apply for my visa right away and come join you in Marbella."

That night we slept curled together, my knees pressing against the back of his thighs. I awoke at one point in the middle of the night, startled by the brightness of moonlight streaming in the window. I changed the position of my head slightly, and that was when I saw the moon, full and golden, a harvest moon in late December. It was bright enough to read my watch: 3:40.

I got up and went to the window. The tile floor radiated cold under my bare feet. I crunched my toes against it and stood there, feeling part of something basic and essential. I was at one with the dark and the light, the earth and the sky, and the seed in my belly was at one with the moon, heavy with promise. I was carrying my baby. I was carrying Juan Ramón's baby.

Yes, I was going to have a baby. The wonder of it, the beauty, the perfection.

But oh God. The terror of it. The joke of it. How had I allowed this to happen to me, who certainly, like any modern woman almost thirty years old, knew how to take precautions? Yet I had not. I roiled with turmoil. Where was all my planning? I thought of Norma, and I thought of all the research for my story. The cosmos was laughing at me.

I lay back down, but sleep didn't come. I willed myself to again focus on the joy, the miracle, for I knew that was what it was, even though I didn't know what was ahead for me or Juan Ramón or this child.

26

ON THE LINE

Nobody had pulled the plug on it. The newsroom of *The Marbella Beacon* droned with the same self-perpetuating hum as always. I set down my briefcase and tried to settle into the familiar feel of my swivel chair. The view across the room from my workstation was still a crazy quilt of computer screens, glowing rectangles with swatches of news stories in stages of assembly. I wasn't ready for re-entry, but I needed to talk to Leland, let him know I was back. For the moment, I had energy only to sit still and dwell on the fact I was no longer anywhere near Juan Ramón or the Mexican countryside. Gone were the pine forests, the green walls of órganos cactus, burros packed with firewood waiting along the roadside, stretches of farmland with volcanoes hunkering in the background. Gone were the melodies in Ixmilco of the knife sharpener's whistle right outside the window, the toot of the pickup truck bringing fresh milk from the ranchos. Gone were out-of-tune school bands practicing their calls to battle, and gone was the comforting smell of tortillas over an open flame.

I had tried to rest over the weekend, my house cold and lonely. I was back to living within parentheses, subordinate clauses, and incomplete thoughts. Here in Marbella my work awaited, and my friends (making a note to call Carole-Ann on her lunch break) and Mama (imperative to see her after work). Start to write a story (until interrupted by a colleague who wanted to talk about how he might jack a raise out of Leland).

The conversation with the colleague would lurch along for a few minutes (until interrupted by the telephone). The telephone call would be interrupted by "call waiting" (when I would start to list items to pick up at the supermarket—something to do after I told Mama my news).

Was it a mere three days ago Juan Ramón had driven me to the airport in Mexico City and I had flown home alone? All weekend long, the wind howled, and the waves slammed the deserted beach.

"I feel desperate to be with you and take care of you," he said at the airport. He explained that he had to visit the embassy in Mexico City and arrange for another six-month tourist visa to the U.S., and that would take days, maybe even a week or more.

We held on to each other in the airport, his jacket yielding under my fingertips. I pulled myself away at the security check and marched toward the metal archway. Juan Ramón wasn't there to hold my hand on takeoff, to smoke and make his comments on the ride up the coast to Marbella as he flicked through the Spanish radio stations, then to fish out his key at the front door and announce "voilá" as he flashed the lights on. Nor was he there to keep me warm when the lights went off again.

I warmed myself with the knowledge that there was the baby.

* * *

"At last," Leland drawled, "the native returns." He sat at his desk, his own computer screen glowing like amber kryptonite behind him. "What did you bring back from Mexico this time?" His eyebrows wagged up and down in mock anticipation.

Wouldn't he be surprised. "Just a cold. And some recipes."

"Recipes? Is this your way of saying you want to change departments? Write for the culinary pages on Wednesday?" The way he drew out "culinary" made it sound downright dirty.

"I can teach you how to make tortillas with your own two hands, Leland."

He got up and came to the front of his desk where he perched on the edge, arms and legs tightly crossed as if cold, his mouth in a wry smile. His earring winked.

I warmed to my recital. "I also brought back the mother of all vinegars." I rattled on, sounding to myself hell-bent on devaluing with flippancy all that had meant so much to me the last seven months, especially the last seven days. To tell Leland, the Arbiter of the Printed Page, what had happened and how I had breathed it into me, that would sound, well, too wobbly. In my circle, it wasn't the fashion to risk being wobbly or, worse yet, corny.

"I would like to have seen your customs declaration."

"I wrote 'Nothing of value.' I lied, of course." It was now that I was lying, and I hated myself for playing the cynical smart-ass.

He unfolded his arms and leaned slightly forward. "How about a drink after work tonight? You can tell me the vinegar recipe."

"My place or yours?" I knew the choreography by heart. One part of me enjoyed falling into the familiar teasing banter with Leland, pseudo-flirting that would horrify Juan Ramón. But Leland and I knew it meant nothing serious—okay, in a way it did, but it was its own end, going nowhere, friendship, nothing more. This repartee was simply a reassurance that things between us, such as they were, had not been changed by this "international escapade," or whatever Leland termed it.

"Ours," Leland said, in response to my question.

"Then it's the Back Street Bar again, is it?" I would have to think up an excuse for ordering a bottle of Perrier instead of my usual mango margarita. I wished Carole-Ann could be with us.

"We can drink a memorial service to Tennessee Williams. Maintain the tradition of writers honoring a great writer's passing."

I placed my hand on my hip in mock exasperation. "Again? We had a memorial drink last year and the year before. We've already ushered him out properly."

"This will be a third-year anniversary."

"Even though he died at the end of February?" I was appalled at how hard it was for me to break a habit. I was playing my part by rote, but only out of courtesy to Leland. Truly, I was just too worn out to go for a drink after work, even of cow's milk. The only place I really wanted to go was home. To bed, to sleep, and perchance to dream. I was even too tired to haul myself to Mama's. I would call her from my bed, under the soft fold of the eiderdown, baby chick phoning in from under the wing of mama-hen substitute.

"To tell you the truth, Leland, I can't make it today. I'm just, well, jet lagged. The time difference in central Mexico, you know."

He made a deliberate pout and sniffed. "That's never stopped you before. I suspect you're casting me aside for someone else." He gave a mock sigh. "Someone tall, dark, and handsome? With a bewildering, I mean bewitching, accent?"

"Stop that."

He let go of the pretend pout. He picked up a blue pencil and played with it like a pool stick. "The enemy always comes from the uncalculated angle, not from the shadows," he said as if he had not heard me, "but right out of the sunshine. I should have known that by sanctioning your trip to Mexico, I myself was waving the flag of your fair hair at every bachelor down there." He sat down in his chair and placed the pencil on his desk with exaggerated precision. "I shouldn't give a rat's ass if you're tired."

We were hovering in a moment where the roulette wheel spun slowly. Was he just bantering, or was he, in his oblique way, telling me it mattered to him more than a "rat's ass" with *whom* I spent my time away from work? Could he actually be jealous? I teetered on whether to nail him down. In that hesitation swung years of waiting, trying to figure things out with every man I had spent time with, waiting for and sometimes dreading moves that didn't happen or declarations that were unclear or didn't come or were only partially birthed or that I had simply misinterpreted.

I managed to say, "Fair hair? Watch yourself, Leland, that's such a stereotype. So predictable."

"Well, I must never be that." He circled back to the glowing face of his computer. I was relieved.

"Oh, by the way," he said over his shoulder, "your Mexico story has moved up and up. It's in the semi-finals of a bigger arena now. I'll fill you in before the staff meeting."

* * *

I stirred under the pile of eiderdown. It was eight fifteen a.m., I had overslept, and the phone was ringing. I wanted it to be Juan Ramón saying he was on his way. I picked up the receiver. "May I ask why you haven't called me yet?"

"Oh, Carole-Ann. You know you're at the top of my list."

"Now I'm relegated to being an item on your to-do list?" I was bursting to tell her my news in person. We agreed to meet the next evening for dinner at El Bandido, her favorite. I had just snuggled back into the eiderdown, even though I was telling myself I really had to get up, when the phone rang again.

An unfamiliar male voice announced he was calling from *The San Diego Union-Tribune* newspaper. "We have been following your story on the birth control issue in rural Mexico. Being right here on the border with Mexico, we're looking to expand our coverage of matters that may be of interest to not only our general readership, but would help us grow our readership among Mexican-Americans," the man said. They wanted to talk to me. He asked if we could arrange a meeting.

I bolted upright, flapping off the eiderdown. "I am interested. Very interested."

We set up an interview for the following week. As soon as we hung up, I sprung from bed, suddenly energized, and began dashing from room to room. I must be dreaming. A move from *The Marbella Beacon* to a major daily newspaper was indeed a dream. I could hardly wait to tell Juan Ramón.

* * *

El Bandido was one of those places throughout Southern California that fried every dish in grease, ladled tomato sauce and melted cheese over it, then bestowed some name ending in o. As I sat across from Carole-Ann, I studied the glittering concoction on her plate. I think it was called a Flying Saucer. It consisted of a fried flour tortilla shaped like a giant mollusk shell, its yawning maw heaped with cheese, beans and enough sour cream to spike anyone's cholesterol count for a week. I didn't recall sighting a Flying Saucer on any menu in Mexico.

"What's doing at the *Beacon?*" asked Carole-Ann. "How's our Leland?"

"He's soon off to Harvard to study current affairs on some kind of fellowship for editors. A Nieman, I think it's called. Rumors are that he'll be promoted soon. Not that he doesn't deserve it." I splashed salsa over my plate of potato skins and cut off a forkful that lay invisible under a blanket of mandarin-yellow cheese.

"Yeah, I've already heard a version of that rumor. So twice circulated must mean it's true. Could you pass that salsa?" She dribbled a thin W of red across the corner of the Flying Saucer, giving the mollusk the cheerful look of wearing lipstick.

"I always knew Leland would make it to the top," she said. "Being married to your job pays off, don't you know?" She launched a hefty bite of the Flying Saucer toward her mouth, then let it hover just outside her lips. "What do you think, Rosie, is he or is he not a eunuch? I mean, all these years and I've never seen him with anyone male or fem—"

She started to sputter and fan her open mouth. "I'm on fire. Why didn't you warn me?"

I didn't even try to suppress a giggle. I actually liked seeing each of my colleagues from the *Beacon* go up in flames.

Carole-Ann took quick gulps of iced water. "If you weren't my beloved friend, I would deem you a fucking sadist. How can you sit there so coolly spooning that stuff in your mouth? You're a sadist *and* a masochist."

"Sorry," I said, trying to sound sincere. I withdrew a pink packet of sugar from the caddy in the center of the table and held it out. "Here, eat some sugar. It'll take away the burn."

"I'd say you've gotten used to a lot of new things."

"It seems the more I melt into Juan Ramón's world, the more apart I feel from this one."

Carole-Ann gave me a strange look. "Melt? You're scaring me. Now don't go making any formless amoeba moves. That's not like you."

The pink sugar packet lay empty and crumpled next to Carole-Ann's plate. She had regained her composure, with only a trace of watery eyes. She cleared her throat. "So how are you feeling about your job? Ready to move up to an editor's slot yet?"

"Surely you jest. I can't see myself riding herd over other writers. I just want to be one of the senior writers. I wouldn't get to do much writing as an editor."

I was itching to tell Carole-Ann about my upcoming interview at the San Diego paper, but I really wanted Juan Ramón to be the first to know and was annoyed he hadn't called yet.

Carole-Ann was studying my face. "You look pale. Are you low in spirits?"

"No. It's—"

"God knows I'm no example. I do think, though, we've got to go through life with our knees bent. Like an athlete. Be ready to respond in a split second. That way, if we get knocked hard, we roll like a ball and bounce right up." She peered sharply at me. "This isn't about your job at all, is it? What's the word on Juan Ramón? Isn't he coming back?"

"He'd better." I hesitated, then said, "I'm pregnant, Carole-Ann."

"Oh, shit." She looked as though she had just swallowed a cup of salsa. She laughed nervously and hastened to control herself. "So much for rolling yourself up in a ball to take life's punches." She sighed and fluffed her ringlets. "What kind of friend am I? I mean, are congratulations in order? Are you happy?"

"Happy? That word is staggering. Overwhelming, in fact. I'm certainly not happy about everything. How could any sane person be happy about everything? I'm not happy about Juan Ramón's sister Ceci. Nor about world hunger. Nor all the poor children who live with abusive parents or go to bed hungry or don't have shoes on their feet."

"For God's sake, you're talking like a beauty queen contestant. Stop the Barbie doll speech. I just want to know if you're happy you're going to have a baby."

I let out my breath. "Juan Ramón isn't here with me. I don't know what comes next. He hasn't told me exactly when he's coming back."

"I repeat. Are you happy you're pregnant?"

"Yes. I feel more complete," I said, suddenly shy and in a voice that embarrassed me with its emotion.

"Well, then, if that's what you want, Rosie, I'm pleased for you." She cleared her throat. "Now, down to business. Let's start with benefit of clergy, if you'll pardon that old-fashioned phrase. Are you and Juan Ramón getting married? I assume it's his baby." She smirked.

I threw up my hands. "Of course it's his baby. As for marriage, we never talk about it."

"Well, why not?"

"I don't know. Maybe we're both nervous about putting each other on the spot. Or we haven't fully absorbed the fact of my being pregnant."

We had finished eating, and Carole-Ann was leaning against the back of the booth. Was I being too sensitive in feeling the distance between us had grown in more ways than one? "It was a turn in the road, wasn't it? My getting a Mexican boyfriend and changing my ways. Now I'm going to be a mother and change my ways even more."

"Will you tell me something? Don't misunderstand me, but what do the two of you talk about? I'm just curious."

"What everybody talks about, like what's for dinner, and where you left the car keys. You know, our little triumphs and annoyances of the day, what we find funny or sad." In the telling of it to Carole-Ann, it didn't come out right. The conversations between Juan Ramón and me did not capture the bond. Unlike my situation with Monty, my feelings for Juan Ramón did not revolve around talk so much. His was an exciting and a comforting presence, both at the same time. That was a lot better than talk. So much of the time, talk trudged about in circles.

I was anxious to go home now. Surely I would hear from Juan Ramón tonight. As we stood up, Carole-Ann said, "Oh, I meant to mention this earlier. I guess you're withstanding the usual jealousies about being in the running for another award."

"Leland mentioned something about the semi-finals for an award. I don't know any details yet."

"Well, congratulations, and just ignore the other stuff. Besides, you've got more vital matters to think about than petty office politics at the *Beacon.*"

* * *

Once home, my desire to have contact with Juan Ramón raged stronger than ever. I made up my mind to call him. No more waiting around for a man, or anyone, if I could help it. I would make something happen, even though I dreaded the frustration of making the call go through. I rummaged through my Rolodex for the series of numbers I needed to phone León. But why León? Juan Ramón could be in line at the embassy in Mexico City. While I was thumbing for the number, the phone startled me with its ring. As if summoned by mental telepathy, Juan Ramón's voice filled my ear along with the static of distance.

"I've missed you so much, *mi preciosa.* How are you feeling?"

"I'm fine, thank you," I said, as if speaking with a stranger. Finally hearing his voice, I felt myself retract. "No, I'm not fine. Why haven't you called? When are you going to leave León?"

"I've already left León."

My heart leapt to think he might have already made the flight and could be calling from Los Angeles International. "Where are you?"

"Tijuana."

"Tijuana? At the border? Why there?" I couldn't imagine the chain of events that could have landed him in that sprawling

Mexican border town, devoid of greenery and charm.

"*Mi amor*, I have had a terrible time. I didn't call you because I did not want you to worry."

"You should have called me anyway because I was worried anyway. What terrible time?"

The problem was his visa. The American Embassy in Mexico City asked for proof that he had a life in Mexico. They had to be sure he would return, not stay in the U.S. He had to present bank statements or check stubs from his job in Mexico to prove he had a real life there.

My hopes sank. He had pretty much emptied his Mexican bank account months back to meet the demands of living in Marbella. And he hadn't been steadily employed in Mexico for some six months, so how could he come up with check stubs or recent bank statements? He had received almost nothing for his work with the earthquake victims, and what he did receive was in cash. I feared what he was about to say: He could not come, that was it.

"I need your help, *chiquita linda*. I'm going to cross the border tomorrow night."

My heart thumped. "What?" The words rushed out. "You are? But how?"

"With my legs, of course."

"How can you be joking at a time like this? I mean, how are you going to get the visa?"

"I cannot. My documents will never be in order because I no longer have the proofs your embassy insists on. And I cannot wait any longer to be with you."

"Oh my God, what are you talking about?"

"I will be okay. People cross the border without papers all the time."

"Juan Ramón, please, you can't do it that way. It's loco, crazy. It's too—it's far too dangerous. What if something happens to you? What if you're caught? Then what?" We were entering another dimension. Nobody I knew did this kind of thing. The most illegal act was speeding or fudging their taxes a little. Such was my tidy world.

"*Mi Rosita*, I have to ask you a big favor. I do not want to do this to you, but it is the surest way." His voice quavered.

I closed my eyes. "Anything." Anything to lessen the fear in his voice and mine.

We arranged it. I was to meet Juan Ramón in San Ysidro, the first U.S. town north of Tijuana. I was to drive to a convenience store. He told me an address somebody had given him. He had been talking to people on the streets. The network was vast, he said, vaster than anyone realized. Hundreds of people studied the U.S. side of the border for safe houses, places to merge into the crowd, gardens to take cover in, ways to disappear into the bubbling stew of Southern California's many cultures.

He said that the store was on a steep hill, and across from it was a large empty lot where I could park my car and stay inside, the doors locked. All I had to do was wait. Once again.

* * *

He leaned against the brick wall of a run-down neighborhood store optimistically called El Porvenir, The Future. Down below, the ocean was sluggish but oddly vivid under the harsh searchlights beaming from the U.S. side. Even from his high vantage point, he could sniff the odor of seaweed decaying on the beach and hear the wash of waves, the sound amplified as it lifted up the eleven or twelve meters to the top of the steep cliff. On the beach below, a knot of men formed and reformed as, young and old, they studied the ocean and calculated their chances of swimming or dashing to *el otro lado*, the other side, as the United States was called. Juan Ramón contemplated the large group of his paisanos. "*Pobres diablos*," he said to himself, then laughed at the irony. For want of the proper papers, here he stood, also one of those poor devils.

He thought of his father, his back straight as the barrel of a rifle, walking kilometers to his factory at six o'clock each morning. His father was well able to drive the Lincoln Continental. He was well able, for that matter, to pay someone to drive him to the place he had been going every day at this hour for the last forty years. The walking was a matter of choice, Don Alejandro insisted. Everything we do is ultimately a matter of choice. Juan Ramón didn't want to think about what his father would say about this choice his son was now making.

Someone tugged at Juan Ramón's sleeve. "Let's go." The man, slim and weasel-like, led Juan Ramón several long blocks away from the sea to a corner dark and unpopulated. Minutes later, a dusty city bus wheezed to a stop beside them. The man signaled, and they both jumped on.

Juan Ramón grasped a pole in the front of the crowded bus. He tried to keep from bumping into a young woman who stood next to him. With one arm crooked around the same pole, she pressed a bright woven bag against it for balance, cradling a baby with the other arm. The bus swayed around the corner as the woman and baby simultaneously swayed toward him. Mother and child gazed at him blankly. Something about the curve of the woman's mouth, a curve repeated in the miniature mouth of the baby, drew him. The wan face of Ceci rose in his mind, her eyes vacant in death.

Then a tug on his sleeve and they were bounding down the metal stairs of the bus, springing from the last step like buck deer and across a barren field to the north. Their feet pounded on the hard-packed ground as they ran uphill. Without explanation or hesitation, the man guided him to a hole in the fence. Quiet as ghosts, they passed through.

"You're in *gringolandia* now, *cabrón*," said the man. Again, quiet as a ghost, the man passed back into Mexico. "Run," he said, and vanished.

Juan Ramón darted across the dirt road that paralleled the length of the border fence.

He began to run hard. Suddenly he saw brilliant light. He dashed behind a bush, eyes and ears alert, heart loud in his chest. Moving pools of light from a helicopter raked the terrain. He pressed himself further into the bush. The helicopter continued to hover, radiating deafening noise. He didn't move. Barely breathed.

The stark circle of light swept away from him. He left the safety of the bush and began to run again, running like a hunted animal. This was not the running of the soccer field in his teenaged years, nor the running of the tennis court in his twenties. He had not run this way for more than nineteen years. Not since he was a boy and had bloodied the nose of his cousin Pepe Chuy, who had sworn to kill him, *hijo de una cabronsísima madre*, for the indignity. He had been eleven years old and slipping down the matted grass of the embankment, daring to glance back over his shoulder and see Pepe Chuy waving the hunting gun as he gained on him, the ire on his cousin's face showing he had forgotten about the quail they had come to shoot, forgotten about everything but settling the score with Juan Ramón in blood.

Now he was slipping again. At the foot of the hill, his feet pressed into something wet and soft. He had landed in mud. Ah yes, the man had told him about patches of watermelon growing in the narrow gulches, planted for his paisanos so those jumping the border could have something wet and sweet to sustain them as they sucked in desperate drafts of the dry air. He doubted the story but felt for a melon anyway in the betraying moonlight. His fingers closed around a dry vine, but it was bare.

He clambered to his feet. The leather of his shoes—the wrong shoes, how stupid, he had worn the wrong shoes for running—made low sucking sounds as he forced them from the mud. He began to run again, his feet heavy, fatigued.

Rosie would be waiting for him. He longed to have this all done with so he could rest and enfold her in his arms. He had to protect her now more than ever.

He zigzagged across fields, passing small farms. He avoided another glaring circle of light, almost supernatural in its distinctness from the night. A helicopter hovered as people were being detained. He thought he glimpsed the bright shopping bag of the young woman with the baby he'd seen on the bus.

His lungs were about to burst. The face of Ceci teased again at the edge of his consciousness. If everything we do is choice, Papá, what choices did Ceci have? How could she possibly have chosen the blood-smeared sheets? He forced his sister's white face from his mind, and instead pictured Rosie, waiting with their baby within her.

And his own choices? He had chosen to give up the clinic, his patients, friends, family, his country. He had chosen not to fight the complications with his visa. Instead, he had chosen to run like prey. Not to do so would have been to choose, by default, a consequence that betrayed every fiber of his Mexican honor. He would not abandon his unborn child. He had chosen Rosie.

Now everything left in him focused on getting to the town of San Ysidro and back to her. He would ensure that everything was all right this time. He would work hard, even harder than before. He needed more money than ever. He had only to get to where she would be waiting as she had promised.

He made a reckless sign of the cross, bowed his head, and ran.

* * *

I looked at my watch: 8:27 p.m. I was in my car, waiting, just as we had agreed. I tapped my fingers on the dashboard, then on the steering wheel, then on my watch face, as if that would bring him faster. Despite the hot Santa Ana wind, I kept the windows rolled up. I felt safer that way.

For weeks I had been dead tired with exhaustion. If I hadn't known I was pregnant, I would have thought I had contracted a fatal disease. Now I was hyperalert. I tried to calm myself with the thoughts of the life growing inside me. Yesterday I had stood riveted to the floor in Waldenbooks, unable to take my eyes from the full-page photographs of an embryo as it evolved over the weeks. By now the baby should be slightly bigger than a glob of spit. Just thimble size. With a quickly beating heart. Was that the real reason Juan Ramón was risking this crossing, coming back for this thimble with a heart?

I glanced at my watch again. The 7-Eleven store cast a bright glow some thirty yards to the right. Customers entered and exited as if on stage. Two teenaged boys in tight jeans pushed the door open as far as it went, guffawing so loudly I could hear them even through the rolled-up windows. Behind them hurried a middle-aged woman with what appeared to be a six-pack cradled in her arms. A wiry man in paint-flecked pants limped toward the door.

As the customers backed their cars out of the lot, their headlights raked my vacant patch of dirt like a lighthouse beacon and, for a split moment, illuminated my hands where I held tight to the steering wheel. Immediately to my other side stretched darkness, but a darkness relieved in the distance below by the jeweled carpet of Tijuana's lights.

The previous night, I had slept fitfully after Juan Ramón's call. I was eager to tell him about my upcoming interview, but the time wasn't right. I lay there willing myself to fall asleep. A tumbling mass of images ensured I did not. I pictured Juan

Ramón pinned in the searchlight of the Border Patrol helicopters, or Juan Ramón jumped by bandits, or Juan Ramón felled by a car as he dared to dart across the freeway. Or, if he came by way of the beach, Juan Ramón churning in the black sea, pulled further out by the infamous riptides off the border's Imperial Beach.

Waiting, that's what we women are supposed to do naturally. If Carl Jung was right, and we carry centuries of ancestral memory within us, this waiting should be something we females are adept at by now.

But my genes were impatient, despite those millennia of women, that unbroken chain of female ancestors, waiting. My genes had already waited with the Ithacan girl-woman who had spun tapestries for ten years after the Trojan War, waiting for her man to come home—and then believed his stories. They had waited with the Roman maiden who bathed and powdered while hoping to see her centurion crest one of the Seven Hills. They were with the medieval lady who hunched over an imperfect map, trying in vain to make out the letters of a place called Asia Minor while feeding six kids and waiting for her crusading knight to ride westward again. They were embedded in the fishwife whose eyes roamed the night seas, waiting long weeks for a wandering husband who still had not sailed home. Despite all this gene training bred into me through the generations, not to mention throughout my own life, I was as nervous and restless as a novice. I waited and I waited.

A sound startled me out of my exhaustion. Footsteps? The sound was coming closer. I started sweating. The amorphous dark took shape. A person was running, actually running, right toward me. I double-checked that the doors were locked. I held my breath. A man lunged at the door handle, rattled it, then swore. The man's face appeared at the window.

I cried out, half in terror, half in relief, to see Juan Ramón.

Jolted with adrenaline, I unlocked the door as quickly as I could and started the engine.

He jumped into the seat. With him came the smell of sweat, salt, dirt, and the acrid odor of fear. He grabbed me to him and kissed me, a kiss that lasted for only a second, fast and hard but long enough to feel the nervous current in his body, the adrenaline in his touch.

"Let's go!"

I threw the car into reverse, then angled forward and crossed the parking lot of the 7-Eleven. No sign of pale green Border Patrol vehicles. Through the windshield, the lights of the lot spotlighted the mud smeared along Juan Ramón's pant leg. He sat unmoving, staring straight ahead, his mouth tight.

"Juan Ramón? Are you okay?"

His voice broke. "I am an animal. An animal running from hunters."

I fought the urge to stop the car and encircle him in my arms. I released my right hand from the steering wheel and rested it for a moment on his leg. "It's over. *Gracias a Dios.* You're safe now." I wasn't so sure, though.

"Let's go!"

I rolled into the street, driving neither fast nor slowly. Best not to call attention. I drove several blocks, listening as Juan Ramón's labored breathing fell back to normal.

After a few more blocks, he asked me to pull over to the curb. As soon as the car stopped, he drew me to him. "*Mi chiquita linda,*" he said. "You have no idea." Then he kissed me, his lips insistent with commitment.

Our mutual fear for what he had just gone through to get back to me and our baby mingled with my hope for a better future together. It also mingled with my uncertainty for what lay ahead.

I was afraid in a new way than I had been while waiting in

the dark. Now he was here illegally. It was more dangerous than ever for him to work. He could be caught up in a sweep and deported at any moment, never allowed to return.

27

GOD MUST BE
A GRINGO

The sun, low in the sky, glinted off the chrome of the cars parked on the lot of Morton's Chevrolet. Juan Ramón had not made a sale all week. His legs ached from so much standing around. The hot, dry Santa Ana winds had been blowing for three days. He wished he could plop down and yank off his shoes, but neither of those two wishes would ride well with the management. He could imagine the Voice. It would come on the loudspeaker and boom all over the lot. The Voice would utter something cryptic enough that the customers would not know what was said, and just menacing enough so Juan Ramón would.

"Ray," the Voice always called him, shortening and anglicizing his name. "Ray, immediate adjustment required. Ray, report to the sales office at once."

The small number of customers, what they referred to here as the "traffic," wasn't the worst thing about this job. The worst thing was the *maldita* Voice. On the second floor of the Chevrolet agency, encased behind walls of tinted glass, presided the sales manager with the Voice. From his high tower in the center of the lot, the sales manager commanded a view of the entirety of Morton's Chevrolet, almost a full acre of vehicles, new and used. The Voice's main purpose during the day was to make sure that each of the salesmen "turned."

Never was a salesman to allow a member of the public to wander off among the cars on his own or simply leave the lot. Even if "just looking," that potential customer must be turned—passed on to another salesperson—who likewise must turn the customer to a fresh salesperson should the customer show signs of hesitancy, or worse yet, start to wander away. Through this strategy of a full-court press with a multiplicity of sales patter and personalities, a perfect match might be found. The right salesman for this particular customer would enter the process at the crucial moment. The right salesperson would complete the grinding down and clinch the sale. Sometimes a pot of beans was about to burn on the stove at home; the customer suddenly remembered and split. Or the customer disappeared into the agency's restroom. When this happened, the Voice would summon: "Ray!"

It cost Juan Ramón a bit of effort to remember that this "Ray" referred to him. He always responded with a start to this new name the sales manager pinned on him. Ray would then make his way to the glass tower to explain what had happened, how the customer had managed to get away without being turned. *Mea culpa, mea culpa, mea maxima culpa.*

Juan Ramón shifted from foot to foot, as if a dancing bear, trying to alleviate the burning that coursed down the back of his legs and into his feet. Southern California sun streamed onto the tarmac with no clouds to soften its intensity, only the Santa Ana winds that put a jagged edge on the already dry air. He glanced over his shoulder and squinted as the sun bounced off the glass tower in a blinding flare. He turned away to seek relief for his strained eyes but saw only more sun as bright beams ricocheted off windshields. At moments like this, the car lot glistened and sparkled in surreal brilliance.

A customer appeared on the left side of the lot where the used cars were located. At once, Juan Ramón went into motion, heading toward the man with a newly acquired gait, not too eager, not too reluctant. Juan Ramón had told Rosie that working at the car lot was like being trapped in an electronic police state. The sales manager saw and heard all from his tower, just as he no doubt was watching this moment from on high as Juan Ramón approached the customer.

Juan Ramón had been back in Marbella almost five weeks now, three of those at Morton's Chevrolet. He reminded himself daily he was passing time on this arid lot only for the money. With his mechanical sense and knowledge of cars, he had believed he would make more money selling cars than shoving tacos into take-out bags. To get the job required little identification. The car agency, close to the barrio on Marbella's main street, had not been fussy about paperwork. Morton's Chevrolet was more interested in getting someone who could speak Spanish, had good "presentation," meaning clean shaven, properly attired and well-spoken, and someone who had few, or no, other options.

The customer stopped in front of a cream-colored 1979 Monte Carlo. The man was of medium height, stocky and broad shouldered, with sleek, dark hair and a neat mustache. He looked to be latino, probably in his early thirties. His long-sleeved polyester shirt was unbuttoned several notches down his chest, and the V of its opening enshrined a large cross set with rhinestones or cubic zirconia or, who could tell, perhaps real diamonds.

Juan Ramón was desperate to make a sale. The baby would need clothes, a crib, car seat, stroller, a walker. He could not let Rosie take sole responsibility for those bills. It bothered him that he couldn't tell her to quit her job, that he could take care of her.

"Good afternoon," Juan Ramón said, then "*Buenas tardes*,"

covering both bases. "I'm Juan Ramón. You can call me Ray." Without taking his eyes off the car, the man returned his greeting in Spanish.

"This one's in great condition," said Juan Ramón, resigned to his sales pitch, now in Spanish. "It's got a 350 engine and only 50,000 miles." The man looked up. His gaze was patient and calculating at the same time. "This isn't what I came to look at, hombre. You should show me the new Corvettes, Ray. And you can call me Francisco."

The sun leapt off the stone in the pinkie ring of Francisco's right hand and tagged the cross on his chest. As the windshields glinted around them, Juan Ramón had the illumined idea that this guy was exactly where he belonged. Francisco had come to just the right gleaming, squinting, sparkly place. Maybe he was only looking. But maybe those really were diamonds set in the cross and several rings that winked and flirted on his stubby fingers.

The twinkle from the stones sparked Juan Ramón's spirits and allowed him to disregard the ache in his legs. If he could clinch the sale of a new Corvette, the commission would go a long way toward a nest egg. The salesmen knew the agency tinkered with the commissions for the used car sales, but what could they do except quit? Twenty percent on the profit, the sales manager said, the salesperson gets twenty percent on the profit. When the salesman's check was drawn, it was always a shock to see how little profit the agency allowed on the car. Turns out it had needed new shock absorbers, balancing of the tires, another clutch, and, of course, a smog check. At least with a new car, the salesman stood a better chance of making more than forty or sixty dollars on the sale, since there was nothing to fix.

Juan Ramón angled in and out of the rows of cars, escorting the man toward the showroom where a new black

Corvette waited, sleek and fierce, its lustrous layers of paint as hypnotic as the pool of Narcissus. Francisco stood and stared at the Corvette. His reflection was unwavering in the lustrous paint. He appeared besotted.

The sales manager suddenly materialized, taking no chances. Francisco said in English to the sales manager, "I will take Ray here for a short ride. I've had the pleasure of driving these Corvettes before. But Ray here, I know he could use a little break."

Juan Ramón backed the Corvette out of the showroom and onto the lot. The constant growl of the engine and the car's hard-edged design spoke the language of masculine power. Juan Ramón turned the car over to Francisco and situated himself in the passenger seat. Francisco accelerated, and with a snarl of reassurance, the Corvette pulled onto a side street of pale stucco houses. He accelerated again, and the car slid into second with a surge and a roar. Keeping his eyes on the street ahead, he said, "Paisano, this is the way to live, no?"

Juan Ramón laughed. *"Pues, sí.* If you've got it to spend, why not? Life is too short." He leaned back his head, rubbed his chin, and considered the neighborhood they were growling through still in second gear. All around stood small houses, some with chain link fences outlining their front yards, some with borders of sea lavender or geranium instead of a fence. Here and there old newspaper pages lay flattened against the fences or hedges, pinned like giant moths. Cars parked on the street were older models, with dents and faded paint in need of washing. Clearly, the people here didn't have *lana*—cash— to spend any more than a country-doctor-turned-car-sales- man. No doubt they too were trying to amass just enough for diapers or a stroller or crib. Here were his people, his patients. But he couldn't attend them.

Francisco circled through the neighborhood and found the entrance to the 101-freeway going north. "I have been very lucky in business, amigo," he said, snapping the car up through the gears. In seconds, the Corvette had surpassed the freeway's fifty-five mile per hour speed limit.

"I imagine so," said Juan Ramón. He didn't ask Francisco how he earned his money. He already had a good idea. The metal reflectors that separated the lanes of cars whizzed by in a solid seam.

"In case you are wondering, Ray, I make investments. The investment business is very good."

He angled the Corvette over to the fast lane, and although the speedometer read eighty-five miles per hour, Juan Ramón could tell only a small part of the Corvette's torque had been unleashed. Francisco switched on the radio and adjusted the knobs until he found a station in Spanish with Mexican ranchero music. The wind through the open window ruffled Juan Ramón's hair and, although warm, gave him the most relief he'd had all day from the unrelenting heat. He hovered on the edge of feeling carefree, but he didn't want the car's speed to get them pulled over.

El Rey, sung by Vicente Fernández, leapt from the radio. Francisco bellowed out the chorus of the song, affirming a man's determination to live life on his own terms.

Juan Ramón raised his voice in unison. What impulse rendered him and his countrymen unable to resist the siren call of music, joining in song wherever and whenever they heard familiar music in Spanish, be they strangers in bars and restaurants, on the street, at parties, united by this urge to meld their sorrows or worries or triumphs in collective harmony? These same strangers belted out lyrics with gusto, burst out with trills and wrenching cries, even sometimes wept together, strangers no longer, joined by universal pain and longing.

El Rey was followed immediately by *Volver, Volver,* a yearning to return to what was. Juan Ramón and Francisco threw back their heads, opened their throats, and cried out the refrain as Juan Ramón prayed he was not, like the man in the song, on his way to locura.

At the end of the song, Francisco said, "*Oye*, Ray, listen, I like to see my paisanos do well here in Yankee land. That's the only way you get the respect."

He kept his eyes trained ahead, never even glancing at Juan Ramón. "You are a man of good presentation, and you seem intelligent. I know ways you can make real money. More money than I am sure you're making in that, permit me to say, *pinche* car lot. Of course, you must have a taste for risk, like any business."

Francisco had exited the freeway and was looping around to catch the same freeway going south, back in the direction of Morton's Chevrolet.

Despite the expensive hum of the car on the open road, the songs, and the wind through the window, Juan Ramón still hadn't managed to make himself carefree. That idealized state of being ran before him faster than the Corvette and more taunting than the ranchero laments.

Juan Ramón said, "I'm sure there are better ways to earn money than sweating like a pig in the sun all day." He was pretty sure where the dialogue was going.

"There are money-making strategies, amigo, and you would be surprised how easy it is." Francisco turned and looked full-face at him now. "Of course, you have to be a man of vision. A man who sees opportunities, sees the future, and doesn't let either get by him." He turned his own vision back to the road. "A man with feet and head as fast as this Hugo Sánchez, no?"

Juan Ramón's throat was dry, but he managed to say, "The best Mexican soccer player in the world, his golden feet now playing for Real Madrid in Spain. A man as fast as this Corvette, no?" He rapidly projected how his days and nights would be in what Francisco termed the investment business. Here in California, he hadn't seen many Mexicans who had made it big. He had seen some Chicanos who by the second or third generation had risen to middle-class status, but they were now Americans, not his paisanos, and they weren't rich either. There were some *ricos* here from Mexico, but they had made their money in the big cities, in Guadalajara, Monterrey, or Mexico City, and then come here to splurge on spacious beach condos, electronics, and top-of-the-line athletic shoes. The huge majority of his fellow Mexicans were poor laborers hungry for a job. Nobody was rich, except a few of those who were *abajo el agua*, or, as was said here, off the books.

He couldn't see himself carefree in Francisco's world, or perhaps any world, even when, seemingly in harmony, he cried out the words of the song with Francisco and the now ninety-mile-per-hour wind parted his hair. Four months since December, and he had not managed to put Ceci out of his daily thoughts. Nor could he stop worrying about Rosie. She should not be working such long hours. Always there was the glaring contradiction between how he thought his life should go and how it was actually going. Francisco's beguiling rings adorning the steering wheel were one more reminder.

Juan Ramón clenched his jaw. What was he doing here, anyway? This wasn't his country. This wasn't his calling. Francisco wasn't his friend. And just being here, working without proper entry papers, he was very much *abajo el agua*, even though he had fooled himself he was not.

The Corvette glided down the off-ramp, and within minutes they were in sight of the tall signs for Morton's Chevrolet. The sun had weakened as afternoon drew on, and now the car lot appeared lackluster as the glass tower threw shadow over it.

To close the deal was a quick matter. Francisco indicated he didn't need financing. The Corvette cost twenty-nine thousand dollars. He would pay half in cash and half by check. In the cubicle where the final papers were signed and where the sales manager continued to preside, Juan Ramón watched with envy as Francisco unpeeled a roll of hundred-dollar bills, his jewelry flashing under the artificial light. He counted out fourteen thousand five hundred dollars, then wrote a check for the balance. He snapped the checkbook shut and took a sip of the coffee Juan Ramón had brought him.

Juan Ramón tried to imagine what it could be like to live with enough money in the bank to be able to buy a Corvette for cash off the showroom floor.

When the sales manager left the room to verify the check, Francisco said, "Let me tell you, Ray. Anytime, I mean *anytime*, you feel you're ready to take the chance and go into the investment business, I got a job for you, Ray." Francisco reached into his pants pocket for his wallet and withdrew a business card. "Take my card. Think about what I told you. Like I tell you, Ray, I want to see my paisanos looking good." He slid along the vowels in "good," making it two syllables for emphasis.

Juan Ramón took the card, and they shook hands. The Corvette was brought forward. It idled loudly, welcoming its new owner. Juan Ramón held open the driver's door. Francisco slid in, turned up the radio, and again ranchero wails floated out the windows. He touched one side of his forehead in salute to Juan Ramón.

Juan Ramón shut the car door gently, and it sounded with the crisp click of an expensive door mechanism. The Corvette lurched from the curb. With a snarling display of thrust, the dark streak of car was down the street before Juan Ramón could finish reading the business card.

Francisco Torres was inscribed on the white parchment in elaborate lettering. In smaller letters underneath, it said sales manager, and there was a phone number. Juan Ramón slipped the card in his shirt pocket. Then he stepped back onto the lot, still car salesman at Morton's Chevrolet, answerable to the Voice. From across the tarmac, the sales manager raised his thumb, indicating Ray had done well. Juan Ramón was glad for the plump commission Francisco had brought him, but that was all as the Santa Ana winds slammed against him.

* * *

It was almost ten o'clock that night before he turned left onto Horizon View Drive and arrived officially back at Marbella Beach. The wind was still blowing hard, just as it had the night Rosie picked him up at the border. On that drive up the coast, he kept turning Rosie's words over in his mind: *It's done, you're safe now.* He had not felt safe. Nor was it over. It was all beginning again, the long road of makeshift jobs and struggles with English, standing outside of Rosie's world, peering in. His euphoria at having made it across the border, at not having let the embassy's denial of his visa stop him from rejoining Rosie, at having found the job selling cars, was now deflated by cold reality.

He sniffed the fishy sea air as he got out of the car. The things he did not tell Rosie were piling up. He had not yet told her he had abandoned the English classes. At first, he had struggled to maintain them. But his schedule at the car lot differed each week. Sometimes he drew split days. Other times he worked mornings, or he drew just the afternoon or evening shift. He would have liked to explain to Mrs. Miller, his English teacher, what was going on. But to acknowledge he was working would be to acknowledge he had violated the terms of his visa. He no longer had the visa, of course, but pretended he did. He was *sin papeles*, without papers, undocumented, as they said in Mexico. Or as they said here, he was an "illegal alien." Two grim words. He would tell Rosie about the sale of the Corvette, but he would not tell her about Francisco's offer. It only reminded him of how low he had sunk.

"How does Mrs. Peebles sound?" Rosie asked as soon as he trudged the stairs to the living room. "It's still open."

"That's fine." Although he never found any dishes to his liking there, tonight he was so hungry he would devour anything these *gabachos* flung before him.

"The beach has a split personality," Rosie had pointed out during his first tour of Marbella, proud of its ability to function as a two-chambered heart. Towering modern houses and new restaurants of several stories rubbed shoulders with the old and homey, the small cottages of just one story built in the thirties and forties.

Only a sprinkling of unpretentious and well-worn restaurants remained from the old days. Mrs. Peebles was one of those, built down on the ground with a minimum of foundation. Sand tracked in from the parking lot extended the ever-windy beach right into the dining area where, in a kind of redundancy, plank wood walls were painted dark blue to suggest the ocean some fifty meters outside. Somehow Mrs. Peebles had managed to secure a beer and wine license, so the restaurant stayed open later than other old ones.

They found a seat in the central dining room. The waitress, a thin beach-blonde with "Marsi" embroidered on her beige blouse, handed them their menus, and rasped in a friendly way suggestive of too many cigarettes that she'd be right back to take their order.

Juan Ramón scowled at the menu. What he wanted was a Presidente brandy with coke chaser. He ordered wine, even though it often left him with a headache. Rosie ordered mineral water with a twist of lemon.

When their drinks came, she raised her glass. "To the baby."

He lifted his glass of wine, meeting her eyes. "To our

baby." He was thirsty and downed his wine quickly. Catching Marsi's eye as she passed, he raised his empty glass, signaling for another.

When it came, Rosie lifted her water glass again: "To your being here. To your having made it home"—she swiftly reworded—"here safely."

She was right not to say he had come home. Neither of them thought for a minute he was home. Marsi reappeared at the table, balancing two plates on a tray. She set poached sea bass before Rosie and grilled skirt steak, a Mrs. Peebles specialty, before him.

As soon as Marsi was out of earshot, he said, "I envy you your job."

Rosie looked uneasy. "Well, it's not—"

"But you've just won another award, Rosie. That's something to be proud of. For . . . what was it? For 'International Focus on Rural Perspectives.' No?"

"That's its fancy name."

"And you even have a job offer in San Diego."

Rosie let out an audible breath. "I'm hoping San Diego has more opportunities for you. Plus, it's closer to Mexico."

He didn't say anything.

She started to poke around in her sea bass as if she'd lost something there. "It's good to be recognized. But to tell you the truth, well, I'm discovering that the awards don't mean that much to me." She kept looking into her plate.

He set his empty wine glass down. "No? Does that mean two are not enough? Now you are after more?" He picked up a napkin and wiped his brow. It was stuffy in here, and the long, hot day weighed on him.

She raised her eyes. "It just means I don't feel the way I thought I would. Nobody at the paper gives a . . . rat's ass . . . about the poverty I described. Or the people I wrote about—Norma, María del Carmen, Fidel. Those people are just a

picturesque opportunity. A chance for somebody to win attention. For the newspaper to look current with the community."

"You achieved something. You're respected."

"It's more like I'm envied. Writing the article hasn't solved
anything. Not really."

"I don't know what that means."

"It means so many things are up in the air still."

"Do you mean San Diego?" He reached for his wine, then
realized it was gone. "Or do you mean us?"

They were aware of Marsi hovering near the table. He held
up his empty glass so she could see it. "Dried out," he said to
Rosie. "Too hot in here." He gestured toward the kitchen. "It's
the grill." What he wanted was for the alcohol to perform surgery on him, to excise the burgeoning pain.

Rosie hadn't answered. She put her fork down. "I'm not
that hungry. Everything smells so strong now. It's all turned
around. All the food I used to like before, I can't stand now. I
can't imagine why I ordered fish."

He tried a softer tone. "That's okay, *chiquita*. It's your hormones adapting to the baby." His questions of a moment hung
between them unanswered, but he didn't pursue them. He
needed to get out into fresh air.

Rosie was of like mind and stood up when he did. He
pulled out his wallet and paid with a pair of twenties left there
among a few pesos.

Outside, perpendicular to Mrs. Peebles' parking lot, began
the expanse of sand, an obscure nothingness under the dark
of night, as vague and formless as he willed his mind to be.
The ocean stretched beyond, a black slab of infinity roughened
by the atypical easterly wind.

He put his arm around Rosie's waist and tugged her in the
direction of the beach. "Let's return to the sea, *mi amor*," he
intoned in mock melodrama. "We came from the ocean. We
return to the ocean."

Rosie didn't move. "I don't know, Juan Ramón. Aren't you tired? I was thinking we could go back to the house. We could lie down together . . . and just be. Just rest."

He pretended he didn't hear her. "Listen, even the wind is calling us home to the saline." He was starting to vibrate with a fine glow. The beautiful alcohol, that sharp liquid knife, was doing its job. "C'mon, Rosie."

"Well, only if I can be a mermaid," she said, attempting to lighten her mood as she gave in. She stepped onto the sand with him.

"You, my love, can be the Queen of the Seven Seas if you want." He bent down and took off Rosie's sandals. Then he undid the laces of his own shoes and kicked them off. He dug his feet down into the rough grit, noticing how it changed from warm on the surface to cool farther down. That pleased him. It was something that made sense. What Rosie had said about the other writers she worked with at the newspaper, that made sense, too, even though he hadn't told her it did.

He looked up, where overhead the stars showed as tiny holes punched in black tar paper. His neck strained with the effort of gazing upward, and he suddenly felt dizzy, as if inside a cosmic kaleidoscope. The sky turned and folded over itself, and his brief euphoria shifted.

They concentrated on walking in the dry sand. Rosie held tightly to his hand, and that, too, pleased him, seemed right, and helped push back what he did not want to think about. Underfoot, the dry sand gave way to wet as their feet crossed the tide line. They picked their way over seaweed, cold and rubbery, washed up by the tide.

The Santa Ana gale that whipped trash through the streets inland had blown out much of its force here at the beach, but still reared up in sporadic easterly gusts that sent phosphorescent spume spiraling up and back from the waves. The wind was strong enough to lift Rosie's hair and push it forward into her face.

He turned and held her at arm's length. "You look like an Eskimo girl, with fur around your face," he said, rocking her back and forth in a gentle motion as if trying to comfort her, or really himself. Anyway, strange notion, Rosie as an Eskimo. Rosie, mother of his Eskimo child. Rosie, innocent possessor of all he, Mexican father of her child, was lacking here: career, friends, a decent salary from work that meant something, her mother, respect.

Rosie looked uncertain, but laughed. "I'd still rather be a mermaid."

And what would he rather be? He looked up again at the night sky and was back inside the kaleidoscope. It swirled and refracted at a jarring, even nauseating, rate.

The wind picked up, buffeting them from behind. It brought with it the long, hot day he had managed to exist through. Even with his having made a fat sale, it was a day not so different from the clotted stream of days he had already endured here.

He opened his mouth, and the swirl of stars and wind spiraled into it. The sky and the ground were rotating away from each other. He felt as if he were choking. He yelled to clear his throat.

Rosie pulled his arm, angling him toward her. "Are you all right?" Her lips opened in a distorted O.

"I shouldn't have had the drinks." They used to inspire him, fuel his long arguments into the night with Eugenio. Here, even the alcohol affected him differently.

"Rosie," he said, steadying himself against her. "Have you ever screamed into the wind?"

She raised her voice. "What?"

He tried to gain hold of himself. He still had the sensation he was dry and choking. "Scream into the wind. That's what I did when I was a boy. When I was upset about something, I would run outside and yell it into the wind. Let's do it."

The wind tore at them now, and they needed each other for balance.

She smiled tentatively. "Well . . . what should I scream?"

"Anything."

She faced the ocean and opened her mouth. Out came a warble, like a yodel.

"Too pretty." He squeezed her arm tightly. "Put your madness into it."

Rosie spun toward him. "What is it, Juan Ramón? Tell me what's wrong."

"Be like a bad opera singer on a high note. Like this." He filled his lungs and threw back his head. The scream was so big it startled both of them. The force of his breath exiting his body jogged something loose within.

He yelled again. For the *fregada* taco shop reeking of overcooked grease, and the *fregada* used car lot baking in the sun, for the *fregada* English that eluded him every day, for this *fregada* world he had no control over and no home in.

The awful image of Ceci, wan in her hospital gown, arose yet again. His little sister, he had no little sister. He, the doctor, attending her by day, sleeping next to her hospital bed by night, had not been able to save her. He was yelling now for the doctor he no longer was, for Eugenio and the clinic and the sick people he had left behind in Ixmilco, and the poor patients in Rosie's article, and for his mother and father, and for his *tierra*.

He sank to his knees and pulled Rosie with him onto the sand.

"No, no, no," she was saying, her head moving back and forth.

He knelt facing her. "Do you know about the mesquite tree, Rosie? I'm like that tough tree in Mexico." He was still loud, but he wanted to make sure the wind wouldn't toss away his words. "It hardly needs water. Its bark is hard as iron. It can stand hot wind and frosts. But one thing about it—"

He tightened his grip on her arms. "It cannot be transplanted, my beloved Rosie. *Se seca.* The mesquite dries up and dies."

Rosie was crying now, and she fished for something in her pant pocket. The sight of her crying made him all the more miserable.

The words his father flung at him that first time he had announced he was going to *el norte* to be with Rosie now resounded. "You will be back, Juan Ramón. You won't be able to last there. You will come back where you belong."

Rosie reached out and rested her arms on his shoulders, a tissue balled in one hand. Her face was fearful, her eyes unblinking. "I know that this place, Marbella—" She stopped, then began again. "This country . . . is not the place for you. I know that."

He held his hands up in front of her. "I have a calling, Rosie. These hands, they can help people. I couldn't help Ceci, but I have taken away pain, and even saved lives. That is my gift, Rosie, from God. I'm not using that gift. I'm useless."

She seized his hands and pressed them between hers.

"You useless? Of all people, how can you say that?" She sounded angry.

"You know very well what I do with these hands now. I make phone calls to sell used Chevrolets. Before this, I dropped fucking greasy tacos into fucking waxed bags." His voice grew huskier. "This is *una locura.* I cannot make even enough money to offer you marriage."

"The money doesn't matter to me."

"It matters to me. I can't take care of you here. I can barely even take care of myself."

"You will. As soon as you pass the medical boards. It's just a few more months. Your English is getting better."

"I haven't been going to class."

"You haven't?"

He was shouting again. "With a schedule that changes every week?"

"But you don't have to work. You can just study. I make enough to support us until—" She dug her nails into his palms. "You forget that I'm an illegal. I can't take the medical boards. *Ay, chiquita linda,* we have to see reality, not what you are wishing for."

The stars in the sky behind her were steady now, no longer spinning. They teased with sudden glints of hope. "Come with me to Mexico, Rosie. Come live with me there. You, me, the baby, we can have a better life."

She stared at him, no longer crying. "You want me to go with you? To quit my work? Mama? Simply leave everything?"

"I cannot make it here."

She touched his shoulder. "Oh, Juan Ramón."

"Come with me. Or should I steal you away in the old Mexican way? Steal my bride on horseback in the night?"

"I have to . . . I have to think about it. It's such a—"

"Locura, no? Crazy to leave your work and your friends and your mother and your language, everything you know?" He stood and pulled her to her feet. "Yes. We know it is crazy. That doesn't mean you shouldn't do it, Rosie."

Rosie was looking out over the water. "I know what you're asking is what you've done for me. Leave everything." She turned to face him. "This just isn't where I thought things with us would go."

He pulled her against him. The life within her belly pressed into him.

Despite his impassioned words about leaving and despite whatever Rosie would decide, and despite all his longing for home and for belonging, he knew he could not leave her and their baby. Not of his own free will. Not ever. He belonged wherever they were, no matter what his problems with this country. Here he remained, a mesquite with strangled roots, buried in the treachery of new soil.

28

GRAFTING ON

Louise returned from her walk, where color hunger had dispatched her on a mission for perfect "goldenrod," what her Crayolas had once labeled "medium yellow." She opened her front door and there in her living room stood Rosie, hands on hips.

"Where have you been?" Rosie's words tumbled out. "I've been calling since before eight, and no answer. I come over and find your door unlocked, and you're not even here."

She started to bristle at Rosie's imperiousness, then realized Rosie wasn't doing well. Her gaze was rotating from one thing to another, and her face was mottled.

"Let's sit in the kitchen, honey. Let me make you tea."

Rosie stood wide-eyed in the middle of the living room and made no move toward the kitchen. "There's something I haven't told you about Juan Ramón's being back."

Louise tried to look neutral in the face of this declaration. "He had problems with his visa."

"Yes, you told me that."

"So he ran the border."

"He what?"

"He's here illegally. Without papers. He paid a coyote."

Louise dropped onto the sofa. "Oh, this is something. This is serious. This changes everything." A jumble of questions sprung to mind. First of all, why was Rosie only now telling her this? And couldn't Juan Ramón have found a better way? Did this mean he couldn't take his board exams? But Louise could manage only: "Is he okay?"

That wasn't the right question. Rosie's words shot out. "Of course he's not. He wants to go back. He says he'll always feel like a foreigner here."

Louise knew what this meant. Desperation was claiming Rosie's face.

"He wants me to go with him."

Louise reeled. This was the moment she had feared for almost a year, ever since she met this Juan Ramón. She held onto the back of a chair. "And—?"

"I don't know, I don't know." Rosie resumed her furtive glancing around the room as if the answer lay there on the mantel, now there at the window, then on the carpet. "I just want to be together. And I don't want to make the wrong decision. But being here is strangling him."

Louise tried to still her own racing thoughts. Rosie leaving. Rosie so far away. Her grandchild so far away. Herself alone. She didn't know if she could bear it, just as she didn't know if she could bear it when Rosie's father had left. But then she still had Rosie.

"Juan Ramón tells me there's so much work to be done in those little clinics in Mexico. He's needed there in a way he'll never be needed here. And you know what, Mama?" Rosie became focused and sure. "He's right."

As Rosie continued to talk, she grew calmer, more certain. She said again, "I know in my heart he's right. He says California doesn't need another rich doctor. He really would like the money. And there are poor people here who need help, too. But Mexico needs him more."

Rosie sank onto the sofa next to Louise and pulled the throw pillows around her stomach. "Oh, Mama." Her voice grew tight, the moment of equanimity gone. "I don't know what to do.

Louise wanted to hold that face in her hands the way she had when Rosie was little.

"What should I do?"

"You know I can't answer that for you."

"I can't leave you alone."

"I will be fine," Louise said. "I am fine," she repeated. "In fact, just yesterday afternoon I got a clean bill of health."

Rosie pushed herself up, the pillows falling to the floor.

"A clean bill of health? You went to the doctor's yesterday?"

"Well," said Louise, flushing now that the focus had shifted to her, "I didn't want to bother you before I knew for sure. It was just a little lump."

"A little lump? What lump? A lump and you didn't tell me? Since when, this 'little lump'?"

"You had a secret. I can't have one, too? I told you, the doctor says I'm healthy. It turns out I do have an allergy. That's what was making me so tired, not the lump. The lump is benign. I have developed, of all things, an allergy to the chemicals in oil paint."

Rosie raised her voice. "You haven't told me that either. How could you not tell me this? I tell you everything!"

"It took you almost three months to tell me you were pregnant. And just now you're telling me Juan Ramón is here illegally. Anyway, you weren't here when I first discovered the lump. It was Christmas time. You were with Juan Ramón's family in Mexico. I wanted to make sure first."

Rosie reached toward her mother. "Oh, Mama, this is exactly what I mean. Juan Ramón can't understand what he's asking. I cannot leave you here by yourself in Marbella. And how can you work if you're allergic to oil paint?"

"There are plenty of other media I can work in." Louise took Rosie by the hand and steered her to the kitchen. "What you're saying is just an excuse, Rosie. You're trying to control my life as well as your own." She guided Rosie into a kitchen chair. "You know what this reminds me of?"

Rosie shook her head. Before answering, Louise busied herself pulling out a bottle of seltzer water from the refrigerator, then stood on tiptoe to reach two of her finest crystal goblets on a high shelf. If she could just focus on what her hands were doing, she would be able to get through this. She had always been able to depend on her hands to carry her through.

"Do you remember when you were around eleven or twelve and I tried to teach you how to do watercolors?"

"Oh God, yes. I never liked them."

"You couldn't stand the way the paint spread on the paper as if it had a mind of its own. You were even afraid to put down a wash because it would start moving in ways you hadn't foreseen. You were so afraid, my darling daughter, to make a decision you couldn't control. You just have to surrender to the situation, Rosie. And trust." Louise realized she could be delivering this advice to herself as well.

She closed her eyes to keep her nerve up. "You and Juan Ramón love each other and want to be together. There's a baby coming. You three belong together."

"Yes, but why not here? I have a home here. You here. A job here, a better job waiting. I have no life there. I want to be near you."

Louise spread her hands on the kitchen table. "This isn't a matter of making a good decision or a bad decision. You work with what you've got, with however the paint spreads."

She turned her back to the table and scrambled for what seemed like a long time through a drawer, her fingers numb with anxiety, until she found a bottle opener. She beat down the voice within crying, "Me. Me. Choose me."

"This occasion calls for a bubbly drink instead of tea." She popped the top off a bottle of seltzer water. She poured the water, cut a tangerine wedge into it, and turned around to face her daughter. She sat down and raised her glass, smiling. Rosie picked up her goblet, sighed, and to Louise's relief, returned the smile, albeit wanly.

"To new life," Louise said. Sun was lighting up the crystal goblets. Refracted light skipped around the room, and in it she saw an artist's palette of possibilities. She touched her glass to Rosie's with a light clink. It would take her awhile, as it might Rosie. Louise swallowed the knot in her throat, grateful she had managed to keep her tears in check.

* * *

Teddy McGee was at it again. Here it was, not even seven thirty on a Saturday morning, and he was whacking with a pair of pruning shears at the small plum tree on his side of the fence. The plum tree grew not too far from where hundreds of red and white tulips had just finished their yearly extravagant bloom. Louise drew her sweater around her, picked up her coffee cup, and stepped into the cool morning air of the front yard. Some idle conversation, some turning outward, could feel good after so much time turned inward.

"Hey there, Teddy," she said as she drew near to where he was working. He was not whacking at all but carefully choosing the spots where he made his cuts.

"Morning, Louise," he called back and let go of the shears with one hand to wave. He was wearing his usual blue flannel work shirt and a pair of carpenter's pants, his outdoor uniform. He paused his pruning as she drew near. "Haven't seen you this week."

It was uncanny how Teddy McGee seemed to keep tabs on

her. Maybe from all those hours spent communing with plants every day he had absorbed some kind of elemental knowing, another sense, organic and mute, the way monarch butterflies know where to migrate south and birds in a flock know when to make instant turns. Could he tell what she had been through these last two months, know of the tumor that turned out not to be a tumor after all, know of her fear run wild? Just in case he could see into her thoughts, she practiced keeping her mind a blank when he came near.

"I hoped you weren't sick or anything."

He was peering at her as if she could use a little horticultural handiwork, a bit of staking or watering or tilling, as if he were itching to get his green thumbs on her. Maybe if she were to look deep into his eyes, she'd see lusty earthworms wriggling there.

She stopped herself. No, that wasn't how he was looking at her at all. That was just what she always assumed before she backed away from a man. She allowed herself to return his gaze and saw only simple kindness and concern.

"How's that daughter of yours doing?"

"Doing okay. She's going to have a baby."

"Lucky you." He unlatched the gate between their two yards. "Come. I want to show you something." He waved his hand to show she should follow him.

She stepped through the gate and let him lead her alongside his house and into the back garden.

He walked with a loping gait, part man, part large animal. They turned the corner of the house and were now on the other side of the screen of trees that were the reason she couldn't see his back property from hers.

With a deprecatory wave of his hand, Teddy indicated that there it all was if she wanted to take a look. The left side of the yard featured a small, newly painted greenhouse, fronted by tidy rows of vegetable garden, the kind once called a victory garden. A small but dense orchard took over the right side of the property. Some eight to ten fruit trees had grown tall and broad enough that there was just room for a man with pruning shears to pass among them. Directly in front of where she and Teddy were standing, a flower garden waved in full vivid bloom, separated into two long sections that ran across the lot. The back flower garden was in the free-flowing English style, the closer one in the formal design of a French garden, planted with well-tended rose bushes in symmetry.

"This is you," Louise said, partly under her breath. She was seeing the essence of Mr. Teddy McGee, his personality and passion depicted in botanical calligraphy. This intimate knowledge was sudden and unanticipated—they had been neighbors for at least nine years, but she had known so little about him.

He motioned her along the gravel path to the greenhouse.

"You think your daughter will be getting married?"

"I don't know if they're even talking about it, she and her boyfriend." The word "boyfriend" didn't do justice anymore to Juan Ramón's role in Rosie's life. "He's from Mexico," she added, surprising herself with how loquacious she had become here in Teddy McGee's private preserve.

"Good," he said. "Good stock."

She wasn't sure what he meant by his talk of "good stock."

Teddy pointed to what looked like the sawed-off stems from several trees. They stood upright in the ground. Stuck in the outer perimeter of each stem were two small sticks. It looked like a project a child might have tired of playing with and abandoned there.

"Grafting," he said. "That's cleft grafting." He squatted next to the sawed-off stems, his knees poking up through his pants legs like sharp stalks. This is the way she had seen him that day months ago when he brought a bouquet of hydrangeas to her door. He had fumbled the bouquet, dropping it as he started to hand it to her, and as he squat down, his knees had poked out in that same stalk-like way.

"For the average yard, you can make a healthier tree if you graft a scion from a different plant onto a strong rootstock," he said. "I'm talking about your average domestic tree, not your commercial orchards. Now in New England, where I come from, you have lots of apple trees. By grafting two different trees, not of the same kind, you make a stronger tree. More productive. Better fruit."

"Like marriage," said Louise, thinking how two sets of bloodlines and histories and hormones combined to produce offspring.

"Like marriage with an outsider. It's best with somebody from far away."

He touched a bony forefinger to the top of each of the two scions. "These here have to be placed just so in the clefts of the rootstocks." He grabbed hold of the stump underneath. "This bigger trunk here, that's the rootstock. See how the scions are shaved on their sides and slip into the cleft? You want the cambium layers of the rootstock to match the cambium layers of the scions."

Louise bent over the tree stumps and stared at them as if that would enable her to see the cambium layers where the two sticks jointed the rootstock. She felt herself a voyeur staring at the act of physical merging.

Teddy said, "The cambium layer refers to the cells underneath the bark or stem of a plant. That's where the bonding takes place."

"This is just, well, marvelous," said Louise, raising back up, suffused with the most purpose she had in weeks. "I really would like to sketch this grafting." She turned and waved her hand toward the rest of the garden. "And all your bountiful plants." In the middle of all this fecundity, she felt herself pulsing with vitality. She didn't add that she would also like to sketch him there amidst it all, but it did occur to her.

"I would like to have you here. Please come back," said Teddy, wiping his hands on his carpenter's pants, looking proud and shy at the same time. "Whenever you want."

29

SAL SI PUEDES II:
LEAVE IF YOU CAN

The ocean was at low tide, silent, seemingly as stymied as I was, mirror flat. I rested on a bench and watched the waves slide in listlessly. It was a lazy Saturday in all ways. My nose wrinkled at the smell of rotting seaweed. I loved the ocean in all its moods—the crashing turbulence, the glassy brilliance, the fog-shrouded invisibility, the receding tides that uncovered treasures along the tideline. Just now I wanted it to give me a sign. Those women in the village outside Ixmilco had their signs. Why couldn't I have mine?

Why was it so damn hard to let go of my life here, the habit of it unsatisfactory though it often was? I had struggled hard to get where I was. I had it all, my house at the beach, a chance to move up to a more prestigious job at a bigger newspaper, friends I could count on, my mother. I also had a baby on the way and Juan Ramón. Gifts all.

The ocean continued its noncommittal quiet. It was balanced on that moment when the low tide had played its way out and the sea would start to swell again. Moving to Mexico was hugely different than spending a few weeks of vacation there over-glorifying it, under the spell of its passionate beauty. Only now could I understand the enormity of what Juan Ramón, who each day still took himself to his job at the car lot, had done for me. I wanted to go home and call him on the spot to confess I was appalled at the extent I had taken that for granted.

But he couldn't take phone calls at work. I walked back to my house and, wavering again, instead dialed Carole-Ann. "Say something that will make it all clear for me," I said as soon as she answered.

"Oh, so now I'm your fortune-teller."

We met later for lunch at the city park not too far from the *Beacon*. Carole-Ann had picked up a carton of broccoli with oyster sauce beef and another of vegetables with shrimp. We huddled side by side on a bench and took turns spearing out mouthfuls with white plastic forks.

I was surprised to see quite a few people in the park. A young mother, her auburn hair in pigtails, pushed a baby stroller past us, going toward the park's playground with her red-haired toddler. An elderly couple sat on a nearby bench, holding hands.

"If only I could be sure, Carole-Ann. What would I do for prenatal care if I were to go?"

"Oh, for God's sake, what's with this 'if I were to go'?"

"That's subjunctive mood. You should recognize it."

"Yeah. Anyway, consider the birth rate. You, of all people, should be able to quote it right from your article. Mexico is a nation of babies, so somebody must know what to do. Anyway, from what I've observed, once a baby is ready to be born, there's little or nothing stopping it. It just plops out."

"I wouldn't say 'just,' as if it's merely a pimple ready to pop. And I used the subjunctive because I am spiraling around and around in the hypothetical. As it were. Besides, I didn't expect you to champion Juan Ramón or my leaving."

"I reserve the right to change," she said. "You've changed, too."

I pushed her fork up and away with mine, parrying her attempt to stab a shrimp before I could. "No fair hunting for the good stuff and leaving the carrots."

"I get certain rights, as your supernatural. Instead of your fortune-teller, consider me your genie. What are your three wishes?"

I sighed. "To be with Juan Ramón and raise our child. To have work I care about."

"Granted."

"C'mon. Just like that? That simple?"

"Yes, that simple."

"Not so fast. What about my work? I have a great chance for a dynamite job."

"We women are usually looking for something beyond what we've got. That's just how we are. We fantasize there's something ahead that's better and that we can control better. There is, in fact, something beyond. It's never what we envision though, and of course it eludes our puny control." Carole-Ann gave a mock sigh. "Anyway, have you forgotten that writing is a portable skill? You can do it anywhere. You can also do it while the baby's napping."

"We won't have much money, a lot less than now."

"Then you'll have to get going with that writing."

"I don't know. What about Mama? That's the hardest part of this."

We watched as the old couple stood and, linking arms, ambled toward a fountain in the middle of the park. They settled themselves on the fountain's ledge, and the woman suddenly leaned toward the water's surface and then quickly straightened up again, flicking water on the man. He laughed and right away dipped his own fingers in the water and flicked bright drops back at her.

"Don't you want that to be you and Juan Ramón, now and in the future?"

"Oh, romantic sabotage. That couple probably just met. Or maybe each is married to someone else, and they are out having a geriatric fling. Or they are even brother and sister. Or they're lost in dementia and think they are teenagers again."

Was I afraid? I didn't like to think of myself this way, but yes, I was afraid of what might lie ahead. "Truly that simple, Carole-Ann?" I wanted to believe it could be.

"Maybe you're just afraid of living in a country with a serious lack of street signs?"

We continued to watch the elderly couple frolic. Demented or not, they were clearly enjoying themselves. Mama had recalled my resistance to watercolors. I must allow myself to be surprised and delighted, not frightened, by how the translucent strokes of paint fanned out, growing naturally, forming and reforming into the unexpected, colors running into each other, changing each other, becoming new blended colors, enriched and created by one another.

* * *

Juan Ramón did not see me as I threaded my way around the cars at Morton's Chevrolet, trying not to waddle with my larger belly. He was engaged with a tall, angular man, a Don Quixote look-alike I assumed was a customer in need of an up-to-date steed. I waited to one side, absently tracing figure eights on my belly. From the other side of the lot, a white-shirted man dressed in the same salesman attire as Juan Ramón was striding swiftly in my direction.

Juan Ramón spotted me. An expression of alarm crossed his face. He said something to Don Quixote, then hurried my way.

His attention went to my hand on my stomach. "Rosie, *mi chiquita linda,* what is it? Are you okay?" He put an arm around me.

A voice boomed on the loudspeaker. "Ray." Juan Ramón gave a slight start at the loud voice, then touched his hand to my face. "What is it, Rosie?"

The other salesman had stopped advancing and stood some five feet off. "Sorry. I didn't realize you know each other."

"Ray!" reverberated the loudspeaker.

"I'm fine. I just wanted to tell you . . ."

The other salesman still stood there, listening.

Now another person materialized, as if by magic, this one wearing a suit and a pinched face. Juan Ramón did not see the man, but I had a pretty good idea who he must be.

Juan Ramón brought his hand up and caressed my hair. "Ray! What is going on?" The sales manager was almost sputtering, and now that he was no longer amplified by the public address system, his voice sounded tinny, almost whining. "Your customer—" He turned and motioned the other salesman toward Don Quixote, who was rubbing the flanks of a like-new Cavalier.

Juan Ramón continued to gaze at me with concern, oblivious to the sales manager, who was practically doing a jig in his annoyance.

"This is a business, Ray. We do not bring our personal life onto the lot. At Morton's Chevrolet, we pride ourselves on acting as professionals. I have no choice but to—"

Juan Ramón spun to face the sales manager. The words shot out like an arrow. "I quit."

I quickly said, "Juan Ramón—that's his name, by the way—has another job. His profession. His true and holy calling." Even though the sales manager had no idea what I was talking about, I had to say it.

Juan Ramón's eyes widened as he looked at me, not the sales manager. Beyond Juan Ramón, the sales manager's face grew redder and tighter by the second.

I squeezed Juan Ramón's hand and addressed the pinched face. "Doctor Juan Ramón, in case you didn't hear him just now, hereby submits his resignation. He has patients in Mexico who desperately need him. We can no longer keep them waiting. He has to go home and pack."

I paused and then added, turning to smile at Juan Ramón, who was starting to grin back at me, "and so do I."

* * *

We sat side by side, our legs pressed hard against each other, on the same bench where I'd sat earlier. The tide was coming in, and the ocean now stirred with purpose, the waves lifting high and sure. The sun poured through one perfect blue-green breaker after another, highlighting the translucent emerald core of each.

"You will miss this."

"Yes."

"You will be—how do you say?—landlocked."

"Yes."

"You will miss your mother."

"Yes."

"You will miss your friends and your job."

"Yes and yes."

"Are you absolutely sure you want to do this for me?"

"No."

He gave a start.

"I want to do this for all three of us."

An unusually tall wave crashed onto the shore, its foam running in several directions at once. As we watched the multi-tone water spread across the beach, I felt myself a brilliant color expanding across the sand, as was Juan Ramón, as was the baby, each of us a vibrant hue, combining to make patterns, inextricable and essential.

It was all there waiting for us in Ixmilco, all the rich color and celebration, along with the shifting shadows I would never understand and, if I could embrace it, the adventure of ambiguity.

IN GRATITUDE

Gracias de todo corazón to the many people who graciously gave of their time, observations, and support:

To Dr. Luis Miguel Villareal Sautto, Dr. José Antonio Correa Sánchez, and Salvador Orozco Guillén for their inspiration;

To those there at the very beginning, Wanda Maureen Miller, Marty Fraser, Gail Tennen, Nadine Goodman;

To class and workshop leaders Caroline Leavitt (twice over) and Judyth Hill (twice over) for their observations and cheerleading;

To Anne Marie Welsh and Nick Fox for their editorial responses and suggestions;

To my San Miguel de Allende writing groups, in particular, those at the *biblioteca*: Geoff Hargreaves, Ken Morrow, Bill Gallacher, Libbe Dennard; Louis Marbre-Cargill; as well as critique sessions with Wendy Bichel, Alice Sperling, Lynn Learned, Judith Jenya, Frank Thoms;

To those who have gone beyond, María Luisa Moreno, known as *La Señora de los Cuentos,* Barbara Faith, who was there at the beginning, Beryl Buchanan, Celia Wakefield, Marni Martin, Naomi Boulton, Deborah Whitehouse;

To Bhakti Ishaya, Andrea Usher, Stephen Slade, and Sandi Steeber for rock bottom faith;

To Judith Jenya, who generously painted the tabachín flower shown on the cover;

To my *familias* in Guadalajara and California for their tender care and love.

About Atmosphere Press

Atmosphere Press is an independent, full-service publisher for excellent books in all genres and for all audiences. Learn more about what we do at atmospherepress.com.

We encourage you to check out some of Atmosphere's latest releases, which are available at Amazon.com and via order from your local bookstore:

Icarus Never Flew 'Round Here, by Matt Edwards
COMFREY, WYOMING: Maiden Voyage, by Daphne Birkmeyer
The Chimera Wolf, by P.A. Power
Umbilical, by Jane Kay
The Two-Blood Lion, by Nick Westfield
Shogun of the Heavens: The Fall of Immortals, by I.D.G. Curry
Hot Air Rising, by Matthew Taylor
30 Summers, by A.S. Randall
Delilah Recovered, by Amelia Estelle Dellos
A Prophecy in Ash, by Julie Zantopoulos
The Killer Half, by JB Blake
Ocean Lessons, by Karen Lethlean
Unrealized Fantasies, by Marilyn Whitehorse
The Mayari Chronicles: Initium, by Karen McClain
Squeeze Plays, by Jeffrey Marshall
JADA: Just Another Dead Animal, by James Morris
Hart Street and Main: Metamorphosis, by Tabitha Sprunger
Karma One, by Colleen Hollis
Ndalla's World, by Beth Franz
Adonai, by Arman Isayan
The Journey, by Khozem Poonawala
Stolen Lives, by Dee Arianne Rockwood

ABOUT THE AUTHOR

Little did Sharon Steeber know where enrolling in a Spanish course back in high school would lead. Years later she went on to raise her children between central Mexico and California. She still divides her time between the two countries. Now retired, she taught college English and co-authored a series of textbooks, *Reading Faster and Understanding More, Books 1, 2,* and *3,* two of which went through five editions. She has also published a family saga, *The Jews,* and magazine and newspaper advice columns for teenagers (before she had any!). More recently, she has had several short plays produced.

*You are invited to visit the website **sharonsteeber.com**.*

Made in the USA
Columbia, SC
20 October 2024

44421946R00217